Everyman, I will go with thee,
and be thy guide

George Eliot

SILAS MARNER
THE LIFTED VEIL
BROTHER JACOB

Edited by
PETER MUDFORD
Birkbeck College, University of London

EVERYMAN
J. M. DENT · LONDON

For Nicola and Chris

Series editor for the Everyman George Eliot
Beryl Gray

Introduction, notes and other critical apparatus
© J M Dent 1996

This edition first published in 1996
All rights reserved

J. M. Dent
Orion Publishing Group
Orion House, 5 Upper St Martin's Lane,
London WC2H 9EA
and
Charles E. Tuttle Co., Inc.
28 South Main Street,
Rutland, Vermont 05701, USA

Typeset in Sabon by CentraCet Ltd, Cambridge
Printed in Great Britain by
The Guernsey Press Co. Ltd, Guernsey, C. I.

British Library Cataloguing-in-Publication Data
is available upon request.

ISBN 0 460 87568 X

CONTENTS

NOTE ON THE AUTHOR AND EDITOR

GEORGE ELIOT was born Mary Anne (later Mary Ann, then Marian) Evans, on 22 November 1819 at Arbury Farm in Warwickshire. When she was five months old the family moved to a farmhouse at Griff, which was her home till she was twenty-one. Her rural upbringing had a profound influence on her imagination. She attended schools at Attleborough and Nuneaton before boarding at the Misses Franklin's school in Coventry, where she studied literature in several languages, excelled in English composition and developed her musical talents.

She left school in 1835, and, after her mother's death, became her father's housekeeper. In 1841 father and daughter moved to Coventry, where Marian was introduced to Charles Bray and his wife Cara. The influence of them and their circle precipitated her move away from dogmatic belief, opening her mind to many new influences. At this time she began her translation of Strauss's *Life of Jesus* (1846): a critical account of the historical veracity of the New Testament. After her father's death in 1849 Marian Evans spent some months in Switzerland, before beginning her life in London as editor of, and contributor to, John Chapman's *Westminster Review*. In 1852 she met G. H. Lewes, with whom she was to live (circumstances made it impossible for them to marry) until his death in 1878. With his encouragement, and using the pen-name of George Eliot to conceal her female identity, she published *Scenes of Clerical Life* and *Adam Bede*, which at once became a triumphant success. *The Lifted Veil*, *The Mill on the Floss*, *Brother Jacob*, *Silas Marner*, *Romola*, *Felix Holt*, *Middlemarch* and *Daniel Deronda* followed over the years, consolidating her reputation and her fame, as well as vanquishing the hostility which her relationship with G. H. Lewes had attracted. Her last work, *The Impressions of Theophrastus Such* was published in 1879; in the following year she married her friend of many years, J. W. Cross, but died a few months later. She is buried close to Lewes in Highgate Cemetery.

PETER MUDFORD is Reader in Modern English Literature at Birkbeck College in the University of London. His book on the European Novella, entitled *Memory and Desire*, will shortly be published by Duckworth. He has also recently completed a book on Graham Greene for the 'Writers and their Work' series, and is editing the 'Shorter Fiction' of Charles Dickens for Everyman. His most recent publication is the chapter on 'British Drama from 1950 to the Present Day' in the *Penguin History of English Literature*, Volume VII.

CHRONOLOGY OF GEORGE ELIOT'S LIFE[*]

Year	Age	Life
1819		Born at South Farm, Arbury, Warwickshire, on 22 November (baptised Mary Anne Evans)
1820	5 months	The Evans family moves to Griff
1824–36	5–16	Attends successively a boarding-school in Attleborough, Miss Wallington's boarding-school in Nuneaton, and the Misses Franklin's school in Coventry
1826	6	Visits Derbyshire and Staffordshire with parents

[*] For a full chronology of George Eliot's life, readers should consult Timothy Hands's *A George Eliot Chronology* (London, 1989)

CHRONOLOGY OF HER TIMES

Year	Literary Context	Historical Events
1818	Walter Scott, *The Heart of Midlothian*	
1819	Birth of Ruskin	Birth of Victoria
1820	Scott, *Ivanhoe*	Death of King George III; accession of George IV
1824	Goethe, *Wilhelm Meisters Lehrjahre* (1795) trans. Carlyle as *Wilhelm Meister's Apprenticeship*	
1825		Opening of Stockton and Darlington railway
1829	Balzac, *Les Chouans*	Catholic Emancipation
1830	Tennyson, *Poems, Chiefly Lyrical*	Death of King George IV; accession of William IV; the 'Bourgeois Revolution' in France: flight of Charles X and accession of Louis-Philippe
1830–3	Charles Lyell, *Principles of Geology*	
1831		First Reform Bill introduced by Lord John Russell rejected; Parliament dissolved; new Parliament elected with a majority for reform; Bill eventually passes
1832	George Sand, *Indiana*	
1833		First Factory Act, regulating child labour; death of William IV; accession of Queen Victoria

Year	Age	Life
1836	16	Death of mother
1837	17	Marriage of sister, Christiana ('Chrissey'). Becomes father's housekeeper
1838	18–19	Reads widely, including many religious works
1839	20	Buys Wordsworth's *Works* – 'I never before met with so many of my own feelings, expressed just as I could like them' (*Letters*, I, 34)
1841	21	Moves, with father, to Coventry. Marriage of brother, Isaac. Introduced to Charles Bray and his wife Caroline (Cara), Charles Hennell's sister. Reads Charles Hennell's *Inquiry*
1842	22	Breaks with orthodox Christianity. Meets Sara Hennell, Cara Bray's sister; friendship generates much correspondence
1844–8	25–8	Translates Strauss's *Das Leben Jesu* (1846). Reading includes Milton, Wordsworth, Dickens, Thackeray, Carlyle, Goethe, Disraeli and Rousseau
1848	28	Meets Emerson. Reading includes Sand and (to her father) Scott
1849	29	Begins to translate Spinoza's *Tractatus theologico-politicus*. Death of father. Visits France, Italy, and Switzerland with Brays; winters in Geneva alone. Begins Journal

Year	Literary Context	Historical Events
1838	Charles Hennell, *An Inquiry into the Origins of Christianity*	Chartists demand suffrage
1840	Birth of Thomas Hardy	Penny Post established Marriage of Queen Victoria to Prince Albert
1841	Carlyle, *Heroes and Hero Worship*	Robert Peel becomes Prime Minister
1842	Wordsworth, *Poems*	Chartist riots
1842–8	Balzac, *La Comédie Humaine* (*The Human Comedy*), 17 vols	
1845	Disraeli, *Sybil, or The Two Nations*	Newman received into the Roman Catholic Church
1846	The Brontës, *Poems*; Ruskin, *Modern Painters*	Repeal of the Corn Laws
1847	Charlotte Brontë, *Jane Eyre*; Emily Brontë, *Wuthering Heights*; Thackeray, *Vanity Fair*; Dickens, *Dombey and Son*	
1848	Elizabeth Gaskell, *Mary Barton*	Revolutions in Europe

Year	Age	Life
1850	30	Returns to England in March but finds the experience painful; decides to earn her living by writing
1851	31	Joins Chapman's household in London; secretly becomes managing editor of his *Westminster Review*, for which she writes articles 'as a man'. Visits Great Exhibition twice
1852	32	Meets and befriends Herbert Spencer (1820–1903), social philosopher and journalist; and George Henry Lewes (1827–78). Attends Covent Garden frequently with Spencer; Spencer rejects her love. Reading includes Aristotle and W. J. Fox's *Lectures Addressed Chiefly to the Working Classes*
1853	33	Much occupied with *Westminster Review*. Reading includes Gaskell's *Ruth*, Charlotte Brontë's *Villette*, Goethe, and Schiller
1854	34	Translates Ludwig Feuerbach's *Das Wesen des Christenthums* (*The Essence of Christianity*). Travels with Lewes to Weimar and Berlin; reports her happiness to Charles Bray
1855	35	Returns to England; sets up house with Lewes in Richmond. Writes and reviews for the *Westminster Review*
1856	36	Begins to write fiction; 'The Sad Fortunes of the Rev. Amos Barton' accepted by *Blackwood's Edinburgh Magazine*. Reading includes Sophocles, accounts (Carlyle and Burke) of the French Revolution, and Jane Austen

Year	Literary Context	Historical Events
1850	First publication of Wordsworth's *Prelude* Death of Wordsworth Herbert Spencer, *Social Statistics*; Dickens, *David Copperfield*	
1851	Ruskin, *The Stones of Venice* (to 1853)	Great Exhibition at the Crystal Palace
1853	Comte, *Cours de philosophie positive* (1830–42) trans. Harriet Martineau as *Positive Philosophy*; Dickens, *Bleak House*; Elizabeth Gaskell, *Cranford, Ruth* Charlotte Brontë, *Villette*	
1854–6		Crimean War
1855	Lewes, *Life of Goethe*; Elizabeth Gaskell, *North and South*; Turgenev, *Russian Life in the Interior or the Experiences of a Sportsman* trans. James D. Meiklejohn	

Year	Age	Life
1857	37	Last contributions to the *Westminster Review* published. 'Amos Barton', 'Mr Gilfil's Love-Story' and 'Janet's Repentance' appear serially in *Blackwood's* (collected and published in 1858 as *Scenes of Clerical Life*). Travels to Scilly Isles with Lewes to continue research for his *Sea-Side Studies*. Tells her family about her relationship with Lewes, and they break off all communication with her
1858	38	Writes *Adam Bede*
1859	39	*Adam Bede* published; has begun *The Mill on the Floss*; writes 'The Lifted Veil', published in *Blackwood's* (July); Dickens expresses his admiration of *Adam Bede*, and invites her to contribute to his weekly periodical, *All The Year Round*
1860	40	*The Mill on the Floss* published; writes 'Brother Jacob'; begins *Silas Marner*
1861	41	*Silas Marner* published; begins research for *Romola*
1862–3	42–3	*Romola* serialized in the *Cornhill Magazine*
1866	46	*Felix Holt* published; continues to write for periodicals (*Pall Mall Gazette* and the *Fortnightly*)
1867	47	Subscribes £50 'from the Author of *Romola*' to the foundation of Girton College, Cambridge
1868	48	*The Spanish Gypsy* published
1869	49	Begins *Middlemarch*; begins correspondence with Harriet Beecher Stowe
1871–2	51–2	*Middlemarch* published in independent parts
1873–6	53–6	Researches and writes *Daniel Deronda*, also published in independent parts

Year	Literary Context	Historical Events
1857	Flaubert, *Madame Bovary*; Elizabeth Gaskell, *The Life of Charlotte Brontë* Dickens, *Little Dorrit*	Indian Mutiny
1859	Charles Darwin, *The Origin of Species* J. S. Mill, *On Liberty*	
1860		Unification of Italy; source of Nile discovered
1861–5		American Civil War
1862	Lev Tolstoy, *Childhood, Boyhood and Youth*, trans. Malwida von Meysenburg	
1863	Elizabeth Gaskell, *Sylvia's Lovers*	
1864–5	Dickens, *Our Mutual Friend*	
1865	Death of Elizabeth Gaskell	Abraham Lincoln assassinated
1866	Elizabeth Gaskell, *Wives and Daughters*	
1867	Turgenev, *Fathers and Sons* (1862), trans. Eugene Schuyler	Second Reform Bill brought in by Disraeli
1869	Turgenev, *Liza* (English version of *A Nest of Gentlefolk*), trans. W. R. S. Ralston; J. S. Mill, *The Subjection of Women*	
1870	Death of Dickens	
1870–1		Franco-Prussian War
1874	Hardy, *Far from the Madding Crowd*	Disraeli becomes Prime Minister

Year	Age	Life
1878	58	Writes *Impressions of Theophrastus Such* (1879). Death of George Henry Lewes
1880	60	Marries John Walter Cross on 6 May. Death in London on 22 December, one month after her 61st birthday

Year	Literary Context	Historical Events
1879	Ibsen, *A Doll's House*	Birth of Trotsky and Stalin
1880	Tennyson, *Ballads and Other Poems*	Parnell demands Home Rule for Ireland

INTRODUCTION

George Eliot and Three Narratives

The short novel and two stories in this volume were first published together, at George Eliot's request, in the Cabinet Edition of 1878. All three date from a period of intense creativity after the publication and immediate popularity of *Adam Bede* in 1859. *The Lifted Veil* appeared in *Blackwood's Edinburgh Magazine* the same summer; *Brother Jacob* was written the following year (though not published until 1864); *Silas Marner* was begun in 1860, and published in 1861. Since the successful publication of *Adam Bede*, she had also written *The Mill on the Floss* and begun the research for *Romola*. Few writers achieve such varied productivity, at this imaginative level, in so short a period of time; but it was characteristic of the intellectual energy which George Eliot showed throughout her life, and her powers of creative reflection.

In all three narratives George Eliot's imagination is drawn to characters who are 'exiles' or 'aliens' from their families or communities, and who know what it is like to be severed from natural human relations. Until she found happiness with G. H. Lewes in 1855, 'exile' in various forms had been well known to Marian Evans. In her childhood she had known the freedom and security of country life, which, as for Wordsworth (1770–1850), had helped to form her moral nature; and for all the intellectual opportunities which life in London was later to bring her, she felt keenly the loss of the happiness she had known in the country with her brother, Isaac, commemorating it in the 'Brother and Sister' sonnets of 1869. Nonetheless, she realised on her return from Switzerland in 1850 that country-living could not nourish the development of her inner life, and that she had to be 'a stranger and a foreigner on the earth for ever more', rather than stay in Warwickshire where the weather, the country and the people were dismal. From then on exile was known to her in many different ways. She had already experienced the loss of her Evangelical faith, as well as the companionship of her father. Soon the severance of ties with her family, as well as social ostracism after she started 'living in sin' with G. H. Lewes, were to contribute to her knowledge of what it was like to feel isolated and estranged. At the same time she shared with the religious writer John Bunyan (1628–88), who deeply influenced her, a trust that the straiht gate is often only discovered along crooked ways. 'There's reasons in things as nobody knows', as Mr Macey puts it in *Silas Marner*.

Adam Bede was published in the same year as Charles Darwin's *On the Origin of Species*. George Eliot read it and commented: 'To me, the Development Theory, and all the other explanations by which processes come to be, produce a feeble impression compared with the mystery that underlies the process.[1] George Eliot's sense of this mystery was closely related to her love of music.[2] What expressed itself in music as harmony, George Eliot perceived as sympathy in its fullest sense between human beings. But she knew that such harmony was not easily achieved; and much of her fiction was concerned with the progress towards it.

Silas Marner suffers from catalepsy, a trance-like state in which he temporarily seems like a man who is dead. This temporary absence of 'soul from body', or 'visitation' as he calls it, has led to his false condemnation for theft in the northern chapel community to which he belongs, and his consequent exile to Raveloe. When we first see Marner, he has been living alone for fifteen years, an 'alien', a member of a 'disinherited race', known and unknown to the villagers of Raveloe, with whom he exchanges few words. 'He invited no comer to step across his door-sill, and he never strolled into the village to drink a pint at the Rainbow, or to gossip at the wheelwright's; he sought no man or woman, save for the purposes of his calling, or in order to supply himself with necessaries; and it was soon clear to the Raveloe lasses that he would never urge one of them to accept him against her will – quite as if he had heard them declare that they would never marry a dead man come to life again' (p. 6). Like Wordsworth's leech-gatherer, he seems like a figure whom Time has forgotten, and who belongs to a narrative which, as George Eliot herself recognised, is 'legendary'. A shaken trust in God and Man which is 'little short of madness' leads to those 'deep sorrows' which the mind cannot always endure, and require a 'marvel' to heal. Marner's return from alienation, and his reintegration into the human community from which he has become an exile, is the subject of George Eliot's narrative.

Brother Jacob, though written after *The Lifted Veil*, originates like *Silas Marner* in rural life. In this short story Jacob and his brother David experience different forms of exile. As a congenital or village idiot, as they were then called, Jacob lives in innocent isolation, forming bonds and affections in his own particular way. David's exile is self-inflicted when he steals his mother's guineas for the purpose of starting a business in the West Indies. After its failure, and David's return to England under another name, Brother Jacob in his innocence becomes the instrument through which David has to confront his crime in public and acknowledge his kinship with his idiot sibling. (As George Eliot herself knew, the failure to do this severs the deepest of human bonds.) But David, revealed for what he is, no longer has a place in the town where he has tried to settle, and is compelled to leave once again. As Silas Marner discovers, belonging to a community means acceptance of its codes, though for Jacob himself this will never be possible.

In *The Lifted Veil*, George Eliot is drawn to another character estranged from normal human relations, and suffering as Marner does from an oddity of consciousness – in this instance the faculty of prevision. Sudden flashes of visual imagining lift the veil on the future, enabling the narrator to foresee his own poisoned marriage and death. This tale, unlike the other two, portrays the lives of the urban rich, and is unique in George Eliot's fiction in exploring an aspect of the supernatural.

The first-person narrator, the younger son of a wealthy banking-family, travels in Europe, as George Eliot's talent had enabled her to do since the late 1840s; but never without that sense of leaving behind what mattered most to her, until she set out for Germany with G. H. Lewes in 1853: 'My heart-ties are not loosened by distance – it is not in the nature of ties to be so; and when I think of my loved ones as those to whom I can be a comforter, and help, I long to be with them again.'[3] The lack of human sympathy in *The Lifted Veil* – powerfully present in the village life of Raveloe – reflects that more hard-hearted social world she had come to know in London and abroad, very different to her own simple upbringing, and which failed to satisfy her need for a deep emotional attachment. At times *The Lifted Veil* also suggests an unusual, but scarcely surprising bitterness at the lack of charity in the society which had turned its back on her. 'We have all a chance of meeting with some pity, some tenderness, some charity, when we are dead: it is the living only who cannot be forgiven' (p. 186).

But this tale of the horror of prevision has other origins too, as Dr Beryl Gray has shown in her excellent 'Afterword' to *The Lifted Veil* (London, 1985). Through her friendship with Charles and Clara Bray in the 1840s, George Eliot had been attracted to the interests of their circle, including phrenology, mesmerism and clairvoyance, about which she had always been sceptical. As she withdrew from her Evangelical faith, in which she had believed with such ardour when young, she was driven to reflect further on the nature of human consciousness. Her prolonged involvement with biblical criticism led to her translation of Spinoza (1632–77) whose nobility of mind was, like George Eliot's, never impaired by his rejection of orthodox beliefs, and whose work, like Eliot's *The Lifted Veil*, raised the question of free-will. Withdrawal from dogma left many questions unanswered about the nature of human consciousness, and the estrangement which could result from perceptions beyond the boundaries of the normal. The epigraph states her wish; 'Give me no light, great Heaven, but such as turns/ To energy of human fellowship'.

Placed side by side, these three tales illustrate how some of George Eliot's intellectual and personal concerns coalesce in this period of fruitfulness. Throughout her twenties she had suffered the isolation which came from being a woman possessed of great intellectual gifts, and had known later what it was like to be rejected on moral grounds. In all three tales the theme of what it is like to be trapped outside, what it felt to be alien, recurs. The narrator of *The Lifted Veil* calls it 'a fatal solitude of soul in the society of one's fellow-men'. For George Eliot it was not fatal, but creative.

Silas Marner

Silas Marner has as its subtitle 'The Weaver of Raveloe'. Marner's occupation in the early years of the nineteenth century is characterised by George Eliot at the opening of the novel: 'those scattered linen-weavers – emigrants from the town into the country – were to the last regarded as aliens by their rustic neighbours, and usually contracted the eccentric habits which belong to a state of loneliness' (p. 4). Marner has come as a wanderer from a town in the industrial North, where community as in 'the old-fashioned village life no longer exists'. George Eliot's narrative tells of the reintegration of Silas into this community through the love brought into his life by a child. The lines from Wordsworth's 'Michael' which George Eliot uses as an epigraph – 'a child, more than all the other gifts that earth can offer to declining man, brings hope with it, and forward-looking thoughts' – are appropriate not just because they indicate the story, but because *Silas Marner* in a more general way is like Wordsworth's tale told in reverse: not the departure from rural life because of the Industrial Revolution, but the return to it as embodying the 'remedial influence of pure natural human relations'. George Eliot's unfulfilled fear that *Silas Marner* would interest no one since Wordsworth was dead, reflects the values which belonged to her own childhood,[4] and which were rapidly being overtaken by the new industrial and commercial age, as can be seen in second part of *Brother Jacob*. Silas Marner arrives in Raveloe in the late 1780s, and Eliot's narration covers more than thirty years of his life: the period of prosperity for weavers during the Napoleonic wars, and subsequent decline of the trade, which would once more drive those less fortunate than Silas Marner back into the factories and towns.

As the title indicates, the portrait of Marner himself matters more to George Eliot than the social history of which he is the product. Nonetheless, the characters of the Rainbow Inn, and the lesser landed gentry who come to celebrate the New Year at the Red House, are portrayed with a directness and humour that make them memorable. George Eliot's ear for the idiom of a Dolly Winthrop or a Priscilla Lammeter is always rhythmical and attuned. But the economy of the narrative is achieved by a poetic intensification of certain events in Marner's life. Outcast from his Dissenting Chapel by the counting of lots, and betrayed in love by his one friend, Silas Marner finds in the contemplation of the gold he receives for his weaving a substitute for the bonds of human fellowship. Its theft from its secret hiding-place beneath the floor of his cottage (itself a metaphor for its psychic value) completes his spiritual death, leaving his 'soul like a forlorn traveller on an unknown desert'. But his terrible grief at the loss of his gold opens the way to a new relationship with the people of Raveloe. 'The repulsion Marner had always created in his neighbours was partly dissipated by the new light in which this misfortune had shown him' (p. 77). In spite of his passionate preoccupation with his loss, a change begins to occur in Marner which George Eliot describes in a metaphor linking human psychological life with that of the seasons: 'Our consciousness rarely registers the beginning of a growth within us any more than that without us: there have been many circulations of the sap before we detect the smallest sign of the bud' (p. 57).

While he is in a cataleptic trance the process of restoration and compensation for his loss is advanced by a 'marvel'. 'Turning towards the hearth, where the two logs had fallen apart, and sent forth only a red uncertain glimmer, he seated himself on his fireside chair, and was stooping to push his logs together, when, to his blurred vision, it seemed as if there were gold on the floor in front of the hearth. Gold! – his own gold – brought back to him as mysteriously as it had been taken away! He felt his heart begin to beat violently, and for a few moments he was unable to stretch out his hand and grasp the restored treasure. The heap of gold seemed to glow and get larger beneath his agitated gaze. He leaned forward at last, and stretched forth his hand; but instead of the hard coin with the familiar resisting outline, his fingers encountered soft warm curls' (p. 110). The child revives a true life in him, linking him with the real world, as opposed to his fantasy life in gold. The 'legendary' narrative parallels and reverses the alchemical process in which base metal is transmuted into gold; here, gold is transmuted into life. For Marner himself, this substitution is an indispensable part of the process of what Jung was later to call 'individuation', and an example of 'synchronicity': a meaningful coincidence of inner and outer events that are not themselves causally connected.[5]

While the narrative looks forward in this way to twentieth-century psychology, it also looks back to mediaeval romance. The arrival of the child in Marner's house is described as a 'marvel', recalling that tradition of story-telling in which, as here, adventures involving the marvellous form part of the process of self-realisation. From the point of view of the future, and of the past, the narrative contains that element of the improbable, and the popularly accepted, associated with legend.

The tale belongs also to the tradition of moral fable, which owes much to Chaucer. In *The Pardoner's Tale*, for example, gold is identified with Death, and greed for it leads to a triple murder. When the Stone-pits are drained in *Silas Marner*, revealing the drowned body of Duncan Cass and the gold he has stolen from Silas, his brother is compelled to point to the moral: 'Everything comes to light . . . sooner or later.' But the emphasis of George Eliot's fable does not fall on the wages of sin; her interest lies in the possibility of human recuperation.

The economy of the narrative enables it, Janus-like, to face both ways in its social stance too: looking back to traditions in village life which were already 'old-fashioned', and looking forward to an England in which the divisiveness of class was increasingly to distort the social structure. The strength of *Silas Marner* lies in its fusing the multiple layers of George Eliot's experience in a narrative which unfolded itself, as she said, from 'the merest millet-seed of thought'.

George Eliot's lack of sympathy with the squirearchy (and this is a tale about how they get their comeuppance) is suggested by the family name. The Casses are crass in varying degrees. On account of the Napoleonic wars, and as a farmer who owns his own land with a tenant or two who treat him like a lord, Squire Cass has illusions about his own superiority, having never met anyone higher on the social scale than himself. The villagers hold it against him that he has kept his sons at home in idleness; and Dunstan in particular – 'a spiteful jeering fellow, who seemed to enjoy his drink the more when other people went dry' – enjoys the privilege of rank, such as it is, without responsibility. When he goes to his death by drowning in the Stone-pits with Marner's gold in his hands, the place and manner of his death accentuate the allegorical as well as the realistic element of the narrative. Bunyan's Slough of Despond casts its shadow upon Squire Cass's deserted stone-pit. Godfrey, the elder brother, for all the good-nature attributed to him, is crass in a different way. Perhaps not altogether to blame for marrying a woman of a different class who becomes an opium-addict and fathering her child, he still attempts to reclaim Eppie from Silas after the latter has cared for her for sixteen years. His coarseness

of feeling and lack of respect for the bond between Silas and
Eppie reflects a class attitude (which was to anger E. M. Forster
fifty years later in *Where Angels Fear to Tread*)[6] that Eppie
would be better off with them. She would not. Eppie chooses
with the decisiveness that goes with natural and instinctive
bonds, and of someone who knows where her affections,
loyalties and roots lie. The rejection of her real father is also a
rejection of his class, and the attitudes which shape it: 'I wasn't
brought up to be a lady, and I can't turn my mind to it. I like
the working-folks, and their victuals, and their ways' (p. 171).

Seen like this, *Silas Marner* contains the seed of a revolutionary fiction, expressing a working-class solidarity against the
moral turpitude and unimaginative heartlessness of the gentry.
But while George Eliot's moral outlook is adamant against the
weaknesses of the Cass family, the tone of *Silas Marner* is deeply
impressed by her love of English rural life, its continuities and
its humour, its qualities of forbearance, simplicity, loyalty and
neighbourly self-reliance. Raveloe life has been forged from the
endurance of many generations of peasants, who have learned
how to preserve their independence and help each other in times
of need – as Dolly Winthrop helps Silas after the theft of his
gold and in the nurturing of Eppie. Together they help him to
return to the inherited wisdom and lore of village life: 'By
seeking what was needful for Eppie, by sharing the effect that
everything produced on her, he had himself come to appropriate
the forms of custom and belief which were the mould of Raveloe
life' (p. 141). While this mould takes cognisance of the Church
it does so lightly, recognising the unseemliness of trying too
hard to get to Heaven before your neighbour; and instead
placing trust in laws which lie beneath dogmatic belief. No one
in Raveloe would be likely to have stolen Marner's gold because
of the impossibility of spending it without the whole village
knowing! Only in exile could the thief profit from his theft, and
the Raveloe life is not one from which anyone moves.

George Eliot's understanding of certain qualities in the English
temperament – an inherited sense of what is decent and seemly
– enables her to characterise the inhabitants of the Rainbow
Inn, Dolly Winthrop and Priscilla Lammeter, with a warmth
and humour which is Shakespearean in its vividness. Priscilla's
sturdy independence – 'As I say, Mr have-your-own-way is
the best husband, and the only one I'd ever promise to obey' –

exemplifies an eccentricity which shows itself in many guises, and at times expresses a philosophy of life. Dolly Winthrop, recalling Marner's false conviction at the hands of the Dissenters in Lantern Yard, comments: 'You were hard done by that once, Master Marner, and it seems you'll never know the rights of it; but that doesn't hinder there *being* a rights, Master Marner, for all it's dark to you and me' (p. 177–8). In the final sentences of *Silas Marner* these rights are expressed in a harmony between human beings, based on mutual sympathy, and the natural world of which they are a part.

> The garden was fenced with stones on two sides, but in front there was an open fence, through which the flowers shone with answering gladness, as the four united people came within sight of them.
>
> 'O father,' said Eppie, 'what a pretty home ours is! I think nobody could be happier than we are'
>
> (p. 181).

In *Silas Marner* George Eliot writes with the assured reflectiveness that comes from 'emotion recollected in tranquillity' about a way of life which was disappearing about the time she was born in 1819. She was able to make a short masterpiece out of *Silas Marner* because it is elegiac, telling of customs and continuities which were dying and which are reborn in creative memory, where the sun still shines on them.

Brother Jacob[7]

Although *Brother Jacob* begins in a rural setting, it is very different in style to *Silas Marner*. It is a cautionary tale, told, as it were, by a schoolmaster, reflecting on the theme of just retribution: 'Among the many fatalities attending the bloom of young desire, that of blindly taking to the confectionary line has not, perhaps, been sufficiently considered' (p. 229). While George Eliot's voice can be heard close behind the narrator of *Silas Marner*, this narrator writes with mock-serious gravity, favouring biblical phrases such as 'in this wise' and 'so it came to pass'. Both the vocabulary and the tone illustrate George Eliot's pleasure in using the mock-serious to humorous effect. But *Brother Jacob* also owes much to Wordsworth and the theme of knowing innocence in 'The Idiot Boy'. This awkward combination is reflected in George Eliot's uncertainty as to whether to call the tale 'Mr David Faux, Confectioner' or 'The Idiot Brother'.[8]

David Faux sees his vocation as making sweetmeats. Having served his apprenticeship, he sees no chance of advancement without helping himself to his mother's guineas and setting up his own business in 'foreign climes'. (His moral nullity is rare in a George Eliot character.) He attempts to hide the guineas under the roots of a hollow ash, but before making his escape he is observed by his idiot brother. Here the mastery of George Eliot in the simple magical effect realises itself: the idiot brother finds equal satisfaction in the golden lozenges which David Faux happens to have in his confectioner's pocket, as in the golden guineas. The affection generated by this transference, of which Brother Jacob does not realise the significance, will lead many years later to the unmasking of his brother's falseness. Food and money, as different yet interchangeable forms of social coinage, control and deepen the narrative as it progresses.

After the failure of his business in the West Indies, David Faux returns to the small town of Grimworth, assuming the new name of Mr Edward Freely. (Names are often significant in George Eliot, whether literally as in the case of 'Faux', or in a more musical and associative way as here: a point also raised in relation to *Silas Marner*.) What had begun as moral fable now also begins to interest George Eliot as a portrait of changing provincial life, which nine years later was to become a major aspect of *Middlemarch*. In the 'old order' Church and Chapel patronised different shops. Now a vagrant spirit (absent in Raveloe!) is drawing the more affluent to the neighbouring town of Cattleton, where business is run on the system of 'small profits and quick returns'. Consumerist and capitalist ideals (such as value for money) are beginning to make the world go round.

The new confectioner's window belonging to Mr Edward Freely in the market square is compared in its colour and allure to a still life of the Dutch school or a 'landscape in Turner's latest style'. The comparison is picturesque, the significance economic, in that the window attracts the purchasing power of the middle classes, tempting wives to buy what they would previously have baked. 'Buying at Freely's' becomes a form of one-upmanship in which neighbours compete with each other, when they wish 'to give an entertainment of some brilliancy'.

What used to be private talents are beginning to be commercialised. Where you shop is also beginning to replace where you worship as an image of social status.

The partial emancipation of women from labour in the kitchen does not lead, however, to any improvement in their quality of life, as the narrator ironically observes:

> And so it came to pass, that the progress of civilisation at Grimworth was not otherwise apparent than in the impoverishment of men, the gossiping idleness of women, and the heightening prosperity of Mr Edward Freely
>
> (p. 247).

George Eliot contrasts the pseudo-sophistication of small-town life with the unaffected natural feeling in Brother Jacob, who after Edward Freely has once again revealed himself to his family by claiming a share of his mother's estate, reenters his brothers's life and unmasks him. Once again the power of the simple image exemplifies George Eliot's narrative gift:

> 'Mother's zinnies?' said Jacob, pointing to a glass jar of yellow lozenges that stood in the window. 'Zive 'em me'
>
> (p. 263).

Jacob's undiminished affection for the brother who once exchanged guineas for lozenges becomes the source of his undoing in Grimworth: 'there would never be any security against his coming back, like a wasp to the honey-pot' (p. 268). The associative nature of the simile continues the organising power of yellow in the narrative, as is also the case in *Silas Marner*. David Faux, having lost the respect and custom of the townspeople, departs to another exile where the narrator does not follow him.

But the morals which our periphrastic narrator draws from his tale are not distant from those implicit in *Silas Marner*: 'And we see in it, I think, an admirable instance of the unexpected forms in which the great Nemesis hides herself' (p. 269). Eppie's rejection of Godfrey Cass was described by George Eliot as a 'mild Nemesis', of which Dunstan's drowning is the more powerful example that pride takes a fall. In all three cases her attraction to laws of life which are classical rather than Christian are apparent, and morality which in its dislike of ostentation, whether in feeling or way of life, has much in common with the civic virtues of Rome.

The Lifted Veil

George Eliot described *The Lifted Veil* as a *'jeu de mélancholie'*.[9] Her *mélancholie* was brought on by recalling in the first chapters of *The Mill on the Floss* her happy childhood years with her brother Isaac before the parting of their ways. 'The exceptional mental character' of the narrator which excludes him from natural human relations mirrors what George Eliot suffered as a result of her unique gifts as a woman and an artist. But because she is an artist, this *mélancholie* is suffused and transformed in a Gothic tale, where the 'double consciousness' of the narrator and the artist are parallel but different.

Latimer, the narrator, suffers from the poet's sensibility without the poet's voice – a 'dumb passion' bringing with it a 'fatal solitude of soul in the society of one's fellow-men'. After a prolonged illness, Latimer's father, who disapproves of his impractical and unscientific son, offers him the chance to recuperate on a European tour. The mention of the word 'Prague' triggers his faculty of prevision: a vision of the city which includes George Eliot's fear of a society unreplenished with 'the energy of human fellowship', living in a 'rigidity of habit' and deprived of the beliefs which nourished it in the past.

The faculty of prevision intensifies Latimer's awareness of how things are. To him people appear as if under a microscope which shows 'all the intermediate frivolities, all the suppressed egoism, all the struggling chaos of puerilities, meanness, vague capricious memories, and indolent make-shift thoughts, from which human words and deeds emerge like leaflets covering a fermenting heap' (p. 196). As a novelist intent upon seeing how certain human lots were woven and interwoven, George Eliot was aware how human perception, with its intermittent alterations of focus and intensity, was the basis of her art, and also, as for Latimer, the burden of the artist.

Worst of all for him is the foreknowledge that he will supplant his brother as husband to Bertha; an event which comes about through his brother's death in a riding accident. After the first passion of being in love with Bertha fades, he begins to see the narrow room of the woman's soul. And as he does so, she will lose the power to dominate him, not possessing his 'gift'. She cannot perceive the cause of the change in him. The veil lifted for him becomes a darkening of the veil for her. Here, George Eliot is beginning to explore the territory which Strindberg was to open up more completely twenty years later: that struggle for psychic domination, achieved by playing upon weaknesses and fears, and which can cause, as in Bertha, rage and hatred when failure is apparent. Her feeble husband possesses the key to her soul without her knowing it. For Latimer, seeing is knowing; for Bertha, it is not. Strindberg's men and women resolve this in a duel to the death; Latimer and Bertha in a less dramatic but more terrifying and mirthless way: 'our alienation, our repulsion from each other, lay within the silence of our own hearts' (p. 215). Whether or not Latimer's prevision gave him the free-will to avoid this fate remains an enigma which the narrative does not attempt to solve.

At the end, though, George Eliot brings about the final revelation by a piece of scientific experimentation which is not only grotesque but also implausible (the more surprising in that the author's faculty of prevision would seem to make it unnecessary). The experiment of transfusing blood from the doctor's artery into the arteries of Bertha's dead servant enables the servant to return from the dead, and reveal Bertha's hatred of her husband and her plan to murder him. This lifting of the veil – by a different means – leads sensibly to their separation, and another form of exile: 'Since then Bertha and I have lived apart – she in her own neighbourhood, the mistress of half our wealth, I as a wanderer in foreign countries' (p. 225). His dark consciousness continues to torment him, as it does all those possessed of high imagination, because it enables him to see not just the future, but those secrets of human heart which, for peace of mind at least, had better remain hidden.

George Eliot chose *The Lifted Veil* to be printed between *Silas Marner* and *Brother Jacob*. It remains the odd-ball of the three; more powerful though less characteristic than *Brother Jacob*. To have ended the volume with it would have ended it in a minor key, lacking that affirming power of sympathy which was the hallmark of George Eliot's humanist vision.

References

1 (p.xx) George Eliot, *Letters* (London, 1954), III, p.227.

2 (p.xx) For a detailed and valuable discussion, see Beryl Gray, *George Eliot and Music* (London, 1989).

3 (p.xxi) Quoted in Joan Bennett, *George Eliot, Her Mind and Art* (Cambridge, 1962), letter of 4 December 1849 to Cara Bray, p.44.

4 (p.xxiii) George Eliot was born in 1819: the period covered by the novel ends about this period. Wordsworth died in 1850.

5 (p.xxiv) For further reading on 'individuation' and 'synchronicity', see *Man and his Symbols* (London, 1964), ed. C. G. Jung. A more extended discussion of 'synchronicity' is to be found in F. D. Peat, *Synchronicity* (New York, 1987).

6 (p.xxvi) E. M. Forster's *Where Angels Fear to Tread* was published in 1905. See p.85, and following.

7 (p.xxvii) I have chosen to discuss *Brother Jacob* before *The Lifted Veil*, in spite of the order in which they are printed, because its rural English setting suggests a natural comparison with *Silas Marner* whereas *The Lifted Veil* does not. This supernatural tale stands on its own within George Eliot's work. See the final paragraph of the Introduction for a suggestion as to why George Eliot had them printed in this order.

8 (p.xxviii) See F. B. Pinion, *A George Eliot Miscellany* (London, 1982), p.103. (*The Lifted Veil* and *Brother Jacob* are reprinted in Chapter 2, with some useful notes to which I am indebted.)

9 (p.xxx) *ibid*, p.28.

NOTE ON THE TEXT

The text used here is that of the Cabinet Edition of 1878, which was approved by George Eliot.

SILAS MARNER

THE WEAVER OF RAVELOE

A child, more than all other gifts
That earth can offer to declining man,
Brings hope with it, and forward-looking thoughts.
                              – WORDSWORTH

PART I

CHAPTER I

In the days when the spinning wheels hummed busily in the farmhouses – and even great ladies, clothed in silk and thread-lace, had their toy spinning-wheels of polished oak – there might be seen in districts far away among the lanes, or deep in the bosom of the hills, certain pallid undersized men, who, by the side of the brawny country-folk, looked like the remnants of a disinherited race. The shepherd's dog barked fiercely when one of these alien-looking men appeared on the upland, dark against the early winter sunset; for what dog likes a figure bent under a heavy bag? – and these pale men rarely stirred abroad without that mysterious burden. The shepherd himself, though he had good reason to believe that the bag held nothing but flaxen thread,[1] or else the long rolls of strong linen spun from that thread, was not quite sure that this trade of weaving, indispensable though it was, could be carried on entirely without the help of the Evil One. In that far-off time superstition clung easily round every person or thing that was at all unwonted, or even intermittent and occasional merely, like the visits of the pedlar[2] or the knife-grinder. No one knew where wandering men had their homes or their origin; and how was a man to be explained unless you at least knew somebody who knew his father and mother? To the peasants[3] of old times, the world outside their own direct experience was a region of vagueness and mystery: to their untravelled thought a state of wandering was a conception as dim as the winter life of the swallows that came back with the spring; and even a settler, if he came from distant parts, hardly ever ceased to be viewed with a remnant of distrust, which would have prevented any surprise if a long course of inoffensive conduct on his part had ended in the commission of a crime; especially if he had any reputation for knowledge, or showed any skill in handicraft. All cleverness, whether in the rapid use of that difficult instrument the tongue, or in some other art unfamiliar to villagers, was in itself suspicious: honest folk, born and bred in a visible manner, were mostly not over-wise or clever – at least, not beyond such a matter as knowing the signs of the weather; and the process by which rapidity and dexterity of any kind were acquired was so wholly hidden, that they partook of the nature of conjuring. In this way it came to pass that those scattered linen-weavers – emigrants from the town into the country – were to the last regarded as aliens by their rustic neighbours, and usually contracted the eccentric habits which belong to a state of loneliness.

In the early years of this century,[4] such a linen-weaver, named Silas Marner, worked at his vocation in a stone cottage that stood among the nutty hedgerows near the village of Raveloe, and not far from the edge of a deserted stone-pit. The question-able sound of Silas's loom, so unlike the natural cheerful trotting of the winnowing-machine, or the simpler rhythm of the flail, had a half-fearful fascination for the Raveloe boys, who would often leave off their nutting or birds'-nesting to peep in at the window of the stone cottage, counterbalancing a certain awe at the mysterious action of the loom, by a pleasant sense of scornful superiority, drawn from the mockery of its alternating noises, along with the bent, tread-mill attitude of the weaver. But sometimes it happened that Marner, pausing to adjust an irregularity in his thread, became aware of the small scoundrels, and, though chary of his time, he liked their intrusion so ill that he would descend from his loom, and, opening the door, would fix on them a gaze that was always enough to make them take to their legs in terror. For how was it possible to believe that those large brown protuberant eyes in Silas Marner's pale face really saw nothing very distinctly that was not close to them, and not rather that their dreadful stare could dart cramp, or rickets, or a wry mouth at any boy who happened to be in the rear? They had, perhaps, heard their fathers and mothers hint that Silas Marner could cure folk's rheumatism if he had a mind, and add, still more darkly, that if you could only speak the devil fair enough, he might save you the cost of the doctor. Such strange lingering echoes of the old demon-worship might per-haps even now be caught by the diligent listener among the grey-haired peasantry; for the rude mind with difficulty associates the ideas of power and benignity. A shadowy conception of power that by much persuasion can be induced to refrain from inflicting harm, is the shape most easily taken by the sense of the Invisible in the minds of men who have always been pressed close by primitive wants, and to whom a life of hard toil has never been illuminated by any enthusiastic religious faith. To them pain and mishap present a far wider range of possibilities than gladness and enjoyment: their imagination is almost barren of the images that feed desire and hope, but is all overgrown by recollections that are a perpetual pasture to fear. 'Is there anything you can fancy that you would like to eat?' I once said to an old labouring man, who was in his last illness, and who had refused all the food his wife had offered him. 'No,' he answered, 'I've never been used to nothing but common victual, and I can't eat that.' Experience had bred no fancies in him that could raise the phantasm of appetite.

And Raveloe was a village where many of the old echoes lingered, undrowned by new voices. Not that it was one of those barren parishes lying on the outskirts of civilisation – inhabited by meagre sheep and thinly-scattered shepherds: on the contrary, it lay in the rich central plain of what we are pleased to call Merry England, and held farms which, speaking from a spiritual point of view, paid highly-desirable tithes.[5] But it was nestled in a snug well-wooded hollow, quite an hour's journey on horse-back from any turnpike,[6] where it was never reached by the vibrations of the coach-horn, or of public opinion. It was an important-looking village, with a fine old church and large churchyard in the heart of it, and two or three large brick-and-stone homesteads, with well-walled orchards and ornamental weathercocks, standing close upon the road, and lifting more imposing fronts than the rectory, which peeped from among the trees on the other side of the churchyard: – a village which showed at once the summits of its social life, and told the practised eye that there was no great park and manor-house in the vicinity, but that there were several chiefs in Raveloe who could farm badly quite at their ease, drawing enough money from their bad farming, in those war times,[7] to live in a rollicking fashion, and keep a jolly Christmas, Whitsun, and Easter tide.

It was fifteen years since Silas Marner had first come to Raveloe; he was then simply a pallid young man, with prominent short-sighted brown eyes, whose appearance would have had nothing strange for people of average culture and experience, but for the villagers near whom he had come to settle it had mysterious peculiarities which corresponded with the exceptional nature of his occupation, and his advent from an unknown region called 'North'ard'. So had his way of life: – he invited no comer to step across his door-sill, and he never strolled into the village to drink a pint at the Rainbow, or to gossip at the wheelwright's: he sought no man or woman, save for the purposes of his calling, or in order to supply himself with necessaries; and it was soon clear to the Raveloe lasses that he would never urge one of them to accept him against her will – quite as if he had heard them declare that they would never marry a dead man come to life again. This view of Marner's personality was not without another ground than his pale face and unexampled eyes; for Jem Rodney, the mole-catcher,[8] averred that one evening as he was returning homeward he saw Silas Marner leaning against a stile with a heavy bag on his back, instead of resting the bag on the stile as a man in his senses would have done; and that, on coming up to him, he saw that Marner's eyes were set like a dead man's, and he spoke to him, and shook him, and his limbs were stiff, and his hands clutched the bag as if they'd been made of iron; but just as he had made up his mind that the weaver was dead, he came all right again, like, as you might say, in the winking of an eye, and said 'Good night,' and walked off. All this Jem swore he had seen, more by token that it was the very day he had been mole-catching on Squire Cass's land, down by the old saw-pit. Some said Marner must have been in a 'fit', a word which seemed to explain things otherwise incredible; but the argumentative Mr Macey, clerk of the parish, shook his head, and asked if anybody was ever known to go off in a fit and not fall down. A fit was a stroke, wasn't it?[9] and it was in the nature of a stroke to partly take away the use of a man's limbs and throw him on the parish, if he'd got no children to look to. No, no; it was no stroke that would let a man stand on his legs, like a horse between the shafts, and then walk off as soon as you can say 'Gee!' But there might be such a thing as a man's soul being loose from his body, and going out and in, like a bird out of its nest and back; and that was how folks got over-wise, for they went to school in this shell-less state to those who could teach them more than their neighbours could learn with their five senses and the parson. And where did Master Marner get his knowledge of herbs from – and charms too, if he liked to give them away? Jem Rodney's story was no more than what might have been expected by anybody who had seen how Marner had cured Sally Oates, and made her sleep like a baby, when her heart had been beating enough to burst her body, for two months and more, while she had been under the doctor's care. He might cure more folks if he would; but he was worth speaking fair, if it was only to keep him from doing you a mischief.

It was partly to this vague fear that Marner was indebted for protecting him from the persecution that his singularities might have drawn upon him, but still more to the fact that, the old linen-weaver in the neighbouring parish of Tarley being dead, his handicraft made him a highly welcome settler to the richer housewives of the district, and even to the more provident cottagers, who had their little stock of yarn at the year's end. Their sense of his usefulness would have counteracted any repugnance or suspicion which was not confirmed by a deficiency in the quality or the tale of the cloth[10] he wove for them. And the years had rolled on without producing any change in the impressions of the neighbours concerning Marner, except the change from novelty to habit. At the end of fifteen years the Raveloe men said just the same things about Silas Marner as at the beginning: they did not say them quite so often, but they believed them much more strongly when they did say them. There was only one important addition which the years had brought: it was, that Master Marner had laid by a fine sight of money somewhere, and that he could buy up 'bigger men' than himself.

But while opinion concerning him had remained nearly stationary, and his daily habits had presented scarcely any visible change, Marner's inward life had been a history and a metamorphosis, as that of every fervid nature must be when it has fled, or been condemned to solitude. His life, before he came to Raveloe, had been filled with the movement, the mental activity, and the close fellowship, which, in that day as in this, marked the life of an artisan early incorporated in a narrow religious sect, where the poorest layman has the chance of distinguishing himself by gifts of speech, and has, at the very least, the weight of a silent voter in the government of his community. Marner was highly thought of in that little hidden world, known to itself as the church assembling in Lantern Yard;[11] he was believed to be a young man of exemplary life and ardent faith; and a peculiar interest had been centred in him ever since he had fallen, at a prayer-meeting, into a mysterious rigidity and suspension of consciousness, which, lasting for an hour or more, had been mistaken for death. To have sought a medical explanation for this phenomenon would have been held by Silas himself, as well as by his minister and fellow-members, a wilful self-exclusion from the spiritual significance that might lie therein. Silas was evidently a brother selected for a peculiar discipline; and though the effort to interpret this discipline was discouraged by the absence, on his part, of any spiritual vision during his outward trance, yet it was believed by himself and others that its effect was seen in an accession of light and fervour. A less truthful man than he might have been tempted into the subsequent creation of a vision in the form of resurgent memory; a less sane man might have believed in such a creation; but Silas was both sane and honest, though, as with many honest and fervent men, culture had not defined any channels for his sense of mystery, and so it spread itself over the proper pathway of inquiry and knowledge. He had inherited from his mother some acquaintance with medicinal herbs and their preparation – a little store of wisdom which she had imparted to him as a solemn bequest – but of late years he had had doubts about the lawfulness of applying this knowledge, believing that herbs could have no efficacy without prayer, and that prayer might suffice without herbs; so that his inherited delight to wander through the fields in search of foxglove and dandelion and coltsfoot, began to wear to him the character of a temptation.

Among the members of his church there was one young man, a little older than himself, with whom he had long lived in such close friendship that it was the custom of their Lantern Yard brethren to call them David and Jonathan.[12] The real name of the friend was William Dane, and he, too, was regarded as a shining instance of youthful piety, though somewhat given to over-severity towards weaker brethren, and to be so dazzled by his own light as to hold himself wiser than his teachers. But whatever blemishes others might discern in William, to his friend's mind he was faultless; for Marner had one of those impressible self-doubting natures which, at an inexperienced age, admire imperativeness and lean on contradiction. The expression of trusting simplicity in Marner's face, heightened by that absence of special observation, that defenceless, deer-like, gaze which belongs to large prominent eyes, was strongly contrasted by the self-complacement suppression of inward triumph that lurked in the narrow slanting eyes and compressed lips of William Dane. One of the most frequent topics of conversation between the two friends was Assurance of salvation:[13] Silas confessed that he could never arrive at anything higher than hope mingled with fear, and listened with longing wonder when William declared that he had possessed unshaken assurance ever since, in the period of his conversion, he had dreamed that he saw the words 'calling and election sure' standing by themselves on a white page in the open Bible. Such colloquies have occupied many a pair of pale-faced weavers, whose unnurtured souls have been like young winged things, fluttering forsaken in the twilight.

It had seemed to the unsuspecting Silas that the friendship had suffered no chill even from his formation of another attachment of a closer kind. For some months he had been engaged to a young servant-woman, waiting only for a little increase to their mutual savings in order to their marriage; and it was a great delight to him that Sarah did not object to William's occasional presence in their Sunday interviews. It was at this point in their history that Silas's cataleptic fit[14] occurred during the prayer-meeting; and amidst the various queries and expressions of interest addressed to him by his fellow-members, William's suggestion alone jarred with the general sympathy towards a brother thus singled out for special dealings. He observed that, to him, this trance looked more like a visitation of Satan than a proof of divine favour, and exhorted his friend to see that he hid no accursed thing within his soul. Silas, feeling bound to accept rebuke and admonition as a brotherly office, felt no resentment, but only pain, at his friend's doubts concerning him; and to this was soon added some anxiety at the perception that Sarah's manner towards him began to exhibit a strange fluctuation between an effort at an increased manifestation of regard and involuntary signs of shrinking and dislike. He asked her if she wished to break off their engagement; but she denied this: their engagement was known to the church, and had been recognised in the prayer-meetings; it could not be broken off without strict investigation, and Sarah could render no reason that would be sanctioned by the feeling of the community. At this time the senior deacon was taken dangerously ill, and, being a childless widower, he was tended night and day by some of the younger brethren or sisters. Silas frequently took his turn in the night-watching with William, the one relieving the other at two in the morning. The old man, contrary to expectation, seemed to be on the way to recovery, when one night Silas, sitting up by his bedside, observed that his usual audible breathing had ceased. The candle was burning low, and he had to lift it to see the patient's face distinctly. Examination convinced him that the deacon was dead – had been dead some time, for the limbs were rigid. Silas asked himself if he had been asleep, and looked at the clock: it was already four in the morning. How was it that William had not come? In much anxiety he went to seek for help, and soon there were several friends assembled in the house, the minister among them, while Silas went away to his work, wishing he could have met William to know the reason of his non-appearance. But at six o'clock, as he was thinking of going to seek his friend, William came, and with him the minister. They came to summon him to Lantern Yard, to meet the church members there; and to his inquiry concerning the cause of the summons the only reply was, 'You will hear.' Nothing further was said until Silas was seated in the vestry, in front of the minister, with the eyes of those who to him represented God's people fixed solemnly upon him. Then the minister, taking out a pocket-knife, showed it to Silas, and asked him if he knew where he had left that knife? Silas said, he did not know that he had left it anywhere out of his own pocket – but he was trembling at this strange interrogation. He was then exhorted not to hide his sin, but to confess and repent. The knife had been found in the bureau by the departed deacon's bedside – found in the place where the little bag of church money had lain, which the minister himself had seen the day before. Some hand had removed that bag; and whose hand could it be, if not that of the man to whom the knife belonged? For some time Silas was mute with astonishment: then he said, 'God will clear me: I know nothing about the knife being there, or the money being gone. Search me and my dwelling; you will find nothing but three pound five of my own savings, which William Dane knows I have had these six months.' At this William groaned, but the minister said, 'The proof is heavy against you, brother Marner. The money was taken in the night last past, and no man was with our departed brother but you, for William Dane declares to us that he was hindered by sudden sickness from going to take his place as usual, and you yourself said that he had not come; and, moreoever, you neglected the dead body.'

'I must have slept,' said Silas. Then after a pause, he added, 'Or I must have had another visitation like that which you have all seen me under, so that the thief must have come and gone while I was not in the body, but out of the body. But, I say again, search me and my dwelling, for I have been nowhere else.'

The search was made, and it ended – in William Dane's finding the well-known bag, empty, tucked behind the chest of drawers in Silas's chamber! On this William exhorted his friend to confess, and not to hide his sin any longer. Silas turned a look of keen reproach on him, and said, 'William, for nine years that we have gone in and out together, have you ever known me tell a lie? But God will clear me.'

'Brother,' said William, 'how do I know what you may have done in the secret chambers of your heart, to give Satan an advantage over you?'

Silas was still looking at his friend. Suddenly a deep flush came over his face, and he was about to speak impetuously, when he seemed checked again by some inward shock, that sent the flush back and made him tremble. But at last he spoke feebly, looking at William.

'I remember now – the knife wasn't in my pocket.'

William said, 'I know nothing of what you mean.' The other persons present, however, began to inquire where Silas meant to say that the knife was, but he would give no further explanation: he only said, 'I am sore stricken; I can say nothing. God will clear me.'

On their return to the vestry there was further deliberation. Any resort to legal measures for ascertaining the culprit was contrary to the principles of the church in Lantern Yard, according to which prosecution was forbidden to Christians, even had the case held less scandal to the community. But the members were bound to take other measures for finding out the truth, and they resolved on praying and drawing lots. This resolution can be a ground of surprise only to those who are unacquainted with that obscure religious life which has gone on in the alleys of our towns. Silas knelt with his brethren, relying on his own innocence being certified by immediate divine interference, but feeling that there was sorrow and mourning behind for him even then – that his trust in man had been cruelly bruised. *The lots declared that Silas Marner was guilty.* He was solemnly suspended from church-membership, and called upon to render up the stolen money: only on confession, as the sign of repentance, could he be received once more within the folds of the church. Marner listened in silence. At last, when every one rose to depart, he went towards William Dane and said, in a voice shaken by agitation –

'The last time I remember using my knife, was when I took it out to cut a strap for you. I don't remember putting it in my pocket again. *You* stole the money, and you have woven a plot to lay the sin at my door. But you may prosper, for all that: there is no just God that governs the earth righteously, but a God of lies, that bears witness against the innocent.'

There was a general shudder at this blasphemy.

William said meekly, 'I leave our brethren to judge whether this is the voice of Satan or not. I can do nothing but pray for you, Silas.'

Poor Marner went out with that despair in his soul – that shaken trust in God and man, which is little short of madness to a loving nature. In the bitterness of his wounded spirit, he said to himself, '*She* will cast me off too.' And he reflected that, if she did not believe the testimony against him, her whole faith must be upset as his was. To people accustomed to reason about the forms in which their religious feeling has incorporated itself, it is difficult to enter into that simple, untaught state of mind in which the form and the feeling have never been severed by an act of reflection. We are apt to think it inevitable that a man in Marner's position should have begun to question the validity of an appeal to the divine judgment by drawing lots; but to him this would have been an effort of independent thought such as he had never known; and he must have made the effort at a moment when all his energies were turned into the anguish of disappointed faith. If there is an angel who records the sorrows of men as well as their sins, he knows how many and deep are the sorrows that spring from false ideas for which no man is culpable.[15]

Marner went home, and for a whole day sat alone, stunned by despair, without any impulse to go to Sarah and attempt to

win her belief in his innocence. The second day he took refuge
from benumbing unbelief, by getting into his loom and working
away as usual; and before many hours were past, the minister
and one of the deacons came to him with the message from
Sarah, that she held her engagement to him at an end. Silas
received the message mutely, and then turned away from the
messengers to work at his loom again. In little more than a
month from that time, Sarah was married to William Dane; and
not long afterwards it was known to the brethren in Lantern
Yard that Silas Marner had departed from the town.

CHAPTER 2

Even people whose lives have been made various by learning, sometimes find it hard to keep a fast hold on their habitual views of life, on their faith in the Invisible, nay, on the sense that their past joys and sorrows are a real experience, when they are suddenly transported to a new land, where the beings around them know nothing of their history, and share none of their ideas – where their mother earth shows another lap, and human life has other forms than those on which their souls have been nourished. Minds that have been unhinged from their old faith and love, have perhaps sought this Lethean influence of exile, in which the past becomes dreamy because its symbols have all vanished, and the present too is dreamy because it is linked with no memories. But even *their* experience may hardly enable them thoroughly to imagine what was the effect on a simple weaver like Silas Marner, when he left his own country and people and came to settle in Raveloe. Nothing could be more unlike his native town, set within sight of the widespread hillsides, than this low, wooded region, where he felt hidden even from the heavens by the screening trees and hedgerows. There was nothing here, when he rose in the deep morning quiet and looked out on the dewy brambles and rank tufted grass, that seemed to have any relation with that life centring in Lantern Yard, which had once been to him the altar-place of high dispensations. The whitewashed walls; the little pews where well-known figures entered with a subdued rustling, and where first one well-known voice and then another, pitched in a peculiar key of petition, uttered phrases at once occult and familiar, like the amulet worn on the heart; the pulpit where the minister delivered unquestioned doctrine, and swayed to and fro, and handled the book in a long-accustomed manner; the very pauses between the couplets of the hymn, as it was given out, and the recurrent swell of voices in song: these things had been the channel of divine influences to Marner – they were the fostering home of his religious emotions – they were Christianity and God's kingdom upon earth. A weaver who finds hard words in his hymn-book knows nothing of abstractions; as the little child knows nothing of parental love, but only knows one face and one lap towards which it stretches its arms for refuge and nurture.

And what could be more unlike that Lantern Yard world than the world in Raveloe? – orchards looking lazy with neglected plenty; the large church in the wide churchyard, which men gazed at lounging at their own doors in service-time; the purple-faced farmers jogging along the lanes or turning in at the Rainbow; homesteads, where men supped heavily and slept in the light of the evening hearth, and where women seemed to be laying up a stock of linen for the life to come. There were no lips in Raveloe from which a word could fall that would stir Silas Marner's benumbed faith to a sense of pain. In the early ages of the world, we know, it was believed that each territory was inhabited and ruled by its own divinities, so that a man could cross the bordering heights and be out of the reach of his native gods, whose presence was confined to the streams and the groves and the hills among which he had lived from his birth. And poor Silas was vaguely conscious of something not unlike the feeling of primitive men, when they fled thus, in fear or in sullenness, from the face of an unpropitious deity. It seemed to him that the Power he had vainly trusted in among the streets and at the prayer-meetings, was very far away from this land in which he had taken refuge, where men lived in careless abundance, knowing and needing nothing of that trust, which, for him, had been turned to bitterness. The little light he possessed spread its beams so narrowly, that frustrated belief was a curtain broad enough to create for him the blackness of night.[1]

His first movement after the shock had been to work in his loom; and he went on with this unremittingly, never asking himself why, now he was come to Raveloe, he worked far on into the night to finish the tale of Mrs Osgood's table-linen sooner than she expected – without contemplating beforehand the money she would put into his hand for the work. He seemed to weave, like the spider, from pure impulse, without reflection. Every man's work, pursued steadily, tends in this way to become an end in itself, and so to bridge over the loveless chasms of his life. Silas's hand satisfied itself with throwing the shuttle, and his eye with seeing the little squares in the cloth complete themselves under his effort. Then there were the calls of hunger; and Silas, in his solitude, had to provide his own breakfast, dinner, and supper, to fetch his own water from the well, and put his own kettle on the fire; and all these immediate promptings helped, along with the weaving, to reduce his life to the unquestioning activity of a spinning insect. He hated the thought of the past; there was nothing that called out his love and fellowship toward the strangers he had come amongst; and the future was all dark, for there was no Unseen Love that cared for him. Thought was arrested by utter bewilderment, now its old narrow pathway was closed, and affection seemed to have died under the bruise that had fallen on its keenest nerves.

But at last Mrs Osgood's table-linen was finished, and Silas was paid in gold. His earnings in his native town, where he worked for a wholesale dealer, had been after a lower rate; he had been paid weekly, and of his weekly earnings a large proportion had gone to objects of piety and charity. Now, for the first time in his life, he had five bright guineas put into his hand; no man expected a share of them, and he loved no man that he should offer him a share. But what were the guineas to him who saw no vista beyond countless days of weaving? It was needless for him to ask that, for it was pleasant to him to feel them in his palm, and look at their bright faces, which were all his own: it was another element of life, like the weaving and the satisfaction of hunger, subsisting quite aloof from the life of belief and love from which he had been cut off. The weaver's hand had known the touch of hard-won money even before the palm had grown to its full breadth; for twenty years, mysterious money had stood to him as the symbol of earthly good, and the immediate object of toil. He had seemed to love it little in the years when every penny had its purpose for him; for he loved the *purpose* then. But now, when all purpose was gone, that habit of looking towards the money and grasping it with a sense of fulfilled effort made a loam that was deep enough for the seeds of desire; and as Silas walked homeward across the fields in the twilight, he drew out the money and thought it was brighter in the gathering gloom.

About this time an incident happened which seemed to open a possibility of some fellowship with his neighbours. One day, taking a pair of shoes to be mended, he saw the cobbler's wife seated by the fire, suffering from the terrible symptoms of heart-disease and dropsy, which he had witnessed as the precursors of his mother's death. He felt a rush of pity at the mingled sight and remembrance, and, recalling the relief his mother had found from a simple preparation of foxglove, he promised Sally Oates to bring her something that would ease her, since the doctor did her no good. In this office of charity, Silas felt, for the first time since he had come to Raveloe, a sense of unity between his past and present life, which might have been the beginning of his rescue from the insect-like existence into which his nature had shrunk. But Sally Oates's disease had raised her into a personage of much interest and importance among the neighbours, and the fact of her having found relief from drinking Silas Marner's 'stuff' became a matter of general discourse. When Doctor Kimble gave physic, it was natural that it should have an effect; but when a weaver, who came from nobody knew where, worked wonders with a bottle of brown waters, the occult character of the process was evident. Such a sort of thing had not been known since the Wise Woman[2] at Tarley died; and she had charms as well as 'stuff': everybody went to her when their children had fits. Silas Marner must be a person of the same sort, for how did he know what would bring back Sally Oates's breath, if he didn't know a fine sight more than that? The Wise Woman had words that she muttered to herself, so that you couldn't hear what they were, and if she tied a bit of red thread round the child's toe the while, it would keep off the water in the head. There were women in Raveloe, at that present time, who had worn one of the Wise Woman's little bags round their necks, and, in consequence, had never had an idiot child, as Ann Coulter had. Silas Marner could very likely do as much, and more; and now it was all clear how he should have come from unknown parts, and be so 'comical-looking'. But Sally Oates must mind and not tell the doctor, for he would be sure to set his face against Marner: he was always angry about the Wise Woman, and used to threaten those who went to her that they should have none of his help any more.

Silas now found himself and his cottage suddenly beset by mothers who wanted him to charm away the hooping-cough, or bring back the milk, and by men who wanted stuff against the rheumatics or the knots in the hands; and, to secure themselves against a refusal, the applicants brought silver in their palms. Silas might have driven a profitable trade in charms as well as in his small list of drugs; but money on this condition was no temptation to him: he had never known an impulse towards falsity, and he drove one after another away with growing irritation, for the news of him as a wise man had spread even to Tarley, and it was long before people ceased to take long walks for the sake of asking his aid. But the hope in his wisdom was at length changed into dread, for no one believed him when he said he knew no charms and could work no cures, and every man and woman who had an accident or a new attack after applying to him, set the misfortune down to Master Marner's ill-will and irritated glances. Thus it came to pass that his movement of pity towards Sally Oates, which had given him a transient sense of brotherhood, heightened the repulsion between him and his neighbours, and made his isolation more complete.

Gradually the guineas, the crowns, and the half-crowns, grew to a heap, and Marner drew less and less for his own wants, trying to solve the problem of keeping himself strong enough to work sixteen hours a-day on as small an outlay as possible. Have not men, shut up in solitary imprisonment, found an interest in marking the moments by straight strokes of a certain length on the wall, until the growth of the sum of straight strokes, arranged, in triangles, has become a mastering purpose? Do we not wile away moments of inanity or fatigued waiting by repeating some trivial movement or sound, until the repetition has bred a want, which is incipient habit? That will help us to understand how the love of accumulating money grows an absorbing passion in men whose imaginations, even in the very beginning of their hoard, showed them no purpose beyond it. Marner wanted the heaps of ten to grow into a square, and then into a larger square; and every added guinea, while it was itself a satisfaction, bred a new desire. In this strange world, made a hopeless riddle to him, he might, if he had had a less intense nature, have sat weaving, weaving – looking towards the end of his pattern, or towards the end of his web, till he forgot the riddle, and everything else but his immediate sensations; but the money had come to mark off his weaving into periods, and the money not only grew, but it remained with him. He began to think it was conscious of him, as his loom was, and he would on no account have exchanged those coins, which had become his familiars,[3] for other coins with unknown faces. He handled them, he counted them, till their form and colour were like the satisfaction of a thirst to him; but it was only in the night, when his work was done, that he drew them out to enjoy their companionship. He had taken up some bricks in his floor underneath his loom, and here he had made a hole in which he set the iron pot that contained his guineas and silver coins, covering the bricks with sand whenever he replaced them. Not that the idea of being robbed presented itself often or strongly to his mind: hoarding was common in country districts in those days; there were old labourers in the parish of Raveloe who were known to have their savings by them, probably inside their flock-beds; but their rustic neighbours, though not all of them as honest as their ancestors in the days of King Alfred, had not imaginations bold enough to lay a plan of burglary. How could they have spent the money in their own village without betraying themselves? They would be obliged to 'run away' – a course as dark and dubious as a balloon journey.

So, year after year, Silas Marner had lived in this solitude, his guineas rising in the iron pot, and his life narrowing and hardening itself more and more into a mere pulsation of desire and satisfaction that had no relation to any other being. His life had reduced itself to the functions of weaving and hoarding, without any contemplation of an end towards which the functions tended. The same sort of process has perhaps been undergone by wiser men, when they have been cut off from faith and love – only, instead of a loom and a heap of guineas, they have had some erudite research, some ingenious project, or some well-knit theory. Strangely Marner's face and figure shrank and bent themselves into a constant mechanical relation to the objects of his life, so that he produced the same sort of impression as a handle or a crooked tube, which has no meaning standing apart. The prominent eyes that used to look trusting and dreamy, now looked as if they had been made to see only one kind of thing that was very small, like tiny grain, for which they hunted everywhere: and he was so withered and yellow, that, though he was not yet forty, the children always called him 'Old Master Marner'.[4]

Yet even in this stage of withering a little incident happened, which showed that the sap of affection was not all gone. It was one of his daily tasks to fetch his water from a well a couple of fields off, and for this purpose, ever since he came to Raveloe, he had had a brown earthenware pot, which he held as his most precious utensil among the very few conveniences he had granted himself. It had been his companion for twelve years, always standing on the same spot, always lending its handle to him in the early morning, so that its form had an expression for him of willing helpfulness, and the impress of its hand on his palm gave a satisfaction mingled with that of having the fresh clear water. One day as he was returning from the well, he stumbled against the step of the stile, and his brown pot, falling with force against the stones that overarched the ditch below him, was broken in three pieces. Silas picked up the pieces and carried them home with grief in his heart. The brown pot could never be of use to him any more, but he stuck the bits together and propped the ruin in its old place for a memorial.

This is the history of Silas Marner, until the fifteenth year after he came to Raveloe. The livelong day he sat in his loom, his ear filled with its monotony, his eyes bent close down on the slow growth of sameness in the brownish web, his muscles moving with such even repetition that their pause seemed almost as much a constraint as the holding of his breath. But at night came his revelry: at night he closed his shutters, and made fast his doors, and drew forth his gold. Long ago the heap of coins had become too large for the iron pot to hold them, and he had made for them two thick leather bags, which wasted no room in their resting-place, but lent themselves flexibly to every corner. How the guineas shone as they came pouring out of the dark leather mouths! The silver bore no large proportion in amount to the gold, because the long pieces of linen which formed his chief work were always partly paid for in gold, and out of the silver he supplied his own bodily wants, choosing always the shillings and sixpences to spend in this way. He loved the guineas best, but he would not change the silver – the crowns and half-crowns that were his own earnings, begotten by his labour; he loved them all. He spread them out in heaps and bathed his hands in them; then he counted them and set them up in regular piles, and felt their rounded outline between his thumb and fingers, and thought fondly of the guineas that were only half earned by the work in his loom, as if they had been unborn children – thought of the guineas that were coming slowly through the coming years, through all his life, which spread far away before him, the end quite hidden by countless days of weaving. No wonder his thoughts were still with his loom and his money when he made his journeys through the fields and the lanes to fetch and carry home his work, so that his steps never wandered to the hedge-banks and the lane-side in search of the once familiar herbs: these too belonged to the past, from which his life had shrunk away, like a rivulet that has sunk far down from the grassy fringe of its old breadth into a little shivering thread, that cuts a groove for itself in the barren sand.

But about the Christmas of that fifteenth year, a second great change came over Marner's life, and his history became blent in a singular manner with the life of his neighbours.

CHAPTER 3

The greatest man in Raveloe was Squire Cass,[1] who lived in the large red house with the handsome flight of stone steps in front and the high stables behind it, nearly opposite the church. He was only one among several landed parishioners, but he alone was honoured with the title of Squire; for though Mr Osgood's family was also understood to be of timeless origin – the Raveloe imagination having never ventured back to that fearful blank when there were no Osgoods – still, he merely owned the farm he occupied; whereas Squire Cass had a tenant or two, who complained of the game to him quite as if he had been a lord.

It was still that glorious war time which was felt to be a peculiar favour of Providence towards the landed interest, and the fall of prices[2] had not yet come to carry the race of small squires and yeomen down that road to ruin for which extravagant habits and bad husbandry were plentifully anointing their wheels. I am speaking now in relation to Raveloe and the parishes that resembled it; for our old-fashioned country life had many different aspects, as all life must have when it is spread over a various surface, and breathed on variously by multitudinous currents, from the winds of heaven to the thoughts of men, which are for ever moving and crossing each other with incalculable results. Raveloe lay low among the bushy trees and the rutted lanes, aloof from the currents of industrial energy and Puritan earnestness: the rich ate and drank freely, accepting gout and apoplexy as things that ran mysteriously in respectable families, and the poor thought that the rich were entirely in the right of it to lead a jolly life; besides, their feasting caused a multiplication of orts,[3] which were the heirlooms of the poor. Betty Jay scented the boiling of Squire Cass's hams, but her longing was arrested by the unctuous liquor in which they were boiled; and when the seasons brought round the great merrymakings, they were regarded on all hands as a fine thing for the poor. For the Raveloe feasts were like the rounds of beef and the barrels of ale – they were on a large scale, and lasted a good while, especially in the winter-time. After ladies had packed up their best gowns and top-knots in bandboxes, and had incurred the risk of fording streams on pillions with the precious burden in rainy or snowy weather, when there was no knowing how high the water would rise, it was not to be supposed that they looked forward to a brief pleasure. On this ground it was always contrived in the dark seasons, when there was little work to be done, and the hours were long, that several neighbours should keep open house in succession. So soon as Squire Cass's standing dishes diminished in plenty and freshness, his guests had nothing to do but to walk a little higher up the village to Mr Osgood's, at the Orchards, and they found hams and chines⁴ uncut, pork pies with the scent of the fire in them, spun butter⁵ in all its freshness – everything, in fact, that appetites at leisure could desire, in perhaps greater perfection, though not in greater abundance, than at Squire Cass's.

For the Squire's wife had died long ago, and the Red House was without that presence of the wife and mother which is the fountain of wholesome love and fear in parlour and kitchen; and this helped to account not only for there being more profusion than finished excellence in the holiday provisions, but also for the frequency with which the proud Squire condescended to preside in the parlour of the Rainbow rather than under the shadow of his own dark wainscot;⁶ perhaps, also, for the fact that his sons had turned out rather ill. Raveloe was not a place where moral censure was severe, but it was thought a weakness in the Squire that he had kept all his sons at home in idleness; and though some licence was to be allowed to young men whose fathers could afford it, people shook their heads at the courses of the second son, Dunstan, commonly called Dunsey Cass, whose taste for swopping and betting might turn out to be a sowing of something worse than wild oats. To be sure, the neighbours said, it was no matter what became of Dunsey – a spiteful jeering fellow, who seemed to enjoy his drink the more when other people went dry – always provided that his doings did not bring trouble on a family like Squire Cass's, with a monument in the church, and tankards older than King George.⁷ But it would be a thousand pities if Mr Godfrey, the eldest, a fine open-faced good-natured young man who was to come into the land some day, should take to going along the same road with his brother, as he had seemed to do of late. If he went on in that way, he would lose Miss Nancy Lammeter; for it was well known that she had looked very shyly on him ever since last Whitsuntide twelvemonth, when there was so much talk about his being away from home days and days together. There was something wrong, more than common – that was quite clear; for Mr Godfrey didn't look half so fresh-coloured and open as he used to do. At one time everybody was saying, What a handsome couple he and Miss Nancy Lammeter would make! and if she could come to be mistress at the Red House, there would be a fine change, for the Lammeters had been brought up in that way, that they never suffered a pinch of salt to be wasted, and yet everybody in their household had of the best, according to his place. Such a daughter-in-law would be a saving to the old Squire, if she never brought a penny to her fortune; for it was to be feared that, notwithstanding his incomings, there were more holes in his pocket than the one where he put his own hand in. But if Mr Godfrey didn't turn over a new leaf, he might say 'Good-bye' to Miss Nancy Lammeter.

It was the once hopeful Godfrey who was standing, with his hands in his side-pockets and his back to the fire, in the dark wainscoted parlour, one late November afternoon in that fifteenth year of Silas Marner's life at Raveloe. The fading grey light fell dimly on the walls decorated with guns, whips, and foxes' brushes, on coats and hats flung on the chairs, on tankards sending forth a scent of flat ale, and on a half-choked fire, with pipes propped up in the chimney-corners; signs of a domestic life destitute of any hallowing charm, with which the look of gloomy vexation on Godfrey's blond face was in sad accordance. He seemed to be waiting and listening for some one's approach, and presently the sound of a heavy step, with an accompanying whistle, was heard across the large empty entrance-hall.

The door opened, and a thick-set, heavy-looking young man entered, with the flushed face and the gratuitously elated bearing which mark the first stage of intoxication. It was Dunsey, and at the sight of him Godfrey's face parted with some of its gloom to take on the more active expression of hatred. The handsome brown spaniel that lay on the hearth retreated under the chair in the chimney-corner.

'Well, Master Godfrey, what do you want with me?' said

Dunsey, in a mocking tone. 'You're my elders and betters, you know; I was obliged to come when you sent for me.'

'Why, this is what I want -- and just shake yourself sober and listen, will you?' said Godfrey, savagely. He had himself been drinking more than was good for him, trying to turn his gloom into uncalculating anger. 'I want to tell you, I must hand over that rent of Fowler's to the Squire, or else tell him I gave it you; for he's threatening to distrain for it, and it'll all be out soon, whether I tell him or not. He said, just now, before he went out, he should send word to Cox to distrain,[8] if Fowler didn't come and pay up his arrears this week. The Squire's short o' cash, and in no humour to stand any nonsense; and you know what he threatened, if ever he found you making away with his money again. So, see and get the money, and pretty quickly, will you?'

'Oh!' said Dunsey, sneeringly, coming nearer to his brother and looking in his face. 'Suppose, now, you get the money yourself, and save me the trouble, eh? Since you was so kind as to hand it over to me, you'll not refuse me the kindness to pay it back for me: it was your brotherly love made you do it, you know.'

Godfrey bit his lips and clenched his fist. 'Don't come near me with that look, else I'll knock you down.'

'Oh no, you won't,' said Dunsey, turning away on his heel, however. 'Because I'm such a good-natured brother, you know. I might get you turned out of house and home, and cut off with a shilling any day. I might tell the Squire how his handsome son was married to that nice young woman, Molly Farren, and was very unhappy because he couldn't live with his drunken wife, and I should slip into your place as comfortable as could be. But you see, I don't do it – I'm so easy and good-natured. You'll take any trouble for me. You'll get the hundred pounds for me – I know you will.'

'How can I get the money?' said Godfrey, quivering. 'I haven't a shilling to bless myself with. And it's a lie that you'd slip into my place: you'd get yourself turned out too, that's all. For if you begin telling tales, I'll follow. Bob's my father's favourite – you know that very well. He'd only think himself well rid of you.'

'Never mind,' said Dunsey, nodding his head sideways as he looked out of the window. 'It 'ud be very pleasant to me to go in your company – you're such a handsome brother, and we've always been so fond of quarrelling with one another, I shouldn't know what to do without you. But you'd like better for us both to stay at home together; I know you would. So you'll manage to get that little sum o' money, and I'll bid you good-bye, though I'm sorry to part.'

Dunstan was moving off, but Godfrey rushed after him and seized him by the arm, saying, with an oath –

'I tell you, I have no money: I can get no money.'

'Borrow of old Kimble.'

'I tell you, he won't lend me any more, and I shan't ask him.'

'Well, then, sell Wildfire.'

'Yes, that's easy talking. I must have the money directly.'

'Well, you've only got to ride him to the hunt tomorrow. There'll be Bryce and Keating there, for sure. You'll get more bids than one.'

'I daresay, and get back home at eight o'clock, splashed up to the chin. I'm going to Mrs Osgood's birthday dance.'

'Oho!' said Dunsey, turning his head on one side, and trying to speak in a small mincing treble. 'And there's sweet Miss Nancy coming; and we shall dance with her, and promise never to be naughty again, and be taken into favour, and – '

'Hold your tongue about Miss Nancy, you fool,' said Godfrey, turning red, 'else I'll throttle you.'

'What for?' said Dunsey, still in an artificial tone, but taking a whip from the table and beating the butt-end of it on his palm. 'You've a very good chance. I'd advise you to creep up her sleeve again: it 'ud be saving time, if Molly should happen to take a drop too much laudanum⁹ some day, and make a widower of you. Miss Nancy wouldn't mind being a second, if she didn't know it. And you've got a good-natured brother, who'll keep your secret well, because you'll be so very obliging to him.'

'I'll tell you what it is,' said Godfrey, quivering, and pale again, 'my patience is pretty near at an end. If you'd a little more sharpness in you, you might know that you may urge a man a bit too far, and make one leap as easy as another. I don't know but what it is so now: I may as well tell the Squire everything myself – I should get you off my back, if I got nothing else. And, after all, he'll know some time. She's been threatening to come herself and tell him. So, don't flatter yourself that your secrecy's worth any price you choose to ask. You drain me of money till I have got nothing to pacify *her* with, and she'll do as she threatens some day. It's all one. I'll tell my father everything myself, and you may go to the devil.'

Dunsey perceived that he had overshot his mark, and that there was a point at which even the hesitating Godfrey might be driven into decision. But he said, with an air of unconcern –

'As you please; but I'll have a draught of ale first.' And ringing the bell, he threw himself across two chairs, and began to rap the window-seat with the handle of his whip.

Godfrey stood, still with his back to the fire, uneasily moving his fingers among the contents of his side-pockets, and looking at the floor. That big muscular frame of his held plenty of animal courage, but helped him to no decision when the dangers to be braved were such as could neither be knocked down nor throttled. His natural irresolution and moral cowardice were exaggerated by a position in which dreaded consequences seemed to press equally on all sides, and his irritation had no sooner provoked him to defy Dunstan and anticipate all possible betrayals, than the miseries he must bring on himself by such a step seemed more unendurable to him than the present evil. The results of confession were not contingent, they were certain; whereas betrayal was not certain. From the near vision of that certainty he fell back on suspense and vacillation with a sense of repose. The disinherited son of a small squire, equally disinclined to dig and to beg, was almost as helpless as an uprooted tree, which, by the favour of earth and sky, has grown to a handsome bulk on the spot where it first shot upward. Perhaps it would have been possible to think of digging with some cheerfulness if Nancy Lammeter were to be won on those terms; but, since he must irrevocably lose *her* as well as the inheritance, and must break every tie but the one that degraded him and left him without motive for trying to recover his better self, he could imagine no future for himself on the other side of confession but that of ''listing for a soldier' – the most desperate step, short of suicide, in the eyes of respectable families. No! he would rather trust to casualties than to his own resolve – rather go on sitting at the feast, and sipping the wine he loved, though with the sword hanging over him and terror in his heart, than rush away into the cold darkness where there was no pleasure left. The utmost concession to Dunstan about the horse began to seem easy, compared with the fulfilment of his own threat. But his pride would not let him recommence the conversation otherwise than by continuing the quarrel. Dunstan was waiting for this, and took his ale in shorter draughts than usual.

'It's just like you,' Godfrey burst out, in a bitter tone, 'to talk about my selling Wildfire in that cool way – the last thing I've got to call my own, and the best bit of horse-flesh I ever had in my life. And if you'd got a spark of pride in you, you'd be ashamed to see the stables emptied, and everybody sneering about it. But it's my belief you'd sell yourself, if it was only for the pleasure of making somebody feel he'd got a bad bargain.'

'Ay, ay,' said Dunstan, very placably, 'you do me justice, I see. You know I'm a jewel for 'ticing people into bargains. For which reason I advise you to let *me* sell Wildfire. I'd ride him to the hunt tomorrow for you, with pleasure. I shouldn't look so handsome as you in the saddle, but it's the horse they'll bid for, and not the rider.'

'Yes, I daresay – trust my horse to you!'

'As you please,' said Dunstan, rapping the window-seat again with an air of great unconcern. 'It's *you* have got to pay Fowler's money; it's none of my business. You received the money from him when you went to Bramcote, and *you* told the Squire it wasn't paid. I'd nothing to do with that; you chose to be so obliging as to give it me, that was all. If you don't want to pay the money, let it alone; it's all one to me. But I was willing to accommodate you by undertaking to sell the horse, seeing it's not convenient to you to go so far tomorrow.'

Godfrey was silent for some moments. He would have liked to spring on Dunstan, wrench the whip from his hand, and flog him to within an inch of his life; and no bodily fear could have deterred him; but he was mastered by another sort of fear, which was fed by feelings stronger even than his resentment. When he spoke again it was in a half-conciliatory tone.

'Well, you mean no nonsense about the horse, eh? You'll sell him all fair, and hand over the money? If you don't, you know, everything 'ull go to smash, for I've got nothing else to trust to. And you'll have less pleasure in pulling the house over my head, when your own skull's to be broken too.'

'Ay, ay,' said Dunstan, rising; 'all right. I thought you'd come round. I'm the fellow to bring old Bryce up to the scratch. I'll get you a hundred and twenty for him, if I get you a penny.'

'But it'll perhaps rain cats and dogs tomorrow, as it did

yesterday, and then you can't go,' said Godfrey, hardly knowing whether he wished for that obstacle or not.

'Not *it*,' said Dunstan. 'I'm always lucky in my weather. It might rain if you wanted to go yourself. You never hold trumps, you know – I always do. You've got the beauty, you see, and I've got the luck, so you must keep me by you for your crooked sixpence; you'll *ne*-ver get along without me.'

'Confound you, hold your tongue!' said Godfrey, impetuously. 'And take care to keep sober tomorrow, else you'll get pitched on your head coming home, and Wildfire might be the worse for it.'

'Make your tender heart easy,' said Dunstan, opening the door. 'You never knew me see double when I'd got a bargain to make; it 'ud spoil the fun. Besides, whenever I fall, I'm warranted to fall on my legs.'

With that, Dunstan slammed the door behind him, and left Godfrey to that bitter rumination on his personal circumstances which was now unbroken from day to day save by the excitement of sporting, drinking, card-playing, or the rarer and less oblivious pleasure of seeing Miss Nancy Lammeter. The subtle and varied pains springing from the higher sensibility that accompanies higher culture, are perhaps less pitiable than that dreary absence of impersonal enjoyment and consolation which leaves ruder minds to the perpetual urgent companionship of their own griefs and discontents. The lives of those rural forefathers, whom we are apt to think very prosaic figures – men whose only work was to ride round their land, getting heavier and heavier in their saddles, and who passed the rest of their days in the half-listless gratification of senses dulled by monotony – had a certain pathos in them nevertheless. Calamities came to *them* too, and their early errors carried hard consequences: perhaps the love of some sweet maiden, the image of purity, order, and calm, had opened their eyes to the vision of a life in which the days would not seem too long, even without rioting; but the maiden was lost, and the vision passed away, and then what was left to them, especially when they had become too heavy for the hunt, or for carrying a gun over the furrows, but to drink and get merry, or to drink and get angry, so that they might be independent of variety, and say over again with eager emphasis the things they had said already any time that twelvemonth? Assuredly, among these flushed and dull-eyed men there were some whom – thanks to their native human-kindness – even riot could never drive into brutality; men who, when their cheeks were fresh, had felt the keen point of sorrow or remorse, had been pierced by the reeds they leaned on, or had lightly put their limbs in fetters from which no struggle could loose them; and under these sad circumstances, common to us all, their thoughts could find no resting-place outside the ever trodden round of their own petty history.[10]

That, at least, was the condition of Godfrey Cass in this six-and-twentieth year of his life. A movement of compunction, helped by those small indefinable influences which every personal relation exerts on a pliant nature, had urged him into a secret marriage, which was a blight on his life. It was an ugly story of low passion, delusion, and waking from delusion, which needs not to be dragged from the privacy of Godfrey's bitter memory. He had long known that the delusion was partly due to a trap laid for him by Dunstan, who saw in his brother's degrading marriage the means of gratifying at once his jealous hate and his cupidity. And if Godfrey could have felt himself simply a victim, the iron bit that destiny had put into his mouth would have chafed him less intolerably. If the curses he muttered half aloud when he was alone had had no other object than Dunstan's diabolical cunning, he might have shrunk less from the consequences of avowal. But he had something else to curse – his own vicious folly, which now seemed as mad and unaccountable to him as almost all our follies and vices do when their promptings have long passed away. For four years he had thought of Nancy Lammeter, and wooed her with tacit patient worship, as the woman who made him think of the future with joy: she would be his wife, and would make home lovely to him, as his father's home had never been; and it would be easy, when she was always near, to shake off those foolish habits that were no pleasures, but only a feverish way of annulling vacancy. Godfrey's was an essentially domestic nature, bred up in a home where the hearth had no smiles, and where the daily habits were not chastised by the presence of household order. His easy disposition made him fall in unresistingly with the family courses, but the need of some tender permanent affection, the longing for some influence that would make the good he preferred easy to pursue, caused the neatness, purity, and liberal orderliness of the Lammeter household, sunned by the smile of

Nancy, to seem like those fresh bright hours of the morning when temptations go to sleep and leave the ear open to the voice of the good angel, inviting to industry, sobriety, and peace. And yet the hope of this paradise had not been enough to save him from a course which shut him out of it for ever. Instead of keeping fast hold of the strong silken rope by which Nancy would have drawn him safe to the green banks where it was easy to step firmly, he had let himself be dragged back into mud and slime, in which it was useless to struggle. He had made ties for himself which robbed him of all wholesome motive and were a constant exasperation.

Still, there was one position worse than the present: it was the position he would be in when the ugly secret was disclosed; and the desire that continually triumphed over every other was that of warding off the evil day, when he would have to bear the consequences of his father's violent resentment for the wound inflicted on his family pride – would have, perhaps, to turn his back on that hereditary ease and dignity which, after all, was a sort of reason for living, and would carry with him the certainty that he was banished for ever from the sight and esteem of Nancy Lammeter. The longer the interval, the more chance there was of deliverance from some, at least, of the hateful consequences to which he had sold himself; the more opportunities remained for him to snatch the strange gratification of seeing Nancy, and gathering some faint indications of her lingering regard. Towards this gratification he was impelled, fitfully, every now and then, after having passed weeks in which he had avoided her as the far-off bright-winged prize that only made him spring forward and find his chain all the more galling. One of those fits of yearning was on him now, and it would have been strong enough to have persuaded him to trust Wildfire to Dunstan rather than disappoint the yearning, even if he had not had another reason for his disinclination towards the morrow's hunt. That other reason was the fact that the morning's meet was near Batherley, the market-town where the unhappy woman lived, whose image became more odious to him every day; and to his thought the whole vicinage was haunted by her. The yoke a man creates for himself by wrong-doing will breed hate in the kindliest nature; and the good-humoured, affectionate-hearted Godfrey Cass was fast becoming a bitter man, visited by cruel wishes, that seemed to

enter, and depart, and enter again, like demons who had found
in him a ready-garnished home.

What was he to do this evening to pass the time? He might as
well go to the Rainbow, and hear the talk about the cock-
fighting:[11] everybody was there, and what else was there to be
done? Though, for his own part, he did not care a button for
cock-fighting. Snuff, the brown spaniel, who had placed herself
in front of him, and had been watching him for some time, now
jumped up in impatience for the expected caress. But Godfrey
thrust her away without looking at her, and left the room,
followed humbly by the unresenting Snuff – perhaps because she
saw no other career open to her.

CHAPTER 4

Dunstan Cass, setting off in the raw morning, at the judiciously quiet pace of a man who is obliged to ride to cover on his hunter, had to take his way along the lane which, at its farther extremity, passed by the piece of unenclosed ground called the Stone-pit, where stood the cottage, once a stone-cutter's shed, now for fifteen years inhabited by Silas Marner. The spot looked very dreary at this season, with the moist trodden clay about it, and the red, muddy water high up in the deserted quarry. That was Dunstan's first thought as he approached it; the second was, that the old fool of a weaver, whose loom he heard rattling already, had a great deal of money hidden somewhere. How was it that he, Dunstan Cass, who had often heard talk of Marner's miserliness, had never thought of suggesting to Godfrey that he should frighten or persuade the old fellow into lending the money on the excellent security of the young Squire's prospects? The resource occurred to him now as so easy and agreeable, especially as Marner's hoard was likely to be large enough to leave Godfrey a handsome surplus beyond his immediate needs, and enable him to accommodate his faithful brother, that he had almost turned the horse's head towards home again. Godfrey would be ready enough to accept the suggestion: he would snatch eagerly at a plan that might save him from parting with Wildfire. But when Dunstan's meditation reached this point, the inclination to go on grew strong and prevailed. He didn't want to give Godfrey that pleasure: he preferred that Master Godfrey should be vexed. Moreover, Dunstan enjoyed the self-important consciousness of having a horse to sell, and the opportunity of driving a bargain, swaggering, and possibly taking somebody in. He might have all the satisfaction attendant on selling his brother's horse, and not the less have the further satisfaction of setting Godfrey to borrow Marner's money. So he rode on to cover.[1]

Bryce and Keating were there, as Dunstan was quite sure they would be – he was such a lucky fellow.

'Heyday!' said Bryce, who had long had his eye on Wildfire, 'you're on your brother's horse today: how's that?'

'Oh, I've swopped with him,' said Dunstan, whose delight in lying, grandly independent of utility, was not to be diminished by the likelihood that his hearer would not believe him – 'Wildfire's mine now.'

'What! has he swopped with you for that big-boned hack of yours?' said Bryce, quite aware that he should get another lie in answer.

'Oh, there was a little account between us,' said Dunsey, carelessly, 'and Wildfire made it even. I accommodated him by taking the horse, though it was against my will, for I'd got an itch for a mare o' Jortin's – as rare a bit o' blood as ever you threw your leg across. But I shall keep Wildfire, now I've got him, though I'd a bid of a hundred and fifty for him the other day, from a man over at Flitton – he's buying for Lord Cromleck – a fellow with a cast in his eye, and a green waistcoat. But I mean to stick to Wildfire: I shan't get a better at a fence in a hurry. The mare's got more blood, but she's a bit too weak in the hind-quarters.'

Bryce of course divined that Dunstan wanted to sell the horse, and Dunstan knew that he divined it (horse-dealing is only one of many human transactions carried on in this ingenious manner); and they both considered that the bargain was in its first stage, when Bryce replied, ironically –

'I wonder at that now; I wonder you mean to keep him; for I never heard of a man who didn't want to sell his horse getting a bid of half as much again as the horse was worth. You'll be lucky if you get a hundred.'

Keating rode up now, and the transaction became more complicated. It ended in the purchase of the horse by Bryce for a hundred and twenty, to be paid on the delivery of Wildfire, safe and sound, at the Batherley stables. It did occur to Dunsey that it might be wise for him to give up the day's hunting, proceed at once to Batherley, and, having waited for Bryce's return, hire a horse to carry him home with the money in his pocket. But the inclination for a run, encouraged by confidence in his luck, and by a draught of brandy from his pocket-pistol[2] at the conclusion of the bargain, was not easy to overcome, especially with a horse under him that would take the fences to the admiration of the field. Dunstan, however, took one fence too many, and got his horse pierced with a hedge-stake. His own ill-favoured person, which was quite unmarketable, escaped without injury; but poor Wildfire, unconscious of his price, turned on his flank and painfully panted his last. It happened that Dunstan, a short time before, having had to get down to arrange his stirrup, had muttered a good many curses at this interruption, which had thrown him in the rear of the hunt near the moment of glory, and under this exasperation had taken the fences more blindly. He would soon have been up with the hounds again, when the fatal accident happened; and hence he was between eager riders in advance, not troubling themselves about what happened behind them, and far-off stragglers, who were as likely as not to pass quite aloof from the line of road in which Wildfire had fallen. Dunstan, whose nature it was to care more for immediate annoyances than for remote consequences, no sooner recovered his legs, and saw that it was all over with Wildfire, than he felt a satisfaction at the absence of witnesses to a position which no swaggering could make enviable. Reinforcing himself, after his shake, with a little brandy and much swearing, he walked as fast as he could to a coppice on his right hand, through which it occurred to him that he could make his way to Batherley without danger of encountering any member of the hunt. His first intention was to hire a horse there and ride home forthwith, for to walk many miles without a gun in his hand and along an ordinary road, was as much out of the question to him as to other spirited young men of his kind. He did not much mind about taking the bad news to Godfrey, for he had to offer him at the same time the resource of Marner's money; and if Godfrey kicked, as he always did, at the notion of making a fresh debt from which he himself got the smallest share of advantage, why, he wouldn't kick long: Dunstan felt sure he could worry Godrey into anything. The idea of Marner's money kept growing in vividness, now the want of it had become immediate; the prospect of having to make his appearance with the muddy boots of a pedestrian at Batherley, and to encounter the grinning queries of stablemen, stood unpleasantly in the way of his impatience to be back at Raveloe and carry out his felicitous plan; and a casual visitation of his waistcoat-pocket, as he was ruminating, awakened his memory to the fact that the two or three small coins his forefinger encountered there, were of too pale a colour to cover that small debt, without payment of which the stable-keeper had declared he would never do any more business with Dunsey Cass. After all, according to the direction in which the run had brought him, he was not so very much farther from home than he was from Batherley; but Dunsey, not being remarkable for clearness of head, was only led to this conclusion by the gradual perception that there were other reasons for choosing the unprecedented course of walking home. It was now nearly four o'clock, and a mist was gathering: the sooner he got into the road the better. He remembered having crossed the road and seen the finger-post only a little while before Wildfire broke down; so, buttoning his coat, twisting the lash of his hunting-whip compactly round the handle, and rapping the tops of his boots with a self-possessed air, as if to assure himself that he was not at all taken by surprise, he set off with the sense that he was undertaking a remarkable feat of bodily exertion, which somehow and at some time he should be able to dress up and magnify to the admiration of a select circle at the Rainbow. When a young gentleman like Dunsey is reduced to so exceptional a mode of locomotion as walking, a whip in his hand is a desirable corrective to a too bewildering dreamy sense of unwontedness in his position; and Dunstan, as he went along through the gathering mist, was always rapping his whip somewhere. It was Godfrey's whip, which he had chosen to take without leave because it had a gold handle; of course no one could see, when Dunstan held it, that the name *Godfrey Cass* was cut in deep letters on that gold handle – they could only see that it was a very handsome whip. Dunsey was not without fear that he might meet some acquaintance in whose eyes he would cut a pitiable figure, for mist is no screen when people get close to each other; but when he at last found himself in the well-known Raveloe lanes without having met a soul, he silently remarked that that was part of his usual good-luck. But now the mist, helped by the evening darkness, was more of a screen than he desired, for it hid the ruts into which his feet were liable to slip – hid everything, so that he had to guide his steps by dragging his whip along the low bushes in advance of the hedgerow. He must soon, he thought, be getting near the opening at the Stone-pits: he should find it out by the break in the hedgerow. He found it out, however, by another circumstance which he had not expected – namely, by certain gleams of light, which he presently guessed to proceed from Silas Marner's cottage. That cottage and the money hidden within it had been in his mind continually during his walk, and he had been imagining ways of cajoling and tempting the weaver to part with the immediate possession of his money for the sake of receiving interest. Dunstan felt as if there must be a little frightening added to the cajolery, for his own arithmetical convictions were not clear enough to afford him any forcible demonstration as to the advantages of interest; and as for security, he regarded it vaguely as a means of cheating a man by making him believe that he would be paid. Altogether, the operation on the miser's mind was a task that Godfrey would be sure to hand over to his more daring and cunning brother: Dunstan had made up his mind to that; and by the time he saw the light gleaming through the chinks of Marner's shutters, the idea of a dialogue with the weaver had become so familiar to him, that it occurred to him as quite a natural thing to make the acquaintance forthwith. There might be several conveniences attending this course: the weaver had possibly got a lantern, and Dunstan was tired of feeling his way. He was still nearly three-quarters of a mile from home, and the lane was becoming unpleasantly slippery, for the mist was passing into rain. He turned up the bank, not without some fear lest he might miss the right way, since he was not certain whether the light were in front or on the side of the cottage. But he felt the ground before him cautiously with his whip-handle, and at last arrived safely at the door. He knocked loudly, rather enjoying the idea that the old fellow would be frightened at the sudden noise. He heard no movement in reply: all was silence in the cottage. Was the weaver gone to bed, then? If so, why had he left a light? That was a strange forgetfulness in a miser. Dunstan knocked still more loudly, and, without pausing for a reply, pushed his fingers through the latch-hole, intending to shake the door and pull the latch-string up and down, not doubting that the door was fastened. But, to his surprise, at this double motion the door opened, and he found himself in front of a bright fire which lip up every corner of the cottage – the bed, the loom, the three chairs, and the table – and showed him that Marner was not there.

Nothing at that moment could be much more inviting to
Dunsey than the bright fire on the brick hearth: he walked in
and seated himself by it at once. There was something in front
of the fire, too, that would have been inviting to a hungry man,
if it had been in a different stage of cooking. It was a small bit
of pork suspended from the kettle-hanger by a string passed
through a large door-key, in a way known to primitive housekeepers unpossessed of jacks.[3] But the pork had been hung at
the farthest extremity of the hanger, apparently to prevent the
roasting from proceeding too rapidly during the owner's
absence. The old staring simpleton had hot meat for his supper,
then? thought Dunstan. People had always said he lived on
mouldy bread, on purpose to check his appetite. But where
could he be at this time, and on such an evening, leaving his
supper in this stage of preparation, and his door unfastened?
Dunstan's own recent difficulty in making his way suggested to
him that the weaver had perhaps gone outside his cottage to
fetch in fuel, or for some such brief purpose, and had slipped
into the Stone-pit. That was an interesting idea to Dunstan,
carrying consequences of entire novelty. If the weaver was dead,
who had a right to his money? Who would know where his
money was hidden? *Who would know that anybody had come
to take it away?* He went no farther into the subtleties of
evidence: the pressing question, 'Where *is* the money?' now took
such entire possession of him as to make him quite forget that
the weaver's death was not a certainty. A dull mind, once
arriving at an inference that flatters a desire, is rarely able to
retain the impression that the notion from which the inference
started was purely problematic. And Dunstan's mind was as
dull as the mind of a possible felon usually is. There were only
three hiding-places where he had ever heard of cottagers' hoards
being found: the thatch, the bed, and a hole in the floor.
Marner's cottage had no thatch; and Dunstan's first act, after a
train of thought made rapid by the stimulus of cupidity, was to
go up to the bed; but while he did so, his eyes travelled eagerly
over the floor, where the bricks, distinct in the fire-light, were
discernible under the sprinkling of sand. But not everywhere;
for there was one spot, and one only, which was quite covered
with sand, and sand showing the marks of fingers, which had
apparently been careful to spread it over a given space. It was
near the treddles of the loom. In an instant Dunstan darted to

that spot, swept away the sand with his whip, and, inserting the thin end of the hook between the bricks, found that they were loose. In haste he lifted up two bricks, and saw what he had no doubt was the object of his search; for what could there be but money in those two leathern bags? And, from their weight, they must be filled with guineas. Dunstan felt round the hole, to be certain that it held no more; then hastily replaced the bricks, and spread the sand over them. Hardly more than five minutes had passed since he entered the cottage, but it seemed to Dunstan like a long while; and though he was without any distinct recognition of the possibility that Marner might be alive, and might re-enter the cottage at any moment, he felt an undefinable dread laying hold on him, as he rose to his feet with the bags in his hand. He would hasten out into the darkness, and then consider what he should do with the bags. He closed the door behind him immediately, that he might shut in the stream of light: a few steps would be enough to carry him beyond betrayal by the gleams from the shutter-chinks and the latch-hole. The rain and darkness had got thicker, and he was glad of it; though it was awkward walking with both hands filled, so that it was as much as he could do to grasp his whip along with one of the bags. But when he had gone a yard or two, he might take his time. So he stepped forward into the darkness.

CHAPTER 5

When Dunstan Cass turned his back on the cottage, Silas Marner was not more than a hundred yards away from it, plodding along from the village with a sack thrown round his shoulders as an over-coat, and with a horn lantern[1] in his hand. His legs were weary, but his mind was at ease, free from the presentiment of change. The sense of security more frequently springs from habit than from conviction, and for this reason it often subsists after such a change in the conditions as might have been expected to suggest alarm. The lapse of time during which a given event has not happened, is, in this logic of habit, constantly alleged as a reason why the event should never happen, even when the lapse of time is precisely the added condition which makes the event imminent. A man will tell you that he has worked in a mine for forty years unhurt by an accident as a reason why he should apprehend no danger, though the roof is beginning to sink; and it is often observable, that the older a man gets, the more difficult it is to him to retain a believing conception of his own death. This influence of habit was necessarily strong in a man whose life was so monotonous as Marner's – who saw no new people and heard of no new events to keep alive in him the idea of the unexpected and the changeful; and it explains simply enough, why his mind could be at ease, though he had left his house and his treasure more defenceless than usual. Silas was thinking with double complacency of his supper: first, because it would be hot and savoury; and secondly, because it would cost him nothing. For the little bit of pork was a present from that excellent housewife, Miss Priscilla Lammeter, to whom he had this day carried home a handsome piece of linen; and it was only on occasion of a present like this, that Silas indulged himself with roast-meat. Supper was his favourite meal, because it came at his time of revelry, when his heart warmed over his gold; whenever he had roast-meat, he always chose to have it for supper. But this evening, he had no sooner ingeniously knotted his string fast round his bit of pork, twisted the string according to rule over his door-key, passed it through the handle, and made it fast on the hanger, than he remembered that a piece of very fine twine was indispensable to his 'setting up' a new piece of work in his loom early in the morning. It had slipped his memory, because, in coming from Mr Lammeter's, he had not had to pass through the village; but to lose time by going on errands in the morning was out of the question. It was a nasty fog to turn out into, but there were things Silas loved better than his own comfort; so, drawing his pork to the extremity of the hanger, and arming himself with his lantern and his old sack, he set out on what, in ordinary weather, would have been a twenty minutes' errand. He could not have locked his door without undoing his well-knotted string and retarding his supper; it was not worth his while to make that sacrifice. What thief would find his way to the Stone-pits on such a night as this? and why should he come on this particular night, when he had never come through all the fifteen years before? These questions were not distinctly present in Silas's mind; they merely serve to represent the vaguely-felt foundation of his freedom from anxiety.

He reached his door in much satisfaction that his errand was done: he opened it, and to his short-sighted eyes everything remained as he had left it, except that the fire sent out a welcome increase of heat. He trod about the floor while putting by his lantern and throwing aside his hat and sack, so as to merge the marks of Dunstan's feet on the sand in the marks of his own nailed boots. Then he moved his pork nearer to the fire, and sat down to the agreeable business of tending the meat and warming himself at the same time.

Any one who had looked at him as the red light shone upon his pale face, strange straining eyes, and meagre form, would perhaps have understood the mixture of contemptuous pity, dread, and suspicion with which he was regarded by his neighbours in Raveloe. Yet few men could be more harmless than poor Marner. In his truthful simple soul, not even the growing greed and worship of gold could beget any vice directly injurious to others. The light of his faith quite put out, and his affections made desolate, he had clung with all the force of his nature to his work and his money; and like all objects to which a man devotes himself, they had fashioned him into correspondence with themselves. His loom, as he wrought in it without ceasing, had in its turn wrought on him, and confirmed more and more the monotonous craving for its monotonous response. His gold, as he hung over it and saw it grow, gathered his power of loving together into a hard isolation like its own.

As soon as he was warm he began to think it would be a long while to wait till after supper before he drew out his guineas, and it would be pleasant to see them on the table before him as he ate his unwonted feast. For joy is the best of wine, and Silas's guineas were a golden wine of that sort.

He rose and placed his candle unsuspectingly on the floor near his loom, swept away the sand without noticing any change, and removed the bricks. The sight of the empty hole made his heart leap violently, but the belief that his gold was gone could not come at once – only terror, and the eager effort to put an end to the terror. He passed his trembling hand all about the hole, trying to think it possible that his eyes had deceived him; then he held the candle in the hole and examined it curiously, trembling more and more. At last he shook so violently that he let fall the candle, and lifted his hands to his head, trying to steady himself, that he might think. Had he put his gold somewhere else, by a sudden resolution last night, and then forgotten it? A man falling into dark waters seeks a momentary footing even on sliding stones; and Silas, by acting as if he believed in false hopes, warded off the moment of despair. He searched in every corner, he turned his bed over, and shook it, and kneaded it; he looked in his brick oven where he laid his sticks. When there was no other place to be searched, he kneeled down again and felt once more all round the hole. There was no untried refuge left for a moment's shelter from the terrible truth.

Yes, there was a sort of refuge which always comes with the prostration of thought under an overpowering passion: it was that expectation of impossibilities, that belief in contradictory images, which is still distinct from madness, because it is capable of being dissipated by the external fact. Silas got up from his knees trembling, and looked round at the table: didn't the gold lie there after all? The table was bare. Then he turned and looked behind him – looked all round his dwelling, seeming to strain his brown eyes after some possible appearance of the bags where he had already sought them in vain. He could see every object in his cottage – and his gold was not there.

Again he put his trembling hands to his head, and gave a wild-ringing scream, the cry of desolation. For a few moments after, he stood motionless; but the cry had relieved him from the first maddening pressure of the truth. He turned, and tottered towards his loom, and got into the seat where he worked, instinctively seeking this as the strongest assurance of reality.

And now that all the false hopes had vanished, and the first shock of certainty was past, the idea of a thief began to present itself, and he entertained it eagerly, because a thief might be caught and made to restore the gold. The thought brought some new strength with it, and he started from his loom to the door. As he opened it the rain beat in upon him, for it was falling more and more heavily. There were no footsteps to be tracked on such a night – footsteps? When had the thief come? During Silas's absence in the daytime the door had been locked, and there had been no marks of any in road on his return by daylight. And in the evening, too, he said to himself, everything was the same as when he had left it. The sand and bricks looked as if they had not been moved. *Was* it a thief who had taken the bags? or was it a cruel power that no hands could reach which had delighted in making him a second time desolate? He shrank from this vaguer dread, and fixed his mind with struggling effort on the robber with hands, who could be reached by hands. His thoughts glanced at all the neighbours who had made any remarks, or asked any questions which he might now regard as a ground of suspicion. There was Jem Rodney, a known poacher, and otherwise disreputable: he had often met Marner in his journeys across the fields, and had said something jestingly about the weaver's money; nay, he had once irritated Marner, by lingering at the fire when he called to light his pipe, instead of going about his business. Jem Rodney was the man – there was ease in the thought. Jem could be found and made to restore the money: Marner did not want to punish him, but only to get back his gold which had gone from him, and left his soul like a forlorn traveller on an unknown desert. The robber must be laid hold of. Marner's ideas of legal authority were confused, but he felt that he must go and proclaim his loss; and the great people in the village – the clergyman, the constable, and Squire Cass – would make Jem Rodney, or somebody else, deliver up the stolen money. He rushed out in the rain, under the stimulus of this hope, forgetting to cover his head, not caring to fasten his door; for he felt as if he had nothing left to lose. He ran swiftly, till want of breath compelled him to slacken his pace as he was entering the village at the turning close to the Rainbow.

The Rainbow, in Marner's view, was a place of luxurious resort for rich and stout husbands, whose wives had superfluous stores of linen; it was the place where he was likely to find the powers and dignities of Raveloe, and where he could most speedily make his loss public. He lifted the latch, and turned into the bright bar or kitchen on the right hand, where the less lofty customers of the house were in the habit of assembling, the parlour on the left being reserved for the more select society in which Squire Cass frequently enjoyed the double pleasure of conviviality and condescension. But the parlour was dark tonight, the chief personages who ornamented its circle being all at Mrs Osgood's birthday dance, as Godfrey Cass was. And in consequence of this, the party on the high-screened seats in the kitchen was more numerous than usual; several personages, who would otherwise have been admitted into the parlour and enlarged the opportunity of hectoring and condescension for their betters, being content this evening to vary their enjoyment by taking their spirits-and-water where they could themselves hector and condescend in company that called for beer.

CHAPTER 6

The conversation, which was at a high pitch of animation when Silas approached the door of the Rainbow, had, as usual, been slow and intermittent when the company first assembled. The pipes began to be puffed in a silence which had an air of severity; the more important customers, who drank spirits and sat nearest the fire, staring at each other as if a bet were depending on the first man who winked; while the beer-drinkers, chiefly men in fustian jackets and smock-frocks,[1] kept their eyelids down and rubbed their hands across their mouths, as if their draughts of beer were a funereal duty attended with embarrassing sadness. At last, Mr Snell, the landlord, a man of a neutral disposition, accustomed to stand aloof from human differences as those of beings who were all alike in need of liquor, broke silence, by saying in a doubtful tone to his cousin the butcher –

'Some folks 'ud say that was a fine beast you druv in yesterday, Bob?'

The butcher, a jolly, smiling, red-haired man, was not disposed to answer rashly. He gave a few puffs before he spat and replied, 'And they wouldn't be fur wrong, John.'

After this feeble delusive thaw, the silence set in as severely as before.

'Was it a red Durham?' said the farrier,[2] taking up the thread of discourse after the lapse of a few minutes.

The farrier looked at the landlord, and the landlord looked at the butcher, as the person who must take the responsibility of answering.

'Red it was,' said the butcher, in his good-humoured husky treble – 'and a Durham it was.'

'Then you needn't tell *me* who you bought it of,' said the farrier, looking round with some triumph; 'I know who it is has got the red Durhams o' this country-side. And she'd a white star on her brow, I'll bet a penny?' The farrier leaned forward with his hands on his knees as he put this question, and his eyes twinkled knowingly.

'Well; yes – she might,' said the butcher, slowly, considering that he was giving a decided affirmative. 'I don't say contrairy.'

'I knew that very well,' said the farrier, throwing himself backward again, and speaking defiantly; 'if *I* don't know Mr Lammeter's cows, I should like to know who does – that's all. And as for the cow you've bought, bargain or no bargain, I've been at the drenching of her[3] – contradick me who will.'

The farrier looked fierce, and the mild butcher's conversational spirit was roused a little.

'I'm not for contradicking no man,' he said; 'I'm for peace and quietness. Some are for cutting long ribs – I'm for cutting 'em short myself; but *I* don't quarrel with 'em. All I say is, it's a lovely carkiss – and anybody as was reasonable, it 'ud bring tears into their eyes to look at it.'

'Well, it's the cow as I drenched, whatever it is,' pursued the farrier, angrily; 'and it was Mr Lammeter's cow, else you told a lie when you said it was a red Durham.'

'I tell no lies,' said the butcher, with the same mild huskiness as before, 'and I contradick none – not if a man was to swear himself black: he's no meat o'mine, nor none o' my bargains. All I say is, it's a lovely carkiss. And what I say I'll stick to; but I'll quarrel wi' no man.'

'No,' said the farrier, with bitter sarcasm, looking at the company generally; 'and p'rhaps you arn't pig-headed; and p'rhaps you didn't say the cow was a red Durham; and p'rhaps you didn't say she'd got a star on her brow – stick to that, now you're at it.'

'Come, come,' said the landlord; 'let the cow alone. The truth lies atween you: you're both right and both wrong, as I allays say. And as for the cow's being Mr Lammeter's, I say nothing to that; but this I say, as the Rainbow's the Rainbow. And for the matter o' that, if the talk is to be o' the Lammeters, *you* know the most upo' that head, eh, Mr Macey? You remember when first Mr Lammeter's father come into these parts, and took the Warrens?'

Mr Macey, tailor and parish-clerk, the latter of which functions rheumatism had of late obliged him to share with a small-featured young man who sat opposite him, held his white head on one side, and twirled his thumbs with an air of complacency, slightly seasoned with criticism. He smiled pityingly, in answer to the landlord's appeal, and said –

'Ay, ay; I know, I know; but I let other folks talk. I've laid by now, and gev up to the young uns. Ask them as have been to school at Tarley: they've learnt pernouncing; that's come up since my day.'

'If you're pointing at me, Mr Macey,' said the deputy-clerk, with an air of anxious propriety, 'I'm nowise a man to speak out of my place. As the psalm says –

> I know what's right, nor only so,
> But also practise what I know.'[4]

'Well, then, I wish you'd keep hold o' the tune, when it's set for you; if you're for prac*tis*ing, I wish you'd prac*tise* that,' said a large jocose-looking man, an excellent wheelwright[5] in his week-day capacity, but on Sundays leader of the choir. He winked, as he spoke, at two of the company, who were known officially as the 'bassoon' and the 'key-bugle',[6] in the confidence that he was expressing the sense of the musical profession in Raveloe.

Mr Tookey, the deputy-clerk, who shared the unpopularity common to deputies, turned very red, but replied, with careful moderation – 'Mr Winthrop, if you'll bring me any proof as I'm in the wrong, I'm not the man to say I won't alter. But there's people set up their own ears for a standard, and expect the whole choir to follow 'em. There may be two opinions, I hope.'

'Ay, ay,' said Mr Macey, who felt very well satisfied with this attack on youthful presumption; 'you're right there, Tookey: there's allays two 'pinions; there's the 'pinion a man has of himsen, and there's the 'pinion other folks have on him. There'd be two 'pinions about a cracked bell, if the bell could hear itself.'

'Well, Mr Macey,' said poor Tookey, serious amidst the general laughter, 'I undertook to partially fill up the office of parish-clerk by Mr Crackenthorp's desire, whenever your infirmities should make you unfitting; and it's one of the rights thereof to sing in the choir – else why have you done the same yourself?'

'Ah! but the old gentleman and you are two folks,' said Ben Winthrop. 'The old gentleman's got a gift. Why, the Squire used to invite him to take a glass, only to hear him sing the "Red Rovier", didn't he, Mr Macey? It's a nat'ral gift. There's my little lad Aaron, he's got a gift – he can sing a tune off straight, like a throstle.[7] But as for you, Master Tookey, you'd better stick to your "Amens": your voice is well enough when you keep it up in your nose. It's your inside as isn't right made for music: it's no better nor a hollow stalk.'

This kind of unflinching frankness was the most piquant form of joke to the company at the Rainbow, and Ben Winthrop's insult was felt by everybody to have capped Mr Macey's epigram.

'I see what it is plain enough,' said Mr Tookey, unable to keep cool any longer. 'There's a consperacy to turn me out o' the choir, as I shouldn't share the Christmas money – that's where it is. But I shall speak to Mr Crackenthorp; I'll not be put upon by no man.'

'Nay, nay, Tookey,' said Ben Winthrop. 'We'll pay you your share to keep out of it – that's what we'll do. There's things folks 'ud pay to be rid on, besides varmin.'

'Come, come,' said the landlord, who felt that paying people for their absence was a principle dangerous to society; 'a joke's a joke. We're all good friends here, I hope. We must give and take. You're both right and you're both wrong, as I say. I agree wi' Mr Macey here, as there's two opinions; and if mine was asked, I should say they're both right. Tookey's right and Winthrop's right, and they've only got to split the difference and make themselves even.'

The farrier was puffing his pipe rather fiercely, in some contempt at this trivial discussion. He had no ear for music himself, and never went to church, as being of the medical profession, and likely to be in requisition for delicate cows. But the butcher, having music in his soul, had listened with a divided desire for Tookey's defeat and for the preservation of the peace.

'To be sure,' he said, following up the landlord's conciliatory view, 'we're fond of our old clerk; it's nat'ral, and him used to be such a singer, and got a brother as is known for the first fiddler in this country-side. Eh, it's a pity but what Solomon lived in our village, and could give us a tune when we liked; eh, Mr Macey? I'd keep him in liver and lights for nothing – that I would.'[8]

'Ay, ay,' said Mr Macey, in the height of complacency; 'our family's been known for musicianers as far back as anybody can tell. But them things are dying out, as I tell Solomon every time he comes round; there's no voices like what there used to be, and there's nobody remembers what we remember, if it isn't the old crows.'

'Ay, you remember when first Mr Lammeter's father come into these parts, don't you, Mr Macey?' said the landlord.

'I should think I did,' said the old man, who had now gone through that complimentary process necessary to bring him up to the point of narration; 'and a fine old gentleman he was – as fine, and finer nor the Mr Lammeter as now is. He came from a bit north'ard, so far as I could ever make out. But there's nobody rightly knows about those parts: only it couldn't be far north'ard, nor much different from this country, for he brought a fine breed o' sheep with him, so there must be pastures there, and everything reasonable. We heared tell as he'd sold his own land to come and take the Warrens, and that seemed odd for a man as had land of his own, to come and rent a farm in a strange place. But they said it was along of his wife's dying; though there's reasons in things as nobody knows on – that's pretty much what I've made out; yet some folks are so wise, they'll find you fifty reasons straight off, and all the while the real reason's winkng at 'em in the corner, and they niver see't. Howsomever, it was soon seen as we'd got a new parish'ner as know'd the rights and customs o' things, and kep a good house, and was well looked on by everybody. And the young man – that's the Mr Lammeter as now is, for he'd niver a sister – soon begun to court Miss Osgood, that's the sister o' the Mr Osgood as now is, and a fine handsome lass she was – eh, you can't think – they pretend this young lass is like her, but that's the way wi' people as don't know what come before 'em. *I* should know, for I helped the old rector, Mr Drumlow as was, I helped him marry 'em.'

Here Mr Macey paused; he always gave his narrative in instalments, expecting to be questioned according to precedent.

'Ay, and a partic'lar thing happened, didn't it, Mr Macey, so as you were likely to remember that marriage?' said the landlord, in a congratulatory tone.

'I should think there did – a *very* partic'lar thing,' said Mr Macey, nodding sideways. 'For Mr Drumlow – poor old gentleman, I was fond on him, though he'd got a bit confused in his head, what wi' age and wi' taking a drop o' summat warm when the service come of a cold morning. And young Mr Lammeter he'd have no way but he must be married in Janiwary, which, to be sure, 's a unreasonable time to be married in, for it isn't like a christening or a burying, as you can't help; and so Mr Drumlow – poor old gentleman, I was fond on him – but when he come to put the questions, he put 'em by the rule o' contrary, like, and he says, "Wilt thou have this man to thy wedded wife?" says he, and then he says, "Wilt thou have this woman to thy wedded husband?" says he. But the partic'larest thing of all is, as nobody took any notice on it but me, and they answered straight off "yes", like as if it had been me saying "Amen" i' the right place, without listening to what went before.'

'But *you* knew what was going on well enough, didn't you, Mr Macey? You were live enough, eh?' said the butcher.

'Lor bless you!' said Mr Macey, pausing, and smiling in pity at the impotence of his hearer's imagination – 'why, I was all of a tremble: it was as if I'd been a coat pulled by the two tails, like; for I couldn't stop the parson, I couldn't take upon me to do that; and yet I said to myself, I says, "Suppose they shouldn't be fast married, 'cause the words are contrary?" and my head went working like a mill, for I was allays uncommon for turning things over and seeing all round 'em; and I says to myself, "Is't the meanin' or the words as makes folks fast i' wedlock?" For the parson meant right, and the bride and bridegroom meant right. But then, when I come to think on it, meanin' goes but a little way i' most things, for you may mean to stick things together and your glue may be bad, and then where are you? And so I says to mysen, "It isn't the meanin', it's the glue." And I was worreted as if I'd got three bells to pull at once, when we went into the vestry, and they begun to sign their names. But where's the use o' talking? – you can't think what goes on in a 'cute man's inside.'

'But you held in for all that, didn't you, Mr Macey?' said the landlord.

'Ay, I held in tight till I was by mysen wi' Mr Drumlow, and then I out wi' everything, but respectful, as I allays did. And he made light on it, and he says, "Pooh, pooh, Macey, make yourself easy," he says; "it's neither the meaning nor the words – it's the re*ges*ter does it – that's the glue." So you see he settled it easy; for parsons and doctors know everything by heart, like, so as they aren't worreted wi' thinking what's the rights and wrongs o' things, as I'n been many and many's the time. And sure enough the wedding turned out all right, on'y poor Mrs Lammeter – that's Miss Osgood as was – died afore the lasses was growed up; but for prosperity and everything respectable, there's no family more looked on.'

Every one of Mr Macey's audience had heard this story many times, but it was listened to as if it had been a favourite tune, and at certain points the puffing of the pipes was momentarily suspended, that the listeners might give their whole minds to the expected words. But there was more to come; and Mr Snell, the landlord, duly put the leading question.

'Why, old Mr Lammeter had a pretty fortin, didn't they say, when he come into these parts?'

'Well, yes,' said Mr Macey; 'but I daresay it's as much as this Mr Lammeter's done to keep it whole. For there was allays a talk as nobody could get rich on the Warrens: though he holds it cheap, for it's what they call Charity Land.'[9]

'Ay, and there's few folks know so well as you how it come to be Charity Land, eh, Mr Macey?' said the butcher.

'How should they?' said the old clerk, with some contempt. 'Why, my grandfather made the grooms' livery for that Mr Cliff as came and built the big stables at the Warrens. Why, they're stables four times as big as Squire Cass's, for he thought o' nothing but hosses and hunting, Cliff didn't – a Lunnon tailor, some folks said, as had gone mad wi' cheating. For he couldn't ride; lor bless you! they said he'd got no more grip o' the hoss than if his legs had been cross-sticks: my grandfather heared old Squire Cass say so many and many a time. But ride he would as if Old Harry had been a-driving him; and he'd a son, a lad o'sixteen; and nothing would his father have him do, but he must ride and ride – though the lad was frighted, they said. And it was a common saying as the father wanted to ride the tailor out o' the lad, and make a gentleman on him – not but what I'm a tailor myself, but in respect as God made me such, I'm proud on it, for "Macey, tailor" 's been wrote up over our door since afore the Queen's heads[10] went out on the shillings. But Cliff, he was ashamed o' being called a tailor, and he was sore vexed as his riding was laughed at, and nobody o' the gentlefolks hereabout could abide him. Howsomever, the poor lad got sickly and died, and the father didn't live long after him, for he got queerer nor ever, and they said he used to go out i' the dead o' the night, wi' a lantern in his hand, to the stables, and set a lot o' lights burning, for he got as he couldn't sleep; and there he'd stand, cracking his whip and looking at his hosses; and they said it was a mercy as the stables didn't get burnt down wi' the poor dumb creaturs in 'em. But at last he died raving, and they found as he'd left all his property, Warrens and all, to a Lunnon Charity, and that's how the Warrens come to be Charity Land; though, as for the stables, Mr Lammeter never uses 'em – they're out o' all charicter – lor bless you! if you was to set the doors a-banging in 'em, it 'ud sound like thunder half o'er the parish.'

'Ay, but there's more going on in the stables than what folks see by daylight, eh, Mr Macey?' said the landlord.

'Ay, ay; go that way of a dark night, that's all,' said Mr Macey, winking mysteriously, 'and then make believe, if you like, as you didn't see lights i' the stables, nor hear the stamping o' the hosses, nor the cracking o' the whips, and howling, too, if it's tow'rt daybreak. "Cliff's Holiday" has been the name of it ever sin' I were a boy; that's to say, some said as it was the holiday Old Harry gev him from roasting, like. That's what my father told me, and he was a reasonable man, though there's folks nowadays know what happened afore they were born better nor they know their own business.'

'What do you say to that, eh, Dowlas?' said the landlord, turning to the farrier, who was swelling with impatience for his cue. 'There's a nut for *you* to crack.'

Mr Dowlas was the negative spirit in the company, and was proud of his position.

'Say? I say what a man *should* say as doesn't shut his eyes to look at a finger-post. I say, as I'm ready to wager any man ten pound, if he'll stand out wi' me any dry night in the pasture before the Warren stables, as we shall neither see lights nor hear noises, if it isn't the blowing of our own noses. That's what I say, and I've said it many a time; but there's nobody 'ull venture a ten-pun' note on their ghos'es as they make so sure of.'

'Why, Dowlas, that's easy betting, that is,' said Ben Winthrop. 'You might as well bet a man as he wouldn't catch the rheumatise if he stood up to's neck in the pool of a frosty night. It 'ud be fine fun for a man to win his bet as he'd catch the rheumatise. Folks as believe in Cliff's Holiday aren't agoing to ventur near it for a matter o' ten pound.'

'If Master Dowlas wants to know the truth on it,' said Mr

Macey, with a sarcastic smile, tapping his thumbs together, 'he's no call to lay any bet – let him go and stan' by himself – there's nobody 'ull hinder him; and then he can let the parish'ners know it they're wrong.'

'Thank you! I'm obliged to you,' said the farrier, with a snort of scorn. 'If folks are fools, it's no business o' mine. *I* don't want to make out the truth about ghos'es: I know it a'ready. But I'm not against a bet – everything fair and open. Let any man bet me ten pound as I shall see Cliff's Holiday, and I'll go and stand by myself. I want no company. I'd as lief do it as I'd fill this pipe.'

'Ah, but who's to watch you, Dowlas, and see you do it? That's no fair bet,' said the butcher.

'No fair bet?' replied Mr Dowlas, angrily. 'I should like to hear any man stand up and say I want to bet unfair. Come now, Master Lundy, I should like to hear you say it.'

'Very like you would,' said the butcher. 'But it's no business o' mine. You're none o' my bargains, and I aren't a-going to try and 'bate your price. If anybody 'll bid for you at your own vallying, let him. I'm for peace and quietness, I am.'

'Yes, that's what every yapping cur is, when you hold a stick up at him,' said the farrier. 'But I'm afraid o' neither man nor ghost, and I'm ready to lay a fair bet. *I* aren't a turn-tail cur.'

'Ay, but there's this in it, Dowlas,' said the landlord, speaking in a tone of much candour and tolerance. 'There's folks, i' my opinion, they can't see ghos'es, not if they stood as plain as a pike-staff before 'em. And there's reason i' that. For there's my wife, now, can't smell, not if she'd the strongest o' cheese under her nose. I never see'd a ghost myself; but then I says to myself, "Very like I haven't got the smell for 'em." I mean, putting a ghost for a smell, or else contrairiways. And so, I'm for holding with both sides; for, as I say, the truth lies between 'em. And if Dowlas was to go and stand, and say he'd never seen a wink o' Cliff's Holiday all the night through, I'd back him; and if anybody said as Cliff's Holiday was certain sure for all that, I'd back *him* too. For the smell's what I go by.'

The landlord's analogical argument was not well received by the farrier – a man intensely opposed to compromise.

'Tut, tut,' he said, setting down his glass with refreshed irritation; 'what's the smell got to do with it? Did ever a ghost give a man a black eye? That's what I should like to know. If

ghos'es want me to believe in 'em, let 'em leave off skulking i'
the dark and i' lone places – let 'em come where there's company
and candles.'

'As if ghos'es 'ud want to be believed in by anybody so
ignirant!' said Mr Macey, in deep disgust at the farrier's crass
incompetence to apprehend the conditions of ghostly
phenomena.

CHAPTER 7

Yet the next moment there seemed to be some evidence that ghosts had a more condescending disposition than Mr Macey attributed to them; for the pale thin figure of Silas Marner was suddenly seen standing in the warm light, uttering no word, but looking round at the company with his strange unearthly eyes. The long pipes gave a simultaneous movement, like the antennae of startled insects, and every man present, not excepting even the sceptical farrier, had an impression that he saw, not Silas Marner in the flesh, but an apparition; for the door by which Silas had entered was hidden by the high-screened seats, and no one had noticed his approach. Mr Macey, sitting a long way off the ghost, might be supposed to have felt an argumentative triumph, which would tend to neutralise his share of the general alarm. Had he not always said that when Silas Marner was in that strange trance of his, his soul went loose from his body? Here was the demonstration: nevertheless, on the whole, he would have been as well contented without it. For a few moments there was a dead silence, Marner's want of breath and agitation not allowing him to speak. The landlord, under the habitual sense that he was bound to keep his house open to all company, and confident in the protection of his unbroken neutrality, at last took on himself the task of adjuring the ghost.

'Master Marner,' he said, in a conciliatory tone, 'what's lacking to you? What's your business here?'

'Robbed!' said Silas, gasping. 'I've been robbed! I want the constable – and the Justice – and Squire Cass – and Mr Crackenthorp.'

'Lay hold on him, Jem Rodney,' said the landlord, the idea of a ghost subsiding; 'he's off his head, I doubt. He's wet through.'

Jem Rodney was the outermost man, and sat conveniently near Marner's standing-place; but he declined to give his services.

'Come and lay hold on him yourself, Mr Snell, if you've a

mind,' said Jem, rather sullenly. 'He's been robbed, and murdered too, for what I know,' he added, in a muttering tone.

'Jem Rodney!' said Silas, turning and fixing his strange eyes on the suspected man.

'Ay, Master Marner, what do ye want wi' me?' said Jem, trembling a little, and seizing his drinking-can as a defensive weapon.

'If it was you stole my money,' said Silas, clasping his hands entreatingly, and raising his voice to a cry, 'give it me back, – and I won't meddle with you. I won't set the constable on you. Give it me back, and I'll let you – I'll let you have a guinea.'

'Me stole your money!' said Jem, angrily. 'I'll pitch this can at your eye if you talk o' *my* stealing your money.'

'Come, come, Master Marner,' said the landlord, now rising resolutely, and seizing Marner by the shoulder, 'if you've got any information to lay, speak it out sensible, and show as you're in your right mind, if you expect anybody to listen to you. You're as wet as a drownded rat. Sit down and dry yourself, and speak straight forrard.'

'Ah, to be sure, man,' said the farrier, who began to feel that he had not been quite on a par with himself and the occasion. 'Let's have no more staring and screaming, else we'll have you strapped for a madman. That was why I didn't speak at the first – thinks I, the man's run mad.'

'Ay, ay, make him sit down,' said several voices at once, well pleased that the reality of ghosts remained still an open question.

The landlord forced Marner to take off his coat, and then to sit down on a chair aloof from every one else, in the centre of the circle and in the direct rays of the fire. The weaver, too feeble to have any distinct purpose beyond that of getting help to recover his money, submitted unresistingly. The transient fears of the company were now forgotten in their strong curiosity, and all faces were turned towards Silas, when the landlord, having seated himself again, said –

'Now then, Master Marner, what's this you've got to say – as you've been robbed? Speak out.'

'He'd better not say again as it was me robbed him,' cried Jem Rodney, hastily. 'What could I ha' done with his money? I could as easy steal the parson's surplice, and wear it.'

'Hold your tongue, Jem, and let's hear what he's got to say,' said the landlord. 'Now then, Master Marner.'

Silas now told his story, under frequent questioning as the mysterious character of the robbery became evident.

This strangely novel situation of opening his trouble to his Raveloe neighbours, of sitting in the warmth of a hearth not his own, and feeling the presence of faces and voices which were his nearest promise of help, had doubtless its influence on Marner, in spite of his passionate preoccupation with his loss. Our consciousness rarely registers the beginning of a growth within us any more than without us: there have been many circulations of the sap before we detect the smallest sign of the bud.

The slight suspicion with which his hearers at first listened to him, gradually melted away before the convincing simplicity of his distress: it was impossible for the neighbours to doubt that Marner was telling the truth, not because they were capable of arguing at once from the nature of his statements to the absence of any motive for making them falsely, but because, as Mr Macey observed, 'Folks as had the devil to back 'em were not likely to be so mushed'[1] as poor Silas was. Rather, from the strange fact that the robber had left no traces, and had happened to know the nick of time, utterly incalculable by mortal agents, when Silas would go away from home without locking his door, the more probable conclusion seemed to be, that his disreputable intimacy in that quarter, if it ever existed, had been broken up, and that, in consequence, this ill turn had been done to Marner by somebody it was quite in vain to set the constable after. Why this preternatural felon should be obliged to wait till the door was left unlocked was a question which did not present itself.

'It isn't Jem Rodney as has done this work, Master Marner,' said the landlord. 'You mustn't be a-casting your eye at poor Jem. There may be a bit of a reckoning against Jem for the matter of a hare or so, if anybody was bound to keep their eyes staring open, and niver to wink; but Jem's been a-sitting here drinking his can, like the decentest man i' the parish, since before you left your house, Master Marner, by your own account.'

'Ay, ay,' said Mr Macey; 'let's have no accusing o' the innicent. That isn't the law. There must be folks to swear again' a man before he can be ta'en up. Let's have no accusing o' the innicent, Master Marner.'

Memory was not so utterly torpid in Silas that it could not be wakened by these words. With a movement of compunction as new and strange to him as everything else within the last hour, he started from his chair and went close up to Jem, looking at him as if he wanted to assure himself of the expression in his face.

'I was wrong,' he said – 'yes, yes – I ought to have thought. There's nothing to witness against you, Jem. Only you'd been into my house oftener than anybody else, and so you came into my head. I don't accuse you – I won't accuse anybody – only,' he added, lifting up his hands to his head, and turning away with bewildered misery, 'I try – I try to think where my guineas can be.'

'Ay, ay, they're gone where it's hot enough to melt 'em, I doubt,' said Mr Macey.

'Tchuh!' said the farrier. And then he asked, with a cross-examining air, 'How much money might there be in the bags, Master Marner?'

'Two hundred and seventy-two pounds, twelve and sixpence, last night when I counted it,' said Silas, seating himself again, with a groan.

'Pooh! why, they'd be none so heavy to carry. Some tramp's been in, that's all; and as for the no footmarks, and the bricks and the sand being all right – why, your eyes are pretty much like a insect's, Master Marner; they're obliged to look so close, you can't see much at a time. It's my opinion as, if I'd been you, or you'd been me – for it comes to the same thing – you wouldn't have thought you'd found everything as you left it. But what I vote is, as two of the sensiblest o' the company should go with you to Master Kench, the constable's – he's ill i' bed, I know that much – and get him to appoint one of us his deppity; for that's the law, and I don't think anybody 'ull take upon him to contradick me there. It isn't much of a walk to Kench's; and then, if it's me as is deppity, I'll go back with you, Master Marner, and examine your premises; and if anybody's got any fault to find with that, I'll thank him to stand up and say it out like a man.'

By this pregnant speech the farrier had re-established his self-complacency, and waited with confidence to hear himself named as one of the superlatively sensible men.

'Let us see how the night is, though,' said the landlord, who also considered himself personally concerned in this proposition. 'Why, it rains heavy still,' he said, returning from the door.

'Well, I'm not the man to be afraid o' the rain,' said the farrier. 'For it'll look bad when Justice Malam hears as respectable men like us had a information laid before 'em and took no steps.'

The landlord agreed with this view, and after taking the sense of the company, and duly rehearsing a small ceremony known in high ecclesiastical life as the *nolo episcopari*,[2] he consented to take on himself the chill dignity of going to Kench's. But to the farrier's strong disgust, Mr Macey now started an objection to his proposing himself as a deputy-constable; for that oracular old gentleman, claiming to know the law, stated, as a fact delivered to him by his father, that no doctor could be a constable.

'And you're a doctor, I reckon, though you're only a cow-doctor – for a fly's a fly, though it may be a hoss-fly,' concluded Mr Macey, wondering a little at his own "cuteness".

There was a hot debate upon this, the farrier being of course indisposed to renounce the quality of doctor, but contending that a doctor could be a constable if he liked – the law meant, he needn't be one if he didn't like. Mr Macey thought this was nonsense, since the law was not likely to be fonder of doctors than of other folks. Moreover, if it was in the nature of doctors more than of other men not to like being constables, how came Mr Dowlas to be so eager to act in that capacity?

'*I* don't want to act the constable,' said the farrier, driven into a corner by this merciless reasoning; 'and there's no man can say it of me, if he'd tell the truth. But if there's to be any jealousy and en*v*ying about going to Kench's in the rain, let them go as like it – you won't get me to go, I can tell you.'

By the landlord's intervention, however, the dispute was accommodated. Mr Dowlas consented to go as a second person disinclined to act officially; and so poor Silas, furnished with some old coverings, turned out with his two companions into the rain again, thinking of the long night-hours before him, not as those do who long to rest, but as those who expect to 'watch for the morning'.

CHAPTER 8

When Godfrey Cass returned from Mrs Osgood's party at midnight, he was not much surprised to learn that Dunsey had not come home. Perhaps he had not sold Wildfire, and was waiting for another chance – perhaps, on that foggy afternoon, he had preferred housing himself at the Red Lion at Batherley for the night, if the run had kept him in that neighbourhood; for he was not likely to feel much concern about leaving his brother in suspense. Godfrey's mind was too full of Nancy Lammeter's looks and behaviour, too full of the exasperation against himself and his lot, which the sight of her always produced in him, for him to give much thought to Wildfire, or to the probabilities of Dunstan's conduct.

The next morning the whole village was excited by the story of the robbery, and Godfrey, like every one else, was occupied in gathering and discussing news about it, and in visiting the Stone-pits. The rain had washed away all possibility of distinguishing foot-marks, but a close investigation of the spot had disclosed, in the direction opposite to the village, a tinder-box,[1] with a flint and steel, half sunk in the mud. It was not Silas's tinder-box, for the only one he had ever had was still standing on his shelf; and the inference generally accepted was, that the tinder-box in the ditch was somehow connected with the robbery. A small minority shook their heads, and intimated their opinion that it was not a robbery to have much light thrown on it by tinder-boxes, that Master Marner's tale had a queer look with it, and that such things had been known as a man's doing himself a mischief, and then setting the justice to look for the doer. But when questioned closely as to their grounds for this opinion, and what Master Marner had to gain by such false pretences, they only shook their heads as before, and observed that there was no knowing what some folks counted gain; moreover, that everybody had a right to their own opinions, grounds or no grounds, and that the weaver, as everybody knew, was partly crazy. Mr Macey, though he joined in the defence of Marner against all suspicions of deceit, also pooh-poohed the tinder-box; indeed, repudiated it as a rather impious suggestion, tending to imply that everything must be done by human hands, and that there was no power which could make away with the guineas without moving the bricks. Nevertheless, he turned round rather sharply on Mr Tookey, when the zealous deputy, feeling that this was a view of the case peculiarly suited to a parish-clerk, carried it still further, and doubted whether it was right to inquire into a robbery at all when the circumstances were so mysterious.

'As if,' concluded Mr Tookey – 'as if there was nothing but what could be made out by justices and constables.'

'Now, don't you be for overshooting the mark, Tookey,' said Mr Macey, nodding his head aside admonishingly. 'That's what you're allays at; if I throw a stone and hit, you think there's summat better than hitting, and you try to throw a stone beyond. What I said was against the tinder-box: I said nothing against justices and constables, for they're o' King George's[2] making, and it 'ud be ill-becoming a man in a parish office to fly out again' King George.'

While these discussions were going on amongst the group outside the Rainbow, a higher consultation was being carried on within, under the presidency of Mr Crackenthorp, the rector, assisted by Squire Cass and other substantial parishioners. It had just occurred to Mr Snell, the landlord – he being, as he observed, a man accustomed to put two and two together – to connect with the tinder-box, which, as deputy-constable, he himself had had the honourable distinction of finding, certain recollections of a pedlar who had called to drink at the house about a month before, and had actually stated that he carried a tinder-box about with him to light his pipe. Here, surely, was a clue to be followed out. And as memory, when duly impregnated with ascertained facts, is sometimes surprisingly fertile, Mr Snell gradually recovered a vivid impression of the effect produced on him by the pedlar's[3] countenance and conversation. He had a 'look with his eye' which fell unpleasantly on Mr Snell's sensitive organism. To be sure, he didn't say anything particular – no, except that about the tinder-box – but it isn't what a man says, it's the way he says it. Moreover, he had a swarthy foreignness of complexion which boded little honesty.

'Did he wear ear-rings?' Mr Crackenthorp wished to know, having some acquaintance with foreign customs.

'Well – stay – let me see,' said Mr Snell, like a docile clairvoyante, who would really not make a mistake if she could help it. After stretching the corners of his mouth and contracting his eyes, as if he were trying to see the ear-rings, he appeared to give up the effort, and said, 'Well, he'd got ear-rings in his box to sell, so it's nat'ral to suppose he might wear 'em. But he called at every house, a'most, in the village; there's somebody else, mayhap, saw 'em in his ears, though I can't take upon me rightly to say.'

Mr Snell was correct in his surmise, that somebody else would remember the pedlar's ear-rings. For on the spread of inquiry among the villagers it was stated with gathering emphasis, that the parson had wanted to know whether the pedlar wore ear-rings in his ears, and an impression was created that a great deal depended on the eliciting of this fact. Of course, every one who heard the question, not having any distinct image of the pedlar as *without* ear-rings, immediately had an image of him *with* ear-rings, larger or smaller, as the case might be; and the image was presently taken for a vivid recollection, so that the glazier's wife, a well-intentioned woman, not given to lying, and whose house was among the cleanest in the village, was ready to declare, as sure as ever she meant to take the sacrament the very next Christmas that was ever coming, that she had seen big ear-rings, in the shape of the young moon, in the pedlar's two ears; while Jinny Oates, the cobbler's daughter, being a more imaginative person, stated not only that she had seen them too, but that they had made her blood creep, as it did at that very moment while there she stood.

Also, by way of throwing further light on this clue of the tinder-box, a collection was made of all the articles purchased from the pedlar at various houses, and carried to the Rainbow to be exhibited there. In fact, there was a general feeling in the village, that for the clearing-up of this robbery there must be a great deal done at the Rainbow, and that no man need offer his wife an excuse for going there while it was the scene of severe public duties.

Some disappointment was felt, and perhaps a little indignation also, when it became known that Silas Marner, on being questioned by the Squire and the parson, had retained no other recollection of the pedlar than that he had called at his door, but had not entered his house, having turned away at once when Silas, holding the door ajar, had said that he wanted nothing. This had been Silas's testimony, though he clutched strongly at the idea of the pedlar's being the culprit, if only because it gave him a definite image of a whereabout for his gold after it had been taken away from its hiding-place: he could see it now in the pedlar's box. But it was observed with some irritation in the village, that anybody but a 'blind creatur' like Marner would have seen the man prowling about, for how came he to leave his tinder-box in the ditch close by, if he hadn't been lingering there? Doubtless, he had made his observations when he saw Marner at the door. Anybody might know – and only look at him – that the weaver was a half-crazy miser. It was a wonder the pedlar hadn't murdered him; men of that sort, with rings in their ears, had been known for murderers often and often; there had been one tried at the 'sizes, not so long ago but what there were people living who remembered it.

Godfrey Cass, indeed, entering the Rainbow during one of Mr Snell's frequently repeated recitals of his testimony, had treated it lightly, stating that he himself had bought a pen-knife of the pedlar, and thought him a merry grinning fellow enough; it was all nonsense, he said, about the man's evil looks. But this was spoken of in the village as the random talk of youth, 'as if it was only Mr Snell who had seen something odd about the pedlar!' On the contrary, there were at least half-a-dozen who were ready to go before Justice Malam, and give in much more striking testimony than any the landlord could furnish. It was to be hoped Mr Godfrey would not go to Tarley and throw cold water on what Mr Snell said there, and so prevent the justice from drawing up a warrant. He was suspected of intending this, when, after midday, he was seen setting off on horseback in the direction of Tarley.

But by this time Godfrey's interest in the robbery had faded before his growing anxiety about Dunstan and Wildfire, and he was going, not to Tarley, but to Batherley, unable to rest in uncertainty about them any longer. The possibility that Dunstan had played him the ugly trick of riding away with Wildfire, to return at the end of a month, when he had gambled away or otherwise squandered the price of the horse, was a fear that urged itself upon him more, even, than the thought of an accidental injury; and now that the dance at Mrs Osgood's was past, he was irritated with himself that he had trusted his horse to Dunstan. Instead of trying to still his fears he encouraged them, with that superstitious impression which clings to us all, that if we expect evil very strongly it is the less likely to come; and when he heard a horse approaching at a trot, and saw a hat rising above a hedge beyond an angle of the lane, he felt as if his conjuration had succeeded. But no sooner did the horse come within sight, than his heart sank again. It was not Wildfire; and in a few moments more he discerned that the rider was not Dunstan, but Bryce, who pulled up to speak, with a face that implied something disagreeable.

'Well, Mr Godfrey, that's a lucky brother of yours, that Master Dunsey, isn't he?'

'What do you mean?' said Godfrey, hastily.

'Why, hasn't he been home yet?' said Bryce.

'Home? no. What has happened? Be quick. What has he done with my horse?'

'Ah, I thought it was yours, though he pretended you had parted with it to him.'

'Has he thrown him down and broken his knees?' said Godfrey, flushed with exasperation.

'Worse than that,' said Bryce. 'You see, I'd made a bargain with him to buy the horse for a hundred and twenty – a swinging price, but I always liked the horse. And what does he do but go and stake him – fly at a hedge with stakes in it, atop of a bank with a ditch before it. The horse had been dead a pretty good while when he was found. So he hasn't been home since, has he?'

'Home? no,' said Godfrey, 'and he'd better keep away. Confound me for a fool! I might have known this would be the end of it.'

'Well, to tell you the truth,' said Bryce, 'after I'd bargained for the horse, it did come into my head that he might be riding and selling the horse without your knowledge, for I didn't believe it was his own. I knew Master Dunsey was up to his tricks sometimes. But where can he be gone? He's never been seen at Batherley. He couldn't have been hurt, for he must have walked off.'

'Hurt?' said Godfrey, bitterly. 'He'll never be hurt – he's made to hurt other people.'

'And so you *did* give him leave to sell the horse, eh?' said Bryce.

'Yes; I wanted to part with the horse – he was always a little too hard in the mouth for me,' said Godfrey; his pride making him wince under the idea that Bryce guessed the sale to be a matter of necessity. 'I was going to see after him – I thought some mischief had happened. I'll go back now,' he added, turning the horse's head, and wishing he could get rid of Bryce; for he felt that the long-dreaded crisis in his life was close upon him. 'You're coming on to Raveloe, aren't you?'

'Well, no, not now,' said Bryce. 'I *was* coming round there, for I had to go to Flitton, and I thought I might as well take you in my way, and just let you know all I knew myself about the horse. I suppose Master Dunsey didn't like to show himself till the ill news had blown over a bit. He's perhaps gone to pay a visit at the Three Crowns, by Whitbridge – I know he's fond of the house.'

'Perhaps he is,' said Godfrey, rather absently. Then rousing himself, he said, with an effort at carelessness, 'We shall hear of him soon enough, I'll be bound.'

'Well, here's my turning,' said Bryce, not surprised to perceive that Godfrey was rather 'down'; 'so I'll bid you good-day, and wish I may bring you better news another time.'

Godfrey rode along slowly, representing to himself the scene of confession to his father from which he felt that there was now no longer any escape. The revelation about the money must be made the very next morning; and if he withheld the rest, Dunstan would be sure to come back shortly, and, finding that he must bear the brunt of his father's anger, would tell the whole story out of spite, even though he had nothing to gain by it. There was one step, perhaps, by which he might still win Dunstan's silence and put off the evil day: he might tell his father that he had himself spent the money paid to him by Fowler; and as he had never been guilty of such an offence before, the affair would blow over after a little storming. But Godfrey could not bend himself to this. He felt that in letting Dunstan have the money, he had already been guilty of a breach of trust hardly less culpable than that of spending the money directly for his own behoof;[4] and yet there was a distinction between the two acts which made him feel that the one was so much more blackening than the other as to be intolerable to him.

'I don't pretend to be a good fellow,' he said to himself; 'but I'm not a scoundrel – at least, I'll stop short somewhere. I'll bear the consequences of what I *have* done sooner than make believe I've done what I never would have done. I'd never have spent the money for my own pleasure – I was tortured into it.'

Through the remainder of this day Godfrey, with only occasional fluctuations, kept his will bent in the direction of a complete avowal to his father, and he withheld the story of Wildfire's loss till the next morning, that it might serve him as an introduction to heavier matter. The old Squire was accustomed to his son's frequent absence from home, and thought neither Dunstan's nor Wildfire's non-appearance a matter calling for remark. Godfrey said to himself again and again, that if he let slip this one opportunity of confession, he might never have another; the revelation might be made even in a more odious way than by Dunstan's malignity: *she* might come as she had threatened to do. And then he tried to make the scene easier to himself by rehearsal: he made up his mind how he would pass from the admission of his weakness in letting Dunstan have the money to the fact that Dunstan had a hold on him which he had been unable to shake off, and how he would work up his father to expect something very bad before he told him the fact. The old Squire was an implacable man: he made resolutions in violent anger, and he was not to be moved from them after his anger had subsided – as fiery volcanic matters cool and harden into rock. Like many violent and implacable men, he allowed evils to grow under favour of his own heedlessness, till they pressed upon him with exasperating force, and then he turned round with fierce severity and became unrelentingly hard. This was his system with his tenants: he allowed them to get into arrears, neglect their fences, reduce their stock, sell their straw, and otherwise go the wrong way, – and then, when he became short of money in consequence of this indulgence, he took the hardest measures and would listen to no appeal. Godfrey knew all this, and felt it with the greater force because he had constantly suffered annoyance from witnessing his father's sudden fits of unrelentingness, for which his own habitual irresolution deprived him of all sympathy. (He was not critical on the faulty indulgence which preceded these fits; *that* seemed to him natural enough.) Still there was just the chance, Godfrey thought, that his father's pride might see this marriage in a light that would induce him to hush it up, rather than turn his son out and make the family the talk of the country for ten miles round.

This was the view of the case that Godfrey managed to keep before him pretty closely till midnight, and he went to sleep thinking that he had done with inward debating. But when he awoke in the still morning darkness he found it impossible to reawaken his evening thoughts; it was as if they had been tired out and were not to be roused to further work. Instead of arguments for confession, he could now feel the presence of nothing but its evil consequences: the old dread of disgrace came back – the old shrinking from the thought of raising a hopeless barrier between himself and Nancy – the old disposition to rely on chances which might be favourable to him, and save him from betrayal. Why, after all, should he cut off the hope of them by his own act? He had seen the matter in a wrong light yesterday. He had been in a rage with Dunsey, and had thought of nothing but a thorough break-up of their mutual understanding; but what it would be really wisest for him to do, was to try and soften his father's anger against Dunstan, and keep things as nearly as possible in their old condition. If Dunsey did not come back for a few days (and Godfrey did not know but that the rascal had enough money in his pocket to enable him to keep away still longer), everything might blow over.

CHAPTER 9

Godfrey rose and took his own breakfast earlier than usual, but lingered in the wainscoted parlour till his younger brothers had finished their meal and gone out; awaiting his father, who always took a walk with his managing-man before breakfast. Every one breakfasted at a different hour in the Red House, and the Squire was always the latest, giving a long chance to a rather feeble morning appetite before he tried it. The table had been spread with substantial eatables nearly two hours before he presented himself – a tall, stout man of sixty, with a face in which the knit brow and rather hard glance seemed contradicted by the slack and feeble mouth. His person showed marks of habital neglect, his dress was slovenly; and yet there was something in the presence of the old Squire distinguishable from that of the ordinary farmers in the parish, who were perhaps every whit as refined as he, but, having slouched their way through life with a consciousness of being in the vicinity of their 'betters', wanted that self-possession and authoritativeness of voice and carriage which belonged to a man who thought of superiors as remote existences with whom he had personally little more to do than with America or the stars. The Squire had been used to parish homage all his life, used to the presupposition that his family, his tankards, and everything that was his, were the oldest and best; and as he never associated with any gentry higher than himself, his opinion was not disturbed by comparison.

He glanced at his son as he entered the room, and said, 'What, sir! haven't *you* had your breakfast yet?' but there was no pleasant morning greeting between them; not because of any unfriendliness, but because the sweet flower of courtesy is not a growth of such homes as the Red House.

'Yes, sir,' said Godfrey, 'I've had my breakfast, but I was waiting to speak to you.'

'Ah! well,' said the Squire, throwing himself indifferently into his chair, and speaking in a ponderous coughing fashion, which was felt in Raveloe to be a sort of privilege of his rank, while he cut a piece of beef, and held it up before the deer-hound that had come in with him. 'Ring the bell for my ale, will you? You youngsters' business is your own pleasure, mostly. There's no hurry about it for anybody but yourselves.'

The Squire's life was quite as idle as his sons', but it was a fiction kept up by himself and his contemporaries in Raveloe that youth was exclusively the period of folly, and that their aged wisdom was constantly in a state of endurance mitigated by sarcasm. Godfrey waited, before he spoke again, until the ale had been brought and the door closed – an interval during which Fleet, the deer-hound, had consumed enough bits of beef to make a poor man's holiday dinner.

'There's been a cursed piece of ill-luck with Wildfire,' he began; 'happened the day before yesterday.'

'What! broke his knees?' said the Squire, after taking a draught of ale. 'I thought you knew how to ride better than that, sir. I never threw a horse down in my life. If I had, I might ha' whistled for another, for *my* father wasn't quite so ready to unstring as some other fathers I know of. But they must turn over a new leaf – *they* must. What with mortgages and arrears, I'm as short o' cash as a roadside pauper. And that fool Kimble says the newspaper's talking about peace. Why, the country wouldn't have a leg to stand on. Prices 'ud run down like a jack, and I should never get my arrears, not if I sold all the fellows up. And there's that damned Fowler, I won't put up with him any longer; I've told Winthrop to go to Cox this very day. The lying scoundrel told me he'd be sure to pay me a hundred last month. He takes advantage because he's on that outlying farm, and thinks I shall forget him.'

The Squire had delivered this speech in a coughing and interrupted manner, but with no pause long enough for Godfrey to make it a pretext for taking up the word again. He felt that his father meant to ward off any request for money on the ground of the misfortune with Wildfire, and that the emphasis he had thus been led to lay on his shortness of cash and his arrears was likely to produce an attitude of mind the utmost unfavourable for his own disclosure. But he must go on, now he had begun.

'It's worse than breaking the horse's knees – he's been staked and killed,' he said, as soon as his father was silent, and had begun to cut his meat. 'But I wasn't thinking of asking you to buy me another horse; I was only thinking I'd lost the means of paying you with the price of Wildfire, as I'd meant to do. Dunsey took him to the hunt to sell him for me the other day, and after he'd made a bargain for a hundred and twenty with Bryce, he went after the hounds, and took some fool's leap or other that did for the horse at once. If it hadn't been for that, I should have paid you a hundred pounds this morning.'

The Squire had laid down his knife and fork, and was staring at his son in amazement, not being sufficiently quick of brain to form a probable guess as to what could have caused so strange an inversion of the paternal and filial relations as this proposition of his son to pay him a hundred pounds.

'The truth is, sir – I'm very sorry – I was quite to blame,' said Godfrey. 'Fowler did pay that hundred pounds. He paid it to me, when I was over there one day last month. And Dunsey bothered me for the money, and I let him have it, because I hoped I should be able to pay it you before this.'

The Squire was purple with anger before his son had done speaking, and found utterance difficult. 'You let Dunsey have it, sir? And how long have you been so thick with Dunsey that you must *collogue*[1] with him to embezzle my money? Are you turning out a scamp? I tell you I won't have it. I'll turn the whole pack of you out of the house together, and marry again. I'd have you to remember, sir, my property's got no entail[2] on it; – since my grandfather's time the Casses can do as they like with their land. Remember that, sir. Let Dunsey have the money! Why should you let Dunsey have the money? There's some lie at the bottom of it.'

'There's no lie, sir,' said Godfrey. 'I wouldn't have spent the money myself, but Dunsey bothered me, and I was a fool, and let him have it. But I meant to pay it, whether he did nor not. That's the whole story. I never meant to embezzle money, and I'm not the man to do it. You never knew me do a dishonest trick, sir.'

'Where's Dunsey, then? What do you stand talking there for? Go and fetch Dunsey, as I tell you, and let him give accont of what he wanted the money for, and what he's done with it. He shall repent it. I'll turn him out. I said I would, and I'll do it. He shan't brave me. Go and fetch him.'

'Dunsey isn't come back, sir.'

'What! did he break his own neck, then?' said the Squire, with some disgust at the idea that, in that case, he could not fulfil his threat.

'No, he wasn't hurt, I believe, for the horse was found dead, and Dunsey must have walked off. I daresay we shall see him again by-and-by. I don't know where he is.'

'And what must you be letting him have my money for? Answer me that,' said the Squire, attacking Godfrey again, since Dunsey was not within reach.

'Well, sir, I don't know,' said Godfrey, hesitatingly. That was a feeble evasion, but Godfrey was not fond of lying, and, not being sufficiently aware that no sort of duplicity can long flourish without the help of vocal falsehoods, he was quite unprepared with invented motives.

'You don't know? I tell you what it is, sir. You've been up to some trick, and you've been bribing him not to tell,' said the Squire, with a sudden acuteness which startled Godfrey, who felt his heart beat violently at the nearness of his father's guess. The sudden alarm pushed him on to take the next step – a very slight impulse suffices for that on a downward road.

'Why, sir,' he said, trying to speak with careless ease, 'it was a little affair between me and Dunsey; it's no matter to anybody else. It's hardly worth while to pry into young men's fooleries: it wouldn't have made any difference to you, sir, if I'd not had the back luck to lose Wildfire. I should have paid you the money.'

'Fooleries! Pshaw! it's time you'd done with fooleries. And I'd have you know, sir, you *must* ha' done with 'em,' said the Squire, frowning and casting an angry glance at his son. 'Your goings-on are not what I shall find money for any longer. There's my grandfather had his stables full o' horses, and kept a good house, too, and in worse times, by what I can make out; and so might I, if I hadn't four good-for-nothing fellows to hang on me like horse-leeches. I've been too good a father to you all – that's what it is. But I shall pull up, sir.'

Godfrey was silent. He was not likely to be very penetrating in his judgments, but he had always had a sense that his father's indulgence had not been kindness, and had had a vague longing for some discipline that would have checked his own errant weakness and helped his better will. The Squire ate his bread and meat hastily, took a deep draught of ale, then turned his chair from the table, and began to speak again.

'It'll be all the worse for you, you know – you'd need try and help me keep things together.'

'Well, sir, I've often offered to take the management of things, but you know you've taken it ill always, and seemed to think I wanted to push you out of your place.'

'I know nothing o' your offering or o' my taking it ill,' said the Squire, whose memory consisted in certain strong impressions unmodified by detail; 'but I know, one while you seemed to be thinking o' marrying, and I didn't offer to put any obstacles in your way, as some fathers would. I'd as lieve you married Lammeter's daughter as anybody. I suppose, if I'd said you nay, you'd ha' kept on with it; but, for want o' contradiction, you've changed your mind. You're a shilly-shally fellow:[3] you take after your poor mother. She never had a will of her own; a woman has no call for one, if she's got a proper man for her husband. But *your* wife had need have one, for you hardly know your own mind enough to make both your legs walk one way. The lass hasn't said downright she won't have you, has she?'

'No,' said Godfrey, feeling very hot and uncomfortable; 'but I don't think she will.'

'Think! why haven't you the courage to ask her? Do you stick to it, you want to have *her* – that's the thing?'

'There's no other woman I want to marry,' said Godfrey, evasively.

'Well, then, let me make the offer for you, that's all, if you haven't the pluck to do it yourself. Lammeter isn't likely to be loath for his daughter to marry into *my* family, I should think. And as for the pretty lass, she wouldn't have her cousin – and there's nobody else, as I see, could ha' stood in your way.'

'I'd rather let it be, please sir, at present,' said Godfrey, in alarm. 'I think she's a little offended with me just now, and I should like to speak for myself. A man must manage these things for himself.'

'Well, speak, then, and manage it, and see if you can't turn over a new leaf. That's what a man must do when he thinks o' marrying.'

'I don't see how I can think of it at present, sir. You wouldn't like to settle me on one of the farms, I suppose, and I don't think she'd come to live in this house with all my brothers. It's a different sort of life to what she's been used to.'

'Not come to live in this house? Don't tell me. You ask her, that's all,' said the Squire, with a short, scornful laugh.

'I'd rather let the thing be, at present, sir,' said Godfrey. 'I hope you won't try to hurry it on by saying anything.'

'I shall do what I choose,' said the Squire, 'and I shall let you know I'm master; else you may turn out, and find an estate to drop into somewhere else. Go out and tell Winthrop not to go to Cox's, but wait for me. And tell 'em to get my horse saddled. And stop: look out and get that hack o' Dunsey's sold, and hand me the money, will you? He'll keep no more hacks at my expense. And if you know where he's sneaking – I daresay you do – you may tell him to spare himself the journey o' coming back home. Let him turn ostler, and keep himself. He shan't hang on me any more.'

'I don't know where he is; and if I did, it isn't my place to tell him to keep away,' said Godfrey, moving towards the door.

'Confound it, sir, don't stay arguing, but go and order my horse,' said the Squire, taking up a pipe.

Godfrey left the room, hardly knowing whether he were more relieved by the sense that the interview was ended without having made any change in his position, or more uneasy that he had entangled himself still further in prevarication and deceit. What had passed about his proposing to Nancy had raised a new alarm, lest by some after-dinner words of his father's to Mr Lammeter he should be thrown into the embarrassment of being obliged absolutely to decline her when she seemed to be within his reach. He fled to his usual refuge, that of hoping for some unforeseen turn of fortune, some favourable chance which would save him from unpleasant consequences – perhaps even justify his insincerity by manifesting its prudence.

In this point of trusting to some throw of fortune's dice, Godfrey can hardly be called old-fashioned. Favourable Chance is the god of all men who follow their own devices instead of obeying a law they believe in. Let even a polished man of these days get into a position he is ashamed to avow, and his mind will be bent on all the possible issues that may deliver him from the calculable results of that position. Let him live outside his income, or shirk the resolute honest work that brings wages, and he will presently find himself dreaming of a possible benefactor, a possible simpleton who may be cajoled into using his interest, a possible state of mind in some possible person not yet forthcoming. Let him neglect the responsibilities of his office, and he will inevitably anchor himself on the chance, that the thing left undone may turn out not to be of the supposed importance. Let him betray his friend's confidence, and he will adore that same cunning complexity called Chance, which gives him the hope that his friend will never know. Let him forsake a decent craft that he may pursue the gentilities of a profession to which nature never called him, and his religion will infallibly be the worship of blessed Chance, which he will believe in as the mighty creator of success. The evil principle deprecated in that religion, is the orderly sequence by which the seed brings forth a crop after its kind.

CHAPTER 10

Justice Malam was naturally regarded in Tarley and Raveloe as a man of capacious mind, seeing that he could draw much wider conclusions without evidence than could be expected of his neighbours who were not on the Commission of the Peace. Such a man was not likely to neglect the clue of the tinder-box, and an inquiry was set on foot concerning a pedlar, name unknown, with curly black hair and a foreign complexion, carrying a box of cutlery and jewellery, and wearing large rings in his ears. But either because inquiry was too slow-footed to overtake him, or because the description applied to so many pedlars that inquiry did not know how to choose among them, weeks passed away, and there was no other result concerning the robbery than a gradual cessation of the excitement it had caused in Raveloe. Dunstan Cass's absence was hardly a subject of remark: he had once before had a quarrel with his father, and had gone off, nobody knew whither, to return at the end of six weeks, take up his old quarters unforbidden and swagger as usual. His own family, who equally expected this issue, with the sole difference that the Squire determined this time to forbid him the old quarters, never mentioned his absence; and when his uncle Kimble or Mr Osgood noticed it, the story of his having killed Wildfire and committed some offence against his father was enough to prevent surprise. To connect the fact of Dunsey's disappearance with that of the robbery occurring on the same day, lay quite away from the track of every one's thought – even Godfrey's, who had better reason than any one else to know what his brother was capable of. He remembered no mention of the weaver between them since the time, twelve years ago, when it was their boyish sport to deride him; and, besides, his imagination constantly created an *alibi* for Dunstan: he saw him continually in some congenial haunt, to which he had walked off on leaving Wildfire – saw him sponging on chance acquaintances, and meditating a return home to the old amusement of tormenting his elder brother. Even if any brain in Raveloe had put the said two facts together, I doubt whether a combination so injurious to the prescriptive respectability of a family with a mural monument and venerable tankards, would not have been suppressed as of unsound tendency. But Christmas puddings, brawn, and abundance of spirituous liquors, throwing the mental orginality into the channel of nightmare, are great preservatives against a dangerous spontaneity of waking thought.

When the robbery was talked of at the Rainbow and else-where, in good company, the balance continued to waver between the rational explanation founded on the tinder-box, and the theory of an impenetrable mystery that mocked investigation. The advocates of the tinder-box-and-pedlar view considered the other side a muddle-headed and credulous set, who, because they themselves were wall-eyed, supposed everybody else to have the same blank outlook; and the adherents of the inexplicable more than hinted that their antagonists were animals inclined to crow before they had found any corn – mere skimming-dishes[1] in point of depth – whose clear-sightedness consisted in supposing there was nothing behind a barn-door because they couldn't see through it; so that, though their controversy did not serve to elicit the fact concerning the robbery, it elicited some true opinions of collateral importance.

But while poor Silas's loss served thus to brush the slow current of Raveloe conversation, Silas himself was feeling the withering desolation of that bereavement about which his neighbours were arguing at their ease. To any one who had observed him before he lost his gold, it might have seemed that so withered and shrunken a life as his could hardly be susceptible of a bruise, could hardly endure any subtraction but such as would put an end to it altogether. But in reality it had been an eager life, filled with immediate purpose which fenced him in from the wide, cheerless unknown. It had been a clinging life; and though the object round which its fibres had clung was a dead disrupted thing, it satisfied the need for clinging. But now the fence was broken down – the support was snatched away. Marner's thoughts could no longer move in their old round, and were baffled by a blank like that which meets a plodding ant when the earth has broken away on its homeward path. The loom was there, and the weaving, and the growing pattern in the cloth; but the bright treasure in the hole under his feet was gone; the prospect of handling and counting it was gone: the evening had no phantasm of delight to still the poor soul's craving. The thought of the money he would get by his actual work could bring no joy, for its meagre image was only a fresh reminder of his loss; and hope was too heavily crushed by the sudden blow, for his imagination to dwell on the growth of a new hoard from that small beginning.

He filled up the blank with grief. As he sat weaving, he every now and then, moaned low, like one in pain: it was the sign that his thoughts had come round again to the sudden chasm – to the empty evening time. And all the evening, as he sat in his loneliness by his dull fire, he leaned his elbows on his knees, and clasped his head with his hands, and moaned very low – not as one who seeks to be heard.

And yet he was not utterly forsaken in his trouble. The repulsion Marner had always created in his neighbours was partly dissipated by the new light in which this misfortune had shown him. Instead of a man who had more cunning than honest folks could come by, and, what was worse, had not the inclination to use that cunning in a neighbourly way, it was now apparent that Silas had not cunning enough to keep his own. He was generally spoken of as a 'poor mushed creature';[2] and that avoidance of his neigbours, which had before been referred to his ill-will and to a probable addiction to worse company, was now considered mere craziness.

This change to a kindlier feeling was shown in various ways. The odour of Christmas cooking being on the wind, it was the season when superfluous pork and black puddings are suggestive of charity in well-to-do families; and Silas's misfortune had brought him uppermost in the memory of housekeepers like Mrs Osgood. Mr Crackenthorp, too, while he admonished Silas that his money had probably been taken from him because he thought too much of it and never came to church, enforced the doctrine by a present of pigs' pettitoes, well calculated to dissipate unfounded prejudices against the clerical character. Neighbours who had nothing but verbal consolation to give showed a disposition not only to greet Silas and discuss his misfortune at some length when they encountered him in the village, but also to take the trouble of calling at his cottage and getting him to repeat all the details on the very spot; and they

would try to cheer him by saying, 'Well, Master Marner, you're
no worse off nor other poor folks, after all; and if you was to be
crippled, the parish 'ud give you a 'lowance.'

I suppose one reason why we are seldom able to comfort our
neighbours with our words is that our goodwill gets adulterated,
in spite of ourselves, before it can pass our lips. We can send
black puddings and pettitoes without giving them a flavour of
our own egoism; but language is a stream that is almost sure to
smack of a mingled soil. There was a fair proportion of kindness
in Raveloe; but it was often of a beery and bungling sort, and
took the shape least allied to the complimentary and
hypocritical.

Mr Macey, for example, coming one evening expressly to let
Silas know that recent events had given him the advantage of
standing more favourably in the opinion of a man whose
judgment was not formed lightly, opened the conversation by
saying, as soon as he had seated himself and adjusted his
thumbs –

'Come, Master Marner, why, you've no call to sit a-moaning.
You're a deal better off to ha' lost your money, nor to ha' kep it
by foul means. I used to think, when you first come into these
parts, as you were no better nor you should be; you were
younger a deal than what you are now; but you were allays a
staring, white-faced creatur, partly like a bald-faced calf, as I
may say. But there's no knowing: it isn't every queer-looksed
thing as Old Harry's had the making of – I mean, speaking o'
toads and such; for they're often harmless, and useful against
varmin. And it's pretty much the same wi' you, as fur as I can
see. Though as to the yarbs[3] and stuff to cure the breathing, if
you brought that sort o' knowledge from distant parts, you
might ha' been a bit freer of it. And if the knowledge wasn't
well come by, why, you might ha' made up for it by coming to
church reg'lar; for as for the children as the Wise Woman[4]
charmed, I've been at the christening of 'em again and again,
and they took the water just as well. And that's reasonable; for
if Old Harry's a mind to do a bit o' kindness for a holiday, like,
who's got anything against it? That's my thinking; and I've been
clerk o' this parish forty year, and I know, when the parson and
me does the cussing of a Ash Wednesday, there's no cussing o'
folks as have a mind to be cured without a doctor, let Kimble
say what he will. And so, Master Marner, as I was saying – for

there's windings i' things as they may carry you to the fur end o' the prayer-book afore you get back to 'em – my advice is, as you keep up your sperrits; for as for thinking you're a deep un, and ha' got more inside you nor 'ull bear daylight, I'm not o' that opinion at all, and so I tell the neighbours. For, says I, you talk o' Master Marner making out a tale – why, it's nonsense, that is: it 'ud take a 'cute man to make a tale like that; and, says I, he looked as scared as a rabbit.'

During this discursive address Silas had continued motionless in his previous attitude, leaning his elbows on his knees, and pressing his hands against his head. Mr Macey, not doubting that he had been listened to, paused, in the expectation of some appreciatory reply, but Marner remained silent. He had a sense that the old man meant to be good-natured and neighbourly; but the kindness fell on him as sunshine falls on the wretched – he had no heart to taste it, and felt that it was very far off him.

'Come, Master Marner, have you got nothing to say to that?' said Mr Macey at last, with a slight accent of impatience.

'Oh,' said Marner, slowly, shaking his head between his hands, 'I thank you – thank you – kindly.'

'Ay, ay, to be sure: I thought you would,' said Mr Macey; 'and my advice is – have you got a Sunday suit?'

'No,' said Marner.

'I doubted it was so,' said Mr Macey. 'Now, let me advise you to get a Sunday suit: there's Tookey, he's a poor creatur, but he's got my tailoring business, and some o' my money in it, and he shall make a suit at a low price, and give you trust, and then you can come to church, and be a bit neighbourly. Why, you've never heared me say "Amen" since you come into these parts, and I recommend you to lose no time, for it'll be poor work when Tookey has it all to himself, for I mayn't be equil to stand i' the desk at all, come another winter.' Here Mr Macey paused, perhaps expecting some sign of emotion in his hearer; but not observing any, he went on. 'And as for the money for the suit o' clothes, why, you get a matter of a pound a-week at your weaving, Master Marner, and you're a young man, eh, for all you look so mushed. Why, you couldn't ha' been five-and-twenty when you come into these parts, eh?'

Silas started a little at the change to a questioning tone, and answered mildly, 'I don't know; I can't rightly say – it's a long while since.'

After receiving such an answer as this, it is not surprising that
Mr Macey observed, later on in the evening at the Rainbow,
that Marner's head was 'all of a muddle', and that it was to be
doubted if he ever knew when Sunday came round, which
showed him a worse heathen than many a dog.

Another of Silas's comforters, besides Mr Macey, came to
him with a mind highly charged on the same topic. This was
Mrs Winthrop, the wheelwright's wife. The inhabitants of
Raveloe were not severely regular in their church-going, and
perhaps there was hardly a person in the parish who would not
have held that to go to church every Sunday in the calendar
would have shown a greedy desire to stand well with Heaven,
and get an undue advantage over their neighbours – a wish to
be better than the 'common run', that would have implied a
reflection on those who had had godfathers and godmothers as
well as themselves, and had an equal right to the burying-
service. At the same time, it was understood to be requisite for
all who were not household servants, or young men, to take the
sacrament at one of the great festivals: Squire Cass himself took
it on Christmas-day; while those who were held to be 'good
livers' went to church with greater, though still with moderate,
frequency.

Mrs Winthrop was one of these: she was in all respects a
woman of scrupulous conscience, so eager for duties that life
seemed to offer them too scantily unless she rose at half-past
four, though this threw a scarcity of work over the more
advanced hours of the morning, which it was a constant problem
with her to remove. Yet she had not the vixenish temper which
is sometimes supposed to be a necessary condition of such
habits: she was a very mild, patient woman, whose nature it was
to seek out all the sadder and more serious elements of life, and
pasture her mind upon them. She was the person always first
thought of in Raveloe when there was illness or death in a
family, when leeches were to be applied, or there was a sudden
disappointment in a monthly nurse. She was a 'comfortable
woman' – good-looking, fresh-complexioned, having her lips
always slightly screwed, as if she felt herself in a sick-room with
the doctor or the clergyman present. But she was never whim-
pering; no one had seen her shed tears; she was simply grave
and inclined to shake her head and sigh, almost imperceptibly,
like a funereal mourner who is not a relation. It seemed

surprising that Ben Winthrop, who loved his quart-pot and his joke, got along so well with Dolly; but she took her husband's jokes and joviality as patiently as everything else, considering that 'men *would* be so', and viewing the stronger sex in the light of animals whom it had pleased Heaven to make naturally troublesome, like bulls and turkey-cocks.

This good wholesome woman could hardly fail to have her mind drawn strongly towards Silas Marner, now that he appeared in the light of a sufferer; and one Sunday afternoon she took her little boy Aaron with her, and went to call on Silas, carrying in her hand some small lard-cakes,[5] flat paste-like articles much esteemed in Raveloe. Aaron, an apple-cheeked youngster of seven, with a clean starched frill which looked like a plate for the apples, needed all his adventurous curiosity to embolden him against the possibility that the big-eyed weaver might do him some bodily injury; and his dubiety was much increased when, on arriving at the Stone-pits, they heard the mysterious sound of the loom.

'Ah, it is as I thought,' said Mrs Winthrop, sadly.

They had to knock loudly before Silas heard them; but when he did come to the door he showed no impatience, as he would once have done, at a visit that had been unasked for and unexpected. Formerly, his heart had been as a locked casket with its treasure inside; but now the casket was empty, and the lock was broken. Left groping in darkness, with his prop utterly gone, Silas had inevitably a sense, though a dull and half-depairing one, that if any help came to him it must come from without; and there was a slight stirring of expectation at the sight of his fellow-men, a faint consciousness of dependence on their goodwill. He opened the door wide to admit Dolly, but without otherwise returning her greeting than by moving the armchair a few inches as a sign that she was to sit down in it. Dolly, as soon, as she was seated, removed the white cloth that covered her lard-cakes, and said I her gravest way –

'I'd a baking yisterday, Master Marner, and the lard-cakes turned out better nor common, and I'd ha' asked you to accept some, if you'd thought well. I don't eat such things myself, for a bit o' bread's what I like from one year's end to the other; but men's stomichs are made so comical, they want a change – they do, I know, God help 'em.'

Dolly sighed gently as she held out the cakes to Silas, who

thanked her kindly and looked very close at them, absently, being accustomed to look so at everything he took into his hand – eyed all the while by the wondering bright orbs of the small Aaron, who had made an outwork[6] of his mother's chair, and was peeping round from behind it.

'There's letters pricked on 'em,' said Dolly. 'I can't read 'em myself, and there's nobody, not Mr Macey himself, rightly knows what they mean; but they've a good meaning, for they're the same as is on the pulpit-cloth at church. What are they, Aaron, my dear?'

Aaron retreated completely behind his outwork.

'Oh go, that's naughty,' said his mother, mildly. 'Well, whativer the letters are, they've a good meaning; and it's a stamp as has been in our house, Ben says, ever since he was a little un, and his mother used to put it on the cakes, and I've allays put it on too; for if there's any good, we've need of it i' this world.'

'It's I. H. S.,'[7] said Silas, at which proof of learning Aaron peeped round the chair again.

'Well, to be sure, you can read 'em off,' said Dolly. 'Ben's read 'em to me many and many a time, but they slip out o' my mind again; the more's the pity, for they're good letters, else they wouldn't be in the church; and so I prick 'em on all the loaves and all the cakes, though sometimes they won't hold, because o' the rising – for, as I said, if there's any good to be got, we've need of it i' this world – that we have; and I hope they'll bring good to you, Master Marner, for it's wi' that will I brought you the cakes; and you see the letters have held better nor common.'

Silas was as unable to interpret the letters as Dolly, but there was no possibility of misunderstanding the desire to give comfort that made itself heard in her quiet tones. He said, with more feeling than before – 'Thank you – thank you kindly.' But he laid down the cakes and seated himself absently – drearily unconscious of any distinct benefit towards which the cake and the letters, or even Dolly's kindness, could tend for him.

'Ah, if there's good anywhere, we've need of it,' repeated Dolly, who did not lightly forsake a serviceable phrase. She looked at Silas pityingly as she went on. 'But you didn't hear the church-bells this morning, Master Marner? I doubt you didn't know it was Sunday. Living so lone here, you lose your count, I daresay; and then, when your loom makes a noise, you can't hear the bells, more partic'lar now the frost kills the sound.'

'Yes, I did; I heard 'em,' said Silas, to whom Sunday bells were a mere accident of the day, and not part of its sacredness. There had been no bells in Lantern Yard.

'Dear heart!' said Dolly, pausing before she spoke again. 'But what a pity it is you should work of a Sunday, and not clean yourself – if you *didn't* go to church; for if you'd a roasting bit, it might be as you couldn't leave it, being a lone man. But there's the bakehus, if you could make up your mind to spend a twopence on the oven now and then – not every week, in course – I shouldn't like to do that myself, – you might carry your bit o' dinner there, for it's nothing but right to have a bit o' summat hot of a Sunday, and not to make it as you can't know your dinner from Saturday. But now, upo' Christmas-day, this blessed Christmas as is ever coming, if you was to take your dinner to the bakehus, and go to church, and see the holly and the yew, and hear the anthim, and then take the sacramen', you'd be a deal the better, and you'd know which end you stood on, and you could put your trust i' Them as knows better nor we do, seein' you'd ha' done what it lies on us all to do.'

Dolly's exhortation, which was an unusually long effort of speech for her, was uttered in the soothing persuasive tone with which she would have tried to prevail on a sick man to take his medicine, or a basin of gruel for which he had no appetite. Silas had never before been closely urged on the point of his absence from church, which had only been thought of as a part of his general queerness; and he was too direct and simple to evade Dolly's appeal.

'Nay, nay,' he said. 'I know nothing o' church. I've never been to church.'

'No!' said Dolly, in a low tone of wonderment. Then bethinking herself of Silas's advent from an unknown country, she said, 'Could it ha' been as they'd no church where you was born?'

'O yes,' said Silas, meditatively, sitting in his usual posture of leaning on his knees, and supporting his head. 'There was churches – a many – it was a big town. But I knew nothing of 'em – I went to chapel.'[8]

Dolly was much puzzled at this new word, but she was rather afraid of inquiring further, lest 'chapel' might mean some haunt of wickedness. After a little thought, she said –

'Well, Master Marner, it's niver too late to turn over a new leaf, and if you've niver had no church, there's no telling the good it'll do you. For I feel so set up and comfortable as niver was, when I've been and heard the prayers, and the singing to the praise and glory o' God, as Mr Macey gives out – and Mr Crackenthorp saying good words, and more partic'lar on Sacramen' Day; and if a bit o' trouble comes, I feel as I can put up wi' it, for I've looked for help i' the right quarter, and gev myself up to Them as we must all give ourselves up to at the last; and if we 'n done our part, it isn't to be believed as Them as are above us 'ull be worse nor we are, and come short o' Their'n.'

Poor Dolly's exposition of her simple Raveloe theology fell rather unmeaningly on Silas's ears, for there was no word in it that could rouse a memory of what he had known as religion, and his comprehension was quite baffled by the plural pronoun, which was no heresy of Dolly's, but only her way of avoiding a presumptuous familiarity. He remained silent, not feeling inclined to assent to the part of Dolly's speech which he fully understood – her recommendation that he should go to church. Indeed, Silas was so unaccustomed to talk beyond the brief questions and answers necessary for the transaction of his simple business, that words did not easily come to him without the urgency of a distinct purpose.

But now, little Aaron, having become used to the weaver's awful presence, had advanced to his mother's side, and Silas, seeming to notice him for the first time, tried to return Dolly's signs of goodwill by offering the lad a bit of lard-cake. Aaron shrank back a little, and rubbed his head against his mother's shoulder, but still thought the piece of cake worth the risk of putting his hand out for it.

'Oh, for shame, Aaron,' said his mother, taking him on her lap, however; 'why, you don't want cake again yet awhile. He's wonderful hearty,' she went on, with a little sigh – 'that he is, God knows. He's my youngest, and we spoil him sadly, for either me or the father must allays hev him in our sight – that we must.'

She stroked Aaron's brown head, and thought it must do Master Marner good to see such a 'pictur of a child'. But Marner, on the other side of the hearth, saw the neat-featured rosy face as a mere dim round, with two dark spots in it.

'And he's got a voice like a bird – you wouldn't think,' Dolly went on; 'he can sing a Christmas carril as his father's taught him; and I take it for a token as he'll come to good, as he can learn the good tunes so quick. Come, Aaron, stan' up and sing the carril to Master Marner, come.'

Aaron replied by rubbing his forehead against his mother's shoulder.

'Oh, that's naughty,' said Dolly, gently. 'Stan' up, when mother tells you, and let me hold the cake till you've done.'

Aaron was not indisposed to display his talents, even to an ogre, under protecting circumstances; and after a few more signs of coyness, consisting chiefly in rubbing the backs of his hands over his eyes, and then peeping between them at Master Marner, to see if he looked anxious for the 'carril', he at length allowed his head to be duly adjusted, and standing behind the table, which let him appear above it only as far as his broad frill, so that he looked like a cherubic head untroubled with a body, he began with a clear chirp, and in a melody that had the rhythm of an industrious hammer –

> God rest you, merry gentlemen,
> Let nothing you dismay,
> For Jesus Christ our Saviour
> Was born on Christmas-day.[9]

Dolly listened with a devout look, glancing at Marner in some confidence that this strain would help to allure him to church.

'That's Christmas music,' she said, when Aaron had ended, and had secured his piece of cake again. 'There's no other music equil to the Christmas music – "Hark the erol angils sing". And you may judge what it is at church, Master Marner, with the bassoon and the voices, as you can't help thinking you've got to a better place a'ready – for I wouldn't speak ill o' this world, seeing as Them put us in it as knows best – but what wi' the drink, and the quarrelling, and the bad illnesses, and the hard dying, as I've seen times and times, one's thankful to hear of a better. The boy sings pretty, don't he, Master Marner?'

'Yes,' said Silas, absently, 'very pretty.'

The Christmas carol, with its hammer-like rhythm, had fallen on his ears as strange music, quite unlike a hymn, and could have none of the effect Dolly contemplated. But he wanted to show her that he was grateful, and the only mode that occurred to him was to offer Aaron a bit more cake.

'Oh no, thank you, Master Marner,' said Dolly, holding down Aaron's willing hands. 'We must be going home now. And so I wish you good-bye, Master Marner; and if you ever feel anyways bad in your inside, as you can't fend for yourself, I'll come and clean up for you, and get you a bit o' victual, and willing. But I beg and pray of you to leave off weaving of a Sunday, for it's bad for soul and body – and the money as comes i' that way 'ull be a bad bed to lie down on at the last, if it doesn't fly away, nobody knows where, like the white frost.[10] And you'll excuse me being that free with you, Master Marner, for I wish you well – I do. Make your bow, Aaron.'

Silas said 'Good-bye, and thank you kindly,' as he opened the door for Dolly, but he couldn't help feeling relieved when she was gone – relieved that he might weave again and moan at his ease. Her simple view of life and its comforts, by which she had tried to cheer him, was only like a report of unknown objects, which his imagination could not fashion. The fountains of human love and of faith in a divine love had not yet been unlocked, and his soul was still the shrunken rivulet, with only this difference, that its little groove of sand was blocked up, and it wandered confusedly against dark obstruction.

And so, notwithstanding the honest persuasions of Mr Macey and Dolly Winthrop, Silas spent his Christmas-day in loneliness, eating his meat in sadness of heart, though the meat had come to him as a neighbourly present. In the morning he looked out on the black frost that seemed to press cruelly on every blade of grass, while the half-icy red pool shivered under the bitter wind; but towards evening the snow began to fall, and curtained from him even that dreary outlook, shutting him close up with his narrow grief. And he sat in his robbed home through the livelong evening, not caring to close his shutters or lock his door, pressing his head between his hands and moaning, till the cold grasped him and told him that his fire was grey.

Nobody in this world but himself knew that he was the same Silas Marner who had once loved his fellow with tender love, and trusted in an unseen goodness. Even to himself that past experience had become dim.

But in Raveloe village the bells rang merrily, and the church was fuller than all through the rest of the year, with red faces among the abundant dark-green boughs – faces prepared for a longer service than usual by an odorous breakfast of toast and ale. Those green boughs, the hymn and anthem never heard but at Christmas – even the Athanasian Creed,[11] which was discriminated from the others only as being longer and of exceptional virtue, since it was only read on rare occasions – brought a vague exulting sense, for which the grown men could as little have found words as the children, that something great and mysterious had been done for them in heaven above and in earth below, which they were appropriating by their presence. And then the red faces made their way through the black biting frost to their own homes, feeling themselves free for the rest of the day to eat, drink, and be merry, and using that Christian freedom without diffidence.

At Squire Cass's family party that day nobody mentioned Dunstan – nobody was sorry for his absence, or feared it would be too long. The doctor and his wife, uncle and aunt Kimble, were there, and the annual Christmas talk was carried through without any omissions, rising to the climax of Mr Kimble's experience when he walked the London hospitals thirty years back, together with striking professional anecdotes then gathered. Whereupon cards followed, with aunt Kimble's annual failure to follow suit, and uncle Kimble's irascibility concerning the odd trick which was rarely explicable to him, when it was not on his side, without a general visitation of tricks to see that they were formed on sound principles: the whole being accompanied by a strong steaming odour of spirits-and-water.

But the party on Christmas-day, being a strictly family party, was not the pre-eminently brilliant celebration of the season at the Red House. It was the great dance on New Year's Eve that made the glory of Squire Cass's hospitality, as of his forefathers', time out of mind. This was the occasion when all the society of Raveloe and Tarley, whether old acquaintances separated by long rutty distances, or cooled acquaintances separated by misunderstandings concerning runaway calves, or acquaintances founded on intermittent condescension, counted on meeting and on comporting themselves with mutual appropriateness. This was the occasion on which fair dames who came on pillions sent their bandboxes before them,[12] supplied with more than their evening costume; for the feast was not to end with a single evening, like a paltry town entertainment, where the whole supply of eatables is put on the table at once, and bedding is scanty. The Red House was provisioned as if for a siege; and as for the spare feather-beds ready to be laid on floors, they were as plentiful as might naturally be expected in a family that had killed its own geese for many generations.

Godfrey Cass was looking forward to this New Year's Eve with a foolish reckless longing, that made him half deaf to his importunate companion, Anxiety.

'Dunsey will be coming home soon: there will be a great blow-up, and how will you bribe his spite to silence?' said Anxiety.

'Oh, he won't come home before New Year's Eve, perhaps,' said Godfrey; 'and I shall sit by Nancy then, and dance with her, and get a kind look from her in spite of herself.'

'But money is wanted in another quarter,' said Anxiety, in a louder voice, 'and how will you get it without selling your mother's diamond pin? And if you don't get it . . . ?'

'Well, but something may happen to make things easier. At any rate, there's one pleasure for me close at hand: Nancy is coming.'

'Yes, and suppose your father should bring matters to a pass that will oblige you to decline marrying her – and to give your reasons?'

'Hold your tongue, and don't worry me. I can see Nancy's eyes, just as they will look at me, and feel her hand in mine already.'

But Anxiety went on, though in noisy Christmas company; refusing to be utterly quieted even by much drinking.

Some women, I grant, would not appear to advantage seated on a pillion, and attired in a drab joseph[1] and a drab beaver-bonnet, with a crown resembling a small stew-pan; for a garment suggesting a coachman's greatcoat, cut out under an exiguity of cloth that would only allow of miniature capes, is not well adapted to conceal deficiencies of contour, nor is drab a colour that will throw sallow cheeks into lively contrast. It was all the greater triumph to Miss Nancy Lammeter's beauty that she looked thoroughly bewitching in that costume, as, seated on the pillion behind her tall, erect father, she held one arm round him, and looked down, with open-eyed anxiety, at the treacherous snow-covered pools and puddles, which sent up formidable splashings of mud under the stamp of Dobbin's foot. A painter would, perhaps, have preferred her in those moments when she was free from self-consciousness; but certainly the bloom on her cheeks was at its highest point of contrast with the surrounding drab when she arrived at the door of the Red House, and saw Mr Godfrey Cass ready to lift her from the pillion. She wished her sister Priscilla had come up at the same time behind the servant, for then she would have contrived that Mr Godfrey should have lifted off Priscilla first, and, in the meantime, she would have persuaded her father to go round to the horse-block instead of alighting at the door-steps. It was very painful, when you had made it quite clear to a young man that you were determined not to marry him, however much he might wish it, that he would still continue to pay you marked attentions; besides why didn't he always show the same attentions, if he meant them sincerely, instead of being so strange as Mr Godfrey Cass was, sometimes behaving as if he didn't want to speak to her, and taking no notice of her for weeks and weeks, and then, all on a sudden, almost making love again? Moreover, it was quite plain he had no real love for her, else he would not let people have *that* to say of him which they did say.

Did he suppose that Miss Nancy Lammeter was to be won by any man, squire or no squire, who led a bad life? That was not what she had been used to see in her own father, who was the soberest and best man in that country-side, only a little hot and hasty now and then, if things were not done to the minute.

All these thoughts rushed through Miss Nancy's mind, in their habitual succession, in the moments between her first sight of Mr Godfrey Cass standing at the door and her own arrival there. Happily, the Squire came out too and gave a loud greeting to her father, so that, somehow, under cover of this noise she seemed to find concealment for her confusion and neglect of any suitably formal behaviour while she was being lifted from the pillion by strong arms which seemed to find her ridiculously small and light. And there was the best reason for hastening into the house at once, since the snow was beginning to fall again, threatening an unpleasant journey for such guests as were still on the road. These were a small minority; for already the afternoon was beginning to decline, and there would not be too much time for the ladies who came from a distance to attire themselves in readiness for the early tea which was to inspirit them for the dance.

There was a buzz of voices through the house, as Miss Nancy entered, mingled with the scrape of a fiddle preluding in the kitchen; but the Lammeters were guests whose arrival had evidently been thought of so much that it had been watched for from the windows, for Mrs Kimble, who did the honours at the Red House on these great occasions, came forward to meet Miss Nancy in the hall, and conduct her upstairs. Mrs Kimble was the Squire's sister, as well as the doctor's wife – a double dignity, with which her diameter was in direct proportion; so that, a journey upstairs being rather fatiguing to her, she did not oppose Miss Nancy's request to be allowed to find her way alone to the Blue Room, where the Miss Lammeters' bandboxes[2] had been deposited on their arrival in the morning.

There was hardly a bedroom in the house where feminine compliments were not passing and feminine toilettes going forward, in various stages, in space made scanty by extra beds spread upon the floor; and Miss Nancy, as she entered the Blue Room, had to make her little formal curtsy to a group of six. On the one hand, there were ladies no less important than the two Miss Gunns, the wine merchant's daughters from Lytherly, dressed in the height of fashion, with the tightest skirts and the shortest waists, and gazed at by Miss Ladbrook (of the Old Pastures) with a shyness not unsustained by inward criticism. Partly, Miss Ladbrook felt that her own skirt must be regarded as unduly lax by the Miss Gunns, and partly, that it was a pity the Miss Gunns did not show that judgment which she herself would show if she were in their place, by stopping a little on this side of the fashion. On the other hand, Mrs Ladbrook was standing in skullcap and front, with her turban in her hand, curtsying and smiling blandly and saying, 'After you ma'am', to another lady in similar circumstances, who had politely offered the precedence at the looking-glass.

But Miss Nancy had no sooner made her curtsy than an elderly lady came forward, whose full white muslin kerchief, and mob-cap round her curls of smooth grey hair, were in daring contrast with the puffed yellow satins and top-knotted caps of her neighbours. She approached Miss Nancy with much primness, and said, with a slow, treble suavity –

'Niece, I hope I see you well in health.' Miss Nancy kissed her aunt's cheek dutifully, and answered, with the same sort of amiable primness, 'Quite well, I thank you, aunt; and I hope I see you the same.'

'Thank you, niece; I keep my health for the present. And how is my brother-in-law?'

These dutiful questions and answers were continued until it was ascertained in detail that the Lammeters were all as well as usual, and the Osgoods likewise, also that niece Priscilla must certainly arrive shortly, and that travelling on pillions in snowy weather was unpleasant, though a joseph was a great protection. Then Nancy was formally introduced to her aunt's visitors, the Miss Gunns, as being the daughters of a mother known to *their* mother, though now for the first time induced to make a journey into these parts; and these ladies were so taken by surprise at finding such a lovely face and figure in an out-of-the-way country place, that they began to feel some curiosity about the dress she would put on when she took off her joseph. Miss Nancy, whose thoughts were always conducted with the propriety and moderation conspicuous in her manners, remarked to herself that the Miss Gunns were rather hard-featured than otherwise, and that such very low dresses as they wore might have been attributed to vanity if their shoulders had been pretty, but that, being as they were, it was not reasonable to suppose that they showed their necks from a love of display, but rather from some obligation not inconsistent with sense and modesty. She felt convinced, as she opened her box, that this must be her aunt Osgood's opinion, for Miss Nancy's mind resembled her aunt's to a degree that everybody said was surprising, considering the kinship was on Mr Osgood's side; and though you might not have supposed it from the formality of their greeting, there was a devoted attachment and mutual admiration between aunt and niece. Even Miss Nancy's refusal of her cousin Gilbert Osgood (on the ground solely that he was her cousin), though it had grieved her aunt greatly, had not in the least cooled the preference which had determined her to leave Nancy several of her hereditary ornaments, let Gilbert's future wife be whom she might.

Three of the ladies quickly retired, but the Miss Gunns were quite content that Mrs Osgood's inclination to remain with her niece gave them also a reason for staying to see the rustic beauty's toilette. And it was really a pleasure – from the first opening of the bandbox, where everything smelt of lavender and rose-leaves, to the clasping of the small coral necklace that fitted closely round her little white neck. Everything belonging to Miss Nancy was of delicate purity and nattiness:[3] not a crease was where it had no business to be, not a bit of her linen professed whiteness without fulfilling its profession; the very pins on her pincushion were stuck in after a pattern from which she was careful to allow no aberration; and as for her own person, it gave the same idea of perfect unvarying neatness as the body of a little bird. It is true that her light-brown hair was cropped behind like a boy's, and was dressed in front in a number of flat rings, that lay quite away from her face; but there was no sort of coiffure that could make Miss Nancy's cheek and neck look otherwise than pretty; and when at last she stood complete in her silvery twilled silk, her lace tucker, her coral necklace, and coral ear-drops, the Miss Gunns could see nothing to criticise except her hands, which bore the traces of butter-making, cheese-crushing, and even still coarser work. But Miss Nancy was not ashamed of that, for while she was dressing she narrated to her aunt how she and Priscilla had packed their boxes yesterday, because this morning was baking morning, and since they were leaving home, it was desirable to make a good supply of meat-pies for the kitchen; and as she concluded this judicious remark, she turned to the Miss Gunns that she might not commit the rudeness of not including them in the conversation. The Miss Gunns smiled stiffly, and thought what a pity it was that these rich country people, who could afford to buy such good clothes (really Miss Nancy's lace and silk were very costly), should be brought up in utter ignorance and vulgarity. She actually said 'mate' for 'meat,' ''appen' for 'perhaps', and 'oss' for 'horse', which, to young ladies living[4] in good Lytherly society, who habitually said 'orse, even in domestic privacy, and only said 'appen on the right occasions, was necessarily shocking. Miss Nancy, indeed, had never been to any school higher than Dame Tedman's: her acquaintance with profane literature hardly went beyond the rhymes she had worked in her large sampler under the lamb and the shepherdess; and in order to balance an account, she was obliged to effect her subtraction by removing visible metallic shillings and sixpences from a visible metallic total. There is hardly a servant-maid in these days who is not better informed than Miss Nancy; yet she had the essential attributes of a lady – high veracity, delicate honour in her dealings, deference to others, and refined personal habits, – and least these should not suffice to convince grammatical fair ones that her feelings can at all resemble theirs, I will add that she was slightly proud and exacting, and as constant in her affection towards a baseless opinion as towards an erring lover.

The anxiety about sister Priscilla, which had grown rather active by the time the coral necklace was clasped, was happily ended by the entrance of that cheerful-looking lady herself, with a face made blowsy by cold and damp. After the first questions and greetings, she turned to Nancy, and surveyed her from head to foot – then wheeled her round, to ascertain that the back view was equally faultless.

'What do you think o' *these* gowns, aunt Osgood?' said Priscilla, while Nancy helped her to unrobe.

'Very handsome indeed, niece,' said Mrs Osgood with a slight increase of formality. She always thought niece Priscilla too rough.

'I'm obliged to have the same as Nancy, you know, for all I'm five years older, and it makes me look yallow; for she never *will* have anything without I have mine just like it, because she wants us to look like sisters. And I tell her, folks 'ull think it's my weakness makes me fancy as I shall look pretty in what she looks pretty in. For I *am* ugly – there's no denying that: I feature my father's family. But, law! I don't mind, do you?' Priscilla here turned to the Miss Gunns, rattling on in too much preoccupation with the delight of talking, to notice that her candour was not appreciated. 'The pretty uns do for fly-catchers – they keep the men off us. I've no opinion o' the men, Miss Gunn – I don't know what *you* have. And as for fretting and stewing about what *they*'ll think of you from morning till night, and making your life uneasy about what they're doing when they're out o' your sight – as I tell Nancy, it's a folly no woman need be guilty of, if she's got a good father and a good home: let her leave it to them as have got no fortin, and can't help themselves. As I say, Mr Have-your-own-way is the best husband, and the only one I'd ever promise to obey. I know it isn't pleasant, when you've been used to living in a big way, and managing hogsheads[5] and all that, to go and put your nose in by somebody else's fireside or to sit down by yourself to a scrag or a knuckle;[6] but, thank God! my father's a sober man and likely to live; and if you've got a man by the chimney-corner, it doesn't matter if he's childish – the business needn't be broke up.'

The delicate process of getting her narrow gown over her head without injury to her smooth curls, obliged Miss Priscilla to pause in this rapid survey of life, and Mrs Osgood seized the opportunity of rising and saying –

'Well, niece, you'll follow us. The Miss Gunns will like to go down.'

'Sister,' said Nancy, when they were alone, 'you've offended the Miss Gunns, I'm sure.'

'What have I done, child?' said Priscilla, in some alarm.

'Why, you asked them if they minded about being ugly – you're so very blunt.'

'Law, did I? Well, it popped out: it's a mercy I said no more, for I'm a bad un to live with folks when they don't like the truth. But as for being ugly, look at me, child, in this silver-coloured silk – I told you how it 'ud be – I look as yellow as a daffadil. Anybody 'ud say you wanted to make a mawkin[7] of me.'

'No, Priscy, don't say so. I begged and prayed of you not to let us have this silk if you'd like another better. I was willing to have *your* choice, you know I was,' said Nancy, in anxious self-vindication.

'Nonsense, child! you know you'd set your heart on this; and reason good, for you're the colour o' cream. It' ud be fine doings for you to dress yourself to suit *my* skin. What I find fault with, is that notion o' yours as I must dress myself just like you. But you do as you like with me – you always did, from when first you begun to walk. If you wanted to go the field's length, the field's length you'd go; and there was no whipping you, for you looked as prim and innicent as a daisy all the while.'

'Priscy,' said Nancy, gently, as she fastened a coral necklace, exactly like her own, round Priscilla's neck, which was very far from being like her own, 'I'm sure I'm willing to give way as far as is right, but who shouldn't dress alike if it isn't sisters? Would you have us go about looking as if we were no kin to one another – us that have got no mother and not another sister in the world? I'd do what was right, if I dressed in a gown dyed with cheese-colouring; and I'd rather you'd choose, and let me wear what pleases you.'

'There you go again! You'd come round to the same thing if one talked to you from Saturday night till Saturday morning. It'll be fine fun to see how you'll master your husband and never raise your voice above the singing o' the kettle all the while. I like to see the men mastered!'

'Don't talk *so*, Priscy,' said Nancy, blushing. 'You know I don't mean ever to be married.'

'Oh, you never mean a fiddlestick's end!' said Priscilla, as she arranged her discarded dress, and closed her bandbox. 'Who shall *I* have to work for when father's gone, if you are to go and take notions in your head and be an old maid, because some folks are no better than they should be? I haven't a bit o' patience with you – sitting on an addled egg for ever, as if there was never a fresh un in the world. One old maid's enough out o' two sisters; and I shall do credit to a single life, for God A'mighty meant me for it. Come, we can go down now. I'm as ready as a mawkin *can* be – there's nothing awanting to frighten the crows, now I've got my ear-droppers in.'

As the two Miss Lammeters walked into the large parlour together, any one who did not know the character of both might certainly have supposed that the reason why the square-shouldered, clumsy, high-featured Priscilla wore a dress the facsimile of her pretty sister's, was either the mistaken vanity of the one, or the malicious contrivance of the other in order to set off her own rare beauty. But the good-natured self-forgetful cheeriness and common-sense of Priscilla would soon have dissipated the one suspicion; and the modest calm of Nancy's speech and manners told clearly of a mind free from all disavowed devices.

Places of honour had been kept for the Miss Lammeters near the head of the principal tea-table in the wainscoted parlour, now looking fresh and pleasant with handsome branches of holly, yew, and laurel, from the abundant growths of the old garden; and Nancy felt an inward flutter, that no firmness of purpose could prevent, when she saw Mr Godfrey Cass advancing to lead her to a seat between himself and Mr Crackenthorp, while Priscilla was called to the opposite side between her father and the Squire. It certainly did make some difference to Nancy that the lover she had given up was the young man of quite the highest consequence in the parish – at home in a venerable and unique parlour, which was the extremity of grandeur in her experience, a parlour where *she* might one day have been mistress, with the consciousness that she was spoke of as 'Madam Cass', the Squire's wife. These circumstances exalted her inward drama in her own eyes, and deepened the emphasis with which she declared to herself that not the most dazzling rank should induce her to marry a man whose conduct showed him careless of his character, but that, 'love once, love always', was the motto of a true and pure woman, and no man should ever have any right over her which would be a call on her to destroy the dried flowers that she treasured, and always would treasure, for Godfrey Cass's sake. And Nancy was capable of keeping her word to herself under very trying conditions. Nothing but a becoming blush betrayed the moving thoughts that urged themselves upon her as she accepted the seat next to Mr Crackenthorp; for she was so instinctively neat and adroit in all her actions, and her pretty lips met each other with such quiet firmness, that it would have been difficult for her to appear agitated.

It was not the Rector's practice to let a charming blush pass without an appropriate compliment. He was not in the least lofty or aristocratic, but simply a merry-eyed, small-featured, grey-haired man, with his chin propped by an ample many-creased white neckcloth which seemed to predominate over every other point in his person, and somehow to impress its peculiar character on his remarks; so that to have considered his amenities apart from his cravat would have been a severe, and perhaps a dangerous, effort of abstraction.

'Ha, Miss Nancy,' he said, turning his head within his cravat and smiling down pleasantly upon her, 'when anybody pretends this has been a severe winter, I shall tell them I saw the roses blooming on New Year's Eve – eh, Godfrey, what do *you* say?'

Godfrey made no reply, and avoided looking at Nancy very markedly; for though these complimentary personalities were held to be in excellent taste in old-fashioned Raveloe society, reverent love has a politeness of its own which it teaches to men otherwise of small schooling. But the Squire was rather impatient at Godfrey's showing himself a dull spark in this way. By this advanced hour of the day, the Squire was always in higher spirits than we have seen him in at the breakfast-table, and felt it quite pleasant to fulfil the hereditary duty of being noisily jovial and patronising: the large silver snuffbox was in active service and was offered without fail to all neighbours from time to time, however often they might have declined the favour. At present, the Squire had only given an express welcome to the heads of families as they appeared; but always as the evening deepened, his hospitality rayed out more widely, till he had tapped the youngest guests on the back and shown a peculiar fondness for their presence, in the full belief that they must feel their lives made happy by their belonging to a parish where there was such a hearty man as Squire Cass to invite them and wish them well. Even in this early stage of the jovial mood, it was natural that he should wish to supply his son's deficiencies by looking and speaking for him.

'Ay, ay,' he began, offering his snuffbox to Mr Lammeter, who for the second time bowed his head and waved his hand in stiff rejection of the offer, 'us old fellows may wish ourselves young tonight when we see the mistletoe-bough in the White Parlour. It's true, most things are gone back'ard in these last thirty years – the country's going down since the old king fell ill. But when I look at Miss Nancy here, I begin to think the lasses keep up their quality; – ding me if I remember a sample to match her, not when I was a fine young fellow, and thought a deal about my pigtail.[8] No offence to you, madam,' he added, bending to Mrs Crackenthorp, who sat by him, 'I didn't know *you* when you were as young as Miss Nancy here.'

Mrs Crackenthorp – a small blinking woman, who fidgeted incessantly with her lace, ribbons, and gold chain, turning her head about and making subdued noises, very much like a guinea-pig that twitches its nose and soliloquises in all company indiscriminately – now blinked and fidgeted towards the Squire, and said, 'Oh no – no offence.'

This emphatic compliment of the Squire's to Nancy was felt by others besides Godfrey to have a diplomatic significance; and her father gave a slight additional erectness to his back, as he looked across the table at her with complacent gravity. That grave and orderly senior was not going to bate a jot of his dignity by seeming elated at the notion of a match between his family and the Squire's: he was gratified by any honour paid to his daughter; but he must see an alteration in several ways before his consent would be vouchsafed. His spare but healthy person, and high-featured firm face, that looked as if it had never been flushed by excess, was in strong contrast, not only with the Squire's, but with the appearance of the Ravloe farmers generally – in accordance with a favourite saying of his own, that 'breed was stronger than pasture'.

'Miss Nancy's wonderful like what her mother was, though; isn't she, Kimble?' said the stout lady of that name, looking round for her husband.

But Doctor Kimble (country apothecaries in old days enjoyed that title without authority of diploma), being a thin and agile man, was flitting about the room with his hands in his pockets, making himself agreeable to his feminine patients, with medical impartiality, and being welcomed everywhere as a doctor by hereditary right – not one of those miserable apothecaries who canvass for practice in strange neighbourhoods, and spend all their income in starving their one horse, but a man of substance, able to keep an extravagant table like the best of his patients. Time out of mind the Raveloe doctor had been a Kimble; Kimble was inherently a doctor's name; and it was difficult to contemplate firmly the melancholy fact that the actual Kimble had no son, so that his practice might one day be handed over to a successor with the incongruous name of Taylor or Johnson. But in that case the wiser people in Raveloe would employ Dr Blick of Flitton – as less unnatural.

'Did you speak to me, my dear?' said the authentic doctor, coming quickly to his wife's side; but, as if foreseeing that she would be too much out of breath to repeat her remark, he went on immediately – 'Ha, Miss Priscilla, the sight of you revives the taste of that super-excellent pork-pie. I hope the batch isn't near an end.'

'Yes, indeed, it is, doctor,' said Priscilla; 'but I'll answer for it the next shall be as good. My pork-pies don't turn out well by chance.'

'Not as your doctoring does, eh, Kimble? – because folks forget to take your physic, eh?' said the Squire, who regarded physic and doctors as many loyal churchmen regard the church and the clergy – tasting a joke against them when he was in health, but impatiently eager for their aid when anything was the matter with him. He tapped his box, and looked round with triumphant laugh.

'Ah, she has a quick wit, my friend Priscilla has,' said the doctor, choosing to attribute the epigram to a lady rather than allow a brother-in-law that advantage over him. 'She saves a little pepper to sprinkle over her talk – that's the reason why she never puts too much into her pies. There's my wife, now, she never has an answer at her tongue's end; but if I offend her, she's sure to scarify my throat with black pepper the next day, or else give me the colic with watery greens. That's an awful tit-for-tat.' Here the vivacious doctor made a pathetic grimace.

'Did you ever hear the like?' said Mrs Kimble, laughing above her double chin with much good-humour, aside to Mrs Crackenthorp, who blinked and nodded, and amiably intended to smile, but the intention lost itself in small twitchings and noises.

'I suppose that's the sort of tit-for-tat adopted in your profession, Kimble, if you've a grudge against a patient,' said the rector.

'Never do have a grudge against our patients,' said Mr Kimble, 'except when they leave us: and then, you see, we haven't the chance of prescribing for 'em. Ha, Miss Nancy,' he continued, suddenly skipping to Nancy's side, 'you won't forget your promise? You're to save a dance for me, you know.'

'Come, come, Kimble, don't you be too for'ard,' said the Squire. 'Give the young uns fair-play. There's my son Godfrey'll be wanting to have a round with you if you run off with Miss Nancy. He's bespoke her for the first dance, I'll be bound. Eh, sir! what do you say?' he continued, throwing himself backward, and looking at Godfrey. 'Haven't you asked Miss Nancy to open the dance with you?'

Godfrey, sorely uncomfortable under this significant insistance about Nancy, and afraid to think where it would end by the time his father had set his usual hospitable example of drinking before and after supper, saw no course open but to turn to Nancy and say, with as little awkwardness as possible –

'No: I've not asked her yet, but I hope she'll consent – if somebody else hasn't been before me.'

'No, I've not engaged myself,' said Nancy, quietly, though blushingly. (If Mr Godfrey founded any hopes on her consenting to dance with him, he would soon be undeceived; but there was no need for her to be uncivil.)

'Then I hope you've no objections to dancing with me,' said Godfrey, beginning to lose the sense that there was anything uncomfortable in this arrangement.

'No, no objections,' said Nancy, in a cold tone.

'Ah, well, you're a lucky fellow, Godfrey,' said uncle Kimble; 'but you're my godson, so I won't stand in your way. Else I'm not so very old, eh, my dear?' he went on, skipping to his wife's side again. 'You wouldn't mind my having a second after you were gone – not if I cried a good deal first?'

'Come, come, take a cup o' tea and stop your tongue, do,' said good-humoured Mrs Kimble, feeling some pride in a husband who must be regarded as so clever and amusing by the company generally. If he had only not been irritable at cards!

While safe, well-tested personalities were enlivening the tea in this way, the sound of the fiddle approaching within a distance at which it could be heard distinctly, made the young people look at each other with sympathetic impatience for the end of the meal.

'Why, there's Solomon in the hall,' said the Squire, 'and playing my fav'rite tune, I believe – "The flaxen-headed ploughboy"[9] – he's for giving us a hint as we aren't enough in a hurry to hear him play. Bob,' he called out to his third long-legged son, who was at the other end of the room, 'open the door, and tell Solomon to come in. He shall give us a tune here.'

Bob obeyed, and Solomon walked in, fiddling as he walked, for he would on no account break off in the middle of a tune.

'Here, Solomon,' said the Squire, with loud patronage.

'Round here, my man. Ah, I knew it was "The flaxen-headed ploughboy": there's no finer tune.'

Solomon Macey, a small hale old man, with an abundant crop of long white hair reaching nearly to his shoulders, advanced to the indicated spot, bowing reverently while he fiddled, as much as to say that he respected the key-note more. As soon as he had repeated the tune and lowered his fiddle, he bowed again to the Squire and the Rector, and said, 'I hope I see your honour and your reverence well, and wishing you health and long life and a happy New Year. And wishing the same to you, Mr Lammeter, sir; and to the other gentlemen, and the madams, and the young lasses.'

As Solomon uttered the last words, he bowed in all directions solicitously, lest he should be wanting in due respect. But thereupon he immediately began to prelude, and fell into the tune which he knew would be taken as a special compliment by Mr Lammeter.

'Thank ye, Solomon, thank ye,' said Mr Lammeter when the fiddle paused again. 'That's "Over the hills and far away", that is. My father used to say to me, whenever we heard that tune, "Ah, lad, *I* come from over the hills and far away." There's a many tunes I don't make head or tail of; but that speaks to me like the blackbird's whistle. I suppose it's the name: there's a deal in the name of a tune.'

But Solomon was already impatient to prelude again and presently broke with much spirit into 'Sir Roger de Coverley', at which there was a sound of chairs pushed back, and laughing voices.

'Ay, ay, Solomon, we know what that means,' said the Squire, rising. 'It's time to begin the dance, eh? Lead the way, then, and we'll all follow you.'[10]

So Solomon, holding his white head on one side, and playing vigorously, marched forward at the head of the gay procession into the White Parlour, where the mistletoe-bough was hung, and multitudinous tallow candles made rather a brilliant effect, gleaming from among the berried holly-boughs, and reflected in the old-fashioned oval mirrors fastened in the panels of the white wainscot. A quaint procession! Old Solomon, in his seedy clothes and long white locks, seemed to be luring that decent company by the magic scream of his fiddle – luring discreet matrons in turban-shaped caps, nay, Mrs Crackenthorp herself,

the summit of whose perpendicular feather was on a level with
the Squire's shoulder – luring fair lasses complacently conscious
of very short waists and skirts blameless of front-folds – luring
burly fathers in large variegated waistcoats, and ruddy sons, for
the most part shy and sheepish, in short nether garments and
very long coat-tails.

Already Mr Macey and a few other privileged villagers, who
were allowed to be spectators on these great occasions, were
seated on benches placed for them near the door; and great was
the admiration and satisfaction in that quarter when the couples
had formed themselves for the dance, and the Squire led off with
Mrs Crackenthorp, joining hands with the Rector and Mrs
Osgood. That was as it should be – that was what everybody
had been used to – and the charter of Raveloe seemed to be
renewed by the ceremony. It was not thought of as an unbecom-
ing levity for the old and middle-aged people to dance a little
before sitting down to cards, but rather as part of their social
duties. For what were these if not to be merry at appropriate
times, interchanging visits and poultry with due frequency,
paying each other old-established compliments in sound traditional phrases, passing well-tried personal jokes, urging your
guests to eat and drink too much out of hospitality, and eating
and drinking too much in your neighbour's house to show that
you liked your cheer? And the parson naturally set an example
in these social duties. For it would not have been possible for
the Raveloe mind, without a peculiar revelation, to know that a
clergyman should be a pale-faced memento of solemnities,
instead of a reasonable faulty man whose exclusive authority to
read prayers and preach, to christen, marry, and bury you,
necessarily coexisted with the right to sell you the ground to be
buried in and to take tithe in kind; on which last point, of
course, there was a little grumbling, but not to the extent of
irreligion – not of deeper significance than the grumbling at the
rain, which was by no means accompanied with a spirit of
impious defiance, but with a desire that the prayer for fine
weather might be read forthwith.

There was no reason, then, why the rector's dancing should
not be received as part of the fitness of things quite as much as
the Squire's, or why, on the other hand, Mr Macey's official
respect should restrain him from subjecting the parson's per-
formance to that criticism with which minds of extraordinary

acuteness must necessarily contemplate the doings of their fallible fellow-men.

'The Squire's pretty springe, considering his weight,' said Mr Macey, 'and he stamps uncommon well. But Mr Lammeter beats 'em all for shapes: you see he holds his head like a sodger,[11] and he isn't so cushiony as most o' the oldish gentlefolks – they run fat in general; and he's got a fine leg. The parson's nimble enough, but he hasn't got much of a leg: it's a bit too thick down'ard, and his knees might be a bit nearer wi'out damage; but he might do worse, he might do worse. Though he hasn't that grand way o'waving his hand as the Squire has.'

'Talk o' nimbleness, look at Mrs Osgood,' said Ben Winthrop, who was holding his son Aaron between his knees. 'She trips along with her little steps, so as nobody can see how she goes – it's like as if she had little wheels to her feet. She doesn't look a day older nor last year: she's the finest-made woman as is, let the next be where she will.'

'I don't heed how the women are made,' said Mr Macey, with some contempt. 'They wear nayther coat nor breeches: you can't make much out o' their shapes.'

'Fayder,' said Aaron, whose feet were busy beating out the tune, 'how does that big cock's-feather stick in Mrs Crackenthorp's yead? Is there a little hole for it, like in my shuttle-cock?'[12]

'Hush, lad, hush; that's the way the ladies dress theirselves, that is,' said the father, adding, however, in an under-tone to Mr Macey, 'It does make her look funny, though – partly like a short-necked bottle wi' a long quill in it. Hey, by jingo, there's the young Squire leading off now, wi' Miss Nancy for partners! There's a lass for you! – like a pink-and-white posy – there's nobody 'ud think as anybody could be so pritty. I shouldn't wonder if she's Madam Cass some day, arter all – and nobody more rightfuller, for they'd made a fine match. You can find nothing against Master Godfrey's shapes, Macey, I'll bet a penny.'

Mr Macey screwed up his mouth, leaned his head further on one side, and twirled his thumbs with a presto movement as his eyes followed Godfrey up the dance. At last he summed up his opinion.

'Pretty well down'ard, but a bit too round i' the shoulder-blades. And as for them coats as he gets from the Flitton tailor, they're a poor cut to pay double money for.'

'Ah, Mr Macey, you and me are two folks,' said Ben, slightly indignant at this carping. 'When I've got a pot o' good ale, I like to swaller it, and do my inside good, i'stead o' smelling and staring at it to see if I can't find faut wi' the brewing. I should like you to pick me out a finer-limbed young fellow nor Master Godfrey – one as 'ud knock you down easier, or 's more pleasanter looksed when he's piert[13] and merry.'

'Tchuh!' said Mr Macey, provoked to increased severity, 'he isn't come to his right colour yet: he's partly like a slack-baked pie. And I doubt he's got a soft place in his head, else why should he be turned round the finger by that offal[14] Dunsey as nobody's seen o' late, and let him kill that fine hunting hoss as was the talk o' the country? And one while he was allays after Miss Nancy, and then it all went off again, like a smell o' hot porridge, as I may say. That wasn't my way when *I* went a-coorting.'

'Ah, but mayhap Miss Nancy hung off like, and your lass didn't,' said Ben.

'I should say she didn't,' said Mr Macey, significantly. 'Before I said "sniff", I took care to know as she'd say "snaff", and pretty quick too. I wasn't a-going to open *my* mouth, like a dog at a fly, and snap it to again, wi' nothing to swaller.'

'Well, I think Miss Nancy's a-coming round again,' said Ben, 'for Master Godfrey doesn't look so down-hearted tonight. And I see he's for taking her away to sit down, now they're at the end o' the dance: that looks like sweethearting, that does.'

The reason why Godfrey and Nancy had left the dance was not so tender as Ben imagined. In the close press of couples a slight accident had happened to Nancy's dress, which, while it was short enough to show her neat ankle in front, was long enough behind to be caught under the stately stamp of the Squire's foot, so as to rend certain stitches at the waist, and cause much sisterly agitation in Priscilla's mind, as well as serious concern in Nancy's. One's thoughts may be much occupied with love-struggles, but hardly so as to be insensible to a disorder in the general framework of things. Nancy had no sooner completed her duty in the figure they were dancing than she said to Godfrey, with a deep blush, that she must go and sit down till Priscilla could come to her; for the sisters had already exchanged a short whisper and an open-eyed glance full of meaning. No reason less urgent than this could have prevailed on Nancy to give Godfrey this opportunity of sitting apart with her. As for Godfrey, he was feeling so happy and oblivious under the long charm of the country-dance with Nancy, that he got rather bold on the strength of her confusion, and was capable of leading her straight away, without leave asked, into the adjoining small parlour, where the card-tables were set.

'O no, thank you,' said Nancy, coldly, as soon as she perceived where he was going, 'not in there. I'll wait here till Priscilla's ready to come to me. I'm sorry to bring you out of the dance and make myself troublesome.'

'Why, you'll be more comfortable here by yourself,' said the artful Godfrey: 'I'll leave you here till your sister can come.' He spoke in an indifferent tone.

That was an agreeable proposition, and just what Nancy desired; why, then, was she a little hurt that Mr Godfrey should make it? They entered, and she seated herself on a chair against one of the card-tables, as the stiffest and most unapproachable position she could choose.

'Thank you, sir,' she said immediately. 'I needn't give you any more trouble. I'm sorry you've had such an unlucky partner.'

'That's very ill-natured of you,' said Godfrey, standing by her without any sign of intended departure, 'to be sorry you've danced with me.'

'Oh no, sir, I don't mean to say what's ill-natured at all,' said Nancy, looking distractingly prim and pretty. 'When gentlemen have so may pleasures, one dance can matter but very little.'

'You know that isn't true. You know one dance with you matters more to me than all the other pleasures in the world.'

It was a long, long while since Godfrey had said anything so direct as that, and Nancy was startled. But her instinctive dignity and repugnance to any show of emotion made her sit perfectly still, and only throw a little more decision into her voice, as she said –

'No, indeed, Mr Godfrey, that's not known to me, and I have very good reasons for thinking different. But if it's true, I don't wish to hear it.'

'Would you never forgive me, then, Nancy – never think well of me, let what would happen – would you never think the present made amends for the past? Not if I turned a good fellow, and gave up everything you didn't like?'

Godfrey was half conscious that this sudden opportunity of

speaking to Nancy alone had driven him beside himself; but blind feeling had got the mastery of his tongue. Nancy really felt much agitated by the possibility Godfrey's words suggested, but this very pressure of emotion that she was in danger of finding too strong for her roused all her power of self-command.

'I should be glad to see a good change in anybody, Mr Godfrey,' she answered, with the slightest discernible difference of tone, 'but it 'ud be better if no change was wanted.'

'You're very hard-hearted, Nancy,' said Godfrey, pettishly. 'You might encourage me to be a better fellow. I'm very miserable – but you've no feeling.'

'I think those have the least feeling that act wrong to begin with,' said Nancy, sending out a flash in spite of herself. Godfrey was delighted with that little flash, and would have liked to go on and make her quarrel with him; Nancy was so exasperatingly quiet and firm. But she was not indifferent to him *yet*.

The entrance of Priscilla, bustling forward and saying, 'Dear heart alive, child, let us look at this gown,' cut off Godfrey's hopes of a quarrel.

'I suppose I must go now,' he said to Priscilla.

'It's no matter to me whether you go or stay,' said that frank lady, searching for something in her pocket, with a preoccupied brow.

'Do *you* want me to go?' said Godfrey, looking at Nancy, who was now standing up by Priscilla's order.

'As you like,' said Nancy, trying to recover all her former coldness, and looking down carefully at the hem of her gown.

'Then I like to stay,' said Godfrey, with a reckless determination to get as much of this joy as he could tonight, and think nothing of the morrow.

CHAPTER 12

While Godfrey Cass was taking draughts of forgetfulness from the sweet presence of Nancy, willingly losing all sense of that hidden bond which at other moments galled and fretted him so as to mingle irritation with the very sunshine, Godfrey's wife was walking with slow uncertain steps through the snow-covered Raveloe lanes, carrying her child in her arms.

This journey on New Year's Eve was a premeditated act of vengeance which she had kept in her heart ever since Godfrey, in a fit of passion, had told her he would sooner die than acknowledge her as his wife. There would be a great party at the Red House on New Year's Eve, she knew: her husband would be smiling and smiled upon, hiding *her* existence in the darkest corner of his heart. But she would mar his pleasure: she would go in her dingy rags, with her faded face, once as handsome as the best, with her little child that had its father's hair and eyes, and disclose herself to the Squire as his eldest son's wife. It is seldom that the miserable can help regarding their misery as a wrong inflicted by those who are less miserable. Molly knew that the cause of her dingy rags was not her husband's neglect, but the demon Opium[1] to whom she was enslaved, body and soul, except in the lingering mother's tenderness that refused to give him her hungry child. She knew this well; and yet, in the moments of wretched unbenumbed consciousness, the sense of her want and degradation transformed itself continually into bitterness towards Godfrey. *He* was well off; and if she had her rights she would be well off too. The belief that he repented his marriage, and suffered from it, only aggravated her vindictiveness. Just and self-reproving thoughts do not come to us too thickly, even in the purest air and with the best lessons of heaven and earth; how should those white-winged delicate messengers make their way to Molly's poisoned chamber, inhabited by no higher memories than those of a barmaid's paradise of pink ribbons and gentlemen's jokes?

She had set out at an early hour, but had lingered on the road, inclined by her indolence to believe that if she waited under a warm shed the snow would cease to fall. She had waited longer than she knew, and now that she found herself belated in the snow-hidden ruggedness of the long lanes, even the animation of a vindictive purpose could not keep her spirit from failing. It was seven o'clock, and by this time she was not very far from Raveloe, but she was not familiar enough with those monotonous lanes to know how near she was to her journey's end. She needed comfort, and she knew but one comforter – the familiar demon in her bosom; but she hesitated a moment, after drawing out the black remnant, before she raised it to her lips. In that moment the mother's love pleaded for painful consciousness rather than oblivion – pleaded to be left in aching weariness, rather than to have the encircling arms benumbed so that they could not feel the dear burden. In another moment Molly had flung something away, but it was not the black remnant – it was an empty phial. And she walked on again under the breaking cloud, from which there came now and then the light of a quickly veiled star, for a freezing wind had sprung up since the snowing had ceased. But she walked always more and more drowsily, and clutched more and more automatically the sleeping child at her bosom.

Slowly the demon was working his will, and cold and weariness were his helpers. Soon she felt nothing but a supreme immediate longing that curtained off all futurity – the longing to lie down and sleep. She had arrived at a spot where her footsteps were no longer checked by a hedgerow, and she had wandered vaguely, unable to distinguish any objects, notwithstanding the wide whiteness around her, and the growing starlight. She sank down against a straggling furze bush,[2] an easy pillow enough; and the bed of snow, too, was soft. She did not feel that the bed was cold, and did not heed whether the child would wake and cry for her. But her arms had not yet relaxed their instinctive clutch; and the little one slumbered on as gently as if it had been rocked in a lace-trimmed cradle.

But the complete torpor came at last: the fingers lost their tension, the arms unbent; then the little head fell away from the bosom, and the blue eyes opened wide on a cold starlight. At first there was a little peevish cry of 'mammy', and an effort to regain the pillowing arm and bosom; but mammy's ear was deaf, and the pillow seemed to be slipping away backward. Suddenly, as the child rolled downward on its mother's knees, all wet with snow, its eyes were caught by a bright glancing light on the white ground, and, with the ready transition of infancy, it was immediately absorbed in watching the bright living thing running towards it, yet never arriving. That bright living thing must be caught; and in a instant the child had slipped on all fours, and held out one little hand to catch the gleam. But the gleam would not be caught in that way, and now the head was held up to see where the cunning gleam came from. It came from a very bright place; and the little one, rising on its legs, toddled through the snow, the old grimy shawl in which it was wrapped trailing behind it, and the queer little bonnet dangling at its back – toddled on to the open door of Silas Marner's cottage, and right up to the warm hearth, where there was a bright fire of logs and sticks, which had thoroughly warmed the old sack (Silas's greatcoat) spread out on the bricks to dry. The little one, accustomed to be left to itself for long hours without notice from its mother, squatted down on the sack and spread its tiny hands towards the blaze, in perfect contentment, gurgling and making many inarticulate communications to the cheerful fire, like a new-hatched gosling[3] beginning to find itself comfortable. But presently the warmth had a lulling effect, and the little golden head sank down on the old sack, and the blue eyes were veiled by their delicate half-transparent lids.

But where was Silas Marner while this strange visitor had come to his hearth? He was in the cottage, but he did not see the child. During the last few weeks, since he had lost his money, he had contracted the habit of opening his door and looking out from time to time, as if he thought that his money might be somehow coming back to him, or that some trace, some news of it, might be mysteriously on the road, and be caught by the listening ear or the straining eye. It was chiefly at night, when he was not occupied in his loom, that he fell into this repetition of an act for which he could have assigned no definite purpose, and which can hardly be understood except by those who have undergone a bewildering separation from a supremely loved object. In the evening twilight, and later whenever the night was not dark, Silas looked out on that narrow prospect round the Stone-pits, listening and gazing, not with hope, but with mere yearning and unrest.

This morning he had been told by some of his neighbours that it was New Year's Eve, and that he must sit up and hear the old year rung out and the new rung in, because that was good luck, and might bring his money back again. This was only a friendly Raveloe-way of jesting with the half-crazy oddities of a miser, but it had perhaps helped to throw Silas into a more than usually excited state. Since the on-coming of twilight he had opened his door again and again, though only to shut it immediately at seeing all distance veiled by the falling snow. But the last time he opened it the snow had ceased, and the clouds were parting here and there. He stood and listened, and gazed for a long while – there was really something on the road coming towards him then, but he caught no sign of it; and the stillness and the wide trackless snow seemed to narrow his solitude, and touched his yearning with the chill of despair. He went in again, and put his right hand on the latch of the door to close it – but he did not close it: he was arrested, as he had been already since his loss, by the invisible wand of catalepsy, and stood like a graven image, with wide but sightless eyes, holding open his door, powerless to resist either the good or evil that might enter there.

When Marner's sensibility returned, he continued the action which had been arrested, and closed his door, unaware of the chasm in his consciousness, unaware of any intermediate change, except that the light had grown dim, and that he was chilled and faint. He thought he had been too long standing at the door and looking out. Turning towards the hearth, where the two logs had fallen apart, and sent forth only a red uncertain glimmer, he seated himself on his fireside chair, and was stooping to push his logs together, when, to his blurred vision, it seemed as if there were gold on the floor in front of the hearth. Gold! – his own gold – brought back to him as mysteriously as it had been taken away! He felt his heart begin to beat violently, and for a few moments he was unable to stretch out his hand and grasp the restored treasure. The heap of gold seemed to glow and get larger beneath his agitated gaze. He leaned forward at last, and stretched forth his hand; but instead of the hard coin with the familiar resisting outline, his fingers encountered soft warm curls. In utter amazement, Silas fell on his knees and bent his head low to examine the marvel: it was a sleeping child – a round, fair thing, with soft yellow rings all over its head. Could this be his little sister come back to him in a dream – his little sister whom he had carried about in his arms for a year before she died, when he was a small boy without shoes or stockings? That was the first thought that darted across Silas's blank wonderment. *Was* it a dream? He rose to his feet again, pushed his logs together, and, throwing on some dried leaves and sticks, raised a flame; but the flame did not disperse the vision – it only lit up more distinctly the little round form of the child, and its shabby clothing. It was very much like his little sister. Silas sank into his chair powerless, under the double presence of an inexplicable surprise and a hurrying influx of memories. How and when had the child come in without his knowledge? He had never been beyond the door. But along with that question, and almost thrusting it away, there was a vision of the old home and the old streets leading to Lantern Yard – and within that vision another, of the thoughts which had been present with him in those far-off scenes. The thoughts were strange to him now, like old friendships impossible to revive; and yet he had a dreamy feeling that this child was somehow a message come to him from that far-off life: it stirred fibres that had never been moved in Raveloe – old quiverings of tenderness – old impressions of awe at the presentiment of some Power presiding over his life; for his imagination had not yet extricated itself from the sense of mystery in the child's sudden presence, and had formed no conjectures of ordinary natural means by which the event could have been brought about.

But there was a cry on the hearth: the child had awaked, and Marner stooped to lift it on his knee. It clung round his neck, and burst louder and louder into that mingling of inarticulate cries with 'mammy' by which little children express the bewilderment of waking. Silas pressed it to him, and almost unconsciously uttered sounds of hushing tenderness, while he bethought himself that some of his porridge, which had got cool by the dying fire, would do to feed the child with if it were only warmed up a little.

He had plenty to do through the next hour. The porridge, sweetened with some dry brown sugar from an old store which he had refrained from using for himself, stopped the cries of the little one, and made her lift her blue eyes with a wide quiet gaze at Silas, as he put the spoon into her mouth. Presently she slipped from his knee and began to toddle about, but with a pretty stagger that made Silas jump up and follow her lest she should fall against anything that would hurt her. But she only fell in a sitting posture on the ground, and began to pull at her boots, looking up at him with a crying face as if the boots hurt her. He took her on his knee again, but it was some time before it occurred to Silas's dull bachelor mind that the wet boots were the grievance, pressing on her warm ankles. He got them off with difficulty, and baby was at once happily occupied with the primary mystery of her own toes, inviting Silas, with much chuckling, to consider the mystery too. But the wet boots had at last suggested to Silas that the child had been walking on the snow, and this roused him from his entire oblivion of any ordinary means by which it could have entered or been brought into his house. Under the prompting of this new idea, and without waiting to form conjectures, he raised the child in his arms, and went to the door. As soon as he had opened it, there was the cry of 'mammy' again, which Silas had not heard since the child's first hungry waking. Bending forward, he could just discern the marks made by the little feet on the virgin snow, and he followed their track to the furze bushes. 'Mammy!' the little one cried again and again, stretching itself forward so as almost to escape from Silas's arms, before he himself was aware that there was something more than the bush before him – that there was a human body, with the head sunk low in the furze, and half-covered with the shaken snow.

CHAPTER 13

It was after the early supper-time at the Red House, and the entertainment was in that stage when bashfulness itself had passed into easy jollity, when gentlemen, conscious of unusual accomplishments, could at length be prevailed on to dance a hornpipe, and when the Squire preferred talking loudly, scattering snuff, and patting his visitors' backs, to sitting longer at the whist-table – a choice exasperating to uncle Kimble, who, being always volatile in sober business hours, became intense and bitter over cards and brandy, shuffled before his adversary's deal with a glare of suspicion, and turned up a mean trump-card with an air of inexpressible disgust, as if in a world where such things could happen one might as well enter on a course of reckless profligacy. When the evening had advanced to this pitch of freedom and enjoyment, it was usual for the servants, the heavy duties of supper being well over, to get their share of amusement by coming to look on at the dancing; so that the back regions of the house were left in solitude.

There were two doors by which the White Parlour was entered from the hall, and they were both standing open for the sake of air; but the lower one was crowded with the servants and villagers, and only the upper doorway was left free. Bob Cass was figuring in a hornpipe, and his father, very proud of this lithe son, whom he repeatedly declared to be just like himself in his young days in a tone that implied this to be the very highest stamp of juvenile merit, was the centre of a group who had placed themselves opposite the performer, not far from the upper door. Godfrey was standing a little way off, not to admire his brother's dancing, but to keep sight of Nancy, who was seated in the group, near her father. He stood aloof, because he wished to avoid suggesting himself as a subject for the Squire's fatherly jokes in connection with matrimony and Miss Nancy Lammeter's beauty, which were likely to become more and more explicit. But he had the prospect of dancing with her again when the hornpipe was concluded, and in the meanwhile it was very pleasant to get long glances at her quite unobserved.

But when Godfrey was lifting his eyes from one of those long glances, they encountered an object as startling to him at that moment as if it had been an apparition from the dead. It *was* an apparition from that hidden life which lies, like a dark by-street, behind the goodly ornamented façade that meets the sunlight and the gaze of respectable admirers. It was his own child carried in Silas Marner's arms. That was his instantaneous impression, accompanied by doubt, though he had not seen the child for months past; and when the hope was rising that he might possibly be mistaken, Mr Crackenthorp and Mr Lammeter had already advanced to Silas, in astonishment at this strange advent. Godfrey joined them immediately, unable to rest without hearing every word – trying to control himself, but conscious that if any one noticed him, they must see that he was white-lipped and trembling.

But now all eyes at that end of the room were bent on Silas Marner; the Squire himself had risen and asked angrily, 'How's this? – what's this – what do you do coming in here in this way?'

'I'm come for the doctor – I want the doctor,' Silas had said, in the first moment, to Mr Crackenthorp.

'Why, what's the matter, Marner?' said the rector. 'The doctor's here; but say quietly what you want him for.'

'It's a woman,' said Silas, speaking low, and half-breathlessly, just as Godfrey came up. 'She's dead, I think – dead in the snow at the Stone-pits – not far from my door.'

Godfrey felt a great throb: there was one terror in his mind at that moment: it was, that the woman might *not* be dead. That was an evil terror – an ugly inmate to have found a nestling-place in Godfrey's kindly disposition; but no disposition is a security from evil wishes to a man whose happiness hangs on duplicity.

'Hush, hush!' said Mr Crackenthorp. 'Go out into the hall there. I'll fetch the doctor to you. Found a woman in the snow – and thinks she's dead,' he added, speaking low, to the Squire. 'Better say as little about it as possible: it will shock the ladies. Just tell them a poor woman is ill from cold and hunger. I'll go and fetch Kimble.'

By this time, however, the ladies had pressed forward, curious to know what could have brought the solitary linen-weaver there under such strange circumstances, and interested in the pretty child, who, half alarmed and half attracted by the brightness and the numerous company, now frowned and hid her face, now lifted up her head again and looked round placably, until a touch or a coaxing word brought back the frown and made her bury her face with new determination.

'What child is it?' said several ladies at once, and, among the rest, Nancy Lammeter, addressing Godfrey.

'I don't know – some poor woman's who has been found in the snow, I believe,' was the answer Godfrey wrung from himself with a terrible effort. ('After all, *am* I certain?' he hastened to add, in anticipation of his own conscience.)

'Why, you'd better leave the child here, then, Master Marner,' said good-natured Mrs Kimble, hesitating, however, to take those dingy clothes into contact with her own ornamented satin boddice. 'I'll tell one o' the girls to fetch it.'

'No – no – I can't part with it, I can't let it go,' said Silas, abruptly. 'It's come to me – I've a right to keep it.'

The proposition to take the child from him had come to Silas quite unexpectedly, and his speech, uttered under a strong sudden impulse, was almost like a revelation to himself: a minute before, he had no distinct intention about the child.

'Did you ever hear the like?' said Mrs Kimble, in mild surprise, to her neighbour.

'Now, ladies, I must trouble you to stand aside,' said Mr Kimble, coming from the card-room, in some bitterness at the interruption, but drilled by the long habit of his profession into obedience to unpleasant calls, even when he was hardly sober.

'It's a nasty business turning out now, eh, Kimble?' said the Squire. 'He might ha' gone for your young fellow – the 'prentice, there – what's his name?'

'Might? ay – what's the use of talking about might?' growled uncle Kimble, hastening out with Marner, and followed by Mr Crackenthorp and Godfrey. 'Get me a pair of thick boots, Godfrey, will you? And stay, let somebody run to Winthrop's and fetch Dolly – she's the best woman to get. Ben was here himself before supper; is he gone?'

'Yes, sir, I met him,' said Marner; 'but I couldn't stop to tell him anything, only I said I was going for the doctor, and he said the doctor was at the Squire's. And I made haste and ran, and there was nobody to be seen at the back o' the house, and so I went in to where the company was.'

The child, no longer distracted by the bright light and the smiling women's faces, began to cry and call for 'mammy', though always clinging to Marner, who had apparently won her thorough confidence. Godfrey had come back with the boots, and felt the cry as if some fibre were drawn tight within him.

'I'll go,' he said, hastily, eager for some movement; 'I'll go and fetch the woman – Mrs Winthrop.'

'O, pooh – send somebody else,' said uncle Kimble, hurrying away with Marner.

'You'll let me know if I can be of any use, Kimble,' said Mr Crackenthorp. But the doctor was out of hearing.

Godfrey, too, had disappeared: he was gone to snatch his hat and coat, having just reflection enough to remember that he must not look like a madman; but he rushed out of the house into the snow without heeding his thin shoes.

In a few minutes he was on his rapid way to the Stone-pits by the side of Dolly, who, though feeling that she was entirely in her place in encountering cold and snow on an errand of mercy, was much concerned at a young gentleman's getting his feet wet under a like impulse.

'You'd a deal better go back, sir,' said Dolly, with respectful compassion. 'You've no call to catch cold; and I'd ask you if you'd be so good as tell my husband to come, on your way back – he's at the Rainbow, I doubt – if you found him anyway sober enough to be o' use. Or else, there's Mrs Snell 'ud happpen send the boy up to fetch and carry, for there may be things wanted from the doctor's.'

'No, I'll stay, now I'm once out – I'll stay outside here,' said Godfrey, when they came opposite Marner's cottage. 'You can come and tell me if I can do anything.'

'Well, sir, you're very good: you've a tender heart,' said Dolly, going to the door.

Godfrey was too painfully preoccupied to feel a twinge of self-reproach at this undeserved praise. He walked up and down, unconscious that he was plunging ankle-deep in snow, unconscious of everything but trembling suspense about what was going on in the cottage, and the effect of each alternative on his future lot. No, not quite unconscious of everything else. Deeper down, and half-smothered by passionate desire and dread, there was the sense that he ought not to be waiting on these alternatives; that he ought to accept the consequences of his deeds, own the miserable wife, and fulfil the claims of the helpless child. But he had not moral courage enough to contemplate that active renunciation of Nancy as possible for him: he had only conscience and heart enough to make him for ever uneasy under the weakness that forbade the renunciation. And at this moment his mind leaped away from all restraint toward the sudden prospect of deliverance from his long bondage.

'Is she dead?' said the voice that predominated over every other within him. 'If she is, I may marry Nancy; and then I shall be a good fellow in future, and have no secrets, and the child – shall be taken care of somehow.' But across that vision came the other possibility – 'She may live, and then it's all up with me.'

Godfrey never knew how long it was before the door of the cottage opened and Mr Kimble came out. He went forward to meet his uncle, prepared to suppress the agitation he must feel, whatever news he was to hear.

'I waited for you, as I'd come so far,' he said, speaking first.

'Pooh, it was nonsense for you to come out: why didn't you send one of the men? There's nothing to be done. She's dead – has been dead for hours, I should say.'

'What sort of woman is she?' said Godfrey, feeling the blood rush to his face.

'A young woman, but emaciated, with long black hair. Some vagrant – quite in rags. She's got a wedding-ring on, however. They must fetch her away to the workhouse tomorrow.[1] Come, come along.'

'I want to look at her,' said Godfrey. 'I think I saw such a woman yesterday. I'll overtake you in a minute or two.'

Mr Kimble went on, and Godfrey turned back to the cottage. He cast only one glance at the dead face on the pillow, which Dolly had smoothed with decent care; but he remembered that last look at his unhappy hated wife so well, that at the end of sixteen years every line in the worn face was present to him when he told the full story of this night.

He turned immediately towards the hearth, where Silas Marner sat lulling the child. She was perfectly quiet now, but not asleep – only soothed by sweet porridge and warmth into that wide-gazing calm which makes us older human beings, with our inward turmoil, feel a certain awe in the presence of a little child, such as we feel before some quiet majesty or beauty in the earth or sky – before a steady glowing planet, or a full-flowered eglantine, or the bending trees over a silent pathway. The wide-open blue eyes looked up at Godfrey's without any uneasiness or sign of recognition: the child could make no visible audible claim on its father; and the father felt a strange mixture of feelings, a conflict of regret and joy, that the pulse of that little heart had no response for the half-jealous yearning in his own, when the blue eyes turned away from him slowly, and fixed themselves on the weaver's queer face, which was bent low down to look at them, while the small hand began to pull Marner's withered cheek with loving disfiguration.

'You'll take the child to the parish tomorrow?' asked Godfrey, speaking as indifferently as he could.

'Who says so?' said Marner, sharply. 'Will they make me take her?'

'Why, you wouldn't like to keep her, should you – an old bachelor like you?'

'Till anybody shows they've a right to take her away from me,' said Marner. 'The mother's dead and I reckon it's got no father: it's a lone thing – and I'm a lone thing. My money's gone, I don't know where – and this is come from I don't know where. I know nothing – I'm partly mazed.'

'Poor little thing!' said Godfrey. 'Let me give something towards finding it clothes.'

He had put his hand in his pocket and found half-a-guinea, and, thrusting it into Silas's hand, he hurried out of the cottage to overtake Mr Kimble.

'Ah, I see it's not the same woman I saw,' he said, as he came up. 'It's a pretty little child: the old fellow seems to want to keep it; that's strange for a miser like him. But I gave him a trifle to help him out: the parish isn't likely to quarrel with him for the right to keep the child.'[1]

'No; but I've seen the time when I might have quarrelled with him for it myself. It's too late now, though. If the child ran into the fire, your aunt's too fat to overtake it: she could only sit and grunt like an alarmed sow. But what a fool you are, Godfrey, to come out in your dancing shoes and stockings in this way – and you one of the beaux of the evening, and at your own house! What do you mean by such freaks, young fellow? Has Miss

Nancy been cruel, and do you want to spite her by spoiling your pumps?'

'O, everything has been disagreeable tonight. I was tired to death of jigging and gallanting, and that bother about the hornpipes. And I'd got to dance with the other Miss Gunn,' said Godfrey, glad of the subterfuge his uncle had suggested to him.

The prevarication and white lies which a mind that keeps itself ambitiously pure is as uneasy under as a great artist under the false touches that no eye detects but his own, are worn as lightly as mere trimmings when once the actions have become a lie.

Godfrey reappeared in the White Parlour with dry feet, and, since the truth must be told, with a sense of relief and gladness that was too strong for painful thoughts to struggle with. For could he not venture now, whenever opportunity offered, to say the tenderest things to Nancy Lammeter – to promise her and himself that he would always be just what she would desire to see him? There was no danger that his dead wife would be recognised: those were not days of active inquiry and wide report; and as for the registry of their marriage, that was a long way off, buried in unturned pages, away from every one's interest but his own. Dunsey might betray him if he came back; but Dunsey might be won to silence.

And when events turn out so much better for a man than he has had reason to dread, is it not a proof that his conduct has been less foolish and blameworthy than it might otherwise have appeared? When we are treated well, we naturally begin to think that we are not altogether unmeritorious, and that it is only just we should treat ourselves well, and not mar our own good fortune. Where, after all, would be the use of his confessing the past to Nancy Lammeter, and throwing away his happiness? – nay, hers? for he felt some confidence that she loved him. As for the child, he would see that it was cared for: he would never forsake it; he would do everything but own it. Perhaps it would be just as happy in life without being owned by its father, seeing that nobody could tell how things would turn out, and that – is there any other reason wanted? – well, then, that the father would be much happier without owning the child.

CHAPTER 14

There was a pauper's burial that week in Raveloe, and up Kench Yard at Batherley it was known that the dark-haired woman with the fair child, who had lately come to lodge there, was gone away again. That was all the express note taken that Molly had disappeared from the eyes of men. But the unwept death which, to the general lot, seemed as trivial as the summer-shed leaf, was charged with the force of destiny to certain human lives that we know of, shaping their joys and sorrows even to the end.

Silas Marner's determination to keep the 'tramp's child' was matter of hardly less surprise and iterated talk in the village than the robbery of his money. That softening of feeling towards him which dated from his misfortune, that merging of suspicion and dislike in a rather contemptuous pity for him as lone and crazy, was now accompanied with a more active sympathy, especially amongst the women. Notable mothers, who knew what it was to keep children 'whole and sweet'; lazy mothers, who knew what it was to be interrrupted in folding their arms and scratching their elbows by the mischievous propensities of children just firm on their legs, were equally interested in conjecturing how a lone man would manage with a two-year-old child on his hands, and were equally ready with their suggestions: the notable chiefly telling him what he had better do, and the lazy ones being emphatic in telling him what he would never be able to do.

Among the notable mothers, Dolly Winthrop was the one whose neighbourly offices were the most acceptable to Marner, for they were rendered without any show of bustling instruction. Silas had shown her the half-guinea given to him by Godfrey, and had asked her what he should do about getting some clothes for the child.

'Eh, Master Marner,' said Dolly, 'there's no call to buy, no more nor a pair o'shoes; for I've got the little petticoats as Aaron wore five years ago, and it's ill spending the money on them baby-clothes, for the child 'ull grow like grass i' May, bless it – that it will.'

And the same day Dolly brought her bundle, and displayed to Marner, one by one, the tiny garments in their due order of succession, most of them patched and darned, but clean and neat as fresh-sprung herbs. This was the introduction to a great ceremony with soap and water, from which baby came out in new beauty, and sat on Dolly's knee, handling her toes and chuckling and patting her palms together with an air of having made several discoveries about herself, which she communicated by alternate sounds of 'gug-gug-gug', and 'mammy'. The 'mammy' was not a cry of need or uneasiness: Baby had been used to utter it without expecting either tender sound or touch to follow.

'Anybody 'ud think the angils in heaven couldn't be prettier,' said Dolly, rubbing the golden curls and kissing them. 'And to think of its being covered wi' them dirty rags – and the poor mother – froze to death; but there's Them as took care of it, and brought it to your door, Master Marner. The door was open, and it walked in over the snow, like as if it had been a little starved robin. Didn't you say the door was open?'

'Yes,' said Silas, meditatively. 'Yes – the door was open. The money's gone I don't know where, and this is come from I don't know where.'

He had not mentioned to any one his unconsciousness of the child's entrance, shrinking from questions which might lead to the fact he himself suspected – namely, that he had been in one of his trances.

'Ah,' said Dolly, with soothing gravity, 'it's like the night and the morning, and the sleeping and the waking, and the rain and the harvest – one goes and the other comes, and we know nothing how nor where. We may strive and scrat[1] and fend, but it's little we can do arter all – the big things come and go wi' no striving o' our'n – they do, that they do; and I think you're in the right on it to keep the little un, Master Marner, seeing as it's been sent to you, though there's folks as thinks different. You'll happen be a bit moithered[2] with it while it's so little; but I'll come, and welcome, and see to it for you: I've a bit o' time to spare most days, for when one gets up betimes i' the morning, the clock seems to stan' still tow'rt ten, afore its time to go about the victual. So, as I say, I'll come and see to the child for you, and welcome.'

'Thank you . . . kindly,' said Silas, hesitating a little. 'I'll be glad if you'll tell me things. But,' he added, uneasily, leaning forward to look at Baby with some jealousy, as she was resting her head backward against Dolly's arm, and eyeing him contentedly from a distance – 'But I want to do things for it myself, else it may get fond o' somebody else, and not fond o' me. I've been used to fending for myself in the house – I can learn, I can learn.'

'Eh, to be sure,' said Dolly, gently. 'I've seen men as are wonderful handy wi' children. The men are awk'ard and contrairy mostly, God help 'em – but when the drink's out of 'em, they aren't unsensible, though they're bad for leeching and bandaging – so fiery and unpatient. You see this goes first, next the skin,' proceeded Dolly, taking up the little shirt, and putting it on.

'Yes,' said Marner, docilely, bringing his eyes very close, that they might be initiated in the mysteries; whereupon Baby seized his head with both her small arms, and put her lips against his face with purring noises.

'See there,' said Dolly, with a woman's tender tact, 'she's fondest o' you. She wants to go o' your lap, I'll be bound. Go, then: take her, Master Marner; you can put the things on, and then you can say as you've done for her from the first of her coming to you.'

Marner took her on his lap, trembling with an emotion mysterious to himself, at something unknown dawning on his life. Thought and feeling were so confused within him, that if he had tried to give them utterance, he could only have said that the child was come instead of the gold – that the gold had turned into the child. He took the garments from Dolly, and put them on under her teaching; interrupted, of course, by Baby's gymnastics.

'There, then! why, you take to it quite easy, Master Marner,' said Dolly; 'but what shall you do when you're forced to sit in your loom? For she'll get busier and mischievouser every day – she will, bless her. It's lucky as you've got that high hearth i'stead of a grate, for that keeps the fire more out of her reach: but if you've got anything as can be spilt or broke, or as is fit to cut her fingers off, she'll be at it – and it is but right you should know.'

Silas meditated a little while in some perplexity. 'I'll tie her to the leg o' the loom,' he said at last – 'tie her with a good long strip o' something.'

'Well, mayhap that'll do, as it's a little gell, for they're easier persuaded to sit i' one place nor the lads. I know what the lads are; for I've had four – four I've had, God knows – and if you was to take and tie 'em up, they'd make a fighting and a crying as if you was ringing the pigs. But I'll bring you my little chair, and some bits o' red rag and things for her to play wi'; an' she'll sit and chatter to 'em as if they was alive. Eh, if it wasn't a sin to the lads to wish 'em made different, bless 'em, I should ha' been glad for one of 'em to be a little gell; and to think as I could ha' taught her to scour, and mend, and the knitting, and everything. But I can teach 'em this little un, Master Marner, when she gets old enough.'

'But she'll be *my* little un,' said Marner, rather hastily. 'She'll be nobody else's.'

'No, to be sure; you'll have a right to her, if you're a father to her, and bring her up according. But,' added Dolly, coming to a point which she had determined beforehand to touch upon, 'you must bring her up like christened folk's children, and take her to church, and let her learn her catechise,[3] as my little Aaron can say off – the "I believe", and everything, and "hurt nobody by word or deed", – as well as if he was the clerk. That's what you must do, Master Marner, if you'd do the right thing by the orphin child.'

Marner's pale face flushed suddenly under a new anxiety. His mind was too busy trying to give some definite bearing to Dolly's words for him to think of answering her.

'And it's my belief,' she went on, 'as the poor little creature has never been christened, and it's nothing but right as the parson should be spoke to; and if you was noways unwilling, I'd talk to Mr Macey about it this very day. For if the child ever went anyways wrong, and you hadn't done your part by it, Master Marner – 'noculation, and everything to save it from harm – it 'ud be a thorn i' your bed for ever o' this side the grave; and I can't think as it 'ud be easy lying down for anybody when they'd got to another world, if they hadn't done their part by the helpless children as come wi'out their own asking.'

Dolly herself was disposed to be silent for some time now, for she had spoken from the depths of her own simple belief, and was much concerned to know whether her words would produce the desired effect on Silas. He was puzzled and anxious, for Dolly's word 'christened' conveyed no distinct meaning to him. He had only heard of baptism, and had only seen the baptism of grown-up men and women.

'What is it as you mean by "christened"?' he said at last, timidly. 'Won't folks be good to her without it?'

'Dear, dear! Master Marner,' said Dolly, with gentle distress and compassion. 'Had you never no father nor mother as taught you to say your prayers, and as there's good words and good things to keep us from harm?'

'Yes,' said Silas, in a low voice; 'I know a deal about that – used to, used to. But your ways are different: my country was a good way off.' He paused a few moments, and then added, more decidedly, 'But I want to do everything as can be done for the child. And whatever's right for it i' this country, and you think 'ull do it good, I'll act according, if you'll tell me.'

'Well, then, Master Marner,' said Dolly, inwardly rejoiced, 'I'll ask Mr Macey to speak to the parson about it; and you must fix on a name for it, because it must have a name giv' it when it's christened.'

'My mother's name was Hephzibah,'⁴ said Silas, 'and my little sister was named after her.'

'Eh, that's a hard name,' said Dolly. 'I partly think it isn't a christened name.'

'It's a Bible name,' said Silas, old ideas recurring.

'Then I've no call to speak again' it,' said Dolly, rather startled by Silas's knowledge on this head; 'but you see I'm no scholard, and I'm slow at catching the words. My husband says I'm allays like as if I was putting the haft⁵ for the handle – that's what he says – for he's very sharp, God help him. But it was awk'ard calling your little sister by such a hard name, when you'd got nothing big to say like – wasn't it, Master Marner?'

'We called her Eppie,' said Silas.

'Well, if it was noways wrong to shorten the name, it 'ud be a deal handier. And so I'll go now, Master Marner, and I'll speak about the christening afore dark; and I wish you the best o' luck, and it's my belief as it'll come to you, if you do what's right by the orphin child; – and there's the 'noculation to be seen to; and as to washing its bits o' things, you need look to nobody but me, for I can do 'em wi' one hand when I've got my

suds[6] about. Eh, the blessed angil! You'll let me bring my Aaron
one o' these days, and he'll show her his little cart as his father's
made for him, and the black-and-white pup as he's got a-
rearing.'

Baby *was* christened, the rector deciding that a double baptism was the lesser risk to incur; and on this occasion Silas,
making himself as clean and tidy as he could, appeared for the
first time within the church, and shared in the observances held
sacred by his neighbours. He was quite unable, by means of
anything he heard or saw, to identify the Raveloe religion with
his old faith; if he could at any time in his previous life have
done so, it must have been by the aid of a strong feeling ready
to vibrate with sympathy, rather than by a comparison of
phrases and ideas: and now for long years that feeling had been
dormant. He had no distinct idea about the baptism and the
church-going, except that Dolly had said it was for the good of
the child; and in this way, as the weeks grew to months, the
child created fresh links between his life and the lives from
which he had hitherto shrunk continually into narrower isolation. Unlike the gold which needed nothing, and must be
worshipped in close-locked solitude – which was hidden away
from the daylight, was deaf to the song of birds, and started to
no human tones – Eppie was a creature of endless claims and
ever-growing desires, seeking and loving sunshine, and living
sounds, and living movements; making trial of everything, with
trust in new joy, and stirring the human kindness in all eyes that
looked on her. The gold had kept his thoughts in an ever-
repeated circle, leading to nothing beyond itself; but Eppie was
an object compacted of changes and hopes that forced his
thoughts onward, and carried them far away from their old
eager pacing towards the same blank limit – carried them away
to the new things that would come with the coming years, when
Eppie would have learned to understand how her father Silas
cared for her; and made him look for images of that time in the
ties and charities that bound together the families of his neighbours. The gold had asked that he should sit weaving longer
and longer, deafened and blinded more and more to all things
except the monotony of his loom and the repetition of his web;
but Eppie called him away from his weaving, and made him
think all its pauses a holiday, reawakening his senses with her
fresh life, even to the old winter-flies that came crawling forth

in the early spring sunshine, and warming him into joy because *she* had joy.

And when the sunshine grew strong and lasting, so that the buttercups were thick in the meadows, Silas might be seen in the sunny midday, or in the late afternoon when the shadows were lengthening under the hedgerows, strolling out with uncovered head to carry Eppie beyond the Stone-pits to where the flowers grew, till they reached some favourite bank where he could sit down, while Eppie toddled to pluck the flowers, and make remarks to the winged things that murmured happily above the bright petals, calling 'Dad-dad's' attention continually by bringing him the flowers. Then she would turn her ear to some sudden bird-note, and Silas learned to please her by making signs of hushed stillness, that they might listen for the note to come again: so that when it came, she set up her small back and laughed with gurgling triumph. Sitting on the banks in this way, Silas began to look for the once familiar herbs again; and as the leaves, with their unchanged outline and markings, lay on his palm, there was a sense of crowding remembrances from which he turned away timidly, taking refuge in Eppie's little world, that lay lightly on his enfeebled spirit.

As the child's mind was growing into knowledge, his mind was growing into memory: as her life unfolded, his soul, long stupefied in a cold narrow prison, was unfolding too, and trembling gradually into full consciousness.

It was an influence which must gather force with every new year: the tones that stirred Silas's heart grew articulate, and called for more distinct answers; shapes and sounds grew clearer for Eppie's eyes and ears, and there was more that 'Dad-dad' was imperatively required to notice and account for. Also, by the time Eppie was three years old, she developed a fine capacity for mischief, and for devising ingenious ways of being troublesome, which found much exercise, not only for Silas's patience, but for his watchfulness and penetration. Sorely was poor Silas puzzled on such occasions by the incompatible demands of love. Dolly Winthrop told him that punishment was good for Eppie, and that, as for rearing a child without making it tingle a little in soft and safe places now and then, it was not to be done.

'To be sure, there's another thing you might do, Master Marner,' added Dolly, meditatively: 'you might shut her up once i' the coal-hole. That was what I did wi' Aaron; for I was that silly wi' the youngest lad, as I could never bear to smack him. Not as I could find i' my heart to let him stay i' the coal-hole more nor a minute, but it was enough to colly[7] him all over, so as he must be new washed and dressed, and it was as good as a rod to him – that was. But I put it upo' your conscience, Master Marner, as there's one of 'em you must choose – ayther smacking or the coal-hole – else she'll get so masterful, there'll be no holding her.'

Silas was impressed with the melancholy truth of this last remark; but his force of mind failed before the only two penal methods open to him, not only because it was painful to him to hurt Eppie, but because he trembled at a moment's contention with her, lest she should love him the less for it. Let even an affectionate Goliath[8] get himself tied to a small tender thing, dreading to hurt it by pulling, and dreading still more to snap the cord, and which of the two, pray, will be master? It was clear that Eppie, with her short toddling steps, must lead father Silas a pretty dance on any fine morning when circumstances favoured mischief.

For example. He had wisely chosen a broad strip of linen as a means of fastening her to his loom when he was busy: it made a broad belt round her waist, and was long enough to allow of her reaching the truckle-bed and sitting down on it, but not long enough for her to attempt any dangerous climbing. One bright summer's morning Silas had been more engrossed than usual in 'setting up' a new piece of work, an occasion on which his scissors were in requisition. These scissors, owing to an especial warning of Dolly's, had been kept carefully out of Eppie's reach; but the click of them had had a peculiar attraction for her ear, and watching the results of the click, she had derived the philosophic lesson that the same cause would produce the same effect. Silas had seated himself in his loom, and the noise of weaving had begun; but he had left his scissors on a ledge which Eppie's arm was long enough to reach; and now, like a small mouse, watching her opportunity, she stole quietly from her corner, secured the scissors, and toddled to the bed again, setting up her back as a mode of concealing the fact. She had a distinct intention as to the use of the scissors; and having cut the linen strip in a jagged but effectual manner, in two moments she had run out at the open door where the sunshine was inviting her, while poor Silas believed her to be a better child than usual. It was not until he happened to need his scissors that the terrible fact burst upon him: Eppie had run out by herself – had perhaps fallen into the Stone-pit. Silas, shaken by the worst fear that could have befallen him, rushed out, calling 'Eppie!' and ran eagerly about the unenclosed space, exploring the dry cavities into which she might have fallen, and then gazing with questioning dread at the smooth red surface of the water. The cold drops stood on his brow. How long had she been out? There was one hope – that she had crept through the stile and got into the fields, where he habitually took her to stroll. But the grass was high in the meadow, and there was no descrying her, if she were there, except by a close search that would be a trespass on Mr Osgood's crop. Still, that misdemeanor must be committed; and poor Silas, after peering all round the hedgerows, traversed the grass, beginning with perturbed vision to see Eppie behind every group of red sorrel, and to see her moving always farther off as he approached. The meadow was searched in vain; and he got over the stile into the next field, looking with dying hope towards a small pond which was now reduced to its summer shallowness, so as to leave a wide margin of good adhesive mud. Here, however, sat Eppie, discoursing cheerfully to her own small boot, which she was using as a bucket to convey the water into a deep hoof-mark, while her little naked foot was planted comfortably on a cushion of olive-green mud. A red-headed calf was observing her with alarmed doubt through the opposite hedge.

Here was clearly a case of aberration in a christened child which demanded severe treatment; but Silas, overcome with convulsive joy at finding his treasure again, could do nothing but snatch her up, and cover her with half-sobbing kisses. It was not until he had carried her home, and had begun to think of the necessary washing, that he recollected the need that he should punish Eppie, and 'make her remember'. The idea that she might run away again and come to harm, gave him unusual resolution, and for the first time he determined to try the coal-hole – a small closet near the hearth.

'Naughty, naughty Eppie,' he suddenly began, holding her on his knee, and pointing to her muddy feet and clothes – 'naughty to cut with the scissors and run away. Eppie must go into the coal-hole for being naughty. Daddy must put her in the coal-hole.'

He half-expected that this would be shock enough, and that Eppie would begin to cry. But instead of that, she began to shake herself on his knee, as if the proposition opened a pleasing novelty. Seeing that he must proceed to extremities, he put her into the coal-hole, and held the door closed, with a trembling sense that he was using a strong measure. For a moment there was silence, but then came a little cry, 'Opy, opy!' and Silas let her out again, saying, 'Now Eppie 'ull never be naughty again, else she must go in the coal-hole – a black naughty place.'

The weaving must stand still a long while this morning, for now Eppie must be washed, and have clean clothes on; but it was to be hoped that this punishment would have a lasting effect, and save time in future – though, perhaps, it would have been better if Eppie had cried more.

In half an hour she was clean again, and Silas having turned his back to see what he could do with the linen band, threw it down again, with the reflection that Eppie would be good without fastening for the rest of the morning. He turned round again, and was going to place her in her little chair near the loom, when she peeped out at him with black face and hands again, and said, 'Eppie in de toal-hole!'

This total failure of the coal-hole discipline shook Silas's belief in the efficacy of punishment. 'She'd take it all for fun,' he observed to Dolly, 'if I didn't hurt her, and that I can't do, Mrs Winthrop. If she makes me a bit o' trouble, I can bear it. And she's got no tricks but what she'll grow out of.'

'Well, that's partly true, Master Marner,' said Dolly, sympathetically; 'and if you can't bring your mind to frighten her off touching things, you must do what you can to keep 'em out of her way. That's what I do wi' the pups as the lads are allays a-rearing. They *will* worry and gnaw – worry and gnaw they will, if it was one's Sunday cap as hung anywhere so as they could drag it. They know no difference, God help 'em: it's the pushing o' the teeth as sets 'em on, that's what it is.'

So Eppie was reared without punishment, the burden of her misdeeds being borne vicariously by father Silas. The stone hut was made a soft nest for her, lined with downy patience: and also in the world that lay beyond the stone hut she knew nothing of frowns and denials.

Notwithstanding the difficulty of carrying her and his yarn or linen at the same time, Silas took her with him in most of his

journeys to the farm-houses, unwilling to leave her behind at
Dolly Winthrop's, who was always ready to take care of her;
and little curly-headed Eppie, the weaver's child, became an
object of interest at several outlying homesteads, as well as in
the village. Hitherto he had been treated very much as if he had
been a useful gnome or brownie[9] – a queer and unaccountable
creature, who must necessarily be looked at with wondering
curiosity and repulsion, and with whom one would be glad to
make all greetings and bargains as brief as possible, but who
must be dealt with in a propitiatory way, and occasionally have
a present of pork or garden stuff to carry home with him, seeing
that without him there was no getting the yarn woven. But now
Silas met with open smiling faces and cheerful questioning, as a
person whose satisfactions and difficulties could be understood.
Everywhere he must sit a little and talk about the child, and
words of interest were always ready for him: 'Ah, Master
Marner, you'll be lucky if she takes the measles soon and easy!
– or, 'Why, there isn't many lone men 'ud ha' been wishing to
take up with a little un like that: but I reckon the weaving makes
you handier than men as do out-door work – you're partly as
handy as a woman, for weaving comes next to spinning.' Elderly
masters and mistresses, seated observantly in large kitchen arm-
chairs, shook their heads over the difficulties attendant on
rearing children, felt Eppie's round arms and legs, and pronounced them remarkably firm, and told Silas that, if she turned
out well (which, however, there was no telling), it would be a
fine thing for him to have a steady lass to do for him when he
got helpless. Servant maidens were fond of carrying her out to
look at the hens and chickens, or to see if any cherries could be
shaken down in the orchard; and the small boys and girls
approached her slowly, with cautious movement and steady
gaze, like little dogs face to face with one of their own kind, till
attraction had reached the point at which the soft lips were put
out for a kiss. No child was afraid of approaching Silas when
Eppie was near him: there was no repulsion around him now,
either for young or old; for the little child had come to link him
once more with the whole world. There was love between him
and the child that blent them into one, and there was love
between the child and the world – from men and women with
parental looks and tones, to the red lady-birds and the round
pebbles.

Silas began now to think of Raveloe life entirely in relation to Eppie: she must have everything that was a good in Raveloe; and he listened docilely, that he might come to understand better what this life was, from which, for fifteen years, he had stood aloof as from a strange thing, wherewith he could have no communion: as some man who has a precious plant to which he would give a nurturing home in a new soil, thinks of the rain, and the sunshine, and all influences, in relation to his nursling, and asks industriously for all knowledge that will help him to satisfy the wants of the searching roots, or to guard leaf and bud from invading harm. The disposition to hoard had been utterly crushed at the very first by the loss of his long-stored gold: the coins he earned afterwards seemed as irrelevant as stones brought to complete a house suddenly buried by an earthquake; the sense of bereavement was too heavy upon him for the old thrill of satisfaction to arise again at the touch of the newly-earned coin. And now something had come to replace his hoard which gave a growing purpose to the earnings, drawing his hope and joy continually onward beyond the money.

In old days there were angels who came and took men by the hand and led them away from the city of destruction.[10] We see no white-winged angels now. But yet men are led away from threatening destruction: a hand is put into theirs, which leads them forth gently towards a calm and bright land, so that they look no more backward; and the hand may be a little child's.

CHAPTER 15

There was one person, as you will believe, who watched with keener though more hidden interest than any other, the prosperous growth of Eppie under the weaver's care. He dared not do anything that would imply a stronger interest in a poor man's adopted child than could be expected from the kindliness of the young Squire, when a chance meeting suggested a little present to a simple old fellow whom others noticed with goodwill; but he told himself that the time would come when he might do something towards furthering the welfare of his daughter without incurring suspicion. Was he very uneasy in the meantime at his inability to give his daughter her birthright? I cannot say that he was. The child was being taken care of, and would very likely be happy, as people in humble stations often were – happier, perhaps, than those brought up in luxury.

That famous ring that pricked its owner when he forgot duty and followed desire – I wonder if it pricked very hard when he set out on the chase, or whether it pricked but lightly then, and only pierced to the quick when the chase had long been ended, and hope, folding her wings, looked backward and became regret?

Godfrey Cass's cheek and eye were brighter than ever now. He was so undivided in his aims, that he seemed like a man of firmness. No Dunsey had come back: people had made up their minds that he was gone for a soldier, or gone 'out of the country', and no one cared to be specific in their inquiries on a subject delicate to a respectable family. Godfrey had ceased to see the shadow of Dunsey across his path; and the path now lay straight forward to the accomplishment of his best, longest-cherished wishes. Everybody said Mr Godfrey had taken the right turn; and it was pretty clear what would be the end of things, for there were not many days in the week that he was not seen riding to the Warrens. Godfrey himself, when he was asked jocosely if the day had been fixed, smiled with the pleasant consciousness of a lover who could say 'yes', if he liked. He felt a reformed man, delivered from temptation; and the vision of his future life seemed to him as a promised land for which he had no cause to fight. He saw himself with all his happiness centred on his own hearth, while Nancy would smile on him as he played with the children.

And that other child, not on the hearth – he would not forget it; he would see that it was well provided for. That was a father's duty.

PART II

CHAPTER 16

It was a bright autumn Sunday, sixteen years after Silas Marner had found his new treasure on the hearth. The bells of the old Raveloe church were ringing the cheerful peal which told that the morning service was ended; and out of the arched doorway in the tower came slowly, retarded by friendly greetings and questions, the richer parishioners who had chosen this bright Sunday morning as eligible for church-going. It was the rural fashion of that time for the more important members of the congregation to depart first, while their humbler neighbours waited and looked on, stroking their bent heads or dropping their curtsies to any large ratepayer who turned to notice them.

Foremost among these advancing groups of well-clad people, there are some whom we shall recognise, in spite of Time, who has laid his hand on them all. The tall blond man of forty is not much changed in feature from the Godfrey Cass of six-and-twenty: he is only fuller in flesh, and has only lost the indefinable look of youth – a loss which is marked even when the eye is undulled and the wrinkles are not yet come. Perhaps the pretty woman, not much younger than he, who is leaning on his arm, is more changed than her husband: the lovely bloom that used to be always on her cheek now comes but fitfully, with the fresh morning air or with some strong surprise; yet to all who love human faces best for what they tell of human experience, Nancy's beauty has a heightened interest. Often the soul is ripened into fuller goodness while age has spread an ugly film, so that mere glances can never divine the preciousness of the fruit. But the years have not been so cruel to Nancy. The firm yet placid mouth, the clear veracious glance of the brown eyes, speak now of a nature that has been tested and has kept its highest qualities; and even the costume, with its dainty neatness and purity, has more significance now the coquetries of youth can have nothing to do with it.

Mr and Mrs Godfrey Cass (any higher title has died away

from Raveloe lips since the old Squire was gathered to his fathers and his inheritance was divided) have turned round to look for the tall aged man and the plainly dressed woman who are a little behind – Nancy having observed that they must wait for 'father and Priscilla' – and now they all turn into a narrower path leading across the churchyard to a small gate opposite the Red House. We will not follow them now; for may there not be some others in this departing congregation whom we should like to see again – some of those who are not likely to be handsomely clad, and whom we may not recognise so easily as the master and mistress of the Red House?

But it is impossible to mistake Silas Marner. His large brown eyes seem to have gathered a longer vision, as is the way with eyes that have been short-sighted in early life, and they have a less vague, a more answering gaze; but in everything else one sees signs of a frame much enfeebled by the lapse of the sixteen years. The weaver's bent shoulders and white hair give him almost the look of advanced age, though he is not more than five-and-fifty; but there is the freshest blossom of youth close by his side – a blond dimpled girl of eighteen, who has vainly tried to chastise her curly auburn hair into smoothness under her brown bonnet: the hair ripples as obstinately as a brooklet under the March breeze, and the little ringlets burst away from the restraining comb behind and show themselves below the bonnet-crown. Eppie cannot help being rather vexed about her hair, for there is no other girl in Raveloe who has hair at all like it, and she thinks hair ought to be smooth. She does not like to be blameworthy even in small things: you see how neatly her prayer-book is folded in her spotted handkerchief.

That good-looking young fellow, in a new fustian[1] suit, who walks behind her, is not quite sure upon the question of hair in the abstract, when Eppie puts it to him, and thinks that perhaps straight hair is the best in general, but he doesn't want Eppie's hair to be different. She surely divines that there is some one behind her who is thinking about her very particularly, and mustering courage to come to her side as soon as they are out in the lane, else why should she look rather shy, and take care not to turn away her head from her father Silas, to whom she keeps murmuring little sentences as to who was at church, and who was not at church, and how pretty the red mountain-ash is over the Rectory wall!

'I wish *we* had a little garden, father, with double daisies in, like Mrs Winthrop's,' said Eppie, when they were out in the lane; 'only they say it 'ud take a deal of digging and bringing fresh soil – and you couldn't do that, could you, father? Anyhow, I shouldn't like you to do it, for it 'ud be too hard work for you.'

'Yes, I could do it, child, if you want a bit o' garden: these long evenings, I could work at taking in a little bit o' the waste, just enough for a root or two o' flowers for you; and again, i' the morning, I could have a turn wi' the spade before I sat down to the loom. Why didn't you tell me before as you wanted a bit o' garden?'

'I can dig it for you, Master Marner,' said the young man in fustian, who was now by Eppie's side, entering into the conversation without the trouble of formalities. 'It'll be play to me after I've done my day's work, or any odd bits o' time when the work's slack. And I'll bring you some soil from Mr Cass's garden – he'll let me, and willing.'

'Eh, Aaron, my lad, are you there?' said Silas; 'I wasn't aware of you; for when Eppie's talking o' things, I see nothing but what she's a-saying. Well, if you could help me with the digging, we might get her a bit o' garden all the sooner.'

'Then if you think well and good,' said Aaron, 'I'll come to the Stone-pits this afternoon, and we'll settle what land's to be taken in, and I'll get up an hour earlier i' the morning, and begin on it.'

'But not if you don't promise me not to work at the hard digging, father,' said Eppie. 'For I shouldn't ha' said anything about it,' she added, half-bashfully half-roguishly, 'only Mrs Winthrop said as Aaron 'ud be so good, and – '

'And you might ha' known it without mother telling you,' said Aaron. 'And Master Marner knows too, I hope, as I'm able and willing to do a turn o' work for him, and he won't do me the unkindness to anyways take it out o' my hands.'

'There, now, father, you won't work in it till it's all easy,' said Eppie, 'and you and me can mark out the beds, and make holes and plant the roots. It'll be a deal livelier at the Stone-pits when we've got some flowers, for I always think the flowers can see us and know what we're talking about. And I'll have a bit o' rosemary, and bergamot, and thyme, because they're so sweet-smelling; but there's no lavender only in the gentlefolks' gardens, I think.'[2]

'That's no reason why you shouldn't have some,' said Aaron,

'for I can bring you slips of anything; I'm forced to cut no end of 'em when I'm gardening, and throw 'em away mostly. There's a big bed o' lavender at the Red House: the missis is very fond of it.'

'Well,' said Silas, gravely, 'so as you don't make free for us, or ask for anything as is worth much at the Red House: for Mr Cass's been so good to us, and built us up the new end o' the cottage, and given us beds and things, as I couldn't abide to be imposin' for garden-stuff or anything else.'

'No, no, there's no imposin',' said Aaron; 'there's never a garden in all the parish but what there's endless waste in it for want o' somebody as could use everything up. It's what I think to myself sometimes, as there need nobody run short o' victuals if the land was made the most on, and there was never a morsel but what could find its way to a mouth. It sets one thinking o' that – gardening does. But I must go back now, else mother 'ull be in trouble as I aren't there.'

'Bring her with you this afternoon, Aaron,' said Eppie; 'I shouldn't like to fix about the garden, and her not know everything from the first – should *you*, father?'

'Ay, bring her if you can, Aaron,' said Silas; 'she's sure to have a word to say as 'll help us to set things on their right end.'

Aaron turned back up the village, while Silas and Eppie went on up the lonely sheltered lane.

'O daddy!' she began, when they were in privacy, clasping and squeezing Silas's arm, and skipping round to give him an energetic kiss. 'My little old daddy! I'm so glad. I don't think I shall want anything else when we've got a little garden; and I knew Aaron would dig it for us,' she went on with roguish triumph – 'I knew that very well.'

'You're a deep little puss, you are,' said Silas, with the mild passive happiness of love-crowned age in his face; but you'll make yourself fine and beholden to Aaron.'

'O no, I shan't,' said Eppie, laughing and frisking; 'he likes it.'

'Come, come, let me carry your prayer-book, else you'll be dropping it, jumping i' that way.'

Eppie was now aware that her behaviour was under observation, but it was only the observation of a friendly donkey, browsing with a log fastened to his foot – a meek donkey, not scornfully critical of human trivialities, but thankful to share in them, if possible, by getting his nose scratched; and Eppie did not fail to gratify him with her usual notice, though it was attended with the inconvenience of his following them, painfully, up to the very door of their home.

But the sound of a sharp bark inside, as Eppie put the key in the door, modified the donkey's views, and he limped away again without bidding. The sharp bark was the sign of an excited welcome that was awaiting them from a knowing brown terrier, who, after dancing at their legs in a hysterical manner, rushed with a worrying noise at a tortoise-shell kitten under the loom, and then rushed back with a sharp bark again, as much as to say, 'I have done my duty by this feeble creature, you perceive'; while the lady-mother of the kitten sat sunning her white bosom in the window, and looked round with a sleepy air of expecting caresses, though she was not going to take any trouble for them.

The presence of this happy animal life was not the only change which had come over the interior of the stone cottage. There was no bed now in the living-room and the small space was well filled with decent furniture, all bright and clean enough to satisfy Dolly Winthrop's eye. The oaken table and three-cornered oaken chair were hardly what was likely to be seen in so poor a cottage: they had come, with the beds and other things, from the Red House; for Mr Godfrey Cass, as every one said in the village, did very kindly by the weaver; and it was nothing but right a man should be looked on and helped by those who could afford it, when he had brought up an orphan child, and been father and mother to her – and had lost his money too, so as he had nothing but what he worked for week by week, and when the weaving was going down too – for there was less and less flax spun – and Master Marner was none so young. Nobody was jealous of the weaver, for he was regarded as an exceptional person, whose claims on neighbourly help were not to be matched in Raveloe. Any superstition that remained concerning him had taken an entirely new colour; and Mr Macey, now a very feeble old man of fourscore and six, never seen except in his chimney-corner or sitting in the sunshine at his door-sill, was of opinion that when a man had done what Silas had done by an orphan child, it was a sign that his money would come to light again, or leastwise that the robber would be made to answer for it – for, as Mr Macey observed of himself, his faculties were as strong as ever.

Silas sat down now and watched Eppie with a satisfied gaze as she spread the clean cloth, and set on it the potato-pie, warmed up slowly in a safe Sunday fashion, by being put into a dry pot over a slowly-dying fire, as the best substitute for an oven. For Silas would not consent to have a grate and oven added to his conveniences: he loved the old brick hearth as he had loved his brown pot – and was it not there when he had found Eppie? The gods of the hearth[3] exist for us still; and let all new faith be tolerant of that fetishism, lest it bruise its own roots.

Silas ate his dinner more silently than usual, soon laying down his knife and fork, and watching half-abstractedly Eppie's play with Snap and the cat, by which her own dining was made rather a lengthy business. Yet it was a sight that might well arrest wandering thoughts: Eppie, with the rippling radiance of her hair and the whiteness of her rounded chin and throat set off by the dark-blue cotton gown, laughing merrily as the kitten held on with her four claws to one shoulder, like a design for a jug-handle, while Snap on the right hand and Puss on the other put up their paws towards a morsel which she held out of the reach of both – Snap occasionally desisting in order to remonstrate with the cat by a cogent worrying growl on the greediness and futility of her conduct; till Eppie relented, caressed them both, and divided the morsel between them.

But at last Eppie, glancing at the clock, checked the play, and said, 'O daddy, you're wanting to go into the sunshine to smoke your pipe. But I must clear away first, so as the house may be tidy when godmother comes. I'll make haste – I won't be long.'

Silas had taken to smoking a pipe daily during the last two years, having been strongly urged to it by the sages of Raveloe, as a practice 'good for the fits'; and this advice was sanctioned by Dr Kimble, on the ground that it was as well to try what could do no harm – a principle which was made to answer for a great deal of work in that gentleman's medical practice. Silas did not highly enjoy smoking, and often wondered how his neighbours could be so fond of it; but a humble sort of acquiescence in what was held to be good, had become a strong habit of that new self which had been developed in him since he had found Eppie on his hearth: it had been the only clew his bewildered mind could hold by in cherishing this young life that had been sent to him out of the darkness into which his gold had departed. By seeking what was needful for Eppie, by sharing the effect that everything produced on her, he had himself come to appropriate the forms of custom and belief which were the mould of Raveloe life; and as, with reawakening sensibilities, memory also reawakened, he had begun to ponder over the elements of his old faith, and blend them with his new impressions, till he recovered a consciousness of unity between his past and present. The sense of presiding goodness and the human trust which come with all pure peace and joy, had given him a dim impression that there had been some error, some mistake, which had thrown that dark shadow over the days of his best years; and as it grew more and more easy to him to open his mind to Dolly Winthrop, he gradually communicated to her all he could describe of his early life. The communication was necessarily a slow and difficult process, for Silas's meagre power of explanation was not aided by any readiness of interpretation in Dolly, whose narrow outward experience gave her no key to strange customs, and made every novelty a source of wonder that arrested them at every step of the narrative. It was only by fragments, and at intervals which left Dolly time to revolve what she had heard till it acquired some familiarity for her, that Silas at last arrived at the climax of the sad story – the drawing of lots, and its false testimony concerning him; and this had to be repeated in several interviews, under new questions on her part as to the nature of this plan for detecting the guilty and clearing the innocent.

'And yourn's the same Bible, you're sure o' that, Master Marner – the Bible as you brought wi' you from that country – it's the same as what they've got at church, and what Eppie's a-learning to read in?'

'Yes,' said Silas, 'every bit the same; and there's drawing o' lots in the Bible, mind you,' he added in a lower tone.

'O dear, dear,' said Dolly in a grieved voice, as if she were hearing an unfavourable report of a sick man's case. She was silent for some minutes; at last she said –

'There's wise folks, happen, as know how it all is; the parson knows, I'll be bound; but it takes big words to tell them things, and such as poor folks can't make much out on. I can never rightly know the meaning o' what I hear at church, only a bit here and there, but I know it's good words – I do. But what lies upo' your mind – it's this, Master Marner: as, if Them above had done the right thing by you, They'd never ha' let you be turned out for a wicked thief when you was innicent.'

'Ah!' said Silas, who had now come to understand Dolly's phraseology, 'that was what fell on me like as if it had been red-hot iron; because, you see, there was nobody as cared for me or clave to me above nor below. And him as I'd gone out and in wi' for ten year and more, since when we was lads and went halves – mine own familiar friend in whom I trusted, had lifted up his heel again' me, and worked to ruin me.'

'Eh, but he was a bad 'un – I can't think as there's another such,' said Dolly. 'But I'm o'er-come, Master Marner; I'm like as if I'd waked and didn't know whether it was night or morning. I feel somehow as sure as I do when I've laid something up though I can't justly put my hand on it, as there was a rights in what happened to you, if one could but make it out; and you'd no call to lose heart as you did. But we'll talk on it again; for sometimes things come into my head when I'm leeching⁴ or poulticing, or such, as I could never think on when I was sitting still.'

Dolly was too useful a woman not to have many opportunities of illumination of the kind she alluded to, and she was not long before she recurred to the subject.

'Master Marner,' she said, one day that she came to bring home Eppie's washing, 'I've been sore puzzled for a good bit wi' that trouble o' yourn and the drawing o' lots; and it got twisted back'ards and for'ards, as I didn't know which end to lay hold on. But it come to me all clear like, that night when I was sitting up wi' poor Bessy Fawkes, as is dead and left her children behind, God help 'em – it come to me as clear as daylight; but whether I've got hold on it now, or can anyways bring it to my tongue's end, that I don't know. For I've often a deal inside me as 'll never come out; and for what you talk o' your folks in your old country niver saying prayers by heart nor saying 'em out of a book, they must be wonderful cliver; for if I didn't know "Our Father", and little bits o' good works as I can carry out o' church wi' me, I might down o' my knees every night, but nothing could I say.'

'But you can mostly say something as I can make sense on, Mrs Winthrop,' said Silas.

'Well, then, Master Marner, it come to me summat like this: I can make nothing o' the drawing o' lots and the answer coming wrong; it 'ud mayhap take the parson to tell that, and he could only tell us i' big words. But what come to me as clear as the daylight, it was when I was troubling over poor Bessy Fawkes, and it allays comes into my head when I'm sorry for folks, and feel as I can't do a power to help 'em, not if I was to get up i' the middle o' the night – it comes into my head as Them above has got a deal tenderer heart nor what I've got – for I can't be anyways better nor Them as made me; and if anything looks hard to me, it's because there's things I don't know on; and for the matter o' that, there may be plenty o' things I don't know on, for it's little as I know – that it is. And so, while I was thinking o' that, you come into my mind, Master Marner, and it all come pouring in: – if *I* felt i' my inside what was the right and just thing by you, and them as prayed and drawed the lots, all but that wicked un, if *they*'d ha' done the right thing by you if they could, isn't there Them as was at the making on us, and knows better and has a better will? And that's all as ever I can be sure on, and everything else is a big puzzle to me when I think on it. For there was the fever come and took off them as were full-growed, and left the helpless children; and there's the breaking o' limbs; and them as 'ud do right and be sober have to suffer by them as are contrairy – eh, there's trouble i' this world, and there's things as we can niver make out the rights on. And all as we've got to do is to trusten, Master Marner – to do the right thing as fur as we know, and to trusten. For if us as knows so little can see a bit o' good and rights, we may be sure as there's a good and a rights bigger nor what we can know – I feel it i' my own inside as it must be so. And if you could but ha' gone on trustening, Master Marner, you wouldn't ha' run away from your fellow-creaturs and been so lone.'

'Ah, but that 'ud ha' been hard,' said Silas, in an under-tone; 'it 'ud ha' been hard to trusten then.'

'And so it would,' said Dolly, almost with compunction; 'them things are easier said nor done; and I'm partly ashamed o' talking.'

'Nay, nay,' said Silas, 'you're i' the right, Mrs Winthrop – you're i' the right. There's good i' this world – I've a feeling o' that now; and it makes a man feel as there's a good more nor he can see, i' spite o' the trouble and the wickedness. That drawing o' the lots is dark; but the child was sent to me: there's dealings with us – there's dealings.'

This dialogue took place in Eppie's earlier years, when Silas had to part with her for two hours every day, that she might learn to read at the dame school,[5] after he had vainly tried himself to guide her in that first step to learning. Now that she was grown up, Silas had often been led, in those moments of quiet outpouring which come to people who live together in perfect love, to talk with *her* too of the past, and how and why he had lived a lonely man until she had been sent to him. For it would have been impossible for him to hide from Eppie that she was not his own child: even if the most delicate reticence on the point could have been expected from Raveloe gossips in her presence, her own questions about her mother could not have been parried, as she grew up, without that complete shrouding of the past which would have made a painful barrier between their minds. So Eppie had long known how her mother had died on the snowy ground, and how she herself had been found on the hearth by father Silas, who had taken her golden curls for his lost guineas brought back to him. The tender and peculiar love with which Silas had reared her in almost inseparable companionship with himself, aided by the seclusion of their dwelling, had preserved her from the lowering influences of the village talk and habits, and had kept her mind in that freshness which is sometimes falsely supposed to be an invariable attribute of rusticity. Perfect love has a breath of poetry which can exalt the relations of the least-instructed human beings; and this breath of poetry had surrounded Eppie from the time when she had followed the bright gleam that beckoned her to Silas's hearth; so that it is not surprising if, in other things besides her delicate prettiness, she was not quite a common village maiden, but had a touch of refinement and fervour which came from no other teaching than that of tenderly-nurtured unvitiated feeling. She was too childish and simple for her imagination to rove into questions about her unknown father; for a long while it did not even occur to her that she must have had a father; and the first time that the idea of her mother having had a husband presented itself to her, was when Silas showed her the wedding-ring which had been taken from the wasted finger, and had been carefully preserved by him in a little lackered box shaped like a shoe. He delivered this box into Eppie's charge when she had grown up, and she often opened it to look at the ring: but still she thought hardly at all about the father of whom it was the symbol. Had she not a father very close to her, who loved her better than any real fathers in the village seemed to love their daughters? On the contrary, who her mother was, and how she came to die in that forlornness, were questions that often pressed on Eppie's mind. Her knowledge of Mrs Winthrop, who was her nearest friend next to Silas, made her feel that a mother must be very precious; and she had again and again asked Silas to tell her how her mother looked, whom she was like, and how he had found her against the furze bush, led towards it by the little footsteps and the outstretched arms. The furze bush was there still; and this afternoon, when Eppie came out with Silas into the sunshine, it was the first object that arrested her eyes and thoughts.

'Father,' she said, in a tone of gentle gravity, which sometimes came like a sadder, slower cadence across her playfulness, 'we shall take the furze bush into the garden; it'll come into the corner, and just against it I'll put snowdrops and crocuses, 'cause Aaron says they won't die out, but'll always get more and more.'

'Ah, child,' said Silas, always ready to talk when he had his pipe in his hand, apparently enjoying the pauses more than the puffs, 'it wouldn't do to leave out the furze bush; and there's nothing prettier to my thinking, when it's yallow with flowers. But it's just come into my head what we're to do for a fence – mayhap Aaron can help us to a thought; but a fence we must have, else the donkeys and things 'ull come and trample everything down. And fencing's hard to be got at, by what I can make out.'

'O, I'll tell you, daddy,' said Eppie, clasping her hands suddenly, after a minute's thought. 'There's lots o' loose stones about, some of 'em not big, and we might lay 'em atop of one another, and make a wall. You and me could carry the smallest, and Aaron 'ud carry the rest – I know he would.'

'Eh, my precious un,' said Silas, 'there isn't enough stones to go all round; and as for you carrying, why, wi' your little arms you couldn't carry a stone no bigger than a turnip. You're dillicate made, my dear,' he added, with a tender intonation – 'that's what Mrs Winthrop says.'

'O, I'm stronger than you think, daddy,' said Eppie; 'and if there wasn't stones enough to go all round, why they'll go part o' the way, and then it 'll be easier to get sticks and things for the rest. See here, round the big pit, what a many stones!'

She skipped forward to the pit, meaning to lift one of the stones and exhibit her strength, but she started back in surprise.

'O, father, just come and look here,' she exclaimed – 'come and see how the water's gone down since yesterday. Why, yesterday the pit was ever so full!'

'Well, to be sure,' said Silas, coming to her side. 'Why, that's the draining they've begun on, since harvest, i' Mr Osgood's fields, I reckon. The foreman said to me the other day, when I passed by 'em, "Master Marner," he said, "I shouldn't wonder if we lay your bit o' waste as dry as a bone." It was Mr Godfrey Cass, he said, had gone into the draining: he'd been taking these fields o' Mr Osgood.'

'How odd it'll seem to have the old pit dried up!' said Eppie, turning away, and stooping to lift rather a large stone. 'See, daddy, I can carry this quite well,' she said, going along with much energy for a few steps, but presently letting it fall.

'Ah, you're fine and strong, arn't you?' said Silas, while Eppie shook her aching arms and laughed. 'Come, come, let us go and sit down on the bank against the stile there, and have no more lifting. You might hurt yourself, child. You'd need have somebody to work for you – and my arm isn't overstrong.'

Silas uttered the last sentence slowly, as if it implied more than met the ear; and Eppie, when they sat down on the bank, nestled close to his side, and, taking hold caressingly of the arm that was not over strong, held it on her lap, while Silas puffed again dutifully at the pipe, which occupied his other arm. An ash in the hedgerow behind made a fretted screen from the sun, and threw happy playful shadows all about them.

'Father,' said Eppie, very gently, after they had been sitting in silence a little while, 'if I was to be married, ought I to be married with my mother's ring?'

Silas gave an almost imperceptible start, though the question fell in with the under-current of thought in his own mind, and then said, in a subdued tone, 'Why, Eppie, have you been a-thinking on it?'

'Only this last week, father,' said Eppie, ingenuously, 'since Aaron talked to me about it.'

'And what did he say?' said Silas, still in the same subdued way, as if he were anxious lest he should fall into the slightest tone that was not for Eppie's good.

'He said he should like to be married, because he was a-going in four-and-twenty, and had got a deal of gardening work, now Mr Mott's given up; and he goes twice a-week regular to Mr Cass's, and once to Mr Osgood's, and they're going to take him on at the Rectory.'

'And who is it as he's wanting to marry?' said Silas, with rather a sad smile.

'Why, me, to be sure, daddy,' said Eppie, with dimpling laughter, kissing her father's cheek; 'as if he'd want to marry anybody else!'

'And you mean to have him, do you?' said Silas.

'Yes, some time,' said Eppie, 'I don't know when. Everybody's married some time, Aaron says. But I told him that wasn't true: for, I said, look at father – he's never been married.'

'No, child,' said Silas, 'your father was a lone man till you was sent to him.'

'But you'll never be lone again, father,' said Eppie, tenderly. 'That was what Aaron said – "I could never think o' taking you away from Master Marner, Eppie." And I said, "It 'ud be no use if you did, Aaron." And he wants us all to live together, so as you needn't work a bit, father, only what's for your own pleasure; and he'd be as good as a son to you – that was what he said.'

'And should you like that, Eppie?' said Silas, looking at her.

'I shouldn't mind it, father,' said Eppie, quite simply. 'And I should like things to be so as you needn't work much. But if it wasn't for that, I'd sooner things didn't change. I'm very happy: I like Aaron to be fond of me, and come and see us often, and behave pretty to you – he always *does* behave pretty to you, doesn't he, father?'

'Yes, child, nobody could behave better,' said Silas, emphatically. 'He's his mother's lad.'

'But I don't want any change,' said Eppie. 'I should like to go on a long, long while, just as we are. Only Aaron does want a change; and he made me cry a bit – only a bit – because he said I didn't care for him, for if I cared for him I should want us to be married, as he did.'

'Eh, my blessed child,' said Silas, laying down his pipe as if it were useless to pretend to smoke any longer, 'you're o'er young to be married. We'll ask Mrs Winthrop – we'll ask Aaron's mother what *she* thinks: if there's a right thing to do, she'll come at it. But there's this to be thought on, Eppie: things *will* change, whether we like it or no; things won't go on for a long while just as they are and no difference. I shall get older and helplesser, and be a burden on you, belike, if I don't go away from you altogether. Not as I mean you'd think me a burden – I know you wouldn't – but it 'ud be hard upon you; and when I look for'ard to that, I like to think as you'd have somebody else besides me – somebody young and strong, as 'll outlast your own life, and take care on you to the end.' Silas paused, and, resting his wrists on his knees, lifted his hands up and down meditatively as he looked on the ground.

'Then, would you like me to be married, father?' said Eppie, with a little trembling in her voice.

'I'll not be the man to say no, Eppie,' said Silas, emphatically; 'but we'll ask your godmother. She'll wish the right thing by you and her son too.'

'There they come then,' said Eppie. 'Let us go and meet 'em. O the Pipe! won't you have it lit again, father?' said Eppie, lifting that medicinal appliance from the ground.

'Nay, child,' said Silas, 'I've done enough for today. I think, mayhap, a little of it does me more good than so much at once.'

CHAPTER 17

While Silas and Eppie were seated on the bank discoursing in the fleckered shade of the ash-tree, Miss Priscilla Lammeter was resisting her sister's arguments, that it would be better to take tea at the Red House, and let her father have a long nap, than drive home to the Warrens so soon after dinner. The family party (of four only) were seated round the table in the dark wainscoted parlour, with the Sunday dessert before them, of fresh filberts,[1] apples, and pears, duly ornamented with leaves by Nancy's own hand before the bells had rung for church.

A great change has come over the dark wainscoted parlour since we saw it in Godfrey's bachelor days, and under the wifeless reign of the old Squire. Now all is polish, on which no yesterday's dust is ever allowed to rest, from the yard's width of oaken boards round the carpet, to the old Squire's gun and whips and walking-sticks, ranged on the stag's antlers above the mantelpiece. All other signs of sporting and outdoor occupation Nancy has removed to another room; but she has brought into the Red House the habit of filial reverence, and preserves sacredly in a place of honour these relics of her husband's departed father. The tankards are on the sidetable still, but the bossed silver is undimmed by handling, and there are no dregs to send forth unpleasant suggestions: the only prevailing scent is of the lavender and rose-leaves that fill the vases of Derbyshire spar.[2] All is purity and order in this once dreary room, for, fifteen years ago, it was entered by a new presiding spirit.

'Now father,' said Nancy, '*is* there any call for you to go home to tea? Mayn't you just as well stay with us? – such a beautiful evening as it's likely to be.'

The old gentleman had been talking with Godfrey about the increasing poor-rate[3] and the ruinous times, and had not heard the dialogue between his daughters.

'My dear, you must ask Priscilla,' he said, in the once firm voice, now become rather broken. 'She manages me and the farm too.'

'And reason good as I should manage you, father,' said Priscilla, 'else you'd be giving yourself your death with rheumatism. And as for the farm, if anything turns out wrong, as it can't but do in these times, there's nothing kills a man so soon as having nobody to find fault with but himself. It's a deal the best way o' being master, to let somebody else do the ordering, and keep the blaming in your own hands. It 'ud save many a man a stroke, I believe.'

'Well, well, my dear,' said her father, with a quiet laugh, 'I didn't say you don't manage for everybody's good.'

'Then manage so as you may stay tea, Priscilla,' said Nancy, putting her hand on her sister's arm affectionately. 'Come now; and we'll go round the garden while father has his nap.'

'My dear child, he'll have a beautiful nap in the gig, for I shall drive. And as for staying tea, I can't hear of it; for there's this dairymaid, now she knows she's to be married, turned Michaelmas, she'd as lief pour the new milk into the pig-trough as into the pans. That's the way with 'em all: it's as if they thought the world 'ud be new-made because they're to be married. So come and let me put my bonnet on, and there'll be time for us to walk round the garden while the horse is being put in.'

When the sisters were treading the neatly-swept garden-walks, between the bright turf that contrasted pleasantly with the dark cones and arches and wall-like hedges of yew, Priscilla said –

'I'm as glad as anything at your husband's making that exchange o' land with cousin Osgood, and beginning the dairying. It's a thousand pities you didn't do it before; for it'll give you something to fill your mind. There's nothing like a dairy if folks want a bit o' worrit to make the days pass. For as for rubbing furniture, when you can once see your face in a table there's nothing else to look for; but there's always something fresh with the dairy; for even in the depths o' winter there's some pleasure in conquering the butter, and making it come whether or no. My dear,' added Priscilla, pressing her sister's hand affectionately as they walked side by side, 'you'll never be low when you've got a dairy.'

'Ah, Priscilla,' said Nancy, returning the pressure with a grateful glance of her clear eyes, 'but it won't make up to Godfrey: a dairy's not so much to a man. And it's only what he cares for that ever makes me low. I'm contented with the blessings we have, if he could be contented.'

'It drives me past patience,' said Priscilla, impetuously, 'that way o' the men – always wanting and wanting, and never easy with what they've got: they can't sit comfortable in their chairs when they've neither ache nor pain, but either they must stick a pipe in their mouths, to make 'em better than well, or else they must be swallowing something strong, though they're forced to make haste before the next meal comes in. But joyful be it spoken, our father was never that sort o' man. And if it had pleased God to make you ugly, like me, so as the men wouldn't ha' run after you, we might have kept to our own family, and had nothing to do with folks as have got uneasy blood in their veins.'

'O don't say so, Priscilla,' said Nancy, repenting that she had called forth this outburst; 'nobody has any occasion to find fault with Godfrey. It's natural he should be disappointed at not having any children: every man likes to have somebody to work for and lay by for, and he always counted so on making a fuss with 'em when they were little. There's many another man 'ud hanker more than he does. He's the best of husbands.'

'O, I know,' said Priscilla, smiling sarcastically, 'I know the way o' wives; they set one on to abuse their husbands, and then they turn round on one and praise 'em as if they wanted to sell 'em. But father'll be waiting for me; we must turn now.'

The large gig with the steady old grey was at the front door, and Mr Lammeter was already on the stone steps, passing the time in recalling to Godfrey what very fine points Speckle had when his master used to ride him.

'I always *would* have a good horse, you know,' said the old gentleman, not liking that spirited time to be quite effaced from the memory of his juniors.

'Mind you bring Nancy to the Warrens before the week's out, Mr Cass,' was Priscilla's parting injunction, as she took the reins, and shook them gently, by way of friendly incitement to Speckle.

'I shall just take a turn to the fields against the Stone-pits, Nancy, and look at the draining,' said Godfrey.

'You'll be in again by tea-time, dear?'

'O yes, I shall be back in an hour.'

It was Godfrey's custom on a Sunday afternoon to do a little contemplative farming in a leisurely walk. Nancy seldom accompanied him, for the women of her generation – unless, like Priscilla, they took to outdoor management – were not given to much walking beyond their own house and garden, finding sufficient exercise in domestic duties. So, when Priscilla was not with her, she usually sat with Mant's Bible[4] before her, and after following the text with her eyes for a little while, she would gradually permit them to wander as her thoughts had already insisted on wandering.

But Nancy's Sunday thoughts were rarely quite out of keeping with the devout and reverential intention implied by the book spread open before her. She was not theologically instructed enough to discern very clearly the relation between the sacred documents of the past which she opened without method, and her own obscure, simple life; but the spirit of rectitude, and the sense of responsibility for the effect of her conduct on others, which were strong elements in Nancy's character, had made it a habit with her to scrutinise her past feelings and actions with self-questioning solicitude. Her mind not being courted by a great variety of subjects, she filled the vacant moments by living inwardly, again and again, through all her remembered experience, especially through the fifteen years of her married time, in which her life and its significance had been doubled. She recalled the small details, the words, tones, and looks, in the critical scenes which had opened a new epoch for her by giving her a deeper insight into the relations and trials of life, or which had called on her for some little effort of forbearance, or of painful adherence to an imagined or real duty – asking herself continually whether she had been in any respect blamable. This excessive rumination and self-questioning is perhaps a morbid habit inevitable to a mind of much moral sensibility when shut out from its due share of outward activity and of practical claims on its affections – inevitable to a noble-hearted, childless woman, when her lot is narrow. 'I can do so little – have I done it all well?' is the perpetually recurring thought; and there are no voices calling her away from that soliloquy, no peremptory demands to divert energy from vain regret or superfluous scruple.

There was one main thread of painful experience in Nancy's married life, and on it hung certain deeply-felt scenes, which were the oftenest revived in retrospect. The short dialogue with

Priscilla in the garden had determined the current of retrospect in that frequent direction this particular Sunday afternoon. The first wandering of her thought from the text, which she still attempted dutifully to follow with her eyes and silent lips, was into an imaginary enlargement of the defence she had set up for her husband against Priscilla's implied blame. The vindication of the loved object is the best balm affection can find for its wounds: – 'A man must have so much on his mind', is the belief by which a wife often supports a cheerful face under rough answers and unfeeling words. And Nancy's deepest wounds had all come from the perception that the absence of children from their hearth was dwelt on in her husband's mind as a privation to which he could not reconcile himself.

Yet sweet Nancy might have been expected to feel still more keenly the denial of a blessing to which she had looked forward with all the varied expectations and preparations, solemn and prettily trivial, which fill the mind of a loving woman when she expects to become a mother. Was there not a drawer filled with the neat work of her hands, all unworn and untouched, just as she had arranged it there fourteen years ago – just, but for one little dress, which had been made the burial-dress? But under this immediate personal trial Nancy was so firmly unmurmuring, that years ago she had suddenly renounced the habit of visiting this drawer, lest she should in this way be cherishing a longing for what was not given.

Perhaps it was this very severity towards any indulgence of what she held to be sinful regret in herself, that made her shrink from applying her own standard to her husband. 'It is very different – it is much worse for a man to be disappointed in that way: a woman can always be satisfied with devoting herself to her husband, but a man wants something that will make him look forward more – and sitting by the fire is so much duller to him than to a woman.' And always, when Nancy reached this point in her meditations – trying, with predetermined sympathy, to see everything as Godfrey saw it – there came a renewal of self-questioning. *Had* she done everything in her power to lighten Godfrey's privation? Had she really been right in the resistance which had cost her so much pain six years ago, and again four years ago – the resistance to her husband's wish that they should adopt a child? Adoption was more remote from the ideas and habits of that time than of our own; still Nancy had her opinion on it. It was as necessary to her mind to have an opinion on all topics, not exclusively masculine, that had come under her notice, as for her to have a precisely marked place for every article of her personal property: and her opinions were always principles to be unwaveringly acted on. They were firm, not because of their basis, but because she held them with a tenacity inseparable from her mental action. On all the duties and proprieties of life, from filial behaviour to the arrangements of the evening toilet, pretty Nancy Lammeter, by the time she was three-and-twenty, had her unalterable little code, and had formed every one of her habits in strict accordance with that code. She carried these decided judgments within her in the most unobtrusive way: they rooted themselves in her mind, and grew there as quietly as grass. Years ago, we know, she insisted on dressing like Priscilla, because 'it was right for sisters to dress alike', and because 'she would do what was right if she wore a gown dyed with cheese-colouring.' That was a trivial but typical instance of the mode in which Nancy's life was regulated.

It was one of those rigid principles, and no petty egoistic feeling, which had been the ground of Nancy's difficult resistance to her husband's wish. To adopt a child, because children of your own had been denied you, was to try and choose your lot in spite of Providence: the adopted child, she was convinced, would never turn out well, and would be a curse to those who had wilfully and rebelliously sought what it was clear that, for some high reason, they were better without. When you saw a thing was not meant to be, said Nancy, it was a bounden duty to leave off so much as wishing for it. And so far, perhaps, the wisest of men could scarcely make more than a verbal improvement in her principle. But the conditions under which she held it apparent that a thing was not meant to be, depended on a more peculiar mode of thinking. She would have given up making a purchase at a particular place if, on three successive times, rain, or some other cause of Heaven's sending, had formed an obstacle; and she would have anticipated a broken limb or other heavy misfortune to any one who persisted in spite of such indications.

'But why should you think the child would turn out ill?' said Godfrey, in his remonstrances. 'She has thriven as well as child can do with the weaver; and *he* adopted her. There isn't such a pretty little girl anywhere else in the parish, or one fitter for the station we could give her. Where can be the likelihood of her being a curse to anybody?'

'Yes, my dear Godfrey,' said Nancy, who was sitting with her hands tightly clasped together, and with yearning, regretful affection in her eyes. 'The child may not turn out ill with the weaver. But, then, he didn't go to seek her, as we should be doing. It will be wrong: I feel sure it will. Don't you remember what that lady we met at the Royston Baths told us about the child her sister adopted? That was the only adopting I ever heard of: and the child was transported when it was twenty-three. Dear Godfrey, don't ask me to do what I know is wrong: I should never be happy again. I know it's very hard for *you* – it's easier for me – but it's the will of Providence.'

It might seem singular that Nancy – with her religious theory pieced together out of narrow social traditions, fragments of church doctrine imperfectly understood, and girlish reasonings on her small experience – should have arrived by herself at a way of thinking so nearly akin to that of many devout people whose beliefs are held in the shape of a system quite remote from her knowledge: singular, if we did not know that human beliefs, like all other natural growths, elude the barriers of system.

Godfrey had from the first specified Eppie, then about twelve years old, as a child suitable for them to adopt. It had never occurred to him that Silas would rather part with his life than with Eppie. Surely the weaver would wish the best to the child he had taken so much trouble with, and would be glad that such good fortune should happen to her: she would always be very grateful to him, and he would be well provided for to the end of his life – provided for as the excellent part he had done by the child deserved. Was it not an appropriate thing for people in a higher station to take a charge off the hands of a man in a lower? It seemed an eminently appropriate thing to Godfrey, for reasons that were known only to himself; and by a common fallacy, he imagined the measure would be easy because he had private motives for desiring it. This was rather a coarse mode of estimating Silas's relations to Eppie; but we must remember that many of the impressions which Godfrey was likely to gather concerning the labouring people around him would favour the idea that deep affections can hardly go along with callous palms and scant means; and he had not had the opportunity, even if he had had the power, of entering intimately into all that was exceptional in the weaver's experience. It was only the want of adequate knowledge that could have made it possible for Godfrey deliberately to entertain an unfeeling project: his natural kindness had outlived that blighting time of cruel wishes, and Nancy's praise of him as a husband was not founded entirely on a wilful illusion.

'I was right,' she said to herself, when she had recalled all their scenes of discussion – 'I feel I was right to say him nay, though it hurt me more than anything; but how good Godfrey has been about it! Many men would have been very angry with me for standing out against their wishes; and they might have thrown out that they'd had ill-luck in marrying me; but Godfrey has never been the man to say me an unkind word. It's only what he can't hide: everything seems so blank to him, I know; and the land – what a difference it 'ud make to him, when he goes to see after things, if he'd children growing up that he was doing it all for! But I won't murmur; and perhaps if he'd married a woman who'd have had children, she'd have vexed him in other ways.'

This possibility was Nancy's chief comfort; and to give it greater strength, she laboured to make it impossible that any other wife should have had more perfect tenderness. She had been *forced* to vex him by that one denial. Godfrey was not insensible to her loving effort, and did Nancy no injustice as to the motives of her obstinacy. It was impossible to have lived with her fifteen years and not be aware that an unselfish clinging to the right, and a sincerity clear as the flower-born dew, were her main characteristics; indeed, Godfrey felt this so strongly, that his own more wavering nature, too averse to facing difficulty to be unvaryingly simple and truthful, was kept in a certain awe of this gentle wife who watched his looks with a yearning to obey them. It seemed to him impossible that he should ever confess to her the truth about Eppie: she would never recover from the repulsion the story of his earlier marriage would create, told to her now, after that long concealment. And the child, too, he thought, must become an object of repulsion: the very sight of her would be painful. The shock to Nancy's mingled pride and ignorance of the world's evil might even be too much for her delicate frame. Since he had married her with that secret on his heart, he must keep it there to the last.

Whatever else he did, he could not make an irreparable breach between himself and this long-loved wife.

Meanwhile, why could he not make up his mind to the absence of children from a hearth brightened by such a wife? Why did his mind fly uneasily to that void, as if it were the sole reason why life was not thoroughly joyous to him? I suppose it is the way with all men and women who reach middle age without the clear perception that life never *can* be thoroughly joyous: under the vague dulness of the grey hours, dissatisfaction seeks a definite object, and finds it in the privation of an untried good. Dissatisfaction seated musingly on a childless hearth, thinks with envy of the father whose return is greeted by young voices – seated at the meal where the little heads rise one above another like nursery plants, it sees a black care hovering behind every one of them, and thinks the impulses by which men abandon freedom, and seek for ties, are surely nothing but a brief madness. In Godfrey's case there were further reasons why his thoughts should be continually solicited by this one point in his lot: his conscience, never thoroughly easy about Eppie, now gave his childless home the aspect of a retribution; and as the time passed on, under Nancy's refusal to adopt her, any retrieval of his error became more and more difficult.

On this Sunday afternoon it was already four years since there had been any allusion to the subject between them, and Nancy supposed that it was for ever buried.

'I wonder if he'll mind it less or more as he gets older,' she thought; 'I'm afraid more. Aged people feel the miss of children: what would father do without Priscilla? And if I die, Godfrey will be very lonely – not holding together with his brothers much. But I won't be over-anxious, and trying to make things out beforehand: I must do my best for the present.'

With that last thought Nancy roused herself from her reverie, and turned her eyes again towards the forsaken page. It had been forsaken longer than she imagined, for she was presently surprised by the appearance of the servant with the tea-things. It was, in fact, a little before the usual time for tea; but Jane had her reasons.

'Is your master come into the yard, Jane?'

'No 'm, he isn't,' said Jane, with a slight emphasis, of which, however, her mistress took no notice.

'I don't know whether you've seen 'em, 'm,' continued Jane,

after a pause, 'but there's folks making haste all one way, afore the front window. I doubt something's happened. There's niver a man to be seen i' the yard, else I'd send and see. I've been up into the top attic, but there's no seeing anything for trees. I hope nobody's hurt, that's all.'

'O, no, I daresay there's nothing much the matter,' said Nancy. 'It's perhaps Mr Snell's bull got out again, as he did before.'

'I wish he mayn't gore anybody then, that's all,' said Jane, not altogether despising a hypothesis which covered a few imaginary calamities.

'That girl is always terrifying me,' thought Nancy; 'I wish Godfrey would come in.'

She went to the front window and looked as far as she could see along the road, with an uneasiness which she felt to be childish, for there were now no such signs of excitement as Jane had spoken of, and Godfrey would not be likely to return by the village road, but by the fields. She continued to stand, however, looking at the placid churchyard with the long shadows of the gravestones across the bright green hillocks, and at the glowing autumn colours of the Rectory trees beyond. Before such calm external beauty the presence of a vague fear is more distinctly felt – like a raven flapping its slow wing across the sunny air. Nancy wished more and more that Godfrey would come in.

CHAPTER 18

Some one opened the door at the other end of the room, and Nancy felt that it was her husband. She turned from the window with gladness in her eyes, for the wife's chief dread was stilled.

'Dear, I'm so thankful you're come,' she said, going towards him. 'I began to get . . .'

She paused abruptly, for Godfrey was laying down his hat with trembling hands, and turned towards her with a pale face and a strange unanswering glance, as if he saw her indeed, but saw her as part of a scene invisible to herself. She laid her hand on his arm, not daring to speak again; but he left the touch unnoticed, and threw himself into his chair.

Jane was already at the door with the hissing urn. 'Tell her to keep away, will you?' said Godfrey; and when the door was closed again he exerted himself to speak more distinctly.

'Sit down, Nancy – there,' he said, pointing to a chair opposite him. 'I came back as soon as I could, to hinder anybody's telling you but me. I've had a great shock – but I care most about the shock it'll be to you.'

'It isn't father and Priscilla?' said Nancy, with quivering lips, clasping her hands together tightly on her lap.

'No, it's nobody living,' said Godfrey, unequal to the considerate skill with which he would have wished to make his revelation. 'It's Dunstan – my brother Dunstan, that we lost sight of sixteen years ago. We've found him – found his body – his skeleton.'

The deep dread Godfrey's look had created in Nancy made her feel these words a relief. She sat in comparative calmness to hear what else he had to tell. He went on:

'The Stone-pit has gone dry suddenly – from the draining, I suppose; and there he lies – has lain for sixteen years, wedged between two great stones. There's his watch and seals, and there's my gold-handled hunting-whip, with my name on: he took it away, without my knowing, the day he went hunting on Wildfire, the last time he was seen.'

Godfrey paused: it was not so easy to say what came next. 'Do you think he drowned himself?' said Nancy, almost wondering that her husband should be so deeply shaken by what had happened all those years ago to an unloved brother, of whom worse things had been augured.

'No, he fell in,' said Godfrey, in a low but distinct voice, as if he felt some deep meaning in the fact. Presently he added: 'Dunstan was the man that robbed Silas Marner.'

The blood rushed to Nancy's face and neck at this surprise and shame, for she had been bred up to regard even a distant kinship with crime as a dishonour.

'O Godfrey!' she said, with compassion in her tone, for she had immediately reflected that the dishonour must be felt still more keenly by her husband.

'There was the money in the pit,' he continued – 'all the weaver's money. Everything's been gathered up, and they're taking the skeleton to the Rainbow. But I came back to tell you: there was no hindering it; you must know.'

He was silent, looking on the ground for two long minutes. Nancy would have said some words of comfort under this disgrace, but she refrained, from an instinctive sense that there was something behind – that Godfrey had something else to tell her. Presently he lifted his eyes to her face, and kept them fixed on her, as he said –

'Everything comes to light, Nancy, sooner or later. When God Almighty wills it, our secrets are found out. I've lived with a secret on my mind, but I'll keep it from you no longer. I wouldn't have you know it by somebody else, and not by me – I wouldn't have you find it out after I'm dead. I'll tell you now. It's been "I will" and "I won't" with me all my life – I'll make sure of myself now.'

Nancy's utmost dread had returned. The eyes of the husband and wife met with awe in them, as at a crisis which suspended affection.

'Nancy,' said Godfrey, slowly, 'when I married you, I hid something from you – something I ought to have told you. That woman Marner found dead in the snow – Eppie's mother – that wretched woman – was my wife: Eppie is my child.'

He paused, dreading the effect of his confession. But Nancy

sat quite still, only that her eyes dropped and ceased to meet his. She was pale and quiet as a meditative statue, clasping her hands on her lap.

'You'll never think the same of me again,' said Godfrey, after a little while, with some tremor in his voice.

She was silent.

'I oughtn't to have left the child unowned: I oughtn't to have kept it from you. But I couldn't bear to give you up, Nancy. I was led away into marrying her – I suffered for it.'

Still Nancy was silent, looking down; and he almost expected that she would presently get up and say she would go to her father's. How could she have any mercy for faults that must seem so black to her, with her simple severe notions?

But at last she lifted up her eyes to his again and spoke. There was no indignation in her voice – only deep regret.

'Godfrey, if you had but told me this six years ago, we could have done some of our duty by the child. Do you think I'd have refused to take her in, if I'd known she was yours?'

At that moment Godfrey felt all the bitterness of an error that was not simply futile, but had defeated its own end. He had not measured this wife with whom he had lived so long. But she spoke again, with more agitation.

'And – O, Godfrey – if we'd had her from the first, if you'd taken to her as you ought, she'd have loved me for her mother – and you'd have been happier with me: I could better have bore my little baby dying, and our life might have been more like what we used to think it 'ud be.'

The tears fell, and Nancy ceased to speak.

'But you wouldn't have married me then, Nancy, if I'd told you,' said Godfrey, urged, in the bitterness of his self-reproach, to prove to himself that his conduct had not been utter folly. 'You may think you would now, but you wouldn't then. With your pride and your father's, you'd have hated having anything to do with me after the talk there'd have been.'

'I can't say what I should have done about that, Godfrey. I should never have married anybody else. But I wasn't worth doing wrong for – nothing is in this world. Nothing is so good as it seems beforehand – not even our marrying wasn't, you see.' There was a faint sad smile on Nancy's face as she said the last words.

'I'm a worse man than you thought I was, Nancy,' said Godfrey, rather tremulously. 'Can you fogive me ever?'

'The wrong to me is but little, Godfrey: you've made it up to me – you've been good to me for fifteen years. It's another you did the wrong to; and I doubt it can never be all made up for.'

'But we can take Eppie now,' said Godfrey. 'I won't mind the world knowing at last. I'll be plain and open for the rest o' my life.'

'It'll be different coming to us, now she's grown up,' said Nancy, shaking her head sadly. 'But it's your duty to acknowledge her and provide for her; and I'll do my part by her, and pray to God Almighty to make her love me.'

'Then we'll go together to Silas Marner's this very night, as soon as everything's quiet at the Stone-pits.'

CHAPTER 19

Between eight and nine o'clock that evening, Eppie and Silas
were seated alone in the cottage. After the great excitement the
weaver had undergone from the events of the afternoon, he had
felt a longing for this quietude, and had even begged Mrs
Winthrop and Aaron, who had naturally lingered behind every
one else, to leave him alone with his child. The excitement had
not passed away: it had only reached that stage when the
keenness of the susceptibility makes external stimulus intolerable – when there is no sense of weariness, but rather an
intensity of inward life, under which sleep is an impossibility.
Any one who has watched such moments in other men remembers the brightness of the eyes and the strange definiteness that
comes over coarse features from that transient influence. It is as
if a new fineness of ear for all spiritual voices had sent wonder-
working vibrations through the heavy mortal frame – as if
'beauty born of murmuring sound'[1] had passed into the face of
the listener.

Silas's face showed that sort of transfiguration, as he sat in his
arm-chair and looked at Eppie. She had drawn her own chair
towards his knees, and leaned forward, holding both his hands,
while she looked up at him. On the table near them, lit by a
candle, lay the recovered gold – the old long-loved gold, ranged
in orderly heaps, as Silas used to range it in the days when it
was his only joy. He had been telling her how he used to count
it every night, and how his soul was utterly desolate till she was
sent to him.

'At first, I'd a sort o' feeling come across me now and then,'
he was saying in a subdued tone, 'as if you might be changed
into the gold again; for sometimes, turn my head which way I
would, I seemed to see the gold; and I thought I should be glad
if I could feel it, and find it was come back. But that didn't last
long. After a bit, I should have thought it was a curse come
again, if it had drove you from me, for I'd got to feel the need o'

your looks and your voice and the touch o' your little fingers.
You didn't know then, Eppie, when you were such a little un –
you didn't know what your old father Silas felt for you.'

'But I know now, father,' said Eppie. 'If it hadn't been for
you, they'd have taken me to the workhouse,[2] and there'd have
been nobody to love me.'

'Eh, my precious child, the blessing was mine. If you hadn't
been sent to save me, I should ha' gone to the grave in my
misery. The money was taken away from me in time; and you
see it's been kept – kept till it was wanted for you. It's wonderful
– our life is wonderful.'

Silas sat in silence a few minutes looking at the money. 'It
takes no hold of me now,' he said, ponderingly – 'the money
doesn't. I wonder if it ever could again – I doubt it might, if I
lost you, Eppie. I might come to think I was forsaken again, and
lose the feeling that God was good to me.'

At that moment there was a knocking at the door; and Eppie
was obliged to rise without answering Silas. Beautiful she
looked, with the tenderness of gathering tears in her eyes and a
slight flush on her cheeks, as she stepped to open the door. The
flush deepened when she saw Mr and Mrs Godfrey Cass. She
made her little rustic curtsy, and held the door wide for them to
enter.

'We're disturbing you very late, my dear,' said Mrs Cass,
taking Eppie's hand, and looking in her face with an expression
of anxious interest and admiration. Nancy herself was pale and
tremulous.

Eppie, after placing chairs for Mr and Mrs Cass, went to
stand against Silas, opposite to them.

'Well, Marner,' said Godfrey, trying to speak with perfect
firmness, 'it's a great comfort to me to see you with your money
again, that you've been deprived of so many years. It was one of
my family did you the wrong – the more grief to me – and I feel
bound to make up to you for it in every way. Whatever I can do
for you will be nothing but paying a debt, even if I looked no
further than the robbery. But there are other things I'm beholden
– shall be beholden to you for, Marner.'

Godfrey checked himself. It had been agreed between him and
his wife that the subject of his fatherhood should be approached
very carefully, and that, if possible, the disclosure should be
reserved for the future, so that it might be made to Eppie

gradually. Nancy had urged this, because she felt strongly the painful light in which Eppie must inevitably see the relation between her father and mother.

Silas, always ill at ease when he was being spoken to by 'betters', such as Mr Cass – tall, powerful, florid men, seen chiefly on horseback – answered with some constraint –

'Sir, I've a deal to thank you for a'ready. As for the robbery, I count it no loss to me. And if I did, you couldn't help it: you aren't answerable for it.'

'You may look at it in that way, Marner, but I never can; and I hope you'll let me act according to my own feeling of what's just. I know you're easily contented: you've been a hard-working man all your life.'

'Yes, sir, yes,' said Marner, meditatively. 'I should ha' been bad off without my work: it was what I held by when everything else was gone from me.'

'Ah,' said Godfrey, applying Marner's words simply to his bodily wants, 'it was a good trade for you in this country, because there's been a great deal of linen-weaving to be done. But you're getting rather past such close work, Marner: it's time you laid by and had some rest. You look a good deal pulled down, though you're not an old man, *are* you?'

'Fifty-five, as near as I can say, sir,' said Silas.

'O, why, you may live thirty years longer – look at old Macey! And that money on the table, after all, is but little. It won't go far either way – whether it's put out to interest, or you were to live on it as long as it would last: it wouldn't go far if you'd nobody to keep but yourself, and you've had two to keep for a good many years now.'

'Eh, sir,' said Silas, unaffected by anything Godfrey was saying, 'I'm in no fear o' want. We shall do very well – Eppie and me 'ull do well enough. There's few working-folks have got so much laid by as that. I don't know what it is to gentlefolks, but I look upon it as a deal – almost too much. And as for us, it's little we want.'

'Only the garden, father,' said Eppie, blushing up to the ears the moment after.

'You love a garden, do you, my dear?' said Nancy, thinking that this turn in the point of view might help her husband. 'We should agree in that: I give a deal of time to the garden.'

'Ah, there's plenty of gardening at the Red House,' said

Godfrey, surprised at the difficulty he found in approaching a proposition which had seemed so easy to him in the distance. 'You've done a good part by Eppie, Marner, for sixteen years. It 'ud be a great comfort to you to see her well provided for, wouldn't it? She looks blooming and healthy, but not fit for any hardships: she doesn't look like a strapping girl come of working parents. You'd like to see her taken care of by those who can leave her well off, and make a lady of her; she's more fit for it than for a rough life, such as she might come to have in a few years' time.'

A slight flush came over Marner's face, and disappeared, like a passing gleam. Eppie was simply wondering Mr Cass should talk so about things that seemed to have nothing to do with reality, but Silas was hurt and uneasy.

'I don't take your meaning, sir,' he answered, not having words at command to express the mingled feelings with which he had heard Mr Cass's words.

'Well, my meaning is this, Marner,' said Godfrey, determined to come to the point. 'Mrs Cass and I, you know, have no children – nobody to be the better for our good home and everything else we have – more than enough for ourselves. And we should like to have somebody in the place of a daughter to us – we should like to have Eppie, and treat her in every way as our own child. It u'd be a great comfort to you in your old age, I hope, to see her fortune made in that way, after you've been at the trouble of bringing her up so well. And it's right you should have every reward for that. And Eppie, I'm sure, will always love you and be grateful to you: she'd come and see you very often, and we should all be on the look-out to do everything we could towards making you comfortable.'

A plain man like Godfrey Cass, speaking under some embarrassment, necessarily blunders on words that are coarser than his intentions, and that are likely to fall gratingly on susceptible feelings. While he had been speaking, Eppie had quietly passed her arm behind Silas's head, and let her hand rest against it caressingly: she felt him trembling violently. He was silent for some moments when Mr Cass had ended – powerless under the conflict of emotions, all alike painful. Eppie's heart was swelling at the sense that her father was in distress; and she was just going to lean down and speak to him, when one struggling dread at last gained the mastery over every other in Silas, and he said, faintly – 'Eppie, my child, speak. I won't stand in your way. Thank Mr and Mrs Cass.'

Eppie took her hand from her father's head, and came forward a step. Her cheeks were flushed, but not with shyness this time: the sense that her father was in doubt and suffering banished that sort of self-consciousness. She dropt a low curtsy, first to Mrs Cass and then to Mr Cass, and said –

'Thank you, ma'am – thank you, sir. But I can't leave my father, nor own anybody nearer than him. And I don't want to be a lady – thank you all the same' (here Eppie dropped another curtsy). 'I couldn't give up the folks I've been used to.'

Eppie's lip began to tremble a little at the last words. She retreated to her father's chair again, and held him round the neck: while Silas, with a subdued sob, put up his hand to grasp hers.

The tears were in Nancy's eyes, but her sympathy with Eppie was, naturally, divided with distress on her husband's account. She dared not speak, wondering what was going on in her husband's mind.

Godfrey felt an irritaion inevitable to almost all of us when we encounter an unexpected obstacle. He had been full of his own penitence and resolution to retrieve his error as far as the time was left to him; he was possessed with all-important feelings, that were to lead to a predetermined course of action which he had fixed on as the right, and he was not prepared to enter with lively appreciation into other people's feelings counteracting his virtuous resolves. The agitation with which he spoke again was not quite unmixed with anger.

'But I've a claim on you, Eppie – the strongest of all claims. It's my duty, Marner, to own Eppie as my child, and provide for her. She's my own child: her mother was my wife. I've a natural claim on her that must stand before every other.'

Eppie had given a violent start, and turned quite pale. Silas, on the contrary, who had been relieved, by Eppie's answer, from the dread lest his mind should be in opposition to hers, felt the spirit of resistance in him set free, not without a touch of parental fierceness. 'Then, sir,' he answered, with an accent of bitterness that had been silent in him since the memorable day when his youthful hope had perished – 'then, sir, why didn't you say so sixteen year ago, and claim her before I'd come to love her, i'stead o' coming to take her from me now, when you might as well take the heart out o' my body? God gave her to me because you turned your back upon her, and He looks upon her as mine: you've no right to her! When a man turns a blessing from his door, it falls to them as take it in.'

'I know that, Marner. I was wrong. I've repented of my conduct in that matter,' said Godfrey, who could not help feeling the edge of Silas's words.

'I'm glad to hear it, sir,' said Marner, with gathering excitement; 'but repentance doesn't alter what's been going on for sixteen year. Your coming now and saying "I'm her father" doesn't alter the feelings inside us. It's me she's been calling her father ever since she could say the word.'

'But I think you might look at the thing more reasonably, Marner,' said Godfrey, unexpectedly awed by the weaver's direct truth-speaking. 'It isn't as if she was to be taken quite away from you, so that you'd never see her again. She'll be very near you, and come to see you very often. She'll feel just the same towards you.'

'Just the same?' said Marner, more bitterly than ever. 'How'll she feel just the same for me as she does now, when we eat o' the same bit, and drink o' the same cup, and think o' the same things from one day's end to another? Just the same? that's idle talk. You'd cut us i' two.'

Godfrey, unqualified by experience to discern the pregnancy of Marner's simple words, felt rather angry again. It seemed to him that the weaver was very selfish (a judgment readily passed by those who have never tested their own power of sacrifice) to oppose what was undoubtedly for Eppie's welfare; and he felt himself called upon, for her sake, to assert his authority.

'I should have thought, Marner,' he said, severely – I should have thought your affection for Eppie would make you rejoice in what was for her good, even if it did call upon you to give up something. You ought to remember your own life's uncertain, and she's at an age now when her lot may soon be fixed in a way very different from what it would be in her father's home: she may marry some low working-man, and then, whatever I might do for her, I couldn't make her well-off. You're putting yourself in the way of her welfare; and though I'm sorry to hurt you after what you've done, and what I've left undone, I feel now it's my duty to insist on taking care of my own daughter. I want to do my duty.'

It would be difficult to say whether it were Silas or Eppie that was more deeply stirred by this last speech of Godfrey's. Thought had been very busy in Eppie as she listened to the contest between her old long-loved father and this new unfamiliar father who had suddenly come to fill the place of that black featureless shadow which had held the ring and placed it on her mother's finger. Her imagination had darted backward in conjectures, and forward in previsions, of what this revealed fatherhood implied; and there were words in Godfrey's last speech which helped to make the previsions especially definite. Not that these thoughts, either of past or future, determined her resolution – *that* was determined by the feelings which vibrated to every word Silas had uttered; but they raised, even apart from these feelings, a repulsion towards the offered lot and the newly-revealed father.

Silas, on the other hand, was again stricken in conscience, and alarmed lest Godfrey's accusation should be true – lest he should be raising his own will as an obstacle to Eppie's good. For many moments he was mute, struggling for the self-conquest necessary to the uttering of the difficult words. They came out tremulously.

'I'll say no more. Let it be as you will. Speak to the child. I'll hinder nothing.'

Even Nancy, with all the acute sensibility of her own affections, shared her husband's view, that Marner was not justifiable in his wish to retain Eppie, after her real father had avowed himself. She felt that it was a very hard trial for the poor weaver, but her code allowed no question that a father by blood must have a claim above that of any foster-father. Besides, Nancy, used all her life to plenteous circumstances and the privileges of 'respectability', could not enter into the pleasures which early nurture and habit connect with all the little aims and efforts of the poor who are born poor: to her mind, Eppie, in being restored to her birthright, was entering on a too long withheld but unquestionable good. Hence she heard Silas's last words with relief, and thought, as Godfrey did, that their wish was achieved.

'Eppie, my dear,' said Godfrey, looking at his daughter, not without some embarrassment, under the sense that she was old enough to judge him, 'it'll always be our wish that you should show your love and gratitude to one who's been a father to you so many years, and we shall want to help you to make him comfortable in every way. But we hope you'll come to love us as well; and though I haven't been what a father should ha' been to you all these years, I wish to do the utmost in my power for you for the rest of my life, and provide for you as my only child. And you'll have the best of mothers in my wife – that'll be a blessing you haven't known since you were old enough to know it.'

'My dear, you'll be a treasure to me,' said Nancy, in her gentle voice. 'We shall want for nothing when we have our daughter.'

Eppie did not come forward and curtsy, as she had done before. She held Silas's hand in hers, and grasped it firmly – it was a weaver's hand, with a palm and finger-tips that were sensitive to such pressure – while she spoke with colder decision than before.

'Thank you, ma'am – thank you, sir, for your offers – they're very great, and far above my wish. For I should have no delight i' life any more if I was forced to go away from my father, and knew he was sitting at home, a-thinking of me and feeling lone. We've been used to be happy together every day, and I can't think o' no happiness without him. And he says he'd nobody i' the world till I was sent to him, and he'd have nothing when I was gone. And he's took care of me and loved me from the first, and I'll cleave to him as long as he lives, and nobody shall ever come between him and me.'

'But you must make sure, Eppie,' said Silas, in a low voice – 'you must make sure as you won't ever be sorry, because you've made your choice to stay among poor folks, and with poor clothes and things, when you might ha' had everything o' the best.'

His sensitiveness on this point had increased as he listened to Eppie's words of faithful affection.

'I can never be sorry, father,' said Eppie. 'I shouldn't know what to think on or to wish for with fine things about me, as I haven't been used to. And it 'ud be poor work for me to put on things, and ride in a gig, and sit in a place at church, as 'ud make them as I'm fond of think me unfitting company for 'em. What could I care for then?'

Nancy looked at Godfrey with a pained questioning glance. But his eyes were fixed on the floor, where he was moving the end of his stick, as if he were pondering on something absently.

She thought there was a word which might perhaps come better from her lips than from his.

'What you say is natural, my dear child – it's natural you should cling to those who've brought you up,' she said, mildly; 'but there's a duty you owe to your lawful father. There's perhaps something to be given up on more sides than one. When your father opens his home to you, I think it's right you shouldn't turn your back on it.'

'I can't feel as I've got any father but one,' said Eppie, impetuously, while the tears gathered. 'I've always thought of a little home where he'd sit i' the corner, and I should fend and do everything for him: I can't think o' no other home. I wasn't brought up to be a lady, and I can't turn my mind to it. I like the working-folks, and their victuals, and their ways. And,' she ended passionately, while the tears fell, 'I'm promised to marry a working-man, as 'll live with father, and help me to take care of him.'

Godfrey looked up at Nancy with a flushed face and smarting dilated eyes. This frustration of a purpose towards which he had set out under the exalted consciousness that he was about to compensate in some degree for the greatest demerit of his life, made him feel the air of the room stifling.

'Let us go,' he said, in an under-tone.

'We won't talk of this any longer now,' said Nancy, rising. 'We're your well-wishers, my dear – and yours too, Marner. We shall come and see you again. It's getting late now.'

In this way she covered her husband's abrupt departure, for Godfrey had gone straight to the door, unable to say more.

CHAPTER 20

Nancy and Godfrey walked home under the starlight in silence. When they entered the oaken parlour, Godfrey threw himself into his chair, while Nancy laid down her bonnet and shawl, and stood on the hearth near her husband, unwilling to leave him even for a few minutes, and yet fearing to utter any word lest it might jar on his feeling. At last Godfrey turned his head towards her, and their eyes met, dwelling in that meeting without any movement on either side. That quiet mutual gaze of a trusting husband and wife is like the first moment of rest or refuge from a great weariness or a great danger – not to be interfered with by speech or action which would distract the sensations from the fresh enjoyment of repose.

But presently he put out his hand, and as Nancy placed hers within it, he drew her towards him, and said –

'That's ended!'

She bent to kiss him, and then said, as she stood by his side, 'Yes, I'm afraid we must give up the hope of having her for a daughter. It wouldn't be right to want to force her to come to us against her will. We can't alter her bringing up and what's come of it.'

'No,' said Godfrey, with a keen decisiveness of tone, in contrast with his usually careless and unemphatic speech – 'there's debts we can't pay like money debts, by paying extra for the years that have slipped by. While I've been putting off and putting off, the trees have been growing – it's too late now. Marner was in the right in what he said about a man's turning away a blessing from his door: it falls to somebody else. I wanted to pass for childless once, Nancy – I shall pass for childless now against my wish.'

Nancy did not speak immediately, but after a little while she asked – 'You won't make it known, then, about Eppie's being your daughter?'

'No: where would be the good to anybody? – only harm. I

must do what I can for her in the state of life she chooses. I must see who it is she's thinking of marrying.'

'If it won't do any good to make the thing known,' said Nancy, who thought she might now allow herself the relief of entertaining a feeling which she had tried to silence before, 'I should be very thankful for father and Priscilla never to be troubled with knowing what was done in the past, more than about Dunsey: it can't be helped, their knowing that.'

'I shall put it in my will – I think I shall put it in my will. I shouldn't like to leave anything to be found out, like this about Dunsey,' said Godfrey, meditatively. 'But I can't see anything but difficulties that 'ud come from telling it now. I must do what I can to make her happy in her own way. I've a notion,' he added, after a moment's pause, 'it's Aaron Winthrop she meant she was engaged to. I remember seeing him with her and Marner going away from church.'

'Well, he's very sober and industrious,' said Nancy, trying to view the matter as cheerfully as possible.

Godfrey fell into thoughtfulness again. Presently he looked up at Nancy sorrowfully, and said –

'She's a very pretty, nice girl, isn't she, Nancy?'

'Yes, dear; and with just your hair and eyes: I wondered it had never struck me before.'

'I think she took a dislike to me at the thought of my being her father: I could see a change in her manner after that.'

'She couldn't bear to think of not looking on Marner as her father,' said Nancy, not wishing to confirm her husband's painful impression.

'She thinks I did wrong by her mother as well as by her. She thinks me worse than I am. But she *must* think it: she can never know all. It's part of my punishment, Nancy, for my daughter to dislike me. I should never have got into that trouble if I'd been true to you – if I hadn't been a fool. I'd no right to expect anything but evil could come of that marriage – and when I shirked doing a father's part too.'

Nancy was silent: her spirit of rectitude would not let her try to soften the edge of what she felt to be a just compunction. He spoke again after a little while, but the tone was rather changed: there was tenderness mingled with the previous self-reproach.

'And I got *you*, Nancy, in spite of all; and yet I've been

grumbling and uneasy because I hadn't something else – as if I deserved it.'

'You've never been wanting to me, Godfrey,' said Nancy, with quiet sincerity. 'My only trouble would be gone if you resigned yourself to the lot that's been given us.'

'Well, perhaps it isn't too late to mend a bit there. Though it *is* too late to mend some things, say what they will.'

CHAPTER 21

The next morning, when Silas and Eppie were seated at their breakfast, he said to her –

'Eppie, there's a thing I've had on my mind to do this two year, and now the money's been brought back to us, we can do it. I've been turning it over and over in the night, and I think we'll set out tomorrow, while the fine days last. We'll leave the house and everything for your godmother to take care on, and we'll make a little bundle o' things and set out.'

'Where to go, daddy?' said Eppie, in much surprise.

'To my old country – to the town where I was born – up Lantern Yard. I want to see Mr Paston, the minister: something may ha' come out to make 'em know I was inincent o' the robbery. And Mr Paston was a man with a deal o' light – I want to speak to him about the drawing o' the lots. And I should like to talk to him about the religion o' this country-side, for I partly think he doesn't know on it.'

Eppie was very joyful, for there was the prospect not only of wonder and delight at seeing a strange country, but also of coming back to tell Aaron all about it. Aaron was so much wiser than she was about most things – it would be rather pleasant to have this little advantage over him. Mrs Winthrop, though possessed with a dim fear of dangers attendant on so long a journey, and requiring many assurances that it would not take them out of the region of carriers' carts and slow waggons, was nevertheless well pleased that Silas should revisit his own country, and find out if he had been cleared from that false accusation.

'You'd be easier in your mind for the rest o' your life, Master Marner,' said Dolly – 'that you would. And if there's any light to be got up the yard as you talk on, we've need of it i' this world, and I'd be glad on it myself, if you could bring it back.'

So on the fourth day from that time, Silas and Eppie, in their Sunday clothes, with a small bundle tied in a blue linen handkerchief, were making their way through the streets of a great manufacturing town. Silas, bewildered by the changes thirty years had brought over his native place, had stopped several persons in succession to ask them the name of this town, that he might be sure he was not under a mistake about it.

'Ask for Lantern Yard, father – ask this gentleman with the tassels on his shoulders a-standing at the shop door; he isn't in a hurry like the rest,' said Eppie, in some distress at her father's bewilderment, and ill at ease, besides, amidst the noise, the movement, and the multitude of strange indifferent faces.

'Eh, my child, he won't know anything about it,' said Silas; 'gentlefolks didn't ever go up the Yard. But happen somebody can tell me which is the way to Prison Street, where the jail is. I know the way out o' that as if I'd seen it yesterday.'

With some difficulty, after many turnings and new inquiries, they reached Prison Street; and the grim walls of the jail, the first object that answered to any image in Silas's memory, cheered him with the certitude, which no assurance of the town's name had hitherto given him, that he was in his native place.

'Ah,' he said, drawing a long breath, 'there's the jail, Eppie; that's just the same: I aren't afraid now. It's the third turning on the left hand from the jail doors – that's the way we must go.'

'O, what a dark ugly place!' said Eppie. 'How it hides the sky! It's worse than the workhouse. I'm glad you don't live in this town now, father. Is Lantern Yard like this street?'

'My precious child,' said Silas, smiling, 'it isn't a big street like this. I never was easy i' this street myself, but I was fond o' Lantern Yard. The shops here are all altered, I think – I can't make 'em out; but I shall know the turning, because it's the third.'

'Here it is,' he said, in a tone of satisfaction, as they came to a narrow alley. 'And then we must go to the left again, and then straight for'ard for a bit, up Shoe Lane: and then we shall be at the entry next to the o'erhanging window, where there's the nick in the road for the water to run. Eh, I can see it all.'

'O father, I'm like as if I was stifled,' said Eppie. 'I couldn't ha' thought as any folks lived i' this way, so close together. How pretty the Stone-pits 'ull look when we get beck!'

'It looks comical to *me*, child, now – and smells bad. I can't think as it usened to smell so.'

Here and there a sallow, begrimed face looked out from a gloomy doorway at the strangers, and increased Eppie's uneasiness, so that it was a longed-for relief when they issued from the alleys into Shoe Lane, where there was a broader strip of sky.

'Dear heart!' said Silas, 'why, there's people coming out o' the Yard as if they'd been to chapel at this time o' day – a weekday noon!'

Suddenly he started and stood still with a look of distressed amazement, that alarmed Eppie. They were before an opening in front of a large factory, from which men and women were streaming for their midday meal.

'Father,' said Eppie, clasping his arm, 'what's the matter?'

But she had to speak again and again before Silas could answer her.

'It's gone, child,' he said, at last, in strong agitation – 'Lantern Yard's gone. It must ha' been here, because here's the house with the o'erhanging window – I know that – it's just the same; but they've made this new opening; and see that big factory! It's all gone – chapel and all.'

'Come into that little brush-shop and sit down, father – they'll let you sit down,' said Eppie, always on the watch lest one of her father's strange attacks should come on. 'Perhaps the people can tell you all about it.'

But neither from the brush-maker, who had come to Shoe Lane only ten years ago, when the factory was already built, nor from any other source within his reach, could Silas learn anything of the old Lantern Yard friends, or of Mr Paston the minister.

'The old place is all swep' away,' Silas said to Dolly Winthrop on the night of his return – 'the little graveyard and everything. The old home's gone; I've no home but this now. I shall never know whether they got at the truth o' the robbery, nor whether Mr Paston could ha' given me any light about the drawing o' the lots. It's dark to me, Mrs Winthrop, that is; I doubt it'll be dark to the last.'

'Well, yes, Master Marner,' said Dolly, who sat with a placid listening face, now bordered by grey hairs; 'I doubt it may. It's the will o' Them above as a many things should be dark to us; but there's some things as I've never felt i' the dark about, and they're mostly what comes i' the day's work. You were hard done by that once, Master Marner, and it seems as you'll never know the rights of it; but that doesn't hinder there *being* a rights, Master Marner, for all it's dark to you and me.'

'No,' said Silas, 'no; that doesn't hinder. Since the time the child was sent to me and I've come to love her as myself, I've had light enough to trusten by; and now she says she'll never leave me, I think I shall trusten till I die.'

CONCLUSION

There was one time of the year which was held in Raveloe to be especially suitable for a wedding. It was when the great lilacs and laburnums in the old-fashioned gardens showed their golden and purple wealth above the lichen-tinted walls, and when there were calves still young enough to want bucketfuls of fragrant milk. People were not so busy then as they must become when the full cheese-making and the mowing had set in; and besides, it was a time when a light bridal dress could be worn with comfort and seen to advantage.

Happily the sunshine fell more warmly than usual on the lilac tufts the morning that Eppie was married, for her dress was a very light one. She had often thought, though with a feeling of renunciation, that the perfections of a wedding-dress would be a white cotton, with the tiniest pink sprig at wide intervals; so that when Mrs Godfrey Cass begged to provide one, and asked Eppie to choose what it should be, previous meditation had enabled her to give a decided answer at once.

Seen at a little distance as she walked across the churchyard and down the village, she seemed to be attired in pure white, and her hair looked like the dash of gold on a lily. One hand was on her husband's arm, and with the other she clasped the hand of her father Silas.

'You won't be giving me away, father,' she had said before they went to church; 'you'll only be taking Aaron to be a son to you.'

Dolly Winthrop walked behind with her husband; and there ended the little bridal procession.

There were many eyes to look at it, and Miss Priscilla Lammeter was glad that she and her father had happened to drive up to the door of the Red House just in time to see this pretty sight. They had come to keep Nancy company today, because Mr Cass had had to go away to Lytherley, for special reasons. That seemed to be a pity, for otherwise he might have gone, as Mr Crackenthorp and Mr Osgood certainly would, to look on at the wedding-feast which he had ordered at the Rainbow, naturally feeling a great interest in the weaver who had been wronged by one of his own family.

'I could ha' wished Nancy had had the luck to find a child like that and bring her up,' said Priscilla to their father, as they sat in the gig; 'I should ha' had something young to think of then, besides the lambs and the calves.'

'Yes, my dear, yes,' said Mr Lammeter; 'one feels that as one gets older. Things look dim to old folks: they'd need have some young eyes about 'em, to let 'em know the world's the same as it used to be.'

Nancy came out now to welcome her father and sister; and the wedding group had passed on beyond the Red House to the humbler part of the village.

Dolly Winthrop was the first to divine that old Mr Macey, who had been set in his arm-chair outside his own door, would expect some special notice as they passed, since he was too old to be at the wedding-feast.

'Mr Macey's looking for a word from us,' said Dolly; 'he'll be hurt if we pass him and say nothing – and him so racked with rheumatiz.'

So they turned aside to shake hands with the old man. He had looked forward to the occasion, and had his premeditated speech.

'Well, Master Marner,' he said, in a voice that quavered a good deal, 'I've lived to see my words come true. I was the first to say there was no harm in you, though your looks might be again' you; and I was the first to say you'd get your money back. And it's nothing but rightful as you should. And I'd ha' said the "Amens", and willing, at the holy matrimony; but Tookey's done it a good while now, and I hope you'll have none the worse luck.'

In the open yard before the Rainbow the party of guests were already assembled, though it was still nearly an hour before the appointed feast-time. But by this means they could not only enjoy the slow advent of their pleasure; they had also ample leisure to talk of Silas Marner's strange history, and arrive by due degrees at the conclusion that he had brought a blessing on himself by acting like a father to a lone motherless child. Even the farrier did not negative this sentiment: on the contrary, he took it up as peculiarly his own, and invited any hardy person present to contradict him. But he met with no contradiction; and all differences among the company were merged in a general agreement with Mr Snell's sentiment, that when a man had deserved his good luck, it was the part of his neighbours to wish him joy.

As the bridal group approached, a hearty cheer was raised in the Rainbow yard; and Ben Winthrop, whose jokes had retained their acceptable flavour, found it agreeable to turn in there and receive congratulations; not requiring the proposed interval of quiet at the Stone-pits before joining the company.

Eppie had a larger garden than she had ever expected there now; and in other ways there had been alterations at the expense of Mr Cass, the landlord, to suit Silas's larger family. For he and Eppie had declared that they would rather stay at the Stone-pits than go to any new home. The garden was fenced with stones on two sides, but in front there was an open fence, through which the flowers shone with answering gladness, as the four united people came within sight of them.

'O father,' said Eppie, 'what a pretty home ours is! I think nobody could be happier than we are.'

THE LIFTED VEIL

Give me no light, great Heaven, but such as turns
To energy of human fellowship;
No powers beyond the growing heritage
That makes completer manhood.[1]

CHAPTER I

The time of my end approaches. I have lately been subject to attacks of *angina pectoris*; and in the ordinary course of things, my physician tells me, I may fairly hope that my life will not be protracted many months. Unless, then, I am cursed with an exceptional physical constitution, as I am cursed with an exceptional mental character, I shall not much longer groan under the wearisome burthen of this earthly existence. If it were to be otherwise – if I were to live on to the age most men desire and provide for – I should for once have known whether the miseries of delusive expectation can outweigh the miseries of true prevision. For I foresee when I shall die, and everything that will happen in my last moments.

Just a month from this day, on the 20th of September 1850, I shall be sitting in this chair, in this study, at ten o'clock at night, longing to die, weary of incessant insight and foresight, without delusions and without hope. Just as I am watching a tongue of blue flame rising in the fire, and my lamp is burning low, the horrible contraction will begin at my chest. I shall only have time to reach the bell, and pull it violently, before the sense of suffocation will come. No one will answer my bell. I know why. My two servants are lovers, and will have quarrelled. My housekeeper will have rushed out of the house in a fury, two hours before, hoping that Perry will believe she has gone to drown herself. Perry is alarmed at last, and is gone out after her. The little scullery-maid is asleep on a bench: she never answers the bell; it does not wake her. The sense of suffocation increases: my lamp goes out with a horrible stench: I make a great effort, and snatch at the bell again. I long for life, and there is no help. I thirsted for the unknown: the thirst is gone. O God, let me stay with the known, and be weary of it: I am content. Agony of pain and suffocation – and all the while the earth, the fields, the pebbly brook at the bottom of the rookery, the fresh scent after the rain, the light of the morning through my chamber-window, the warmth of the hearth after the frosty air – will darkness close over them for ever?

Darkness – darkness – no pain – nothing but darkness: but I am passing on and on through the darkness: my thought stays in the darkness, but always with a sense of moving onward . . .

Before that time comes, I wish to use my last hours of ease and strength in telling the strange story of my experience. I have never fully unbosomed myself to any human being; I have never been encouraged to trust much in the sympathy of my fellow-men. But we have all a chance of meeting with some pity, some tenderness, some charity, when we are dead: it is the living only who cannot be forgiven – the living only from whom men's indulgence and reverence are held off, like the rain by the hard east wind. While the heart beats, bruise it – it is your only opportunity; while the eye can still turn towards you with moist timid entreaty, freeze it with an icy unanswering gaze; while the ear, that delicate messenger to the inmost sanctuary of the soul, can still take in the tones of kindness, put it off with hard civility, or sneering compliment, or envious affection of indifference; while the creative brain can still throb with the sense of injustice, with the yearning for brotherly recognition – make haste – oppress it with your ill-considered judgments, your trivial comparisons, your careless misrepresentations. The heart will by-and-by be still – *ubi sœva indignatio ulterius cor lacerare nequit*;[2] the eye will cease to entreat; the ear will be deaf; the brain will have ceased from all wants as well as from all work. Then your charitable speeches may find vent; then you may remember and pity the toil and the struggle and the failure; then you may give due honour to the work achieved; then you may find extenuation for errors, and may consent to bury them.

That is a trivial schoolboy text; why do I dwell on it? It has little reference to me, for I shall leave no works behind me for men to honour. I have no near relatives who will make up, by weeping over my grave, for the wounds they inflicted on me when I was among them. It is only the story of my life that will perhaps win a little more sympathy from strangers when I am dead, than I ever believed it would obtain from my friends while I was living.

My childhood perhaps seems happier to me than it really was, by contrast with all the after-years. For then the curtain of the future was as impenetrable to me as to other children: I had all their delight in the present hour, their sweet indefinite hopes for the morrow; and I had a tender mother: even now, after the dreary lapse of long years, a slight trace of sensation accompanies the remembrance of her caress as she held me on her knee – her arms round my little body, her cheek pressed on mine. I had a complaint of the eyes that made me blind for a little while, and she kept me on her knee from morning till night. That unequalled love soon vanished out of my life, and even to my childish consciousness it was as if that life had become more chill. I rode my little white pony with the groom by my side as before, but there were no loving eyes looking at me as I mounted, no glad arms opened to me when I came back. Perhaps I missed my mother's love more than most children of seven or eight would have done, to whom the other pleasures of life remained as before; for I was certainly a very sensitive child. I remember still the mingled trepidation and delicious excitement with which I was affected by the tramping of the horses on the pavement in the echoing stables, by the loud resonance of the grooms' voices, by the booming bark of the dogs as my father's carriage thundered under the archway of the courtyard, by the din of the gong as it gave notice of luncheon and dinner. The measured tramp of soldiery which I sometimes heard – for my father's house lay near a county town where there were large barracks – made me sob and tremble; and yet when they were gone past, I longed for them to come back again.

I fancy my father thought me an odd child, and had little fondness for me; though he was very careful in fulfilling what he regarded as a parent's duties. But he was already past the middle of life, and I was not his only son. My mother had been his second wife, and he was five-and-forty when he married her. He was a firm, unbending, intensely orderly man, in root and stem a banker, but with a flourishing graft of the active landholder, aspiring to county influence: one of those people who are always like themselves from day to day, who are uninfluenced by the weather, and neither know melancholy nor high spirits. I held him in great awe, and appeared more timid and sensitive in his presence than at other times; a circumstance which, perhaps, helped to confirm him in the intention to educate me on a different plan from the prescriptive one with which he had complied in the case of my elder brother, already a tall youth at Eton. My brother was to be his representative and successor; he must go to Eton and Oxford, for the sake of making connections, of course: my father was not a man to underrate the bearing of Latin satirists or Greek dramatists on the attainment of an aristocratic position. But, intrinsically, he had slight esteem for 'those dead but sceptred spirits'; having qualified himself for forming an independent opinion by reading Potter's 'Æschylus', and dipping into Francis's 'Horace'.[3] To this negative view he added a positive one, derived from a recent connection with mining speculations; namely, that a scientific education was the really useful training for a younger son.[4] Moreover, it was clear that a shy, sensitive boy like me was not fit to encounter the rough experience of a public school. Mr Letherall had said so very decidedly. Mr Letherall was a large man in spectacles, who one day took my small head between his large hands, and pressed it here and there in an exploratory, suspicious manner – then placed each of his great thumbs on my temples,[5] and pushed me a little way from him, and stared at me with glittering spectacles. The contemplation appeared to displease him, for he frowned sternly, and said to my father, drawing his thumbs across my eyebrows –

'The deficiency is there, sir – there; and here,' he added, touching the upper sides of my head, 'here is the excess. That must be brought out, sir, and this must be laid to sleep.'

I was in a state of tremor, partly at the vague idea that I was the object of reprobation, partly in the agitation of my first hatred – hatred of this big, spectacled man, who pulled my head about as if he wanted to buy and cheapen it.

I am not aware how much Mr Letherall had to do with the system afterwards adopted towards me, but it was presently clear that private tutors, natural history, science, and the modern languages, were the appliances by which the defects of my organisation were to be remedied. I was very stupid about machines, so I was to be greatly occupied with them; I had no memory for classification, so it was particularly necessary that I should study systematic zoology and botany; I was hungry for human deeds and human emotions, so I was to be plentifully crammed with the mechanical powers, the elementary bodies, and the phenomena of electricity and magnetism. A better-constituted boy would certainly have profited under my intelligent tutors, with their scientific apparatus; and would, doubtless, have found the phenomena of electricity and magnetism as fascinating as I was, every Thursday, assured they were. As it was, I could have paired off, for ignorance of whatever was taught me, with the worst Latin scholar that was ever turned out of a classical academy. I read Plutarch,[6] and Shakespeare, and Don Quixote by the sly, and supplied myself in that way with wandering thoughts, while my tutor was assuring me that 'an improved man, as distinguished from an ignorant one, was a man who knew the reason why water ran down-hill'. I had no desire to be this improved man; I was glad of the running water; I could watch it and listen to it gurgling among the pebbles, and bathing the bright green water-plants, by the hour together. I did not want to know *why* it ran; I had perfect confidence that there were good reasons for what was so very beautiful.

There is no need to dwell on this part of my life. I have said enough to indicate that my nature was of the sensitive, unpractical order, and that it grew up in an uncongenial medium, which could never foster it into happy, healthy development. When I was sixteen I was sent to Geneva to complete my course of education; and the change was a very happy one to me, for the first sight of the Alps, with the setting sun on them, as we descended the Jura, seemed to me like an entrance into heaven; and the three years of my life there were spent in a perpetual sense of exaltation, as if from a draught of delicious wine, at the presence of Nature in all her awful loveliness. You will think, perhaps, that I must have been a poet, from this early sensibility to Nature. But my lot was not so happy as that. A poet pours forth his song and *believes* in the listening ear and answering soul, to which his song will be floated sooner or later. But the poet's sensibility without his voice – the poet's sensibility that finds no vent but in silent tears on the sunny bank, when the noonday light sparkles on the water, or in an inward shudder at the sound of harsh human tones, the sight of a cold human eye – this dumb passion brings with it a fatal solitude of soul in the society of one's fellow-men. My least solitary moments were those in which I pushed off in my boat, at evening, towards the centre of the lake; it seemed to me that the sky, and the glowing mountain-tops, and the wide blue water, surrounded me with a cherishing love such as no human face had shed on me since my mother's love had vanished out of my life. I used to do as Jean Jacques did – lie down in my boat and let it glide where it would, while I looked up at the departing glow leaving one mountain-top after the other, as if the prophet's chariot of fire were passing over them on its way to the home of light.[7] Then, when the white summits were all sad and corpse-like, I had to push homeward, for I was under careful surveillance, and was allowed no late wanderings. This disposition of mine was not favourable to the formation of intimate friendships among the numerous youths of my own age who are always to be found studying at Geneva. Yet I made *one* such friendship; and, singularly enough, it was with a youth whose intellectual tendencies were the very reverse of my own. I shall call him Charles Meunier; his real surname – an English one, for he was of English extraction – having since become celebrated. He was an orphan, who lived on a miserable pittance while he pursued the medical studies for which he had a special genius. Strange! that with my vague mind, susceptible and unobservant, hating inquiry and given up to contemplation, I should have been drawn towards a youth whose strongest passion was science. But the bond was not an intellectual one; it came from a source that can happily blend the stupid with the brilliant, the dreamy with the practical: it came from community of feeling. Charles was poor and ugly, derided by Genevese *gamins*,[8] and not acceptable in drawing-rooms. I saw that he was isolated, as I was, though from a different cause, and, stimulated by a sympathetic resentment, I made timid advances towards him. It is enough to say that there sprang up as much comradeship between us as our different habits would allow; and in Charles's rare holidays we went up the Salève together, or took the boat to Vevay, while I listened dreamily to the monologues in which he unfolded his bold conceptions of future experiment and discovery. I mingled them confusedly in my thought with glimpses of blue water and delicate floating cloud, with the notes of birds and the distant glitter of the glacier. He knew quite well that my mind was half absent, yet he liked to talk to me in this way; for don't we talk of our hopes and our projects even to dogs and birds, when they love us? I have mentioned this one friendship because of its connection with a strange and terrible scene which I shall have to narrate in my subsequent life.

This happier life at Geneva was put an end to by a severe illness, which is partly a blank to me, partly a time of dimly-remembered suffering, with the presence of my father by my bed

from time to time. Then came the languid monotony of conva-
lescence, the days gradually breaking into variety and distinctness as my strength enabled me to take longer and longer drives.
On one of these more vividly remembered days, my father said
to me, as he sat beside my sofa –

'When you are quite well enough to travel, Latimer, I shall
take you home with me. The journey will amuse you and do
you good, for I shall go through the Tyrol and Austria, and you
will see many new places. Our neighbours, the Filmores, are
come; Alfred will join us at Basle, and we shall all go together
to Vienna, and back by Prague . . .'

My father was called away before he had finished his sentence,
and he left my mind resting on the word *Prague*, with a strange
sense that a new and wondrous scene was breaking upon me: a
city under the broad sunshine, that seemed to me as if it were
the summer sunshine of a long-past century arrested in its course
– unrefreshed for ages by the dews of night, or the rushing rain-
cloud; scorching the dusty, weary, time-eaten grandeur of a
people doomed to live on in the stale repetition of memories,
like deposed and superannuated kings in their regal gold-
inwoven tatters. The city looked so thirsty that the broad river
seemed to me a sheet of metal; and the blackened statues, as I
passed under their blank gaze, along the unending bridge, with
their ancient garments and their saintly crowns, seemed to me
the real inhabitants and owners of this place, while the busy,
trivial men and women, hurrying to and fro, were a swarm of
ephemeral visitants infesting it for a day. It is such grim, stony
beings as these, I thought, who are the fathers of ancient faded
children, in those tanned time-fretted dwellings that crowd the
steep before me; who pay their court in the worn and crumbling
pomp of the palace which stretches its monotonous length on
the height; who worship wearily[9] in the stifling air of the
churches, urged by no fear or hope, but compelled by their
doom to be ever old and undying, to live on in the rigidity of
habit, as they live on in perpetual midday, without the repose of
night or the new birth of morning.

A stunning clang of metal suddenly thrilled through me, and I
became conscious of the objects in my room again: one of the
fire-irons had fallen as Pierre opened the door to bring me my
draught. My heart was palpitating violently, and I begged Pierre
to leave my draught beside me; I would take it presently.

As soon as I was alone again, I began to ask myself whether I had been sleeping. Was this a dream – this wonderfully distinct vision – minute in its distinctness down to a patch of rainbow light on the pavement, transmitted through a coloured lamp in the shape of a star – of a strange city, quite unfamiliar to my imagination? I had seen no picture of Prague: it lay in my mind as a mere name, with vaguely-remembered historical assocations – ill-defined memories of imperial grandeur and religious wars.

Nothing of this sort had ever occurred in my dreaming experience before, for I had often been humiliated because my dreams were only saved from being utterly disjointed and commonplace by the frequent terrors of nightmare. But I could not believe that I had been asleep, for I remembered distinctly the gradual breaking-in of the vision upon me, like the new images in a dissolving view, or the growing distinctness of the landscape as the sun lifts up the veil of the morning mist. And while I was conscious of this incipient vision, I was also conscious that Pierre came to tell my father Mr Filmore was waiting for him, and that my father hurried out of the room. No, it was not a dream; was it – the thought was full of tremulous exultation – was it the poet's nature in me, hitherto only a trouble yearning sensibility, now manifesting itself suddenly as spontaneous creation? Surely it was in this way that Homer saw the plain of Troy, that Dante saw the abodes of the departed, that Milton saw the earthward flight of the Tempter.[10] Was it that my illness had wrought some happy change in my organisation – given a firmer tension to my nerves – carried off some dull obstruction? I had often read of such effects – in works of fiction at least. Nay; in genuine biographies I had read of the subtilising or exalting influence of some diseases on the mental powers. Did not Novalis[11] feel his inspiration intensified under the progress of consumption?

When my mind had dwelt for some time on this blissful idea, it seemed to me that I might perhaps test it by an exertion of my will. The vision had begun when my father was speaking of our going to Prague. I did not for a moment believe it was really a representation of that city; I believed – I hoped it was a picture that my newly-liberated genius had painted in fiery haste, with the colours snatched from lazy memory. Suppose I were to fix my mind on some other place – Venice, for example, which was far more familiar to my imagination than Prague: perhaps the same sort of result would follow. I concentrated my thoughts on Venice; I stimulated my imagination with poetic memories, and strove to feel myself present in Venice, as I had felt myself present in Prague. But in vain. I was only colouring the Canaletto[12] engravings that hung in my old bedroom at home; the picture was a shifting one, my mind wandering uncertainly in search of more vivid images; I could see no accident of form or shadow without conscious labour after the necessary conditions. It was all prosaic effort, not rapt passivity, such as I had experienced half an hour before. I was discouraged; but I remembered that inspiration was fitful.

For several days I was in a state of excited expectation, watching for a recurrence of my new gift. I sent my thoughts ranging over my world of knowledge, in the hope that they would find some object which would send a reawakening vibration through my slumbering genius. But no; my world remained as dim as ever, and that flash of strange light refused to come again, though I watched for it with palpitating eagerness.

My father accompanied me every day in a drive, and a gradually lengthening walk as my powers of walking increased; and one evening he had agreed to come and fetch me at twelve the next day, that we might go together to select a musical box, and other purchases rigorously demanded of a rich Englishman visiting Geneva. He was one of the most punctual of men and bankers, and I was always nervously anxious to be quite ready for him at the appointed time. But, to my surprise, at a quarter past twelve he had not appeared. I felt all the impatience of a convalescent who has nothing particular to do, and who has just taken a tonic in the prospect of immediate exercise that would carry off the stimulus.

Unable to sit still and reserve my strength, I walked up and down the room, looking out on the current of the Rhone, just where it leaves the dark-blue lake; but thinking all the while of the possible causes that could detain my father.

Suddenly I was conscious that my father was in the room, but not alone: there were two persons with him. Strange! I had heard no footstep, I had not seen the door open; but I saw my father, and at his right hand our neighbour Mrs Filmore, whom I remembered very well, though I had not seen her for five years. She was a commonplace middle-aged woman, in silk and cashmere; but the lady on the left of my father was not more than twenty, a tall, slim, willowy figure, with luxuriant blond hair, arranged in cunning braids and folds that looked almost too massive for the slight figure and the small-featured, thin-lipped face they crowned. But the face had not a girlish expression: the features were sharp, the pale grey eyes at once acute, restless, and sarcastic. They were fixed on me in half-smiling curiosity, and I felt a painful sensation as if a sharp wind were cutting me. The pale-green dress, and the green leaves that seemed to form a border about her pale blond hair, made me think of a Water-Nixie,[13] – for my mind was full of German lyrics, and this pale, fatal-eyed woman, with the green weeds, looked like a birth from some cold sedgy stream, the daughter of an aged river.

'Well, Latimer, you thought me long,' my father said . . .

But while the last word was in my ears, the whole group vanished, and there was nothing between me and the Chinese painted folding-screen that stood before the door. I was cold and trembling; I could only totter forward and throw myself on the sofa. This strange new power had manifested itself again . . . But *was* it a power? Might it not rather be a disease – a sort of intermittent delirium, concentrating my energy of brain into moments of unhealthy activity, and leaving my saner hours all the more barren? I felt a dizzy sense of unreality in what my eye rested on; I grasped the bell convulsively, like one trying to free himself from nightmare, and rang it twice. Pierre came with a look of alarm in his face.

'*Monsieur ne se trouve pas bien?*' he said, anxiously.

'I'm tired of waiting, Pierre,' I said, as distinctly and emphatically as I could, like a man determined to be sober in spite of wine; 'I'm afraid something has happened to my father – he's usually so punctual. Run to the Hôtel des Bergues and see if he is there.'

Pierre left the room at once, with a soothing '*Bien, Monsieur*'; and I felt the better for this scene of simple, waking prose. Seeking to calm myself still further, I went into my bedroom, adjoining the *salon*, and opened a case of eau-de-Cologne; took out a bottle; went through the process of taking out the cork very neatly, and then rubbed the reviving spirit over my hands and forehead, and under my nostrils, drawing a new delight from the scent because I had procured it by slow details of labour, and by no strange sudden madness. Already I had begun to taste something of the horror that belongs to the lot of a human being whose nature is not adjusted to simple human conditions.

Still enjoying the scent, I returned to the *salon*, but it was not unoccupied, as it had been before I left it. In front of the Chinese folding-screen there was my father, with Mrs Filmore on his right hand, and on his left – the slim blond-haired girl, with the keen face and the keen eyes fixed on me in half-smiling curiosity.

'Well, Latimer, you thought me long,' my father said . . .

I heard no more, felt no more, till I became conscious that I was lying with my head low on the sofa, Pierre and my father by my side. As soon as I was thoroughly revived, my father left the room, and presently returned, saying –

'I've been to tell the ladies how you are, Latimer. They were waiting in the next room. We shall put off our shopping expedition today.'

Presently he said, 'That young lady is Bertha Grant, Mrs Filmore's orphan niece. Filmore has adopted her, and she lives with them, so you will have her for a neighbour when we go home – perhaps for a near relation; for there is a tenderness between her and Alfred, I suspect, and I should be gratified by the match, since Filmore means to provide for her in every way as if she were his daughter. It had not occurred to me that you knew nothing about her living with the Filmores.'

He made no further allusion to the fact of my having fainted at the moment of seeing her, and I would not for the world have told him the reason: I shrank from the idea of disclosing to any one what might be regarded as a pitiable peculiarity, most of all from betraying it to my father, who would have suspected my sanity ever after.

I do not mean to dwell with particularity on the details of my experience. I have described these two cases at length, because they had definite, clearly traceable results in my after-lot.

Shortly after this last occurrence – I think the very next day – I began to be aware of a phase in my abnormal sensibility, to which, from the languid and slight nature of my intercourse with others since my illness, I had not been alive before. This was the obtrusion on my mind of the mental process going forward in first one person, and then another, with whom I happened to be in contact: the vagrant, frivolous ideas and emotions of some uninteresting acquaintance – Mrs Filmore, for example – would force themselves on my consciousness like an importunate, ill-played musical instrument, or the loud activity of an imprisoned insect. But this unpleasant sensibility was fitful, and left me moments of rest, when the souls of my companions were once more shut out from me, and I felt a relief such as silence brings to wearied nerves. I might have believed this importunate insight to be merely a diseased activity of the imagination, but that my prevision of incalculable words and actions proved it to have a fixed relation to the mental process in other minds. But this superadded consciousness, wearying and annoying enough when it urged on me the trivial experience of indifferent people, became an intense pain and grief when it seemed to be opening to me the souls of those who were in a close relation to me – when the rational talk, the graceful attentions, the wittily-turned phrases, and the kindly deeds, which used to make the web of their characters, were seen as if thrust asunder by a microscopic vision, that showed all the intermediate frivolities, all the suppressed egoism, all the struggling chaos of puerilities, meanness, vague capricious memories, and indolent make-shift thoughts, from which human words and deeds emerge like leaflets covering a fermenting heap.

At Basle we were joined by my brother Alfred, now a handsome self-confident man of six-and-twenty – a thorough contrast to my fragile, nervous, ineffectual self. I believe I was held to have a sort of half-womanish, half-ghostly beauty; for the portrait-painters, who are thick as weeds at Geneva, had often asked me to sit to them, and I had been the model of a dying minstrel in a fancy picture. But I thoroughly disliked my own *physique*, and nothing but the belief that it was a condition of poetic genius would have reconciled me to it. That brief hope was quite fled, and I saw in my face now nothing but the stamp of a morbid organisation, framed for passive suffering – too feeble for the sublime resistance of poetic production. Alfred, from whom I had been almost constantly separated, and who, in his present stage of character and appearance, came before me as a perfect stranger, was bent on being extremely friendly and brother-like to me. He had the superficial kindness of a good-humoured, self-satisfied nature, that fears no rivalry, and has encountered no contrarieties. I am not sure that my disposition was good enough for me to have been quite free from envy towards him, even if our desires had not clashed, and if I had been in the healthy human condition which admits of generous confidence and charitable construction. There must always have been an antipathy between our natures. As it was, he became in a few weeks an object of intense hatred to me; and when he entered the room, still more when he spoke, it was as if a sensation of grating metal had set my teeth on edge. My diseased consciousness was more intensely and continually occupied with his thoughts and emotions, than with those of any other person who came in my way. I was perpetually exasperated with the petty promptings of his conceit and his love of patronage, with his self-complacent belief in Bertha Grant's passion for him, with his half-pitying contempt for me – seen not in the ordinary indications of intonation and phrase and slight action, which an acute and suspicious mind is on the watch for, but in all their naked skinless complication.

For we were rivals, and our desires clashed, though he was not aware of it. I have said nothing yet of the effect Bertha Grant produced in me on a nearer acquaintance. That effect was chiefly determined by the fact that she made the only exception, among all the human beings about me, to my unhappy gift of insight. About Bertha I was always in a state of uncertainty: I could watch the expression of her face, and speculate on its meaning; I could ask for her opinion with the real interest of ignorance; I could listen for her words and watch for her smile with hope and fear: she had for me the fascination of an unravelled destiny. I say it was this fact that chiefly determined the strong effect she produced on me: for, in the abstract, no womanly character could seem to have less affinity for that of a shrinking, romantic, passionate youth than Bertha's. She was keen, sarcastic, unimaginative, prematurely cynical, remaining critical and unmoved in the most impressive scenes, inclined to dissect all my favourite poems, and especially contemptuous towards the German lyrics which were my pet literature at that time. To this moment I am unable to define my feeling towards her: it was not ordinary boyish admiration, for she was the very opposite, even to the colour of her hair, of the ideal woman who still remained to me the type of loveliness; and she was without that enthusiasm for the great and good, which, even at the moment of her strongest dominion over me, I should have declared to be the highest element of character. But there is no

tyranny more complete than that which a self-centred negative
nature exercises over a morbidly sensitive nature perpetually
craving sympathy and support. The most independent people
feel the effect of a man's silence in heightening their value for
his opinion – feel an additional triumph in conquering the
reverence of a critic habitually captious and satirical: no wonder,
then, that an enthusiastic self-distrusting youth should watch
and wait before the closed secret of a sarcastic woman's face, as
if it were the shrine of the doubtfully benignant deity who ruled
his destiny. For a young enthusiast is unable to imagine the total
negation in another mind of the emotions which are stirring his
own: they may be feeble, latent, inactive, he thinks, but they are
there – they may be called forth; sometimes, in moments of
happy hallucination, he believes they may be there in all the
greater strength because he sees no outward sign of them. And
this effect, as I have intimated, was heightened to its utmost
intensity in me, because Bertha was the only being who remained
for me in the mysterious seclusion of soul that renders such
youthful delusion possible. Doubtless there was another sort of
fascination at work – that subtle physical attraction which
delights in cheating our psychological predictions, and in com-
pelling the men who paint sylphs, to fall in love with some
bonne et brave femme, heavy-heeled and freckled.

Bertha's behaviour towards me was such as to encourage all
my illusions, to heighten my boyish passion, and make me more
and more dependent on her smiles. Looking back with my
present wretched knowledge, I conclude that her vanity and love
of power were intensely gratified by the belief that I had fainted
on first seeing her purely from the strong impression her person
had produced on me. The most prosaic woman likes to believe
herself the object of a violent, a poetic passion; and without a
grain of romance in her, Bertha had that spirit of intrigue which
gave piquancy to the idea that the brother of the man she meant
to marry was dying with love and jealousy for her sake. That
she meant to marry my brother, was what at that time I did not
believe; for though he was assiduous in his attentions to her,
and I knew well enough that both he and my father had made
up their minds to this result, there was not yet an understood
engagement – there had been no explicit declaration; and Bertha
habitually, while she flirted with my brother, and accepted his
homage in a way that implied to him a thorough recognition of

its intention, made me believe, by the subtlest looks and phrases – feminine nothings which could never be quoted against her – that he was really the object of her secret ridicule; that she thought him, as I did, a coxcomb, whom she would have pleasure in disappointing. Me she openly petted in my brother's presence, as if I were too young and sickly ever to be thought of as a lover; and that was the view he took of me. But I believe she must inwardly have delighted in the tremors into which she threw me by the coaxing way in which she patted my curls, while she laughed at my quotations. Such caresses were always given in the presence of our friends; for when we were alone together, she affected a much greater distance towards me, and now and then took the opportunity, by words or slight actions, to stimulate my foolish timid hope that she really preferred me. And why should she not follow her inclination? I was not in so advantageous a position as my brother, but I had fortune, I was not a year younger than she was, and she was an heiress, who would soon be of age to decide for herself.

The fluctuations of hope and fear, confined to this one channel, made each day in her presence a delicious torment. There was one deliberate act of hers which especially helped to intoxicate me. When we were at Vienna her twentieth birthday occurred, and as she was very fond of ornaments, we all took the opportunity of the splendid jewellers' shops in that Teutonic Paris to purchase her a birthday present of jewellery. Mine, naturally, was the least expensive; it was an opal ring – the opal was my favourite stone, because it seems to blush and turn pale as if it had a soul. I told Bertha so when I gave it her, and said that it was an emblem of the poetic nature, changing with the changing light of heaven and of woman's eyes. In the evening she appeared elegantly dressed, and wearing conspicuously all the birthday presents except mine. I looked eagerly at her fingers, but saw no opal. I had no opportunity of noticing this to her during the evening; but the next day, when I found her seated near the window alone, after breakfast, I said, 'You scorn to wear my poor opal. I should have remembered that you despised poetic natures, and should have given you coral, or turquoise, or some other opaque unresponsive stone.' 'Do I despise it?' she answered, taking hold of a delicate gold chain which she always wore round her neck and drawing out the end from her bosom with my ring hanging on it; 'it hurts me a little, I can tell you,' she said, with her usual dubious smile, 'to wear it in that secret place; and since your poetical nature is so stupid as to prefer a more public position, I shall not endure the pain any longer.'

She took off the ring from the chain and put it on her finger, smiling still, while the blood rushed to my cheeks, and I could not trust myself to say a word of entreaty that she would keep the ring where it was before.

I was completely fooled by this, and for two days shut myself up in my room whenever Bertha was absent, that I might intoxicate myself afresh with the thought of this scene and all it implied.

I should mention that during these two months – which seemed a long life to me from the novelty and intensity of the pleasures and pains I underwent – my diseased participation in other people's consciousness continued to torment me; now it was my father, and now my brother, now Mrs Filmore or her husband, and now our German courier, whose stream of thought rushed upon me like a ringing in the ears not to be got rid of, though it allowed my own impulses and ideas to continue their uninterrupted course. It was like a preternaturally heightened sense of hearing, making audible to one a roar of sound where others find perfect stillness. The weariness and disgust of this involuntary intrusion into other souls was counteracted only by my ignorance of Bertha, and my growing passion for her; a passion enormously stimulated, if not produced, by that ignorance. She was my oasis of mystery in the dreary desert of knowledge. I had never allowed my diseased condition to betray itself, or to drive me into any unusual speech or action, except once, when, in a moment of peculiar bitterness against my brother, I had forestalled some words which I knew he was going to utter – a clever observation, which he had prepared beforehand. He had occasionally a slightly-affected hesitation in his speech, and when he paused an instant after the second word, my impatience and jealousy impelled me to continue the speech for him, as if it were something we had both learned by rote. He coloured and looked astonished, as well as annoyed; and the words had no sooner escaped my lips than I felt a shock of alarm lest such an anticipation of words – very far from being words of course, easy to divine – should have betrayed me as an exceptional being, a sort of quiet energumen,[14] whom every one, Bertha above all, would shudder at and avoid. But I magnified, as usual, the impression any word or deed of mine could produce on others; for no one gave any sign of having noticed my interruption as more than a rudeness, to be forgiven me on the score of my feeble nervous condition.

While this superadded consciousness of the actual was almost constant with me, I had never had a recurrence of that distinct prevision which I have described in relation to my first interview with Bertha; and I was waiting with eager curiosity to know whether or not my vision of Prague would prove to have been an instance of the same kind. A few days after the incident of the opal ring, we were paying one of our frequent visits to the Lichtenberg Palace. I could never look at many pictures in succession; for pictures, when they are at all powerful, affect me so strongly that one or two exhaust all my capability of contemplation. This morning I had been looking at Giorgione's[15] picture of the cruel-eyed woman, said to be a likeness of Lucrezia Borgia.[16] I had stood long alone before it, fascinated by the terrible reality of that cunning, relentless face, till I felt a strange poisoned sensation, as if I had long been inhaling a fatal odour, and was just beginning to be conscious of its effects. Perhaps even then I should not have moved away, if the rest of the party had not returned to this room, and announced that they were going to the Belvedere Gallery[17] to settle a bet which had arisen between my brother and Mr Filmore about a portrait. I followed them dreamily, and was hardly alive to what occurred till they had all gone up to the gallery, leaving me below; for I refused to come within sight of another picture that day. I made my way to the Grand Terrace, since it was agreed that we should saunter in the gardens when the dispute had been decided. I had been sitting here a short space, vaguely conscious of trim gardens, with a city and green hills in the distance, when, wishing to avoid the proximity of the sentinel, I rose and walked down the broad stone steps, intending to seat myself farther on in the gardens. Just as I reached the gravel-walk, I felt an arm slipped within mine, and a light hand gently pressing my wrist. In the same instant a strange intoxicating numbness passed over me, like the continuance or climax of the sensation I was still feeling from the gaze of Lucrezia Borgia. The gardens, the summer sky, the consciousness of Bertha's arm being within mine, all vanished, and I seemed to be suddenly in darkness, out of which there gradually broke a dim firelight, and I felt myself sitting in my father's leather chair in the library at home. I knew the fireplace – the dogs for the wood-fire[18] – the black marble chimney-piece with the white marble medallion of the dying Cleopatra in the centre. Intense and hopeless misery was pressing on my soul; the light became stronger, for Bertha was entering with a candle in her hand – Bertha, my wife – with cruel eyes, with green jewels and green leaves on her white ball-dress; every hateful thought within her present to me . . . 'Madman, idiot! why don't you kill yourself, then?' It was a moment of hell. I saw into her pitiless soul – saw its barren worldliness, its scorching hate – and felt it clothe me round like an air I was obliged to breathe. She came with her candle and stood over me with a bitter smile of contempt; I saw the great emerald brooch on her bosom, a studded serpent with diamond eyes. I shuddered – I despised this woman with the barren soul and mean thoughts; but I felt helpless before her, as if she clutched my bleeding heart, and would clutch it till the last drop of life-blood ebbed away. She was my wife, and we hated each other. Gradually the hearth, the dim library, the candle-light disappeared – seemed to melt away into a background of light, the green serpent with the diamond eyes remaining a dark image on the retina. Then I had a sense of my eyelids quivering, and the living daylight broke in upon me; I saw gardens, and heard voices; I was seated on the steps of the Belvedere Terrace, and my friends were round me.

The tumult of mind into which I was thrown by this hideous vision made me ill for several days, and prolonged our stay at Vienna. I shuddered with horror as the scene recurred to me; and it recurred constantly, with all its minutiæ, as if they had been burnt into my memory; and yet, such is the madness of the human heart under the influence of its immediate desires, I felt a wild hell-braving joy that Bertha was to be mine; for the fulfilment of my former prevision concerning her first appearance before me, left me little hope that this last hideous glimpse of the future was the mere diseased play of my own mind, and had no relation to external realities. One thing alone I looked towards as a possible means of casting doubt on my terrible conviction – the discovery that my vision of Prague had been false – and Prague was the next city on our route.

Meanwhile, I was no sooner in Bertha's society again, than I was as completely under her sway as before. What if I saw into the heart of Bertha, the matured woman – Bertha, my wife? Bertha, the *girl*, was a fascinating secret to me still: I trembled under her touch; I felt the witchery of her presence; I yearned to be assured of her love. The fear of poison is feeble against the sense of thirst. Nay, I was just as jealous of my brother as before – just as much irritated by his small patronising ways; for my pride, my diseased sensibility, were there as they had always been, and winced as inevitably under every offence as my eye winced from an intruding mote. The future, even when brought within the compass of feeling by a vision that made me shudder, had still no more than the force of an idea, compared with the force of present emotion – of my love for Bertha, of my dislike and jealousy towards my brother.

It is an old story, that men sell themselves to the tempter, and sign a bond with their blood, because it is only to take effect at a distant day; then rush on to snatch the cup their souls thirst after with an impulse not the less savage because there is a dark shadow beside them for evermore.[19] There is no short cut, no patent tram-road, to wisdom: after all the centuries of invention, the soul's path lies through the thorny wilderness which must be still trodden in solitude, with bleeding feet, with sobs for help, as it was trodden by them of old time.

My mind speculated eagerly on the means by which I should become my brother's successful rival, for I was still too timid, in my ignorance of Bertha's actual feeling, to venture on any step that would urge from her an avowal of it. I thought I should gain confidence even for this, if my vision of Prague proved to have been veracious; and yet, the horror of that certitude! Behind the slim girl Bertha, whose words and looks I watched for, whose touch was bliss, there stood continually that Bertha with the fuller form, the harder eyes, the more rigid mouth, – with the barren selfish soul laid bare; no longer a fascinating secret, but a measured fact, urging itself perpetually on my unwilling sight. Are you unable to give me your sympathy – you who read this? Are you unable to imagine this double consciousness at work within me, flowing on like two parallel streams which never mingle their waters and blend into a common hue? Yet you must have known something of the presentiments that spring from an insight at war with passion; and my visions were only like presentiments intensified to horror. You have known the powerlessness of ideas before the might of impulse; and my visions, when once they had passed into memory, were mere ideas – pale shadows that beckoned in vain, while my hand was grasped by the living and the loved.

In after-days I thought with bitter regret that if I had foreseen something more or something different – if instead of that hideous vision which poisoned the passion it could not destroy, or if even along with it I could have had a foreshadowing of that moment when I looked on my brother's face for the last time, some softening influence would have been shed over my feeling towards him: pride and hatred would surely have been subdued into pity, and the record of those hidden sins would have been shortened. But this is one of the vain thoughts with which we men flatter ourselves. We try to believe that the egoism within us would have easily been melted, and that it was only the narrowness of our knowledge which hemmed in our generosity, our awe, our human piety, and hindered them from submerging our hard indifference to the sensations and emotions of our fellow. Our tenderness and self-renunciation seem strong when our egoism has had its day – when, after our mean striving for a triumph that is to be another's loss, the triumph comes suddenly, and we shudder at it, because it is held out by the chill hand of death.

Our arrival in Prague happened at night, and I was glad of this, for it seemed like a deferring of a terribly decisive moment, to be in the city for hours without seeing it. As we were not to remain long in Prague, but to go on speedily to Dresden, it was proposed that we should drive out the next morning and take a general view of the place, as well as visit some of its specially interesting spots, before the heat became oppressive – for we were in August, and the season was hot and dry. But it happened that the ladies were rather late at their morning toilet, and to my father's politely-repressed but perceptible annoyance, we were not in the carriage till the morning was far advanced. I thought with a sense of relief, as we entered the Jews' quarter, where we were to visit the old synagogue, that we should be kept in this flat, shut-up part of the city, until we should all be too tired and too warm to go farther, and so we should return without seeing more than the streets through which we had already passed. That would give me another day's suspense – suspense, the only form in which a fearful spirit knows the solace of hope. But, as I stood under the blackened, groined

arches of that old synagogue, made dimly visible by the seven
thin candles in the sacred lamp, while our Jewish cicerone[20]
reached down the Book of the Law, and read to us in its ancient
tongue, – I felt a shuddering impression that this strange
building, with its shrunken lights, this surviving withered remnant of medieval Judaism, was of a piece with my vision. Those
darkened dusty Christian saints, with their loftier arches and
their larger candles, needed the consolatory scorn with which
they might point to a more shrivelled death-in-life than their
own.

As I expected, when we left the Jews' quarter the elders of our
party wished to return to the hotel. But now, instead of rejoicing
in this, as I had done beforehand, I felt a sudden overpowering
impulse to go on at once to the bridge, and put an end to the
suspense I had been wishing to protract. I declared, with unusual
decision, that I would get out of the carriage and walk on alone;
they might return without me. My father, thinking this merely a
sample of my usual 'poetic nonsense', objected that I should
only do myself harm by walking in the heat; but when I
persisted, he said angrily that I might follow my own absurd
devices, but that Schmidt (our courier) must go with me. I
assented to this, and set off with Schmidt towards the bridge. I
had no sooner passed from under the archway of the grand old
gate leading on to the bridge, than a trembling seized me, and I
turned cold under the midday sun; yet I went on; I was in search
of something – a small detail which I remembered with special
intensity as part of my vision. There it was – the patch of
rainbow light on the pavement transmitted through a lamp in
the shape of a star.

CHAPTER 2

Before the autumn was at an end, and while the brown leaves still stood thick on the beeches in our park, my brother and Bertha were engaged to each other, and it was understood that their marriage was to take place early in the next spring. In spite of the certainty I had felt from that moment on the bridge at Prague, that Bertha would one day be my wife, my constitutional timidity and distrust had continued to benumb me, and the words in which I had sometimes premeditated a confession of my love, had died away unuttered. The same conflict had gone on within me as before – the longing for an assurance of love from Bertha's lips, the dread lest a word of contempt and denial should fall upon me like a corrosive acid. What was the conviction of a distant necessity to me? I trembled under a present glance, I hungered after a present joy, I was clogged and chilled by a present fear. And so the days passed on: I witnessed Bertha's engagement and heard her marriage discussed as if I were under a conscious nightmare – knowing it was a dream that would vanish, but feeling stifled under the grasp of hard-clutching fingers.

When I was not in Bertha's presence – and I was with her very often, for she continued to treat me with a playful patronage that wakened no jealousy in my brother – I spent my time chiefly in wandering, in strolling, or taking long rides while the daylight lasted, and then shutting myself up with my unread books; for books had lost the power of chaining my attention. My self-consciousness was heightened to that pitch of intensity in which our own emotions take the form of a drama which urges itself imperatively on our contemplation, and we begin to weep, less under the sense of our suffering than at the thought of it. I felt a sort of pitying anguish over the pathos of my own lot: the lot of a being finely organised for pain, but with hardly any fibres that responded to pleasure – to whom the idea of future evil robbed the present of its joy, and for whom the idea of future good did not still the uneasiness of a present yearning or a present dread. I went dumbly through that stage of the poet's suffering, in which he feels the delicious pang of utterance, and makes an image of his sorrows.

I was left entirely without remonstrance concerning this dreamy wayward life: I knew my father's thought about me: 'That lad will never be good for anything in life: he may waste his years in an insignificant way on the income that falls to him: I shall not trouble myself about a career for him.'

One mild morning in the beginning of November, it happened that I was standing outside the portico patting lazy old Cæsar, a Newfoundland almost blind with age, the only dog that ever took any notice of me – for the very dogs shunned me, and fawned on the happier people about me – when the groom brought up my brother's horse which was to carry him to the hunt, and my brother himself appeared at the door, florid, broad-chested, and self-complacent, feeling what a good-natured fellow he was not to behave insolently to us all on the strength of his great advantages.

'Latimer, old boy,' he said to me in a tone of compassionate cordiality, 'what a pity it is you don't have a run with the hounds now and then! The finest thing in the world for low spirits!'

'Low spirits!' I thought bitterly, as he rode away; 'that is the sort of phrase with which coarse, narrow natures like yours think to describe experience of which you can know no more than your horse knows. It is to such as you that the good of this world falls: ready dulness, healthy selfishness, good-tempered conceit – these are the keys to happiness.'

The quick thought came, that my selfishness was even stronger than his – it was only a suffering selfishness instead of an enjoying one. But then, again, my exasperating insight into Alfred's self-complacent soul, his freedom from all the doubts and fears, the unsatisfied yearnings, the exquisite tortures of sensitiveness, that had made the web of my life, seemed to absolve me from all bonds towards him. This man needed no pity, no love; those fine influences would have been as little felt by him as the delicate white mist is felt by the rock it caresses. There was no evil in store for *him*: if he was not to marry Bertha, it would be because he had found a lot pleasanter to himself.

Mr Filmore's house lay not more than half a mile beyond our own gates, and whenever I knew my brother was gone in an another direction, I went there for the chance of finding Bertha at home. Later on in the day I walked thither. By a rare accident she was alone, and we walked out in the grounds together, for she seldom went on foot beyond the trimly-swept gravel-walks. I remember what a beautiful sylph she looked to me as the low November sun shone on her blond hair, and she tripped along teasing me with her usual light banter, to which I listened half fondly, half moodily; it was all the sign Bertha's mysterious inner self ever made to me. Today perhaps the moodiness predominated, for I had not yet shaken off the access of jealous hate which my brother had raised in me by his parting patronage. Suddenly I interrupted and startled her by saying, almost fiercely, 'Bertha, how can you love Alfred?'

She looked at me with surprise for a moment, but soon her light smile came again, and she answered sarcastically, 'Why do you suppose I love him?'

'How can you ask that, Bertha?'

'What! your wisdom thinks I must love the man I'm going to marry? The most unpleasant thing in the world. I should quarrel with him; I should be jealous of him; our *ménage* would be conducted in a very ill-bred manner. A little quiet contempt contributes greatly to the elegance of life.'

'Bertha, that is not your real feeling. Why do you delight in trying to deceive me by inventing such cynical speeches?'

'I need never take the trouble of invention in order to deceive you, my small Tasso'[1] – (that was the mocking name she usually gave me). 'The easiest way to deceive a poet is to tell him the truth.'

She was testing the validity of her epigram in a daring way, and for a moment the shadow of my vision – the Bertha whose soul was no secret to me – passed between me and the radiant girl, the playful sylph whose feelings were a fascinating mystery. I suppose I must have shuddered, or betrayed in some other way my momentary chill of horror.

'Tasso!' she said, seizing my wrist, and peeping round into my face, 'are you really beginning to discern what a heartless girl I am? Why, you are not half the poet I thought you were; you are actually capable of believing the truth about me.'

The shadow passed from between us, and was no longer the

object nearest to me. The girl whose light fingers grasped me, whose elfish charming face looking into mine – who, I thought, was betraying an interest in my feelings that she would not have directly avowed, – this warm-breathing presence again possessed my senses and imagination like a returning syren melody which had been overpowered for an instant by the roar of threatening waves. It was a moment as delicious to me as the waking up to a consciousness of youth after a dream of middle age. I forgot everything but my passion, and said with swimming eyes –

'Bertha, shall you love me when we are first married? I wouldn't mind if you really loved me only for a little while.'

Her look of astonishment, as she loosed my hand and started away from me recalled me to a sense of my strange, my criminal indiscretion.

'Forgive me,' I said, hurriedly, as soon as I could speak again; 'I did not know what I was saying.'

'Ah, Tasso's mad fit has come on, I see,' she answered quietly, for she had recovered herself sooner than I had. 'Let him go home and keep his head cool. I must go in, for the sun is setting.'

I left her – full of indignation against myself. I had let slip words which, if she reflected on them, might rouse in her a suspicion of my abnormal mental condition – a suspicion which of all things I dreaded. And besides that, I was ashamed of the apparent baseness I had committed in uttering them to my brother's betrothed wife. I wandered home slowly, entering our park through a private gate instead of by the lodges. As I approached the house, I saw a man dashing off at full speed from the stableyard across the park. Had any accident happened at home? No; perhaps it was only one of my father's peremptory business errands that required this headlong haste. Nevertheless I quickened my pace without any distinct motive, and was soon at the house. I will not dwell on the scene I found there. My brother was dead – had been pitched from his horse, and killed on the spot by a concussion of the brain.

I went up to the room where he lay, and where my father was seated beside him with a look of rigid despair. I had shunned my father more than any one since our return home, for the radical antipathy between our natures made my insight into his inner self a constant affliction to me. But now, as I went up to him, and stood beside him in sad silence, I felt the presence of a new element that blended us as we had never been blent before.

My father had been one of the most successful men in the money-getting world: he had had no sentimental sufferings, no illness. The heaviest trouble that had befallen him was the death of his first wife. But he married my mother soon after; and I remember he seemed exactly the same, to my keen childish observation, the week after her death as before. But now, at last, a sorrow had come – the sorrow of old age, which suffers the more from the crushing of its pride and its hopes, in proportion as the pride and hope are narrow and prosaic. His son was to have been married soon – would probably have stood for the borough at the next election. That son's existence was the best motive that could be alleged for making new purchases of land every year to round off the estate. It is a dreary thing to live on doing the same things year after year, without knowing why we do them. Perhaps the tragedy of disappointed youth and passion is less piteous than the tragedy of disappointed age and worldliness.

As I saw into the desolation of my father's heart, I felt a movement of deep pity towards him, which was the beginning of a new affection – an affection that grew and strengthened in spite of the strange bitterness with which he regarded me in the first month or two after my brother's death. If it had not been for the softening influence of my compassion for him – the first deep compassion I had ever felt – I should have been stung by the perception that my father transferred the inheritance of an eldest son to me with a mortified sense that fate had compelled him to the unwelcome course of caring for me as an important being. It was only in spite of himself that he began to think of me with anxious regard. There is hardly any neglected child for whom death has made vacant a more favoured place, who will not understand what I mean.

Gradually, however, my new deference to his wishes, the effect of that patience which was born of my pity for him, won upon his affection, and he began to please himself with the endeavour to make me fill my brother's place as fully as my feebler personality would admit. I saw that the prospect which by-and-by presented itself of my becoming Bertha's husband was welcome to him, and he even contemplated in my case what he had not intended in my brother's – that his son and daughter-in-law should make one household with him. My softened feeling towards my father made this the happiest time I had known since childhood; – these last months in which I retained the delicious illusion of loving Bertha, of longing and doubting and hoping that she might love me. She behaved with a certain new consciousness and distance towards me after my brother's death; and I too was under a double constraint – that of delicacy towards my brother's memory, and of anxiety as to the impression my abrupt words had left on her mind. But the additional screen this mutual reserve erected between us only brought me more completely under her power: no matter how empty the adytum,[2] so that the veil be thick enough. So absolute is our soul's need of something hidden and uncertain for the maintenance of that doubt and hope and effort which are the breath of its life, that if the whole future were laid bare to us beyond today, the interest of all mankind would be bent on the hours that lie between; we should pant after the uncertainties of our one morning and our one afternoon; we should rush fiercely to the Exchange for our last possibility of speculation, of success, of disappointment; we should have a glut of political prophets foretelling a crisis or a no-crisis within the only twenty-four hours left open to prophecy. Conceive the condition of the human mind if all propositions whatsoever were self-evident except one, which was to become self-evident at the close of a summer's day, but in the meantime might be the subject of question, of hypothesis, of debate. Art and philosophy, literature and science, would fasten like bees on that one proposition which had the honey of probability in it, and be the more eager because their enjoyment would end with sunset. Our impulses, our spiritual activities, no more adjust themselves to the idea of their future nullity, than the beating of our heart, or the irritability of our muscles.

Bertha, the slim, fair-haired girl, whose present thoughts and emotions were an enigma to me amidst the fatiguing obviousness of the other minds around me, was as absorbing to me as a single unknown today – as a single hypothetic proposition to remain problematic till sunset; and all the cramped, hemmed-in belief and disbelief, trust and distrust, of my nature, welled out in this one narrow channel.

And she made me believe that she loved me. Without ever quitting her tone of *badinage* and playful superiority, she intoxicated me with the sense that I was necessary to her, that she was never at ease unless I was near her, submitting to her playful tyranny. It costs a woman so little effort to besot us in this way! A half-repressed word, a moment's unexpected silence, even an easy fit of petulance on our account, will serve us as *hashish*[3] for a long while. Out of the subtlest web of scarcely perceptible signs, she set me weaving the fancy that she had always unconsciously loved me better than Alfred, but that, with the ignorant fluttered sensibility of a young girl, she had been imposed on by the charm that lay for her in the distinction of being admired and chosen by a man who made so brilliant a figure in the world as my brother. She satirised herself in a very graceful way for her vanity and ambition. What was it to me that I had the light of my wretched prevision on the fact that now it was I who possessed at least all but the personal part of my brother's advantages? Our sweet illusions are half of them conscious illusions, like effects of colour that we know to be made up of tinsel, broken glass, and rags.

We were married eighteen months after Alfred's death, one cold, clear morning in April, when there came hail and sunshine both together; and Bertha, in her white silk and pale-green leaves, and the pale hues of her hair and face, looked like the spirit of the morning. My father was happier than he had thought of being again: my marriage, he felt sure, would complete the desirable modification of my character, and make me practical and worldly enough to take my place in society among sane men. For he delighted in Bertha's tact and acuteness, and felt sure she would be mistress of me, and make me what she chose: I was only twenty-one, and madly in love with her. Poor father! He kept that hope a little while after our first year of marriage, and it was not quite extinct when paralysis came and saved him from utter disappointment.

I shall hurry through the rest of my story, not dwelling so much as I have hitherto done on my inward experience. When people are well known to each other, they talk rather of what befalls them externally, leaving their feelings and sentiments to be inferred.

We lived in a round of visits for some time after our return home, giving splendid dinner-parties, and making a sensation in our neighbourhood by the new lustre of our equipage, for my father had reserved this display of his increased wealth for the period of his son's marriage; and we gave our acquaintances liberal opportunity for remarking that it was a pity I made so poor a figure as an heir and a bridegroom. The nervous fatigue of this existence, the insincerities and platitudes which I had to live through twice over – through my inner and outward sense – would have been maddening to me, if I had not had that sort of intoxicated callousness which came from the delights of a first passion. A bride and bridegroom, surrounded by all the appliances of wealth, hurried through the day by the whirl of society, filling their solitary moments with hastily-snatched caresses, are prepared for their future life together as the novice is prepared for the cloister – by experiencing its utmost contrast.

Through all these crowded excited months, Bertha's inward self remained shrouded from me, and I still read her thoughts only through the language of her lips and demeanour: I had still the human interest of wondering whether what I did and said pleased her, of longing to hear a word of affection, of giving a delicious exaggeration of meaning to her smile. But I was conscious of a growing difference in her manner towards me; sometimes strong enough to be called haughty coldness, cutting and chilling me as the hail had done that came across the sunshine on our marriage morning; sometimes only perceptible in the dexterous avoidance of a *tête-à-tête* walk or dinner to which I had been looking forward. I had been deeply pained by this – had even felt a sort of crushing of the heart, from the sense that my brief day of happiness was near its setting; but still I remained dependent on Bertha, eager for the last rays of a bliss that would soon be gone for ever, hoping and watching for some after-glow more beautiful from the impending night.

I remember – how should I not remember? – the time when that dependence and hope utterly left me, when the sadness I had felt in Bertha's growing estrangement became a joy that I looked back upon with longing, as a man might look back on the last pains in a paralysed limb. It was just after the close of my father's last illness, which had necessarily withdrawn us from society and thrown us more upon each other. It was the evening of my father's death. On that evening the veil which had shrouded Bertha's soul from me – had made me find in her alone among my fellow-beings the blessed possibility of mystery, and doubt, and expectation – was first withdrawn. Perhaps it was the first day since the beginning of my passion for her, in which that passion was completely neutralised by the presence of an absorbing feeling of another kind. I had been watching by

my father's deathbed: I had been witnessing the last fitful
yearning glance his soul had cast back on the spent inheritance
of life – the last faint consciousness of love he had gathered
from the pressure of my hand. What are all our personal loves
when we have been sharing in that supreme agony? In the first
moments when we come away from the presence of death, every
other relation to the living is merged, to our feeling, in the great
relation of a common nature and a common destiny.

In that state of mind I joined Bertha in her private sitting-
room. She was seated in a leaning posture on a settee, with her
back towards the door; the great rich coils of her pale blond
hair surmounting her small neck, visible above the back of the
settee. I remember, as I closed the door behind me, a cold
tremulousness seizing me, and a vague sense of being hated and
lonely – vague and strong, like a presentiment. I know how I
looked at that moment, for I saw myself in Bertha's thought as
she lifted her cutting grey eyes, and looked at me: a miserable
ghost-seer, surrounded by phantoms in the noon-day, trembling
under a breeze when the leaves were still, without appetite for
the common objects of human desire, but pining after the
moonbeams. We were front to front with each other, and judged
each other. The terrible moment of complete illumination had
come to me, and I saw that the darkness had hidden no
landscape from me, but only a blank prosaic wall: from that
evening forth, through the sickening years which followed, I
saw all round the narrow room of this woman's soul – saw
petty artifice and mere negation where I had delighted to believe
in coy sensibilities and in wit at war with latent feeling – saw
the light floating vanities of the girl defining themselves into the
systematic coquetry, the scheming selfishness, of the woman –
saw repulsion and antipathy harden into cruel hatred, giving
pain only for the sake of wreaking itself.

For Bertha too, after her kind, felt the bitterness of disillusion.
She had believed that my wild poet's passion for her would
make me her slave; and that, being her slave, I should execute
her will in all things. With the essential shallowness of a
negative, unimaginative nature, she was unable to conceive the
fact that sensibilities were anything else than weaknesses. She
had thought my weaknesses would put me in her power, and
she found them unmanageable forces. Our positions were
reversed. Before marriage she had completely mastered my

imagination, for she was a secret to me; and I created the unknown thought before which I trembled as if it were hers. But now that her soul was laid open to me, now that I was compelled to share the privacy of her motives, to follow all the petty devices that preceded her words and acts, she found herself powerless with me, except to produce in me the chill shudder of repulsion – powerless, because I could be acted on by no lever within her reach. I was dead to worldly ambitions, to social vanities, to all the incentives within the compass of her narrow imagination, and I lived under influences utterly invisible to her.

She was really pitiable to have such a husband, and so all the world thought. A graceful, brilliant woman, like Bertha, who smiled on morning callers, made a figure in ball-rooms, and was capable of that light repartee which, from such a woman, is accepted as wit, was secure of carrying off all sympathy from a husband who was sickly, abstracted, and, as some suspected, crack-brained. Even the servants in our house gave her the balance of their regard and pity. For there were no audible quarrels between us; our alienation, our repulsion from each other, lay within the silence of our own hearts; and if the mistress went out a great deal, and seemed to dislike the master's society, was it not natural, poor thing? The master was odd. I was kind and just to my dependants, but I excited in them a shrinking, half-contemptuous pity; for this class of men and women are but slightly determined in their estimate of others by general considerations, or even experience, of character. They judge of persons as they judge of coins, and value those who pass current at a high rate.

After a time I interfered so little with Bertha's habits, that it might seem wonderful how her hatred towards me could grow so intense and active as it did. But she had begun to suspect, by some involunatary betrayals of mine, that there was an abnormal power of penetration in me – that fitfully, at least, I was strangely cognisant of her thoughts and intentions, and she began to be haunted by a terror of me, which alternated every now and then with defiance. She meditated continually how the incubus[4] could be shaken off her life – how she could be freed from this hateful bond to a being whom she at once despised as an imbecile, and dreaded as an inquisitor. For a long while she lived in the hope that my evident wretchedness would drive me to the commission of suicide; but suicide was not in my nature.

I was too completely swayed by the sense that I was in the grasp
of unknown forces, to believe in my power of self-release.
Towards my own destiny I had become entirely passive; for my
one ardent desire had spent itself, and impulse no longer
predominated over knowledge. For this reason I never thought
of taking any steps towards a complete separation, which would
have made our alienation evident to the world. Why should I
rush for help to a new course, when I was only suffering from
the consequences of a deed which had been the act of my
intensest will? That would have been the logic of one who had
desires to gratify, and I had no desires. But Bertha and I lived
more and more aloof from each other. The rich find it easy to
live married and apart.

That course of our life which I have indicated in a few
sentences filled the space of years. So much misery – so slow and
hideous a growth of hatred and sin, may be compressed into a
sentence! And men judge of each other's lives through this
summary medium. They epitomise the experience of their
fellow-mortal, and pronounce judgment on him in neat syntax,
and feel themselves wise and virtuous – conquerors over the
temptations they define in well-selected predicates. Seven years
of wretchedness glide glibly over the lips of the man who has
never counted them out in moments of chill disappointment, of
head and heart throbbings, of dread and vain wrestling, of
remorse and despair. We learn *words* by rote, but not their
meaning; *that* must be paid for with our life-blood, and printed
in the subtle fibres of our nerves.

But I will hasten to finish my story. Brevity is justified at once
to those who readily understand, and to those who will never
understand.

Some years after my father's death, I was sitting by the dim
firelight in my library one January evening – sitting in the leather
chair that used to be my father's – when Bertha appeared at the
door, with a candle in her hand, and advanced towards me. I
knew the ball-dress she had on – the white ball-dress, with the
green jewels, shone upon by the light of the wax candle which
lit up the medallion of the dying Cleopatra on the mantelpiece.
Why did she come to me before going out? I had not seen her in
the library, which was my habitual place, for months. Why did
she stand before me with the candle in her hand, with her cruel
contemptuous eyes fixed on me, and the glittering serpent, like

a familiar demon, on her breast? For a moment I thought this fulfilment of my vision at Vienna marked some dreadful crisis in my fate, but I saw nothing in Bertha's mind, as she stood before me, except scorn for the look of overwhelming misery with which I sat before her ... 'Fool, idiot, why don't you kill yourself, then?' – that was her thought. But at length her thoughts reverted to her errand, and she spoke aloud. The apparently indifferent nature of the errand seemed to make a ridiculous anticlimax to my prevision and my agitation.

'I have had to hire a new maid. Fletcher is going to be married, and she wants me to ask you to let her husband have the public-house and farm at Molton. I wish him to have it. You must give the promise now, because Fletcher is going tomorrow morning – and quickly, because I'm in a hurry.'

'Very well; you may promise her,' I said, indifferently, and Bertha swept out of the library again.

I always shrank from the sight of a new person, and all the more when it was a person whose mental life was likely to weary my reluctant insight with worldly ignorant trivialities. But I shrank especially from the sight of this new maid, because her advent had been announced to me at a moment to which I could not cease to attach some fatality: I had a vague dread that I should find her mixed up with the dreary drama of my life – that some new sickening vision would reveal her to me as an evil genius. When at last I did unavoidably meet her, the vague dread was changed into definite disgust. She was a tall, wiry, dark-eyed woman, this Mrs Archer, with a face handsome enough to give her coarse hard nature the odious finish of bold, self-confident coquetry. That was enough to make me avoid her, quite apart from the contemptuous feeling with which she contemplated me. I seldom saw her; but I perceived that she rapidly became a favourite with her mistress, and, after the lapse of eight or nine months, I began to be aware that there had arisen in Bertha's mind towards this woman a mingled feeling of fear and dependence, and that this feeling was associated with ill-defined images of candle-light scenes in her dressing-room, and the locking-up of something in Bertha's cabinet. My interviews with my wife had become so brief and so rarely solitary, that I had no opportunity of perceiving these images in her mind with more definiteness. The recollections of the past become contracted in the rapidity of thought till they sometimes bear hardly a more distinct resemblance to the external reality than the forms of an oriental alphabet to the objects that suggested them.

Besides, for the last year or more a modification had been going forward in my mental condition, and was growing more and more marked. My insight into the minds of those around me was becoming dimmer and more fitful, and the ideas that crowded my double consciousness became less and less dependent on any personal contact. All that was personal in me seemed to be suffering a gradual death, so that I was losing the organ through which the personal agitations and projects of others could affect me. But along with this relief from wearisome insight, there was a new development of what I concluded – as I have since found rightly – to be a prevision of external scenes. It was as if the relation between me and my fellow-men was more and more deadened, and my relation to what we call the inanimate was quickened into new life. The more I lived apart from society, and in proportion as my wretchedness subsided from the violent throb of agonised passion into the dulness of habitual pain, the more frequent and vivid became such visions as that I had had of Prague – of strange cities, of sandy plains, of gigantic ruins, of midnight skies with strange bright constellations, of mountain-passes, of grassy nooks flecked with the afternoon sunshine through the boughs: I was in the midst of such scenes, and in all of them one presence seemed to weigh on me in all these mighty shapes – the presence of something unknown and pitiless. For continual suffering had annihilated religious faith within me: to the utterly miserable – the unloving and the unloved – there is no religion possible, no worship but a worship of devils. And beyond all these, and continually recurring, was the vision of my death – the pangs, the suffocation, the last struggle, when life would be grasped at in vain.

Things were in this state near the end of the seventh year. I had become entirely free from insight, from my abnormal cognisance of any other consciousness than my own, and instead of intruding involuntarily into the world of other minds, was living continually in my own solitary future. Bertha was aware that I was greatly changed. To my surprise she had of late seemed to seek opportunities of remaining in my society, and had cultivated that kind of distant yet familiar talk which is customary between a husband and wife who live in polite and

irrevocable alienation. I bore this with languid submission, and
without feeling enough interest in her motives to be roused into
keen observation; yet I could not help perceiving something
triumphant and excited in her carriage and the expression of her
face – something too subtle to express itself in words or tones,
but giving one the idea that she lived in a state of expectation or
hopeful suspense. My chief feeling was satisfaction that her
inner self was once more shut out from me; and I almost revelled
for the moment in the absent melancholy that made me answer
her at cross purposes, and betray utter ignorance of what she
had been saying. I remember well the look and the smile with
which she one day said, after a mistake of this kind on my part:
'I used to think you were a clairvoyant, and that was the reason
why you were so bitter against other clairvoyants, wanting to
keep your monopoly; but I see now you have become rather
duller than the rest of the world.'

I said nothing in reply. It occurred to me that her recent
obtrusion of herself upon me might have been prompted by the
wish to test my power of detecting some of her secrets; but I let
the thought drop again at once: her motives and her deeds had
no interest for me, but whatever pleasures she might be seeking,
I had no wish to balk her. There was still pity in my soul for
every living thing, and Bertha was living – was surrounded with
possibilities of misery.

Just at this time there occurred an event which roused me
somewhat from my inertia, and gave me an interest in the
passing moment that I had thought impossible for me. It was a
visit from Charles Meunier, who had written me word that he
was coming to England for relaxation from too strenuous
labour, and would like to see me. Meunier had now a European
reputation; but his letter to me expressed that keen remembrance
of an early regard, an early debt of sympathy, which is inseparable from nobility of character: and I too felt as if his presence
would be to me like a transient resurrection into a happier pre-
existence.

He came, and as far as possible, I renewed our old pleasure of
making *tête-à-tête* excursions, though, instead of mountains and
glaciers and the wide blue lake, we had to content ourselves
with mere slopes and ponds and artificial plantations. The years
had changed us both, but with what different result! Meunier
was now a brilliant figure in society, to whom elegant women

pretended to listen, and whose acquaintance was boasted of by noblemen ambitious of brains. He repressed with the utmost delicacy all betrayal of the shock which I am sure he must have received from our meeting, or of a desire to penetrate into my condition and circumstances, and sought by the utmost exertion of his charming social powers to make our reunion agreeable. Bertha was much struck by the unexpected fascinations of a visitor whom she had expected to find presentable only on the score of his celebrity, and put forth all her coquetries and accomplishments. Apparently she succeeded in attracting his admiration, for his manner towards her was attentive and flattering. The effect of his presence on me was so benignant, especially in those renewals of our old *tête-à-tête* wanderings, when he poured forth to me wonderful narratives of his professional experience, that more than once, when his talk turned on the psychological relations of disease, the thought crossed my mind that, if his stay with me were long enough, I might possibly bring myself to tell this man the secrets of my lot. Might there not lie some remedy for *me*, too, in his science? Might there not at least lie some comprehension and sympathy ready for me in his large and susceptible mind? But the thought only flickered feebly now and then, and died out before it could become a wish. The horror I had of again breaking in on the privacy of another soul, made me, by an irrational instinct, draw the shroud of concealment more closely around my own, as we automatically perform the gesture we feel to be wanting in another.

When Meunier's visit was approaching its conclusion, there happened an event which caused some excitement in our household, owing to the surprsingly strong effect it appeared to produce on Bertha – on Bertha, the self-possessed, who usually seemed inaccessible to feminine agitations, and did even her hate in a self-restrained hygienic manner. This event was the sudden severe illness of her maid, Mrs Archer. I have reserved to this moment the mention of a circumstance which had forced itself on my notice shortly before Meunier's arrival, namely, that there had been some quarrel between Bertha and this maid, apparently during a visit to a distant family, in which she had accompanied her mistress. I had overheard Archer speaking in a tone of bitter insolence, which I should have thought an adequate reason for immediate dismissal. No dismissal followed;

on the contrary, Bertha seemed to be silently putting up with personal inconveniences from the exhibitions of this woman's temper. I was the more astonished to observe that her illness seemed a cause of strong solicitude to Bertha; that she was at the bedside night and day, and would allow no one else to officiate as head-nurse. It happened that our family doctor was out on a holiday, an accident which made Meunier's presence in the house doubly welcome, and he apparently entered into the case with an interest which seemed so much stronger than the ordinary professional feeling, that one day when he had fallen into a long fit of silence after visiting her, I said to him –

'Is this a very peculiar case of disease, Meunier?'

'No,' he answered, 'it is an attack of peritonitis, which will be fatal, but which does not differ physically from many other cases that have come under my observation. But I'll tell you what I have on my mind. I want to make an experiment on this woman, if you will give me permission. It can do her no harm – will give her no pain – for I shall not make it until life is extinct to all purposes of sensation. I want to try the effect of transfusing blood into her arteries after the heart has ceased to beat for some minutes. I have tried the experiment again and again with animals that have died of this disease, with astounding results, and I want to try it on a human subject. I have the small tubes necessary, in a case I have with me, and the rest of the apparatus could be prepared readily. I should use my own blood – take it from my own arm. This woman won't live through the night, I'm convinced, and I want you to promise me your assistance in making the experiment. I can't do without another hand, but it would perhaps not be well to call in a medical assistant from among your provincial doctors. A disagreeable foolish version of the thing might get abroad.'

'Have you spoken to my wife on the subject?' I said, 'because she appears to be peculiarly sensitive about this woman: she has been a favourite maid.'

'To tell you the truth,' said Meunier, 'I don't want her to know about it. There are always insuperable difficulties with women in these matters, and the effect on the supposed dead body may be startling. You and I will sit up together, and be in readiness. When certain symptoms appear I shall take you in, and at the right moment we must manage to get every one else out of the room.'

I need not give our farther conversation on the subject. He entered very fully into the details, and overcame my repulsion from them, by exciting in me a mingled awe and curiosity concerning the possible results of his experiment.

We prepared everything, and he instructed me in my part as assistant. He had not told Bertha of his absolute conviction that Archer would not survive through the night, and endeavoured to persuade her to leave the patient and take a night's rest. But she was obstinate, suspecting the fact that death was at hand, and supposing that he wished merely to save her nerves. She refused to leave the sick-room. Meunier and I sat up together in the library, he making frequent visits to the sick-room, and returning with the information that the case was taking precisely the course he expected. Once he said to me, 'Can you imagine any cause of ill feeling this woman has against her mistress, who is so devoted to her?'

'I think there was some misunderstanding between them before her illness. Why do you ask?'

'Because I have observed for the last five or six hours – since, I fancy, she has lost all hope of recovery – there seems a strange prompting in her to say something which pain and failing strength forbid her to utter; and there is a look of hideous meaning in her eyes, which she turns continually towards her mistress. In this disease the mind often remains singularly clear to the last.'

'I am not surprised at an indication of malevolent feeling in her,' I said. 'She is a woman who has always inspired me with distrust and dislike, but she managed to insinuate herself into her mistress's favour.' He was silent after this, looking at the fire with an air of absorption, till he went upstairs again. He stayed away longer than usual, and on returning, said to me quietly, 'Come now.'

I followed him to the chamber where death was hovering. The dark hangings of the large bed made a background that gave a strong relief to Bertha's pale face as I entered. She started forward as she saw me enter, and then looked at Meunier with an expression of angry inquiry; but he lifted up his hand as if to impose silence, while he fixed his glance on the dying woman and felt her pulse. The face was pinched and ghastly, a cold perspiration was on the forehead, and the eyelids were lowered so as almost to conceal the large dark eyes. After a minute or two, Meunier walked round to the other side of the bed where Bertha stood, and with his usual air of gentle politeness towards her begged her to leave the patient under our care – everything should be done for her – she was no longer in a state to be conscious of an affectionate presence. Bertha was hesitating, apparently almost willing to believe his assurance and to comply. She looked round at the ghastly dying face, as if to read the confirmation of that assurance, when for a moment the lowered eyelids were raised again, and it seemed as if the eyes were looking towards Bertha, but blankly. A shudder passed through Bertha's frame, and she returned to her station near the pillow, tacitly implying that she would not leave the room.

The eyelids were lifted no more. Once I looked at Bertha as she watched the face of the dying one. She wore a rich *peignoir*, and her blond hair was half covered by a lace cap: in her attire she was, as always, an elegant woman, fit to figure in a picture of modern aristocratic life: but I asked myself how that face of hers could ever have seemed to me the face of a woman born of woman, with memories of childhood, capable of pain, needing to be fondled? The features at that moment seemed so preternaturally sharp, the eyes were so hard and eager – she looked like a cruel immortal, finding her spiritual feast in the agonies of a dying race. For across those hard features there came something like a flash when the last hour had been breathed out, and we all felt that the dark veil had completely fallen. What secret was there between Bertha and this woman? I turned my eyes from her with a horrible dread lest my insight should return, and I should be obliged to see what had been breeding about two unloving women's hearts. I felt that Bertha had been watching for the moment of death as the sealing of her secret: I thanked Heaven it could remain sealed for me.

Meunier said quietly, 'She is gone.' He then gave his arm to Bertha, and she submitted to be led out of the room.

I suppose it was at her order that two female attendants came into the room, and dismissed the younger one who had been present before. When they entered, Meunier had already opened the artery in the long thin neck that lay rigid on the pillow, and I dismissed them, ordering them to remain at a distance till we rang: the doctor, I said, had an operation to perform – he was not sure about the death. For the next twenty minutes I forgot everything but Meunier and the experiment in which he was so absorbed, that I think his senses would have been closed against all sounds or sights which had no relation to it. It was my task at first to keep up the artificial respiration in the body after the transfusion had been effected, but presently Meunier relieved me, and I could see the wondrous slow return of life; the breast began to heave, the inspirations became stronger, the eyelids quivered, and the soul seemed to have returned beneath them. The artificial respiration was withdrawn: still the breathing continued, and there was a movement of the lips.[5]

Just then I heard the handle of the door moving: I suppose Bertha had heard from the women that they had been dismissed: probably a vague fear had arisen in her mind, for she entered with a look of alarm. She came to the foot of the bed and gave a stifled cry.

The dead woman's eyes were wide open, and met hers in full recognition – the recognition of hate. With a sudden strong effort, the hand that Bertha had thought for ever still was pointed towards her, and the haggard face moved. The gasping eager voice said –

'You mean to poison your husband ... the poison is in the black cabinet ... I got it for you ... you laughed at me, and told lies about me behind my back, to make me disgusting ... because you were jealous ... are you sorry ... now?'

The lips continued to murmur, but the sounds were no longer distinct. Soon there was no sound – only a slight movement: the flame had leaped out, and was being extinguished the faster. The wretched woman's heart-strings had been set to hatred and vengeance; the spirit of life had swept the chords for an instant, and was gone again for ever. Great God! Is this what it is to live again ... to wake up with our unstilled thirst upon us, with our unuttered curses rising to our lips, with our muscles ready to act out their half-committed sins?

Bertha stood pale at the foot of the bed, quivering and helpless, despairing of devices, like a cunning animal whose hiding-places are surrounded by swift-advancing flame. Even Meunier looked paralysed: life for that moment ceased to be a scientific problem to him. As for me, this scene seemed of one texture with the rest of my existence: horror was my familiar, and this new revelation was only like an old pain recurring with new circumstances.

*

Since then Bertha and I have lived apart – she in her own neighbourhood, the mistress of half our wealth, I as a wanderer in foreign countries, until I came to this Devonshire nest to die. Bertha lives pitied and admired; for what had I against that charming woman, whom every one but myself could have been happy with? There had been no witness of the scene in the dying room except Meunier, and while Meunier lived his lips were sealed by a promise to me.

Once or twice, weary of wandering, I rested in a favourite spot, and my heart went out towards the men and women and children whose faces were becoming familiar to me: but I was driven away again in terror at the approach of my old insight – driven away to live continually with the one Unknown Presence revealed and yet hidden by the moving curtain of the earth and sky. Till at last disease took hold of me and forced me to rest here – forced me to live in dependence on my servants. And then the curse of insight – of my double consciousness, came again, and has never left me. I know all their narrow thoughts, their feeble regard, their half-wearied pity.

It is the 20th of September 1850. I know these figures I have just written, as if they were a long familiar inscription. I have seen them on this page in my desk unnumbered times, when the scene of my dying struggle has opened upon me . . .

BROTHER JACOB

Trompeurs, c'est pour vous que j'écris,
Attendez vous à la pareille
LA FONTAINE[1]

CHAPTER I

Among the many fatalities attending the bloom of young desire, that of blindly taking to the confectionery line[2] has not, perhaps, been sufficiently considered. How is the son of a British yeoman,[3] who has been fed principally on salt pork and yeast dumplings, to know that there is satiety for the human stomach even in a paradise of glass jars full of sugared almonds and pink lozenges, and that the tedium of life can reach a pitch where plum-buns at discretion cease to offer the slightest enticement? Or how, at the tender age when a confectioner seems to him a very prince whom all the world must envy, – who breakfasts on macaroons, dines on marengs,[4] sups on twelfth-cake, and fills up the intermediate hours with sugar-candy or peppermint, – how is he to foresee the day of sad wisdom, when he will discern that the confectioner's calling is not socially influential, or favourable to a soaring ambition? I have known a man who turned out to have a metaphysical genius, incautiously, in the period of youthful buoyancy, commence his career as a dancing-master; and you may imagine the use that was made of this initial mistake by opponents who felt themselves bound to warn the public against his doctrine of the Inconceivable. He could not give up his dancing-lessons, because he made his bread by them, and metaphysics would not have found him in so much as salt to his bread. It was really the same with Mr David Faux and the confectionery business. His uncle, the butler at the great house close by Brigford, had made a pet of him in his early boyhood, and it was on a visit to this uncle that the confectioners' shops in that brilliant town had, on a single day, fired his tender imagination. He carried home the pleasing illusion that a confectioner must be at once the happiest and the foremost of men, since the things he made were not only the most beautiful to behold, but the very best eating, and such as the Lord Mayor must always order largely for his private recreation; so that when his father declared he must be put to a trade, David chose

his line without a moment's hesitation; and, with a rashness
inspired by a sweet tooth, wedded himself irrevocably to confectionery. Soon, however, the tooth lost its relish and fell into
blank indifference; and all the while, his mind expanded, his
ambition took new shapes, which could hardly be satisfied
within the sphere his youthful ardour had chosen. But what was
he to do? He was a young man of much mental activity, and,
above all, gifted with a spirit of contrivance; but then, his
faculties would not tell with great effect in any other medium
than that of candied sugars, conserves, and pastry. Say what
you will about the identity of the reasoning process in all
branches of thought, or about the advantage of coming to
subjects with a fresh mind the adjustment of butter to flour, and
of heat to pastry, is *not* the best preparation for the office of
prime minister; besides, in the present imperfectly-organised
state of society, there are social barriers. David could invent
delightful things in the way of drop-cakes, and he had the widest
views of the sugar department; but in other directions he
certainly felt hampered by the want of knowledge and practical
skill; and the world is so inconveniently constituted, that the
vague consciousness of being a fine fellow is no guarantee of
success in any line of business.

This difficulty pressed with some severity on Mr David Faux,
even before his apprenticeship was ended. His soul swelled with
an impatient sense that he ought to become something very
remarkable – that it was quite out of the question for him to
put up with a narrow lot as other men did: he scorned the idea
that he could accept an average. He was sure there was nothing
average about him: even such a person as Mrs Tibbits, the
washer-woman, perceived it, and probably had a preference for
his linen. At that particular period he was weighing out ginger-
bread-nuts; but such an anomaly could not continue. No
position could be suited to Mr David Faux that was not in the
highest degree easy to the flesh and flattering to the spirit. If he
had fallen on the present times, and enjoyed the advantages of
a Mechanics' Institute,[5] he would certainly have taken to
literature and have written reviews; but his education had not
been liberal. He had read some novels from the adjoining
circulating library, and had even bought the story of 'Inkle and
Yarico',[6] which had made him feel very sorry for poor Mr
Inkle; so that his ideas might not have been below a certain

mark of the literary calling; but his spelling and diction were too unconventional.

When a man is not adequately appreciated or comfortably placed in his own country, his thoughts naturally turn towards foreign climes; and David's imagination circled round and round the utmost limits of his geographical knowledge, in search of a country where a young gentleman of pasty visage, lipless mouth, and stumpy hair, would be likely to be received with the hospitable enthusiasm which he had a right to expect. Having a general idea of America as a country where the population was chiefly black, it appeared to him the most propitious destination for an emigrant who, to begin with, had the broad and easily recognisable merit of whiteness; and this idea gradually took such strong possession of him that Satan seized the opportunity of suggesting to him that he might emigrate under easier circumstances, if he supplied himself with a little money from his master's till. But that evil spirit, whose understanding, I am convinced, has been much overrated, quite wasted his time on this occasion. David would certainly have liked well to have some of his master's money in his pocket, if he had been sure his master would have been the only man to suffer for it; but he was a cautious youth, and quite determined to run no risks on his own account. So he stayed out his apprenticeship, and committed no act of dishonesty that was at all likely to be discovered, reserving his plan of emigration for a future opportunity. And the circumstances under which he carried it out were in this wise. Having been at home a week or two partaking of the family beans,[7] he had used his leisure in ascertaining a fact which was of considerable importance to him, namely, that his mother had a small sum in guineas painfully saved from her maiden perquisites, and kept in the corner of a drawer where her baby-linen had reposed for the last twenty years – ever since her son David had taken to his feet, with a slight promise of bow-legs which had not been altogether unfulfilled. Mr Faux, senior, had told his son very frankly, that he must not look to being set-up in business by *him*: with seven sons, and one of them a very healthy and well-developed idiot, who consumed a dumpling about eight inches in diameter every day, it was pretty well if they got a hundred apiece at his death. Under these circumstances, what was David to do? It was certainly hard that he should take his mother's money; but he saw no other ready means of getting any, and it was not to be expected that a young man of his merit should put up with inconveniences that could be avoided. Besides, it is not robbery to take property belonging to your mother: she doesn't prosecute you. And David was very well behaved to his mother; he comforted her by speaking highly of himself to her, and assuring her that he never fell into the vices he saw practised by other youths of his own age, and that he was particularly fond of honesty. If his mother would have given him her twenty guineas as a reward of this noble disposition, he really would not have stolen them from her, and it would have been more agreeable to his feelings. Nevertheless, to an active mind like David's, ingenuity is not without its pleasures: it was rather an interesting occupation to become stealthily acquainted with the wards of his mother's simple key (not in the least like Chubb's patent),[8] and to get one that would do its work equally well; and also to arrange a little drama by which he would escape suspicion, and run no risk of forfeiting the prospective hundred at his father's death, which would be convenient in the improbable case of his *not* making a large fortune in the 'Indies'.

First, he spoke freely of his intention to start shortly for Liverpool and take ship for America; a resolution which cost his good mother some pain, for, after Jacob the idiot, there was not one of her sons to whom her heart clung more than to her youngest-born, David. Next, it appeared to him that Sunday afternoon, when everybody was gone to church except Jacob and the cow-boy, was so singularly favourable an opportunity for sons who wanted to appropriate their mothers' guineas, that he half thought it must have been kindly intended by Providence for such purposes. Especially the third Sunday in Lent; because Jacob had been out on one of his occasional wanderings for the last two days; and David, being a timid young man, had a considerable dread and hatred of Jacob, as of a large personage who went about habitually with a pitchfork in his hand.

Nothing could be easier, then, than for David on this Sunday afternoon to decline going to church, on the ground that he was going to tea at Mr Lunn's, whose pretty daughter Sally had been an early flame of his, and, when the church-goers were at a safe distance, to abstract the guineas from their wooden box and slip them into a small canvas bag – nothing easier than to call to the cow-boy that he was going, and tell him to keep an eye on the house for fear of Sunday tramps. David thought it would be easy, too, to get to a small thicket and bury his bag in a hole he had already made and covered up under the roots of an old hollow ash, and he had, in fact, found the hole without a moment's difficulty, had uncovered it, and was about gently to drop the bag into it, when the sound of a large body rustling towards him with something like a bellow was such a surprise to David, who, as a gentleman gifted with much contrivance, was naturally only prepared for what he expected, that instead of dropping the bag gently he let it fall so as to make it untwist and vomit forth the shining guineas. In the same moment he looked up and saw his dear brother Jacob close upon him, holding the pitchfork so that the bright smooth prongs were a yard in advance of his own body, and about a foot off David's. (A learned friend, to whom I once narrated this history, observed that it was David's guilt which made these prongs formidable, and that the *mens nil conscia sibi*[9] strips a pitchfork of all terrors. I thought this idea so valuable, that I obtained his leave to use it on condition of suppressing his name.) Nevertheless, David did not entirely lose his presence of mind; for in that case he would have sunk on the earth or started backward; whereas he kept his ground and smiled at Jacob, who nodded his head up and down, and said, 'Hoich, Zavy!' in a painfully equivocal manner. David's heart was beating audibly, and if he had had any lips they would have been pale; but his mental activity, instead of being paralysed, was stimulated. While he was inwardly praying (he always prayed when he was much frightened), – 'Oh, save me this once, and I'll never get into danger again!' – he was thrusting his hand into his pocket in search of a box of yellow lozenges, which he had brought with him from Brigford among other delicacies of the same portable kind, as a means of conciliating proud beauty, and more particularly the beauty of Miss Sarah Lunn. Not one of these delicacies had he ever offered to poor Jacob, for David was not a young man to waste his jujubes and barley-sugar in giving pleasure to people from whom he expected nothing. But an idiot with equivocal intentions and a pitchfork is a well worth flattering and cajoling as if he were Louis Napoleon.[10] So David, with a promptitude equal to the occasion, drew out his box of yellow lozenges, lifted the lid, and performed a pantomine with his mouth and fingers, which was meant to imply that he was delighted to see his dear brother Jacob, and seized the opportunity of making him a small present, which he would find particularly agreeable to the taste. Jacob, you understand, was not an intense idiot, but within a certain limited range knew how to choose the good and reject the evil: he took one lozenge, by way of test, and sucked it as if he had been a philosopher; then, in as great an ecstasy as its new and complex savour as Caliban at the taste of Trinculo's wine,[11] chuckled and stroked this suddenly beneficent brother, and held out his hand for more; for, except in fits of anger, Jacob was not ferocious or needlessly predatory. David's courage half returned, and he left off praying; pouring a dozen lozenges into Jacob's palm, and trying to look very fond of him. He congratulated himself that he had formed the plan of going to see Miss Sally Lunn this afternoon, and that, as a consequence, he had brought with him these propitiatory delicacies: he was certainly a lucky fellow; indeed, it was always likely Providence should be fonder of him than of other apprentices, and since he *was* to be interrupted, why, an idiot was preferable to any other sort of witness. For the first time in his life, David thought he saw the advantage of idiots.

As for Jacob, he had thrust his pitchfork into the ground, and had thrown himself down beside it, in thorough abandonment to the unprecedented pleasure of having five lozenges in his mouth at once, blinking meanwhile, and making inarticulate sounds of gustative content. He had not yet given any sign of noticing the guineas, but in seating himself he had laid his broad right hand on them, and unconsciously kept it in that position, absorbed in the sensations of his palate. If he could only be kept so occupied with the lozenges as not to see the guineas before David could manage to cover them! That was David's best hope of safety; for Jacob knew his mother's guineas; it had been part of their common experience as boys to be allowed to look at these handsome coins, and rattle them in their box on high days and holidays, and among all Jacob's narrow experiences as to money, this was likely to be the most memorable.

'Here, Jacob,' said David, in an insinuating tone, handing the box to him, 'I'll give 'em all to you. Run! – make haste! – else somebody 'll come and take 'em.'

David, not having studied the psychology of idiots, was not aware that they are not to be wrought upon by imaginative fears. Jacob took the box with his left hand, but saw no necessity for running away. Was ever a promising young man wishing to lay the foundation of his fortune by appropriating his mother's guineas obstructed by such a day-mare as this? But the moment must come when Jacob would move his right hand to draw off the lid of the tin box, and then David would sweep the guineas into the hole with the utmost address and swiftness, and immediately seat himself upon them. Ah, no! It's of no use to have foresight when you are dealing with an idiot: he is not to be calculated upon. Jacob's right hand was given to vague clutching and throwing; it suddenly clutched the guineas as if they had been so many pebbles, and was raised in an attitude which promised to scatter them like seed over a distant bramble, when, from some prompting or other – probably of an unwonted sensation – it paused, descended to Jacob's knee, and opened slowly under the inspection of Jacob's dull eyes. David began to pray again, but immediately desisted – another resource having occurred to him.

'Mother! zinnies!' exclaimed the innocent Jacob. Then, looking at David, he said, interrogatively, 'Box?'

'Hush! hush!' said David, summoning all his ingenuity in this severe strait. 'See, Jacob!' He took the tin box from his brother's hand, and emptied it of the lozenges, returning half of them to Jacob, but secretly keeping the rest in his own hand. Then he held out the empty box, and said, 'Here's the box, Jacob! The box for the guineas!' gently sweeping them from Jacob's palm into the box.

This procedure was not objectionable to Jacob; on the contrary, the guineas clinked so pleasantly as they fell, that he wished for a repetition of the sound, and seizing the box, began to rattle it very gleefully. David, seizing the opportunity, deposited his reserve of lozenges in the ground and hastily swept some earth over them. 'Look, Jacob!' he said, at last. Jacob paused from his clinking, and looked into the hole, while David began to scratch away the earth, as if in doubtful expectation. When the lozenges were laid bare, he took them out one by one, and gave them to Jacob.

'Hush!' he said, in a loud whisper, 'Tell nobody – all for Jacob – hush – sh – sh! Put guineas in the hole – they'll come out like this!' To make the lesson more complete, he took a guinea, and lowering it into the hole, said, 'Put in *so*.' Then, as he took the last lozenge out, he said, 'Come out *so*,' and put the lozenge into Jacob's hospitable mouth.

Jacob turned his head on one side, looked first at his brother and then at the hole, like a reflective monkey, and, finally, laid the box of guineas in the hole with much decision. David made haste to add every one of the stray coins, put on the lid, and covered it well with earth, saying in his most coaxing tone –

'Take 'm out tomorrow, Jacob; all for Jacob! Hush – sh – sh!'

Jacob, to whom this once indifferent brother had all at once become a sort of sweet-tasted fetish, stroked David's best coat with his adhesive fingers, and then hugged him with an accompaniment of that mingled chuckling and gurgling by which he was accustomed to express the milder passions. But if he had chosen to bite a small morsel out of his beneficent brother's cheek, David would have been obliged to bear it.

And here I must pause, to point out to you the short-sightedness of human contrivance. This ingenious young man, Mr David Faux, thought he had achieved a triumph of cunning when he had associated himself in his brother's rudimentary mind with the flavour of yellow lozenges. But he had yet to learn that it is a dreadful thing to make an idiot fond of you, when you yourself are not of an affectionate disposition: especially an idiot with a pitchfork – obviously a difficult friend to shake off by rough usage.

It may seem to you rather a blundering contrivance for a clever young man to bury the guineas. But, if everything had turned out as David had calculated, you would have seen that his plan was worthy of his talents. The guineas would have lain safely in the earth while the theft was discovered, and David, with the calm of conscious innocence, would have lingered at home, reluctant to say good-bye to his dear mother while she was in grief about her guineas; till at length, on the eve of his departure, he would have disinterred them in the strictest privacy, and carried them on his own person without inconvenience. But David, you perceive, had reckoned without his host, or, to speak more precisely, without his idiot brother – an item of so uncertain and fluctuating a character, that I doubt whether he would not have puzzled the astute heroes of M. de Balzac,[12] whose foresight is so remarkably at home in the future.

It was clear to David now that he had only one alternative before him: he must either renounce the guineas, by quietly putting them back in his mother's drawer (a course not unattended with difficulty); or he must leave more than a suspicion behind him, by departing early the next morning without giving notice, and with the guineas in his pocket. For if he gave notice that he was going, his mother, he knew, would insist on fetching from her box of guineas the three she had always promised him as his share; indeed, in his original plan, he had counted on this as a means by which the theft would be discovered under circumstances that would themselves speak for his innocence; but now, as I need hardly explain, that well-combined plan was completely frustrated. Even if David could have bribed Jacob with perpetual lozenges, an idiot's secrecy is itself betrayal. He dared not even go to tea at Mr Lunns', for in that case he would have lost sight of Jacob, who, in his impatience for the crop of lozenges, might scratch up the box again while he was absent, and carry it home – depriving him at once of reputation and guineas. No! he must think of nothing all the rest of this day, but of coaxing Jacob and keeping him out of mischief. It was a fatiguing and anxious evening to David; nevertheless, he dared not go to sleep without tying a piece of string to his thumb and great toe, to secure his frequent waking; for he meant to be up with the first peep of dawn, and be far out of reach before breakfast-time. His father, he thought, would certainly cut him off with a shilling; but what then? Such a striking young man as he would be sure to be well received in the West Indies: in foreign countries there are always openings – even for cats. It was probable that some Princess Yarico[13] would want him to marry her, and make him presents of very large jewels beforehand; after which, he needn't marry her unless he liked. David had made up his mind not to steal any more, even from people who were fond of him: it was an unpleasant way of making your fortune in a world where you were likely to be surprised in the act by brothers. Such alarms did not agree with David's constitution, and he had felt so much nausea this evening that no doubt his liver was affected. Besides, he would have been greatly hurt not to be thought well of in the world: he always meant to make a figure, and be thought worthy of the best seats and the best morsels.

Ruminating to this effect on the brilliant future in reserve for him, David by the help of his check-string kept himself on the alert to seize the time of earliest dawn for his rising and departure. His brothers, of course, were early risers, but he should anticipate them by at least an hour and a half, and the little room which he had to himself as only an occasional visitor, had its window over the horse-block,[14] so that he could slip out through the window without the least difficulty. Jacob, the horrible Jacob, had an awkward trick of getting up before everybody else, to stem his hunger by emptying the milk-bowl that was 'duly set' for him; but of late he had taken to sleeping in the hay-loft, and if he came into the house, it would be on the opposite side to that from which David was making his exit. There was no need to think of Jacob; yet David was liberal enough to bestow a curse on him – it was the only thing he ever did bestow gratuitously. His small bundle of clothes was ready packed, and he was soon treading lightly on the steps of the horse-block, soon walking at a smart pace across the fields towards the thicket. It would take him no more than two minutes to get out the box; he could make out the tree it was under by the pale strip where the bark was off, although the dawning light was rather dimmer in the thicket. But what, in the name of – burnt pastry – was that large body with a staff planted beside it, close at the foot of the ash-tree? David paused, not to make up his mind as to the nature of the apparition – he had not the happiness of doubting for a moment that the staff was Jacob's pitchfork – but to gather the self-command necessary for addressing his brother with a sufficiently honeyed accent. Jacob was absorbed in scratching up the earth, and had not heard David's approach.

'I say, Jacob,' said David in a loud whisper, just as the tin box was lifted out of the hole.

Jacob looked up, and discerning his sweet-flavoured brother, nodded and grinned in the dim light in a way that made him seem to David like a triumphant demon. If he had been of an impetuous disposition, he would have snatched the pitchfork from the ground and impaled this fraternal demon. But David was by no means impetuous; he was a young man greatly given to calculate consequences, a habit which has been held to be the foundation of virtue. But somehow it had not precisely that effect in David: he calculated whether an action would harm himself, or whether it would only harm other people. In the former case he was very timid about satisfying his immediate desires, but in the latter he would risk the result with much courage.

'Give it *me*, Jacob,' he said, stooping down and patting his brother. 'Let us see.'

Jacob, finding the lid rather tight, gave the box to his brother in perfect faith. David raised the lid, and shook his head, while Jacob put his finger in and took out a guinea to taste whether the metamorphosis into lozenges was complete and satisfactory.

'No, Jacob; too soon, too soon,' said David, when the guinea had been tasted. 'Give it me; we'll go and bury it somewhere else; we'll put it in yonder,' he added, pointing vaguely toward the distance.

David screwed on the lid, while Jacob, looking grave, rose and grasped his pitchfork. Then, seeing David's bundle, he snatched it, like a too officious Newfoundland, stuck his pitchfork into it and carried it over his shoulder in triumph as he accompanied David and the box out of the thicket.

What on earth was David to do? It would have been easy to frown at Jacob, and kick him, an order him to get away; but David dared as soon have kicked the bull. Jacob was quiet as long as he was treated indulgently; but on the slightest show of anger, he became unmanageable, and was liable to fits of fury which would have made him formidable even without his pitchfork. There was no mastery to be obtained over him except by kindness or guile. David tried guile.

'Go, Jacob,' he said, when they were out of the thicket – pointing towards the house as he spoke; 'go and fetch me a spade – a spade. But give *me* the bundle, he added, trying to reach it from the fork, where it hung high above, Jacob's tall shoulder.

But Jacob showed as much alacrity in obeying as a wasp shows in leaving a sugar-basin. Near David, he felt himself in the vicinity of lozenges: he chuckled and rubbed his brother's back, brandishing the bundle higher out of reach. David, with an inward groan, changed his tactics, and walked on as fast as he could. It was not safe to linger. Jacob would get tired of following him, or, at all events, could be eluded. If they could once get to the distant highroad, a coach would overtake them, David would mount it, having previously by some ingenious means secured his bundle, and then Jacob might howl and flourish his pitchfork as much as he liked. Meanwhile he was under the fatal necessity of being very kind to this ogre, and of providing a large breakfast for him when they stopped at a roadside inn. It was already three hours since they had started, and David was tired. Would no coach be coming up soon? he inquired. No coach for the next two hours. But there was a carrier's cart to come immediately, on its way to the next town. If he could slip out, even leaving his bundle behind, and get into the cart without Jacob! But there was a new obstacle. Jacob had recently discovered a remnant of sugar-candy in one of his brother's tail-pockets; and, since then, had cautiously kept his hold on that limb of the garment, perhaps with an expectation that there would be a further development of sugar-candy after a longer or shorter interval. Now every one who has worn a coat will understand the sensibilities that must keep a man from starting away in a hurry when there is a grasp on his coat-tail. David looked forward to being well received among strangers, but it might make a difference if he had only one tail to his coat.

He felt himself in a cold perspiration. He would walk no more: he must get into the cart and let Jacob get in with him. Presently a cheering idea occurred to him: after so large a breakfast, Jacob would be sure to go to sleep in the cart; you see at once that David meant to seize his bundle, jump out, and be free. His expectation was partly fulfilled: Jacob did go to sleep in the cart, but it was in a peculiar attitude – it was with his arms tightly fastened round his dear brother's body; and if ever David attempted to move, the grasp tightened with the force of an affectionate boa-constrictor.

'Th'innicent's fond on you,' observed the carrier, thinking that David was probably an amiable brother, and wishing to pay him a compliment.

David groaned. The ways of thieving were not ways of pleasantness.[15] Oh, why had he an idiot brother? Or why, in general, was the world so constituted that a man could not take his mother's guineas comfortably? David became grimly speculative.

Copious dinner at noon for Jacob; but little dinner, because little appetite, for David. Instead of eating, he plied Jacob with beer; for through this liberality he descried a hope. Jacob fell into a dead sleep, at last, *without* having his arms round David, who paid the reckoning, took his bundle, and walked off. In another half-hour he was on the coach on his way to Liverpool, smiling the smile of the triumphant wicked. He was rid of Jacob – he was bound for the Indies, where a gullible princess awaited him. He would never steal any more, but there would be no need; he would show himself so deserving, that people would make him presents freely. He must give up the notion of his father's legacy; but it was not likely he would ever want that trifle; and even if he did – why, it was a compensation to think that in being for ever divided from his family he was divided from Jacob, more terrible than Gorgon or Demogorgon[16] to David's timid green eyes. Thank heaven, he should never see Jacob any more!

It was nearly six years after the departure of Mr David Faux for the West Indies, that the vacant shop in the market-place at Grimworth was understood to have been let to the stranger with a sallow complexion and a buff cravat, whose first appearance had caused some excitement in the bar of the Woolpack, where he had called to wait for the coach.

Grimworth, to a discerning eye, was a good place to set up shopkeeping in. There was no competition in it at present; the Church-people had their own grocer and draper; the Dissenters had theirs; and the two or three butchers found a ready market for their joints without strict reference to religious persuasion – except that the rector's wife had given a general order for the veal sweet-breads and the mutton kidneys, while Mr Rodd, the Baptist minister, had requested that, so far as was compatible with the fair accommodation of other customers, the sheep's trotters might be reserved for him. And it was likely to be a growing place, for the trustees of Mr Zephaniah Crypt's Charity, under the stimulus of late visitation by commissioners, were beginning to apply long-accumulating funds to the rebuilding of the Yellow Coat School,[1] which was henceforth to be carried forward on a greatly-extended scale, the testator having left no restrictions concerning the curriculum, but only concerning the coat.

The shopkeepers at Grimworth were by no means unanimous as to the advantages promised by this prospect of increased population and trading, being substantial men, who liked doing a quiet business in which they were sure of their customers, and could calculate their returns to a nicety. Hitherto, it had been held a point of honour by the families in Grimworth parish, to buy their sugar and their flannel at the shops where their fathers and mothers had bought before them; but, if new-comers were to bring in the system of neck-and-neck trading, and solicit feminine eyes by gown-pieces laid in fan-like folds, and surmounted by artificial flowers, giving them a factitious charm (for on what human figure would a gown sit like a fan, or what female head was like a bunch of China-asters?), or, if new grocers were to fill their windows with mountains of currants and sugar, made seductive by contrast and tickets, – what security was there for Grimworth, that a vagrant spirit in shopping, once introduced, would not in the end carry the most important families to the larger market town of Cattleton, where, business being done on a system of small profits and quick returns, the fashions were of the freshest, and goods of all kinds might be bought at an advantage?

With this view of the times predominant among the trades-people at Grimworth, their uncertainty concerning the nature of the business which the sallow-complexioned stranger was about to set up in the vacant shop, naturally gave some additional strength to the fears of the less sanguine. If he was going to sell drapery, it was probably that a pale-faced fellow like that would deal in showy and inferior articles – printed cottons and muslins which would leave their dye in the wash-tub, jobbed[2] linen full of knots, and flannel that would soon look like gauze. If grocery, then it was to be hoped that no mother of a family would trust the teas of an untried grocer. Such things had been known in some parishes as tradesmen going about canvassing for custom with cards in their pockets: when people came from nobody knew where, there was no knowing what they might do. It was a thousand pities that Mr Moffat, the auctioneer and broker, had died without leaving anybody to follow him in the business, and Mrs Cleve's trustee ought to have known better than to let a shop to a stranger. Even the discovery that ovens were being put up on the premises, and that the shop was, in fact, being fitted up for a confectioner and pastry-cook's business, hitherto unknown in Grimworth, did not quite suffice to turn the scale in the new-comer's favour, though the landlady at the Woolpack defended him warmly, said he seemed to be a very clever young man, and from what she could make out, came of a very good family; indeed, was most likely a good many people's betters.

It certainly made a blaze of light and colour, almost as if a rainbow had suddenly descended into the market-place, when, one fine morning, the shutters were taken down from the new shop, and the two windows displayed their decorations. On one side, there were the variegated tints of collared and marbled meats, set off by bright green leaves, the pale brown of glazed pies, the rich tones of sauces and bottled fruits enclosed in their veil of glass – altogether a sight to bring tears into the eyes of a Dutch painter; and on the other, there was a predominance of the more delicate hues of pink, and white, and yellow, and buff, in the abundant lozenges, candies, sweet biscuits and icings, which to the eyes of a bilious person might easily have been blended into a faëry landscape in Turner's[3] latest style. What a sight to dawn upon the eyes of Grimworth children! They almost forgot to go to their dinner that day, their appetites being preoccupied with imaginary sugar-plums; and I think even Punch,[4] setting up his tabernacle in the market-place, would not have succeeded in drawing them away from those shop-windows, where they stood according to gradations of size and strength, the biggest and strongest being nearest the window, and the little ones in the outermost rows lifting wide-open eyes and mouths towards the upper tier of jars, like small birds at meal-time.

The elder inhabitants pished and pshawed a little at the folly of the new shopkeeper in venturing on such an outlay in goods that would not keep; to be sure, Christmas was coming, but what housewife in Grimworth would not think shame to furnish forth her table with articles that were not home-cooked? No, no. Mr Edward Freely, as he called himself, was deceived, if he thought Grimworth money was to flow into his pockets on such terms.

Edward Freely was the name that shone in gilt letters on a mazarine[5] ground over the doorplace of the new shop – a generous-sounding name, that might have belonged to the open-hearted, improvident hero of an old comedy, who would have delighted in raining sugared almonds, like a new manna-gift, among that small generation outside the windows. But Mr Edward Freely was a man whose impulses were kept in due subordination: he held that the desire for sweets and pastry must only be satisfied in a direct ratio with the power of paying for them. If the smallest child in Grimworth would go to him with a halfpenny in its tiny fist, he would, after ringing the halfpenny, deliver a just equivalent in 'rock'. He was not a man to cheat even the smallest child – he often said so, observing at the same time that he loved honesty, and also that he was very tender-hearted, though he didn't show his feelings as some people did.

Either in reward of such virtue, or according to some more hidden law of sequence, Mr Freely's business, in spite of prejudice, started under favourable auspices. For Mrs Chaloner, the rector's wife, was among the earliest customers at the shop, thinking it only right to encourage a new parishioner who had made a decorous appearance at church; and she found Mr Freely a most civil, obliging young man, and intelligent to a surprising degree for a confectioner; well-principled, too, for in giving her useful hints about choosing sugars he had thrown much light on the dishonesty of other tradesmen. Moreover, he had been in the West Indies, and had seen the very estate which had been her poor grandfather's property; and he said the missionaries were the only cause of the negro's discontent – an observing young man, evidently. Mrs Chaloner ordered wine-biscuits and olives, and gave Mr Freely to understand that she should find his shop a great convenience. So did the doctor's wife, and so did Mrs Gate, at the large carding-mill,[6] who, having high connections frequently visiting her, might be expected to have a large consumption of ratafias[7] and macaroons.

The less aristocratic matrons of Grimworth seemed likely at first to justify their husbands' confidence that they would never pay a percentage of profits on drop-cakes, instead of making their own, or get up a hollow show of liberal housekeeping by purchasing slices of collared meat when a neighbour came in for supper. But it is my task to narrate the gradual corruption of Grimworth manners from their primitive simplicity – a melancholy task, if it were not cheered by the prospect of the fine peripateia[8] or downfall by which the progress of the corruption was ultimately checked.

It was young Mrs Steene, the veterinary surgeon's wife, who first gave way to temptation. I fear she had been rather over-educated for her station in life, for she knew by heart many passages in 'Lalla Rookh', the 'Corsair', and the 'Siege of Corinth',[9] which had given her a distaste for domestic occupations, and caused her a withering disappointment at the discovery that Mr Steene, since his marriage, had lost all interest in the 'bulbul',[10] openly preferred discussing the nature of spavin[11] with a coarse neighbour, and was angry if the pudding turned out watery – indeed, was simply a top-booted 'vet', who came in hungry at dinner-time; and not in the least like a nobleman turned Corsair out of pure scorn for his race, or like a renegade[12] with a turban and crescent, unless it were in the irritability of his temper. And scorn is such a very different thing in top-boots!

This brutal man had invited a supper-party for Christmas eve, when he would expect to see mince-pies on the table. Mrs Steene had prepared her mince-meat, and had devoted much butter, fine flour, and labour, to the making of a batch of pies in the morning; but they proved to be so very heavy when they came out of the oven, that she could only think with trembling of the moment when her husband should catch sight of them on the supper-table. He would storm at her, she was certain; and before all the company; and then she should never help crying: it was so dreadful to think she had come to that, after the bulbul and everything! Suddenly the thought darted through her mind that *this once* she might send for a dish of mince-pies from Freely's: she knew he had some. But what was to become of the eighteen heavy mince-pies? Oh, it was of no use thinking about that; it was very expensive – indeed, making mince-pies at all was a great expense, when they were not sure to turn out well: it would be much better to buy them ready-made. You paid a little more for them, but there was no risk of waste.

Such was the sophistry with which this misguided young woman – enough. Mrs Steene sent for the mince-pies, and, I am grieved to add, garbled her household accounts in order to conceal the fact from her husband. This was the second step in a downward course, all owing to a young woman's being out of harmony with her circumstances, yearning after renegades and bulbuls, and being subject to claims from a veterinary surgeon fond of mince-pies. The third step was to harden herself by telling the fact of the bought mince-pies to her intimate friend Mrs Mole, who had already guessed it, and who subsequently encouraged herself in buying a mould of jelly, instead of exerting her own skill, by the reflection that 'other people' did the same sort of thing. The infection spread; soon there was a party of clique in Grimworth on the side of 'buying at Freely's'; and many husbands, kept for some time in the dark on this point, innocently swallowed at two mouthfuls a tart on which they were paying a profit of a hundred per cent, and as innocently encouraged a fatal disingenuousness in the partners of their bosoms by praising the pastry. Others, more keen-sighted, winked at the too frequent presentation on washing-days, and at impromptu suppers, of superior spiced-beef, which flattered their palates more than the cold remnants they had formerly been contented with. Every housewife who had once 'bought at Freely's' felt a secret joy when she detected a similar perversion in her neighbour's practice, and soon only two or three old-fashioned mistresses of families held out in the protest against the growing demoralisation, saying to their neighbours who came to sup with them, 'I can't offer you Freely's beef, or Freely's cheese-cakes; everything in our house is home-made; I'm afraid you'll hardly have any appetite for our plain pastry.' The doctor, whose cook was not satisfactory, the curate, who kept no cook, and the mining agent, who was a great *bon vivant*, even began to rely on Freely for the greater part of their dinner, when they wished to give an entertainment of some brilliancy. In short, the business of manufacturing the more fanciful viands was fast passing out of the hands of maids and matrons in private families, and was becoming the work of a special commercial organ.

I am not ignorant that this sort of thing is called the inevitable course of civilisation, division of labour,[13] and so forth, and that the maids and matrons may be said to have had their hands set free from cookery to add to the wealth of society in some other way. Only it happened at Grimworth, which, to be sure, was a low place, that the maids and matrons could do nothing with their hands at all better than cooking; not even those who had always made heavy cakes and leathery pastry. And so it came to pass, that the progress of civilisation at Grimworth was not otherwise apparent than in the impoverishment of men, the gossiping idleness of women, and the heightening prosperity of Mr Edward Freely.

The Yellow Coat School was a double source of profit to the calculating confectioner; for he opened an eating-room for the superior workmen employed on the new school, and he accommodated the pupils at the old school by giving great attention to the fancy-sugar department. When I think of sweet-tasted swans and other ingenious white shapes crunched by the small teeth of that rising generation, I am glad to remember that a certain amount of calcareous food has been held good for young creatures whose bones are not quite formed; for I have observed these delicacies to have an inorganic flavour which would have recommended them greatly to that young lady of the

'Spectator's'[14] acquaintance who habitually made her dessert on the stems of tobacco-pipes.

As for the confectioner himself, he made his way gradually into Grimworth homes, as his commodities did, in spite of some initial repugnance. Somehow or other, his reception as a guest seemed a thing that required justifying, like the purchasing of his pastry. In the first place, he was a stranger, and therefore open to suspicion; secondly, the confectionery business was so entirely new at Grimworth, that its place in the scale of rank had not been distinctly ascertained. There was no doubt about drapers and grocers, when they came of good old Grimworth families, like Mr Luff and Mr Prettyman: they visited with the Palfreys, who farmed their own land, played many a game at whist with the doctor, and condescended a little towards the timber-merchant, who had lately taken to the coal-trade also, and had got new furniture; but whether a confectioner should be admitted to this higher level of respectability, or should be understood to find his associates among butchers and bakers, was a new question on which tradition threw no light. His being a bachelor was in his favour, and would perhaps have been enough to turn the scale, even if Mr Edward Freely's other personal pretensions had been of an entirely insignificant cast. But so far from this, it very soon appeared that he was a remarkable young man, who had been in the West Indies, and had seen many wonders by sea and land, so that he could charm the ears of Grimworth Desdemonas[15] with stories of strange fishes, especially sharks, which he had stabbed in the nick of time by bravely plunging overboard just as the monster was turning on his side to devour the cook's mate; of terrible fevers which he had undergone in a land where the wind blows from all quarters at once; of rounds of toast cut straight from the bread-fruit trees; of toes bitten off by land-crabs; of large honours that had been offered to him as a man who knew what was what, and was therefore particularly needed in a tropical climate; and of a Creole heiress who had wept bitterly at his departure. Such conversational talents as these, we know, will overcome disadvantages of complexion; and young Towers, whose cheeks were of the finest pink, set off by a fringe of dark whisker, was quite eclipsed by the presence of the sallow Mr Freely. So exceptional a confectioner elevated his business, and might well begin to make disengaged hearts flutter a little.

Fathers and mothers were naturally more slow and cautious in their recognition of the new-comer's merits.

'He's an amusing fellow,' said Mr Prettyman, the highly respectable grocer. (Mrs Prettyman was a Miss Fothergill, and her sister had married a London mercer.)[16] 'He's an amusing fellow; and I've no objection to his making one at the Oyster Club; but he's a bit too fond of riding the high horse. He's uncommonly knowing, I'll allow; but how came he to go to the Indies? I should like that answered. It's unnatural in a confectioner. I'm not fond of people that have been beyond seas, if they can't give a good account how they happened to go. When folks go so far off, it's because they've got little credit nearer home – that's my opinion. However, he's got some good rum; but I don't want to be hand and glove with him, for all that.'

It was this kind of dim suspicion which beclouded the view of Mr Freely's qualities in the maturer minds of Grimworth through the early months of his residence there. But when the confectioner ceased to be a novelty, the suspicions also ceased to be novel, and people got tired of hinting at them, especially as they seemed to be refuted by his advancing prosperity and importance. Mr Freely was becoming a person of influence in the parish; he was found useful as an overseer of the poor, having great firmness in enduring other people's pain, which firmness, he said, was due to his great benevolence; he always did what was good for people in the end. Mr Chaloner had even selected him as clergyman's churchwarden, for he was a very handy man, and much more of Mr Chaloner's opinion in everything about church business than the older parishioners. Mr Freely was a very regular churchman, but at the Oyster Club he was sometimes a little free in his conversation, more than hinting at a life of Sultanic self-indulgence which he had passed in the West Indies, shaking his head now and then and smiling rather bitterly, as men are wont to do when they intimate that they have become a little too wise to be instructed about a world which has long been flat and stale to them.

For some time he was quite general in his attentions to the fair sex, combining the gallantries of a lady's man with a severity of criticism on the person and manners of absent belles, which tended rather to stimulate in the feminine breast the desire to conquer the approval of so fastidious a judge. Nothing short of the very best in the department of female charms and virtues could suffice to kindle the ardour of Mr Edward Freely, who had become familiar with the most luxuriant and dazzling beauty in the West Indies. It may seem incredible that a confectioner should have ideas and conversation so much resembling those to be met with in a higher walk of life, but it must be remembered that he had not merely travelled, he had also bow-legs and a sallow, small-featured visage, so that nature herself had stamped him for a fastidious connoisseur of the fair sex.

At last, however, it seemed clear that Cupid had found a sharper arrow than usual, and that Mr Freely's heart was pierced. It was the general talk among the young people at Grimworth. But was it really love? and not rather ambition? Miss Fullilove, the timber-merchant's daughter, was quite sure that if *she* were Miss Penny Palfrey, she would be cautious; it was not a good sign when men looked so much above themselves for a wife. For it was no less a person than Miss Penelope Palfrey, second daughter of the Mr Palfrey who farmed his own land, that had attracted Mr Freely's peculiar regard, and conquered his fastidiousness; and no wonder; for the Ideal, as exhibited in the finest waxwork, was perhaps never so closely approached by the Real as in the person of the pretty Penelope. Her yellowish flaxen hair did not curl naturally, I admit, but its bright crisp ringlets were such smooth, perfect miniature tubes, that you would have longed to pass your little finger through them, and feel their soft elasticity. She wore them in a crop, for in those days, when society was in a healthier state, young ladies wore crops long after they were twenty, and Penelope was not yet nineteen. Like the waxen ideal, she had round blue eyes, and round nostrils in her little nose, and teeth such as the ideal would be seen to have, if it ever showed them. Altogether, she was a small, round thing, as neat as a pink and white double daisy, and as guileless; for I hope it does not argue guile in a pretty damsel of nineteen, to think that she should like to have a beau and be 'engaged', when her elder sister had already been in that position a year and a half. To be sure, there was young Towers always coming to the house; but Penny felt convinced he only came to see her brother, for he never had anything to say to her, and never offered her his arm, and was as awkward and silent as possible.

It is not unlikely that Mr Freely had early been smitten by

Penny's charms, as brought under his observation at church, but he had to make his way in society a little before he could come into nearer contact with them; and even after he was well received in Grimworth families, it was a long while before he could converse with Penny otherwise than in an incidental meeting at Mr Luff's. It was not so easy to get invited to Long Meadows, the residence of the Palfreys; for though Mr Palfrey had been losing money of late years, not being able quite to recover his feet after the terrible murrain[17] which forced him to borrow, his family were far from considering themselves on the same level even as the old-established tradespeople with whom they visited. The greatest people, even kings and queens, must visit with somebody, and the equals of the great are scarce. They were especially scarce at Grimworth, which, as I have before observed, was a low parish, mentioned with the most scornful brevity in gazetteers. Even the great people there were far behind those of their own standing in other parts of this realm. Mr Palfrey's farmyard doors had the paint all worn off them, and the front garden walks had long been merged in a general weediness. Still, his father had been called Squire Palfrey, and had been respected by the last Grimworth generation as a man who could afford to drink too much in his own house.

Pretty Penny was not blind to the fact that Mr Freely admired her, and she felt sure that it was he who had sent her a beautiful valentine; but her sister seemed to think so lightly of him (all young ladies think lightly of the gentlemen to whom they are not engaged), that Penny never dared mention him, and trembled and blushed whenever they met him, thinking of the valentine, which was very strong in its expressions, and which she felt guilty of knowing by heart. A man who had been to the Indies, and knew the sea so well, seemed to her a sort of public character, almost like Robinson Crusoe or Captain Cook; and Penny had always wished her husband to be a remarkable personage, likely to be put in Mangnall's Questions,[16] with which register of the immortals she had become acquainted during her one year at a boarding-school. Only it seemed strange that a remarkable man should be a confectioner and pastry-cook, and this anomaly quite disturbed Penny's dreams. Her brothers, she knew, laughed at men who could't sit on horseback well, and called them tailors; but her brothers were very rough, and were quite without that power of anecdote which made Mr

Freely such a delightful companion. He was a very good man, she thought, for she had heard him say at Mr Luff's, one day, that he always wished to do his duty in whatever state of life he might be placed; and he knew a great deal of poetry, for one day he had repeated a verse of a song. She wondered if he had made the words of the valentine! – it ended in this way:

> Without thee, it is pain to live,
> But with thee, it were sweet to die.[19]

Poor Mr Freely! her father would very likely object – she felt sure he would, for he always called Mr Freely 'that sugar-plum fellow'. Oh, it was very cruel, when true love was crossed in that way, and all because Mr Freely was a confectioner: well, Penny would be true to him, for all that, and since his being a confectioner gave her an opportunity of showing her faithfulness, she was glad of it. Edward Freely was a pretty name, much better than John Towers. Young Towers had offered her a rose out of his button-hole the other day, blushing very much; but she refused it, and thought with delight how much Mr Freely would be comforted if he knew her firmness of mind.

Poor little Penny! the days were so very long among the daisies on a grazing farm, and thought is so active – how was it possible that the inward drama should not get the start of the outward? I have known young ladies, much better educated, and with an outward world diversified by instructive lectures, to say nothing of literature and highly-developed fancy-work, who have spun a cocoon of visionary joys and sorrows for themselves, just as Penny did. Her elder sister Letitia, who had a prouder style of beauty, and a more worldly ambition, was engaged to a wool-factor, who came all the way from Cattelton to see her; and everybody knows that a wool-factor[20] takes a very high rank, sometimes driving a double-bodied gig.[21] Letty's notions got higher every day, and Penny never dared to speak of her cherished griefs to her lofty sister – never dared to propose that they should call at Mr Freely's to buy liquorice, though she had prepared for such an incident by mentioning a slight sore throat. So she had to pass the shop on the other side of the market-place, and reflect, with a suppressed sigh, that behind those pink and white jars somebody was thinking of her tenderly, unconscious of the small space that divided her from him.

And it was quite true that, when business permitted, Mr Freely thought a great deal of Penny. He thought her prettiness comparable to the loveliest things in confectionery; he judged her to be of submissive temper – likely to wait upon him as well as if she had been a negress, and to be silently terrified when his liver made him irritable; and he considered the Palfrey family quite the best in the parish, possessing marriageable daughters. On the whole, he thought her worthy to become Mrs Edward Freely, and all the more so, because it would probably require some ingenuity to win her. Mr Palfrey was capable of horse-whipping a too rash pretender to his daughter's hand; and, moreover, he had three tall sons: it was clear that a suitor would be at a disadvantage with such a family, unless travel and natural acumen had given him a countervailing power of contrivance. And the first idea that occurred to him in the matter was, that Mr Palfrey would object less if he knew that the Freelys were a much higher family than his own. It had been foolish modesty in him hitherto to conceal the fact that a branch of the Freelys held a manor in Yorkshire, and to shut up the portrait of his great uncle the admiral, instead of hanging it up where a family portrait should be hung – over the mantelpiece in the parlour. Admiral Freely, K.C.B., once placed in this conspicuous position, was seen to have had one arm only, and one eye, – in these points resembling the heroic Nelson,[22] while a certain pallid insignificance of feature confirmed the relationship between himself and his grand-newphew.

Next, Mr Freely was seized with an irrepressible ambition to possess Mrs Palfrey's receipt for brawn,[23] hers being pronounced on all hands to be superior to his own – as he informed her in a very flattering letter carried by his errand-boy. Now Mrs Palfrey, like other geniuses, wrought by instinct rather than by rule, and possessed no receipts, – indeed, despised all people who used them, observing that people who pickled by book, must pickle by weights and measures, and such nonsense; as for herself, her weights and measures were the tip of her finger and the tip of her tongue, and if you went nearer, why, of course, for dry goods like flour and spice, you went by handfuls and pinches, and for wet, there was a middle-sized jug – quite the best thing whether for much or little, because you might know how much a teacupful was if you'd got any use of your senses, and you might be sure it would take five middle-sized jugs to make a gallon. Knowledge of this kind is like Titian's[24] colouring, difficult to communicate; and as Mrs Palfrey, once remarkably handsome, and now become rather stout and asthmatical, and scarcely ever left home, her oral teaching could hardly be given anywhere except at Long Meadows. Even a matron is not insusceptible to flattery, and the prospect of a visitor whose great object would be to listen to her conversation, was not without its charms to Mrs Palfrey. Since there was no receipt to be sent in reply to Mr Freely's humble request, she called on her more docile daughter, Penny, to write a note, telling him that her mother would be glad to see him and talk with him on brawn, any day that he could call at Long Meadows. Penny obeyed with a trembling hand, thinking how wonderfully things came about in this world.

In this way, Mr Freely got himself introduced into the home of the Palfreys, and notwithstanding a tendency in the male part of the family to jeer at him a little as 'peaky' and bow-legged, he presently established his position as an accepted and frequent guest. Young Towers looked at him with increasing disgust when they met at the house on a Sunday, and secretly longed to try his ferret upon him, as a piece of vermin which that valuable animal would be likely to tackle with unhesitating vigour. But – so blind sometimes are parents – neither Mr nor Mrs Palfrey suspected that Penny would have anything to say to a tradesman of questionable rank whose youthful bloom was much withered. Young Towers, they thought, had an eye to her, and *that* was likely enough to be a match some day; but Penny was a child at present. And all the while Penny was imagining the circumstances under which Mr Freely would make her an offer: perhaps down by the row of damson-trees, when they were in the garden before tea; perhaps by letter – in which case, how would the letter begin? 'Dearest Penelope?' or 'My dear Miss Penelope?' or straight off, without dear anything, as seemed the most natural when people were embarrassed? But, however he might make the offer, she would not accept it without her father's consent: she would always be true to Mr Freely, but she would not disobey her father. For Penny was a good girl, though some of her female friends were afterwards of opinion that it spoke ill for her not to have felt an instinctive repugnance to Mr Freely.

But he was cautious, and wished to be quite sure of the

ground he trod on. His views in marriage were not entirely sentimental, but were as duly mingled with considerations of what would be advantageous to a man in his position, as if he had had a very large amount of money spent on his education. He was not a man to fall in love in the wrong place; and so, he applied himself quite as much to conciliate the favour of the parents, as to secure the attachment of Penny. Mrs Palfrey had not been inaccessible to flattery, and her husband, being also of mortal mould, would not, it might be hoped, be proof against rum – that very fine Jamaica rum of which Mr Freely expected always to have a supply sent him from Jamaica. It was not easy to get Mr Palfrey into the parlour behind the shop, where a mild back-street light fell on the features of the heroic admiral; but by getting hold of him rather late one evening as he was about to return home from Grimworth, the aspiring lover succeeded in persuading him to sup on some collared beef which, after Mrs Palfrey's brawn, he would find the very best of cold eating.

From that hour Mr Freely felt sure of success: being in privacy with an estimable man old enough to be his father, and being rather lonely in the world, it was natural he should unbosom himself a little on subjects which he could not speak of in a mixed circle – especially concerning his expectations from his uncle in Jamaica, who had no children, and loved his nephew Edward better than any one else in the world, though he had been so hurt at his leaving Jamaica, that he had threatened to cut him off with a shilling. However, he had since written to state his full forgiveness, and though he was an eccentric old gentleman and could not bear to give away money during his life, Mr Edward Freely could show Mr Palfrey the letter which declared, plainly enough, who would be the affectionate uncle's heir. Mr Palfrey actually saw the letter, and could not help admiring the spirit of the nephew who declared that such brilliant hopes as these made no difference to his conduct; he should work at his humble business and make his modest fortune at it all the same. If the Jamaica estate was to come to him – well and good. It was nothing very surprising for one of the Freely family to have an estate left him, considering the lands that family had possessed in time gone by, – nay, still possessed in the Northumberland branch. Would not Mr Palfrey take another glass of rum? and also look at the last year's balance of the accounts? Mr Freely was a man who cared to possess personal virtues, and did not pique himself on his family, though some men would.

We know how easily the great Leviathan may be led, when once there is a hook in his nose or a bridle in his jaws.[25] Mr Palfrey was a large man, but, like Leviathan's, his bulk went against him when once he had taken a turning. He was not a mercurial man, who easily changed his point of view. Enough. Before two months were over, he had given his consent to Mr Freely's marriage with his daughter Penny, and having hit on a formula by which he could justify it, fenced off all doubts and objections, his own included. The formula was this: 'I'm not a man to put my head up an entry before I know where it leads.'

Little Penny was very proud and fluttering, but hardly so happy as she expected to be in an engagement. She wondered if young Towers cared much about it, for he had not been to the house lately, and her sister and brothers were rather inclined to sneer than to sympathise. Grimworth rang with the news. All men extolled Mr Freely's good fortune; while the women, with the tender solicitude characteristic of the sex, wished the marriage might turn out well.

While affairs were at this triumphant juncture, Mr Freely one morning observed that a stone-carver who had been breakfasting in the eating-room had left a newspaper behind. It was the 'X – shire Gazette', and X – shire being a county not unknown to Mr Freely, he felt some curiosity to glance over it, and especially over the advertisements. A slight flush came over his face as he read. It was produced by the following announcement: 'If David Faux, son of Jonathan Faux, late of Gilsbrook, will apply at the office of Mr Strutt, attorney, of Rodham, he will hear of something to his advantage.'

'Father's dead!' exclaimed Mr Freely, involuntarily. 'Can he have left me a legacy?'

Perhaps it was a result quite different from your expectations, that Mr David Faux should have returned from the West Indies only a few years after his arrival there, and have set up in his old business, like any plain man who had never travelled. But these cases do occur in life. Since, as we know, men change their skies and see new constellations without changing their souls, it will follow sometimes that they don't change their business under those novel circumstances.

Certainly, this result was contrary to David's own expectations. He had looked forward, you are aware, to a brilliant career among 'the blacks'; but, either because they had already seen too many white men, or for some other reason, they did not at once recognise him as a superior order of human being; besides, there were no princesses among them. Nobody in Jamaica was anxious to maintain David for the mere pleasure of his society; and those hidden merits of a man which are so well known to himself were as little recognised there as they notoriously are in the effete society of the Old World. So that in the dark hints that David threw out at the Oyster Club about that life of Sultanic self-indulgence spent by him in the luxurious Indies, I really think he was doing himself a wrong; I believe he worked for his bread, and, in fact, took to cooking again, as, after all, the only department in which he could offer skilled labour. He had formed several ingenious plans by which he meant to circumvent people of large fortune and small faculty; but then he never met with exactly the right people under exactly the right circumstances. David's devices for getting rich without work had apparently no direct relation with the world outside him, as his confectionery receipts had. It is possible to pass a great many bad halfpennies and bad half-crowns, but I believe there has no instance been known of passing a halfpenny or a half-crown as a sovereign. A sharper[1] can drive a brisk trade in this world: it is undeniable that there may be a fine career for him, if he will dare consequences; but David was too timid to be a sharper, or venture in any way among the man-traps of the law. He dared rob nobody but his mother. And so he had to fall back on the genuine value there was in him – to be content to pass as a good halfpenny, or, to speak more accurately, as a good confectioner. For in spite of some additional reading and observation, there was nothing else he could make so much money by; nay, he found in himself even a capability of extending his skill in this direction, and embracing all forms of cookery; while, in other branches of human labour, he began to see that it was not possible for him to shine. Fate was too strong for him; he had thought to master her inclination and had fled over the seas to that end; but she caught him, tied an apron round him, and snatching him from all other devices, made him devise cakes and patties in a kitchen at Kingstown. He was getting submissive to her, since she paid him with tolerable gains; but fevers and prickly heat, and other evils incidental to cooks in ardent climates, made him long for his native land; so he took ship once more, carrying his six years' savings, and seeing distinctly, this time, what were Fate's intentions as to his career. If you question me closely as to whether all the money with which he set up at Grimworth consisted of pure and simple earnings, I am obliged to confess that he got a sum or two for charitably abstaining from mentioning some other people's misdemeanours. Altogether, since no prospects were attached to his family name, and since a new christening seemed a suitable commencement of a new life, Mr David Faux thought it as well to call himself Mr Edward Freely.

But lo! now, in opposition to all calculable probability, some benefit appeared to be attached to the name of David Faux. Should he neglect it, as beneath the attention of prosperous tradesman? It might bring him into contact with his family again, and he felt no yearnings in that direction: moreover, he had small belief that the 'something to his advantage' could be anything considerable. On the other hand, even a small gain is pleasant, and the promise of it in this instance was so surprising, that David felt his curiosity awakened. The scale dipped at last on the side of writing to the lawyer, and, to be brief, the correspondence ended in an appointment for a meeting between David and his eldest brother at Mr Strutt's, the vague 'something' having been defined as a legacy from his father of eighty-two pounds three shillings.

David, you know, had expected to be disinherited; and so he would have been, if he had not, like some other indifferent sons, come of excellent parents, whose conscience made them scrupulous where much more highly-instructed people often feel themselves warranted in following the bent of their indignation. Good Mrs Faux could never forget that she had brought this ill-conditioned son into the world when he was in that entirely helpless state which excluded the smallest choice on his part; and, somehow or other, she felt that his going wrong would be his father's and mother's fault, if they failed in one tittle of their parental duty. Her notion of parental duty was not of a high and subtle kind, but it included giving him his due share of the family property; for when a man had got a little honest money of his own, was he so likely to steal? To cut the dilinquent son off with a shilling, was like delivering him over to his evil propensities. No; let the sum of twenty guineas which he had stolen be deducted from his share, and then let the sum of three guineas be put back from it, seeing that his mother had always considered three of the twenty guineas as his; and, though he had run away, and was, perhaps, gone across the sea, let the money be left to him all the same, and be kept in reserve for his possible return. Mr Faux agreed to his wife's views, and made a codicil to his will accordingly, in time to die with a clear conscience. But for some time his family thought it likely that David would never reappear; and the eldest son, who had the charge of Jacob on his hands, often thought it a little hard that David might perhaps be dead, and yet, for want of certitude on that point, his legacy could not fall to his legal heir. But in this state of things the opposite certitude – namely, that David was still alive and in England – seemed to be brought by the testimony of a neighbour, who, having been on a journey to Cattleton, was pretty sure he had seen David in a gig, with a stout man driving by his side. He could 'swear it was David', though he could 'give no account why, for he had no marks on him; but no more had a white dog, and that didn't hinder folks from knowing a white dog'. It was this incident which had led to the advertisement.

The legacy was paid, of course, after a few preliminary disclosures as to Mr David's actual position. He begged to send his love to his mother, and to say that he hoped to pay her a dutiful visit by-and-by; but, at present, his business and near prospect of marriage made it difficult for him to leave home. His brother replied with much frankness.

'My mother may do as she likes about having you to see her, but, for my part, I don't want to catch sight of you on the premises again. When folks have taken a new name, they'd better keep to their new 'quintance.'

David pocketed the insult along with the eighty-two pounds three, and travelled home again in some triumph at the ease of a transaction which had enriched him to this extent. He had no intention of offending his brother by further claims on his fraternal recognition, and relapsed with full contentment into the character of Mr Edward Freely, the orphan, scion of a great but reduced family, with an eccentric uncle in the West Indies. (I have already hinted that he had some acquaintance with imaginative literature; and being of a practical turn, he had, you perceive, applied even this form of knowledge to practical purposes.)

It was little more than a week after the return from his fruitful journey, that the day of his marriage with Penny having been fixed, it was agreed that Mrs Palfrey should overcome her reluctance to move from home, and that she and her husband should bring their two daughters to inspect little Penny's future abode and decide on the new arrangements to be made for the reception of the bride. Mr Freely meant her to have a house so pretty and comfortable that she need not envy even a wool-factor's wife. Of course, the upper room over the shop was to be the best sitting-room; but also the parlour behind the shop was to be made a suitable bower for the lovely Penny, who would naturally wish to be near her husband, though Mr Freely declared his resolution never to allow *his* wife to wait in the shop. The decisions about the parlour furniture were left till last, because the party was to take tea there; and, about five o'clock, they were all seated there with the best muffins and buttered buns before them, little Penny blushing and smiling, with her 'crop' in the best order, and a blue frock showing her little white shoulders, while her opinion was being always asked and never given. She secretly wished to have a particular sort of chimney ornaments, but she could not have brought herself to mention it. Seated by the side of her yellow and rather withered lover, who, though he had not reached his thirtieth year, had already crow's-feet about his eyes, she was quite tremulous at the greatness of her lot in being married to a man who had travelled so much – and before her sister Letty! The handsome Letitia looked rather proud and contemptuous, thought her future brother-in-law an odious person, and was vexed with her father and mother for letting Penny marry him. Dear little Penny! She certainly did look like a fresh white-heart cherry going to be bitten off the stem by that lipless mouth. Would no deliverer come to make a slip between that cherry and that mouth without a lip?

'Quite a family likeness between the admiral and you, Mr Freely,' observed Mrs Palfrey, who was looking at the family portrait for the first time. 'It's wonderful! and only a grand-uncle. Do you feature the rest of your family, as you know of?'

'I can't say,' said Mr Freely, with a sigh. 'My family have mostly thought themselves too high to take any notice of me.'

At this moment an extraordinary disturbance was heard in the shop, as of a heavy animal stamping about and making angry noises, and then of a glass vessel falling in shivers, while the voice of the apprentice was heard calling 'Master' in great alarm.

Mr Freely rose in anxious astonishment, and hastened into the shop, followed by the four Palfreys, who made a group at the parlour-door, transfixed with wonder at seeing a large man in a smock-frock,[2] with a pitchfork in his hand, rush up to Mr Freely and hug him, crying out, – 'Zavy, Zavy, b'other Zavy!'

It was Jacob, and for some moments David lost all presence of mind. He felt arrested for having stolen his mother's guineas. He turned cold, and trembled in his brother's grasp.

'Why, how's this?' said Mr Palfrey, advancing from the door. 'Who is he?'

Jacob supplied the answer by saying over and over again, —

'I'se Zacob, b'other Zacob. Come 'o zee Zavy' – till hunger prompted him to relax his grasp, and to seize a large raised pie, which he lifted to his mouth.

By this time David's power of device had begun to return, but it was a very hard task for his prudence to master his rage and hatred towards poor Jacob.

'I don't know who he is; he must be drunk,' he said, in a low tone to Mr Palfrey. 'But he's dangerous with that pitchfork. He'll never let it go.' Then checking himself on the point of betraying too great an intimacy with Jacob's habits, he added, '*You* watch him, while I run for the constable.' And he hurried out of the shop.

'Why, where do you come from, my man?' said Mr Palfrey, speaking to Jacob in a conciliatory tone. Jacob was eating his pie by large mouthfuls, and looking round at the other good things in the shop, while he embraced his pitchfork with his left arm and laid his left hand on some Bath buns. He was in the rare position of a person who recovers a long absent friend and finds him richer than ever in the characteristics that won his heart.

'I's Zacob – b'other Zacob – 't home. I love Zavy – b'other Zavy,' he said, as soon as Mr Palfrey had drawn his attention. 'Zavy come back from z' Indies – got mother's zinnies. Where's Zavy?' he added, looking round and then turning to the others with a questioning air, puzzled by David's disappearance.

'It's very odd,' observed Mr Palfrey to his wife and daughters. 'He seems to say Freely's his brother come back from th' Indies.'

'What a pleasant relation for us!' said Letitia, sarcastically. 'I think he's a good deal like Mr Freely. He's got just the same sort of nose, and his eyes are the same colour.'

Poor Penny was ready to cry.

But now Mr Freely re-entered the shop without the constable. During his walk of a few yards he had had time and calmness enough to widen his view of consequences, and he saw that to get Jacob taken to the workhouse or to the lock-up house as an offensive stranger, might have awkward effects if his family took the trouble of inquiring after him. He must resign himself to more patient measures.

'On second thoughts,' he said, beckoning to Mr Palfrey and whispering to him while Jacob's back was turned, 'he's a poor half-witted fellow. Perhaps his friends will come after him. I don't mind giving him something to eat, and letting him lie down for the night. He's got it into his head that he knows me – they do get these fancies, idiots do. He'll perhaps go away again in an hour or two, and make no more ado. I'm a kind-hearted man *myself* – I shouldn't like to have the poor fellow ill-used.'

'Why, he'll eat a sovereign's worth in no time,' said Mr

Palfrey, thinking Mr Freely a little too magnificent in his generosity.

'Eh, Zavy, come back?' exclaimed Jacob, giving his dear brother another hug, which crushed Mr Freely's features inconveniently against the stale of the pitchfork.

'Ay, ay,' said Mr Freely, smiling, with every capability of murder in his mind, except the courage to commit it. He wished the Bath buns might by chance have arsenic in them.

'Mother's zinnies?' said Jacob, pointing to a glass jar of yellow lozenges that stood in the window. 'Zive 'em me.'

David dared not do otherwise than reach down the glass jar and give Jacob a handful. He received them in his smock-frock, which he held out for more.

'They'll keep him quiet a bit, at any rate,' thought David, and emptied the jar. Jacob grinned and mowed with delight.

'You're very good to this stranger, Mr Freely,' said Letitia; and then spitefully, as David joined the party at the parlour-door, 'I think you could hardly treat him better, if he was really your brother.'

'I've always thought it a duty to be good to idiots,' said Mr Freely, striving after the most moral view of the subject. 'We might have been idiots ourselves – everybody might have been born idiots, instead of having their right senses.'

'I don't know where there'd ha' been victual for us all then,' observed Mrs Palfrey, regarding the matter in a housewifely light.

'But let us sit down again and finish our tea,' said Mr Freely. 'Let us leave the poor creature to himself.'

They walked into the parlour again; but Jacob, not apparently appreciating the kindness of leaving him to himself, immediately followed his brother, and seated himself, pitchfork grounded, at the table.

'Well,' said Miss Letitia, rising, 'I don't know whether *you* mean to stay, mother; but I shall go home.'

'Oh, me too,' said Penny, frightened to death at Jacob, who had begun to nod and grin at her.

'Well, I think we *had* better be going, Mr Palfrey,' said the mother, rising more slowly.

Mr Freely, whose complexion had become decidedly yellower during the last half-hour, did not resist this proposition. He hoped they should meet again 'under happier circumstances'.

'It's my belief the man is his brother,' said Letitia, when they were all on their way home.

'Letty, it's very ill-natured of you,' said Penny, beginning to cry.

'Nonsense!' said Mr Palfrey. 'Freely's got no brother – he's said so many and many a time; he's an orphan; he's got nothing but uncles – leastwise, one. What's it matter what an idiot says? What call had Freely to tell lies?'

Letitia tossed her head and was silent.

Mr Freely, left alone with his affectionate brother Jacob, brooded over the possibility of luring him out of the town early the next morning, and getting him conveyed to Gilsbrook without further betrayals. But the thing was difficult. He saw clearly that if he took Jacob away himself, his absence, conjoined with the disappearance of the stranger, would either cause the conviction that he was really a relative, or would oblige him to the dangerous course of inventing a story to account for his disappearance, and his own absence at the same time. David groaned. There come occasions when falsehood is felt to be inconvenient. It would, perhaps, have been a longer-headed device, if he had never told any of those clever fibs about his uncles, grand and otherwise; for the Palfreys were simple people, and shared the popular prejudice against lying. Even if he could get Jacob away this time, what security was there that he would not come again, having once found the way? O guineas! O lozenges! what enviable people those were who had never robbed their mothers, and had never told fibs! David spent a sleepless night, while Jacob was snoring close by. Was this the upshot of travelling to the Indies, and acquiring experience combined with anecdote?

He rose at break of day, as he had once before done when he was in fear of Jacob, and took all gentle means to rouse this fatal brother from his deep sleep; he dared not be loud, because his apprentice was in the house, and would report everything. But Jacob was not to be roused. He fought out with his fist at the unknown cause of disturbance, turned over, and snored again. He must be left to wake as he would. David, with a cold perspiration on his brow, confessed to himself that Jacob could not be got away that day.

Mr Palfrey came over to Grimworth before noon, with a natural curiosity to see how his future son-in-law got on with the stranger to whom he was so benevolently inclined. He found a crowd round the shop. All Grimworth by this time had heard how Freely had been fastened on by an idiot, who called him 'Brother Zavy'; and the younger population seemed to find the singular stranger an unwearying source of fascination, while the householders dropped in one by one to inquire into the incident.

'Why don't you send him to the workhouse?' said Mr Prettyman. 'You'll have a row with him and the children presently, and he'll eat you up. The workhouse is the proper place for him; let his kin claim him, if he's got any.'

'Those may be *your* feelings, Mr Prettyman,' said David, his mind quite enfeebled by the torture of his position.

'What! *is* he your brother, then?' said Mr Prettyman, looking at his neighbour Freely rather sharply.

'All men are our brothers, and idiots particular so,' said Mr Freely, who, like many other travelled men, was not master of the English language.

'Come, come, if he's your brother, tell the truth, man,' said Mr Prettyman, with growing suspicion. 'Don't be ashamed of your own flesh and blood.'

Mr Palfrey was present, and also had his eye on Freely. It is difficult for a man to believe in the advantage of a truth which will disclose him to have been a liar. In this critical moment, David shrank from this immediate disgrace in the eyes of his future father-in-law.

'Mr Prettyman,' he said, 'I take your observations as an insult. I've no reason to be otherwise than proud of my own flesh and blood. If this poor man was my brother more than all men are, I should say so.'

A tall figure darkened the door, and David, lifting his eyes in that direction, saw his eldest brother, Jonathan, on the door-sill.

'I'll stay wi' Zavy,' shouted Jacob, as he, too, caught sight of his eldest brother; and, running behind the counter, he clutched David hard.

'What, he *is* here?' said Jonathan Faux, coming forward. 'My mother would have no nay, as he'd been away so long, but I must see after him. And it struck me he was very like come after you, because we'd been talking of you o' late, and where you lived.'

David saw there was no escape; he smiled a ghastly smile.

'What! is this a relation of yours, sir?' said Mr Palfrey to Jonathan.

'Ay, it's my innicent of a brother, sure enough,' said honest Jonathan. 'A fine trouble and cost he is to us, in th' eating and other things, but we must bear what's laid on us.'

'And your name's Freely, is it?' said Mr Prettyman.

'Nay, nay, my name's Faux, I know nothing o' Freelys,' said Jonathan, curtly. 'Come,' he added, turning to David, 'I must take some news to mother about Jacob. Shall I take him with me, or will you undertake to send him back?'

'Take him, if you can make him loose his hold of me,' said David, feebly.

'Is this gentleman here in the confectionery line your brother, then, sir?' said Mr Prettyman, feeling that it was an occasion on which formal language must be used.

'*I* don't want to own him,' said Jonathan, unable to resist a movement of indignation that had never been allowed to satisfy itself. 'He run away from home with good reasons in his pocket years ago: he didn't want to be owned again, I reckon.'

Mr Palfrey left the shop; he felt his own pride too severely wounded by the sense that he had let himself be fooled, to feel curiosity for further details. The most pressing business was to go home and tell his daughter that Freely was a poor sneak, probably a rascal, and that her engagement was broken off.

Mr Prettyman stayed, with some internal self-gratulation that *he* had never given in to Freely, and that Mr Chaloner would see now what sort of fellow it was that he had put over the heads of older parishioners. He considered it due from him (Mr Prettyman) that, for the interests of the parish, he should know all that was to be known about this 'interloper'. Grimworth would have people coming from Botany Bay[3] to settle in it, if things went on in this way.

It soon appeared that Jacob could not be made to quit his dear brother David except by force. He understood, with a clearness equal to that of the most intelligent mind, that Jonathan would take him back to skimmed milk, apple-dumpling, broad-beans, and pork. And he had found a paradise in his brother's shop. It was a difficult matter to use force with Jacob, for he wore heavy nailed boots; and if his pitchfork had been mastered, he would have resorted without hesitation to kicks. Nothing short of using guile to bind him hand and foot would have made all parties safe.

'Let him stay,' said David, with desperate resignation, frightened above all things at the idea of further disturbances in his shop, which would make his exposure all the more conspicuous. '*You* go away again, and tomorrow I can, perhaps, get him to go to Gilsbrook with me. He'll follow me fast enough, I daresay,' he added, with a half-groan.

'Very well,' said Jonathan, gruffly. 'I don't see why *you* shouldn't have some trouble and expense with him as well as the rest of us. But mind you bring him back safe and soon, else mother 'll never rest.'

On this arrangement being concluded, Mr Prettyman begged Mr Jonathan Faux to go and take a snack with him, an invitation which was quite acceptable; and as honest Jonathan had nothing to be ashamed of, it is probable that he was very frank in his communications to the civil draper, who, pursuing the benefit of the parish, hastened to make all the information he could gather about Freely common parochial property. You may imagine that the meeting of the Club at the Woolpack that evening was unusually lively. Every member was anxious to prove that he had never liked Freely, as he called himself. Faux was his name, was it? Fox would have been more suitable. The majority expressed a desire to see him hooted out of the town.

Mr Freely did not venture over his door-sill that day, for he knew Jacob would keep at his side, and there was every probability that they would have a train of juvenile followers. He sent to engage the Woolpack gig for an early hour the next morning; but this order was not kept religiously a secret by the landlord. Mr Freely was informed that he could not have the gig till seven; and the Grimworth people were early risers. Perhaps they were more alert than usual on this particular morning; for when Jacob, with a bag of sweets in his hand, was induced to mount the gig with his brother David, the inhabitants of the market-place were looking out of their doors and windows, and at the turning of the street there was even a muster of apprentices and schoolboys, who shouted as they passed in what Jacob took to be a very merry and friendly way, nodding and grinning in return. 'Huzzay, David Faux! how's your uncle?' was their morning's greeting. Like other pointed things, it was not altogether impromptu.

Even this public derision was not so crushing to David as the horrible thought that though he might succeed now in getting Jacob home again there would never be any security against his coming back, like a wasp to the honey-pot. As long as David lived at Grimworth, Jacob's return would be hanging over him. But could he go on living at Grimworth – an object of ridicule, discarded by the Palfreys, after having revelled in the consciousness that he was an envied and prosperous confectioner? David liked to be envied; he minded less about being loved.

His doubts on this point were soon settled. The mind of Grimworth became obstinately set against him and his viands, and the new school being finished, the eating-room was closed. If there had been no other reason, sympathy with the Palfreys, that respectable family who had lived in the parish time out of mind, would have determined all well-to-do people to decline Freely's goods. Besides, he had absconded with his mother's guineas: who knew what else he had done, in Jamaica or elsewhere, before he came to Grimworth, worming himself into families under false pretences? Females shuddered. Dreadful suspicions gathered round him: his green eyes, his bow-legs, had a criminal aspect. The rector disliked the sight of a man who had imposed upon him; and all boys who could not afford to purchase, hooted 'David Faux' as they passed his shop. Certainly no man now would pay anything for the 'goodwill' of Mr Freely's business, and he would be obliged to quit it without a peculium so desirable towards defraying the expense of moving.

In a few months the shop in the market-place was again to let, and Mr David Faux, *alias* Mr Edward Freely, had gone – nobody at Grimworth knew whither. In this way the demoralisation of Grimworth women was checked. Young Mrs Steene renewed her efforts to make light mince-pies, and having at last made a batch so excellent that Mr Steene looked at her with complacency as he ate them, and said they were the best he had ever eaten in his life, she thought less of bulbuls and renegades ever after. The secrets of the finer cookery were revived in the breasts of matronly housewives, and daughters were again anxious to be initiated in them.

You will further, I hope, be glad to hear, that some purchases of drapery made by pretty Penny, in preparation for her marriage with Mr Freely, came in quite as well for her wedding with young Towers as if they had been made expressly for the latter occasion. For Penny's complexion had not altered, and blue always became it best.

Here ends the story of Mr David Faux, confectioner, and his brother Jacob. And we see in it, I think, an admirable instance of the unexpected forms in which the great Nemesis hides herself.

NOTES

Like all editors I am indebted to previous editions, in particular to Q. D. Leavis's edition of *Silas Marner* (Penguin, 1967).

Silas Marner

Chapter 1

1 (p.3) **flax:** used for the weaving of table- and bed-linen. Silas Marner works at home, and is better off than those who worked for a master, or later in factories. During the Napoleonic Wars weaving was a well-rewarded trade; Silas would have no difficulty in amassing his gold, as a result of his long hours of labour.

2 (p.3) **pedlar:** someone who goes from place to place selling goods.

3 (p.3) **peasants:** agricultural labourers who attempted to support their families on the land they cultivated, which was often rented, and with a proportion of the produce being payable in rent. As a class, peasants still survive in some parts of Europe, but their way of life is rapidly disappearing as a result of bureaucratic agricultural policies.

4 (p.4) **In the early years:** Silas Marner arrives in Raveloe in the late 1780s.

5 (p.5) **tithes:** a tenth part of produce or income which had to be contributed for the support of the Church and clergy.

6 (p.5) **turnpike:** a road on which tolls were payable, introduced in England in the eighteenth century.

7 (p.5) **war times:** the Napoleonic Wars, prosperous for land-owners like the Cass family, who began to suffer after 1815.

8 (p.6) **mole-catcher:** mole-catching was a skilled trade; moles were killed as a pest, and their skins were sold for articles of clothing. They were familiar figures in rural England of the period.

9 (p.6) **A fit was a stroke**: Silas suffers from catalepsy – a state of prolonged rigid seizure, which can ressemble rigor mortis.

10 (p.7) **tale of the cloth**: reckoning of its value.

11 (p.7) **church assembling in Lantern Yard**: This Church was an extreme dissenting sect, influenced by Calvinism. Members of the Church would have been expected to marry within the community of the elect.

12 (p.8) **David and Jonathan**: David was the second King of the Hebrews, about 1000 B.C. Jonathan was his closest friend who was killed in battle; see 2 Samuel 1: 19–26.

13 (p.9) **Assurance of salvation**: Assurance of Salvation was the basis of religious certainty. 'Election' was a fact of religious experience; the soul was saved by divine grace.

14 (p.9) **cataleptic fit**: see note 9.

15 (p.12) **To people accustomed to reason ... is culpable**: Silas Marner would have stood a better chance of being declared 'not guilty' if he had stood trial. The 'church' did not approve of trial under the law. George Eliot represents this Church as being rigorous and repressive, open only to its own view of truth. Silas Marner, unwisely, relied on his innocence being certified by divine intervention.

Chapter 2

1 (p.15) **Even people ... the blackness of night**: This opening passage reflects George Eliot's interest in the classical, or pagan, as well as the Christian world. Bewilderment was the means by which the Greek gods worked upon the minds of men.

2 (p.17) **Wise Woman**: The traditions associated with the Wise Woman of the village, with her knowledge of herbs and charms, was still alive in rural England. Even 'Dr' Kimble has no proper medical training. Not until Pasteur (1822–95) discovered bacteria as a cause of infection was there any real understanding of many forms of illness.

3 (p.19) **familiars**: a supernatural spirit supposed to attend a witch.

4 (p.19) **Master**: a respectful form of address used for craftsmen. The gentry were called Mr, unless intentionally left out. Master was also used of the male children of gentry.

Chapter 3

1 (p.22) **Squire:** The Squire was the main landowner in a rural community, though he was not necessarily high in the wider social hierarchy. This is true of Squire Cass.

2 (p.22) **fall of prices:** after 1815, at the end of the Napoleonic Wars.

3 (p.22) **orts:** left-overs to which the poor were traditionally entitled. The ideal of 'waste not, want not' conflicted with this tradition of charity through excess; the more so as the puritan doctrine of thrift played an increasingly important part in 'middle-class morality' during the nineteenth century.

4 (p.23) **chines:** the meaty backbone of an animal, which was cut for cooking.

5 (p.23) **spun butter:** butter spun for ornamental purposes.

6 (p.23) **wainscot:** wood-panelling around the bottom of the walls of a room.

7 (p.23) **King George:** George III (1760–1820)

8 (p.25) **distrain:** to seize property as a security for debt.

9 (p.26) **laudanum:** medicine of which opium was the main ingredient, and so highly addictive.

10 (p.30) **lives of rural forefathers ... own petty history:** George Eliot's knowledge of the rural past of England derived from her own childhood, as well as her reading.

11 (p.32) **cock-fighting:** a fight between two gamecocks, fitted with sharp metal spurs, popular in England at the time. It was made illegal in 1892.

Chapter 4

1 (p.33) **cover:** the place from which the hunt began after the fox was drawn from its cover.

2 (p.34) **pocket-pistol:** flask.

3 (p.38) **jacks:** a machine used to turn the spit in order to rotate the meat on it.

Chapter 5

1 (p.40) **horn lantern**: lanterns were originally made from horn, hence horn lantern and lanthorn.

Chapter 6

1 (p.45) **fustian jackets and smock-frocks**: Fustian was made of a mixture of flax and cotton, a cloth worn by labourers because it was very hard wearing. A smock-frock was a loose-fitting garment of coarse linen, worn by farm-labourers.

2 (p.45) **farrier**: person who shoes horses.

3 (p.46) **drenching**: a dose of liquid medicine given to an animal.

4 (p.47) **I know what's right . . .**: metrical version of Psalm 119.

5 (p.47) **wheelwright**: a person who makes or mends wheels.

6 (p.47) **key-bugle**: a bugle fitted with keys to increase the number of its sounds.

7 (p.48) **throstle**: another name for the song-thrush.

8 (p.48) **liver and lights**: liver and lungs

9 (p.51) **Charity Land**: land for the benefit of the poor.

10 (p.51) **Queen's heads**: Queen Anne died in 1714.

Chapter 7

1 (p.57) **mushed**: subdued, depressed. A musher is a hammer or pestle used for crushing.

2 (p.59) *nolo episcopari*: 'I am unwilling to accept nomination as a bishop', i.e. formal rejection of election.

Chapter 8

1 (p.60) **tinder-box**: a box used for holding tinder which might be fitted with flint or steel, for making a spark.

2 (p.61) **King George's**: see ch. 3, n. 7.

3 (p.61) **pedlar's**: see ch. 1, n. 2.

4 (p.65) **behoof**: advantage or profit.

Chapter 9

1 (p.70) *collogue*: conspire.

2 (p.70) entail: a legal restriction upon the inheritance of an estate. As there is none, Squire Cass does not to have to leave it to his son.

3 (p.72) shilly-shally: indecisive – reduplication of 'shall I'.

Chapter 10

1 (p.76) skimming-dishes: dishes used for skimming milk.

2 (p.77) 'poor mushed creatur': see ch. 7, n. 1.

3 (p.78) yarbs: dialect form of 'herbs'.

4 (p.78) Wise Woman: see ch. 2, n. 2.

5 (p.81) lard-cakes: more usually, lardy-cakes; an oblong flat cake, crossed with lines, made of dough, lard, sugar and spices; considered a delicacy of the country-poor.

6 (p.82) outwork: work done outside the house, i.e. as though it were outside the house in this instance.

7 (p.82) I. H. S.: standing for the Latin phrase *Iesus Hominum Salvator*, which means 'Jesus Saviour of Mankind'.

8 (p.83) I went to chapel: Silas makes the distinction between Church (the Church of England) and chapel to which dissenters go. This also reflects a class distinction.

9 (p.85) 'God rest you, merry gentlemen': a traditional Christmas carol.

10 (p.86) leave off weaving of a Sunday: According to rural tradition, money earned on Sunday leads to damnation; also money earned in the wrong way becomes a bad bed to lie down on. Rural traditions combined the pagan and the Christian as a matter of attitude rather than dogma.

11 (p.87) Athanasian Creed: profession of faith used in the Christian Church, originally attributed to Athanasius (A.D.296–373?) who championed Christian orthodoxy against Arianism.

12 (p.87) bandboxes: a bandbox was a box for collars, hats, etc. It was originally designed in the seventeenth century as a container for bands or ruffs.

Chapter 11

1 (p.89) **joseph**: long riding-coat worn by ladies in the eighteenth century.

2 (p.90) **bandboxes**: see ch. 10, n.12.

3 (p.92) **nattiness**: smartness, spruceness.

4 (p.93) **She actually said 'mate' for 'meat'**: Nancy's country speech contrasts with the way she speaks in other parts of the book, as heroine. In reality, the Casses speech would have been closer to Raveloe speech than the idealisation of the heroine suggests elsewhere. Class in rural England was still more a matter of deference than speech. (See 'Note on Dialect' in *Silas Marner* (Harmondsworth, 1967) p.245.)

5 (p.94) **hogsheads**: large casks.

6 (p.94) **scrag or a knuckle**: a scrag is a lean end of a neck of veal or mutton; a knuckle, a joint of meat.

7 (p.94) **mawkin**: a slut. (Priscilla is using the word humorously.)

8 (p.97) **pigtail**: plait of hair, fashionable in the period.

9 (p.100) **'The flaxen-headed ploughboy'**: probably the song published in S. Baring-Gould's *English Minstrelsie* (Edinburgh, 1895–99) as 'The Ploughboy'.

10 (p.101) **Lead the way ... we'll all follow you**: In this passage George Eliot reflects the hierarchical order in the English village, and the customs by which it was reasserted every year.

11 (p.103) **sodger**: dialect form of soldier.

12 (p.103) **shuttle-cock**: a light cone with feathered flights.

13 (p.104) **piert**: brisk, lively, cheerful, in good health.

14 (p.104) **offal**: here used in the sense of rubbish, illustrating the villagers' attitude to Duncan Cass, although he is the Squire's son.

Chapter 12

1 (p.107) **demon Opium**: extracted from the seeds of the opium poppy. The Opium Wars of the eighteenth century remain one of the

worst examples of the commercial exploitation of China by the West, with results which, as here, proved disastrous for the poor in the West. Drug-trafficking today follows the same course of indifference to human suffering for the sake of insatiable greed. George Eliot's use of the word 'demon' reflects the moral indignation she felt.

2 (p.108) furze bush: another name for gorse.

3 (p.109) gosling: young goose.

Chapter 13

1 (p.117) the workhouse: an institution in which paupers were lodged, and the able-bodied were set to work. The conditions in them were usually pitiable, even compared to prisons. 'Most well-regulated Bridewells are paradises compared to the Oxford workhouse' (see OED entry for 'workhouse'; the quote dates from 1797).

2 (p.118) the parish isn't likely to quarrel: the parish fulfilled in those days the role of the social services. Marner would not be allowed to keep the child now; but for better or worse? The desire to save money remains unchanged.

Chapter 14

1 (p.121) scrat: scratch

2 (p.121) moithered: broken into very small flakes, metaphorically 'worried'.

3 (p.123) catechise: form of 'catechism'. Instruction by a series of questions and answers, especially in relation to the doctrine of the Christian Church.

4 (p.124) Hephzibah: 'My delight is in her' in Hebrew. See *Isaiah* 62: 4.

5 (p.124) haft: handle of an axe or knife.

6 (p.125) suds: soapy water.

7 (p.127) colly: blacken, soil.

8 (p.127) Goliath: Philistine giant, killed by David with a stone from his sling: 1 *Samuel* 17.

9 (p.130) gnome or brownie: gnomes are said to live in the earth and guard buried treasure; brownies are said to do helpful work at night.

10 (p.131) In old days there were angels: Lot was taken away from Sodom by an angel, before the city was destroyed: *Genesis* 19.

Chapter 16

1 (p.136) **fustian:** see ch. 6, n. 1.

2 (p.137) **no lavender only in the gentlefolks' gardens:** As well as the herbs used for cooking, a lavender-bed or hedge was traditionally planted for a bride, so that the linen would be sweet-smelling. The garden is intended to be practical as well as picturesque.

3 (p.140) **gods of the hearth:** In Roman times, these were known as the *lares et penates*. As mentioned before, George Eliot associates Raveloe with a culture which is both pagan and Christian.

4 (p.142) **leeching:** use of leeches to suck blood as a treatment for disease.

5 (p.144) **dame school:** small school offering basic education, usually run from home.

Chapter 17

1 (p.149) **filberts:** nuts named after a Frankish Abbot of the seventh century. The nuts were said to ripen on his feast day, August 22.

2 (p.149) **spar:** minerals which are easily cleavable.

3 (p.149) **poor-rate:** levy raised in the parish to 'look after' the poor.

4 (p.152) **Mant's Bible:** a three-volume, illustrated Bible, published in 1816.

Chapter 19

1 (p.163) **'beauty born of murmuring sound':** see Wordsworth, 'Three years she grew'. Wordsworth's influence on George Eliot was profoiund. She read and loved him from her childhood until the end of her life.

2 (p.164) **the workhouse:** see ch. 13, n. 1.

The Lifted Veil

Chapter 1

1 (p.184) **Give me no light:** The epigraph was written by George Eliot to give 'sufficient indication' of the idea which inspired *The Lifted Veil*.

See *The Letters of George Eliot*, ed. G. S. Haight (New Haven, 1954–78) vol. v, p.380.

2 (p.186) *ubi sœva indignatio ... nequit*: inscription on Dean Swift's tombstone in Dublin: 'where savage indignation can no longer lacerate the heart'.

3 (p.188) Potter's 'Æschylus' ... Francis's 'Horace': A classical education was then considered a preparation for life. Robert Potter's *The Tragedies of Æschylus* (1777) and Philip Francis's *Horace* (1757) were standard commentaries.

4 (p.188) a scientific education: The School of Mines was established in 1851. Writers like T. H. Huxley, known as Darwin's 'Bulldog', popularised science, advocated the advantages of a scientific education in the 1860s.

5 (p.188) his great thumbs on my temples: Mr Letherall is a phrenologist, who advises on careers by studying the bumps on the skull overlying the parts of the brain thought to be responsible for particular faculties. George Eliot had read George Combe's *Elements of Phrenology* in the 1840s.

6 (p.189) Plutarch: Roman historian (c. 50 B.C.–A.D. 120). Important as a source for Shakespeare's Roman Plays.

7 (p.189–90) Jean Jacques ... home of light: Jean-Jacques Rousseau, whom George Eliot said had influenced her more than any other thinker. The incident referred to is related in the Fifth Walk, *Reveries of a Solitary Walker* (Harmondsworth, 1979), p.85.

8 (p.190) *gamins*: street Arabs.

9 (p.191) who worship wearily: This passage reflects George Eliot's own view of the stultifying effect of religious dogmatism.

10 (p.192) Homer ... Dante ... Milton: George Eliot had read widely from an early age, and knew Homer's *Iliad*, Dante's *Divine Comedy* and Milton's *Paradise Lost* thoroughly.

11 (p.192) Novalis: German Romantic poet (1772–1801) who died of consumption.

12 (p.193) Canaletto: Antonio Canale (1697–1768), Venetian painter.

13 (p.194) Water-Nixie: a nymph or elph, usually unfriendly to human beings. Often mentioned in German myths and lyrics.

14 (p.200) **energumen**: one possessed by a devil. (George Eliot was influenced by Walter Scott. See *The Abbott* (London, 1969), ch. 42.

15 (p.201) **Giorgione**: a Venetian painter (1478–1510), only a score of whose works survive.

16 (p.201) **Lucrezia Borgia**: Italian noblewoman (1480–1519), represented as wanton, murderous and expert with poisons by her political and personal enemies, though respected by her subjects.

17 (p.201) **Belvedere Gallery**: the Belvedere in Vienna's Lichtenberg Palace.

18 (p.202) **dogs for the wood-fire**: one of a pair of irons for supporting burning wood.

19 (p.203) **an old story**: the Faust legend; G. H. Lewes with whom George Eliot lived had written the life of Goethe in 1855.

20 (p.205) **cicerone**: a guide who shows curiosities or antiquities to strangers, derived from Cicero.

Chapter 2

1 (p.208) **Tasso**: Italian poet (1544–95), author of the *Gerusalemme Liberata*.

2 (p.211) **adytum**: private chamber or sanctum.

3 (p.212) *hashish*: powdered hemp leaves, used as a narcotic.

4 (p.215) **incubus**: evil spirit or daemon.

5 (p.224) **the experiment in which he was so absorbed**: This experiment is of course wholly unscientific, and adds a Gothic climax to the tale. In stories like 'Unprofessional', Rudyard Kipling also showed a liking for the pseudo-scientific: a narrative device without plausibility. George Eliot does not actually need it here, as the faculty of prevision would suffice.

Brother Jacob

Chapter 1

1 (p.228) **Trompeurs**: Epigraph from *La Fontaine* (1621–95), *Le Renard et la Cigogne*': 'Deceivers, I write for you; expect a similar fate.'

2 (p.229) **confectionery**: A confection is any sweet preparation.

3 (p.229) **yeoman**: a small freeholder who cultivated his own land.

4 (p.229) **marengs**: dialect form of meringue.

5 (p.230) **Mechanics' Institute**: In Glasgow and London Mechanics' Institutions were established in the 1820s under the inspiration of George Birkbeck. Their aim was self-help and self-improvement. Birkbeck's name is commemorated in the College of London University of which he was the first President. Birkbeck College still exists to provide a university education for those who have not been able to go to university for various reasons, before starting their working lives.

6 (p.230) **'Inkle and Yarico'**: This was a popular story in England and Europe, based on the eleventh paper in Richard Steele's *The Spectator* (1711–14). Thomas Inkle puts self-interest first, selling Yorico, an American-Indian girl who has loved him devotedly, to a Barbadian merchant for money.

7 (p.231) **beans**: French *biens*: goods or property.

8 (p.232) **Chubb**: well known, then and now, for patent-locks.

9 (p.233) *mens nil conscia sibi*: 'mind free from guilt':
Virgil, *Aeneid*, I. 604.

10 (p.233) **Louis Napoleon**: nephew of Napoleon, and Emperor of France, when the story was written.

11 (p.234) **Caliban ... Trinculo**: for Caliban and Trinculo, see Shakespeare's *The Tempest*.

12 (p.236) **Balzac**: French novelist (1799–1850), author of *Le Père Goriot* and many other novels.

13 (p.237) **Princess Yarico**: see n. 6.

14 (p.238) **horse-block**: a small platform, of three or four steps, used in mounting a horse.

15 (p.240) **The ways of thieving were not ways of pleasantness**: Proverbs 3:17 – 'Her ways are ways of pleasantness, and all her paths are peace.'

16 (p.241) **Gorgon or Demogorgon**: Spenser, *Faerie Queene*, I.i.37.

Chapter 2

1 (p.242) **Yellow Coat School**: named after long robe worn in some charity schools.

2 (p.243) **jobbed**: bought from a middle-man.

3 (p.244) **Turner's**: J. M. W. Turner (1775–1851), English painter, whose later style was characterised by colours which reproduced the effects of light.

4 (p.244) **Punch**: as in the Punch and Judy show.

5 (p.244) **mazarine**: deep rich blue.

6 (p.245) **carding-mill**: mills where wool was prepared for spinning by combing out with a card.

7 (p.245) **ratafias**: cakes or biscuits flavoured with ratafia cordial, made from almonds or fruit.

8 (p.245) **peripateia**: a peripeteia – a sudden change or reversal of fortune.

9 (p.245) **'Lalla Rookh', the 'Corsair', and the 'Siege of Corinth'**: Byron established a fashion for oriental tales in verse with 'The Corsair' (1814) and 'The Siege of Corinth' (1816). Thomas Moore followed with 'Lalla Rookh' in 1817.

10 (p.245) **'bulbul'**: nightingale.

11 (p.245) **spavin**: inflammation of the cartilage in horses.

12 (p.246) **renegade**: someone who has turned away from his faith; in this case adopted Muslim dress.

13 (p.247) **division of labour**: see Adam Smith, *An Enquiry into the Nature and Causes of the Wealth of Nations* (1776). Division of labour implies specialisation.

14 (p.248) **'Spectator's'**: Richard Steele, *The Spectator*, 15 July 1712.

15 (p.248) **Desdemonas**: see Shakespeare's *Othello*, II. iii. 126–68.

16 (p.249) **mercer**: dealer in textile fabrics and fine cloth.

17 (p.251) **murrain**: plague-like disease of cattle, from French, *morir*, to die.

18 (p.251) **Mangnall's Questions**: Richmal Mangnall (1769–1820),

Headmistress of Crofton Hall, wrote *Historical and Miscellaneous Questions for the Use of Young People* (1800). This had reached its eighty-fourth impression by 1857.

19 (p.252) **Without thee ... sweet to die:** Faux ('Mr Freely') has adapted lines from the hymn, 'Sun of My Soul, Thou Saviour Dear' from 'Evening' in Keble's *The Christian Year* (1827).

20 (p.252) **wool-factor:** a factor was someone who transacted business on someone else's behalf.

21 (p.252) **gig:** a two-wheeled one horse carriage.

22 (p.253) **Nelson:** Horatio Nelson (1758–1805), British Admiral during the Napoleonic Wars who destroyed French Naval power at the Battle of the Nile (1798), and died at Trafalgar (1805).

23 (p.253) **brawn:** jellied loaf made from head of pig or calf.

24 (p.254) **Titian:** Venetian painter (c.1488–1576), renowned among other things for the subtlety and beauty of his use of colour.

25 (p.256) **the great Leviathan ... a bridle in his jaws:** mock serious allusion to Job 41.

Chapter 3

1 (p.257) **sharper:** a person who cheats or swindles, especially at cards.

2 (p.261) **smock-frock:** a loose protective overgarment, decorated with smocking or ornamental needlework, worn especially by farmworkers.

3 (p.266) **Botany Bay:** a penal settlement in New South Wales, Australia, to which convicts were sent.

GEORGE ELIOT AND HER CRITICS

All three narratives have met with a mixed critical response. *Silas Marner* was admired by almost all critics when it first appeared; in more recent times critics have often passed over it, and the other tales, with a certain reticence. Even F. R. Leavis could only find to say of *Silas Marner* that it was a 'charming minor masterpiece'. G. H. Lewes thought *The Lifted Veil* 'very striking and original', but the publisher, John Blackwood, found it 'horribly painful', and did not want to include it in the uniform edition. But George Eliot insisted, and wrote the epigraph to enlighten Blackwood:

> Give me no light, great Heaven, but such as turns
> To energy of human fellowship;
> No powers beyond the growing heritage
> That makes complete manhood.

John Blackwood praised *Brother Jacob* for being as 'clever as can be', but found in both *Brother Jacob* and *The Lifted Veil* 'a perfect want of light'. The narrative tone and style of *Brother Jacob* is not characteristic of George Eliot, but she wanted it published together with *Silas Marner* and *The Lifted Veil*, as here.

George Eliot: Letter to John Blackwood, 24 February 1861; reprinted in *The Letters of George Eliot*, p.380:

I don't wonder at your finding my story (i.e. *Silas Marner*), as far as you have read it, rather sombre: indeed, I should not have believed that any one would have been interested in it but myself (since William Wordsworth is dead) if Mr Lewes had not been strongly arrested by it. But I hope you will not find it at all a sad story, as a whole, since it sets – or is intended to set – in a strong light the remedial influences of pure, natural, human relations. The Nemesis is a very mild one. I have felt all through as if the story would have lent itself best to metrical rather than prose fiction, especially in all that relates to the psychology of Silas; except that, under that treatment, there could not be an equal play of humour. It came to me first of all, quite suddenly as a sort of legendary tale, suggested by my recollection of having once, in my early childhood, seen a linen-weaver with a bag on his back; but, as my mind dwelt on the subject, I became inclined to a more realistic treatment.

My chief reason for wishing to publish the story now, is, that I like my writings to appear in the order in which they are written, because they belong to successive mental phases, and when they are a year behind me, I can no longer feel that thorough identification with them which gives zest to their sense of authorship.

The reviewer in *Dublin University Magazine* for April 1862 complained of *Silas Marner* that 'a duller book it has seldom been our lot to read through'; but the majority of critics praised it for its depiction of character – especially that of the poor – and more generally its depiction of country life. The reviewer in the *Westminster Review* of July 1861 wrote:

The most remarkable peculiarity and distinguishing excellence of *Silas Marner*, is the complete correlation between the characters and their circumstances; the actors in this story come before us like the flowers of their own fields, native to the soil and varying with each constituent of the earth from which they spring, with every difference that is implied in defective or excessive nutriment, but yet not more the creatures of blind chance, each asserting his own individuality after his kind, and none overstepping the possibilities of culture furnished by such a world-forgotten village as Raveloe. It is impossible to dissociate any of the characters from the village in which they were born and bred – they form an organic whole with Raveloe; they are not connected with it by any external, or even humorous bands, but by vital threads that will not bear disruption. The stranger Silas is at last assimilated by the little society, and only truly lives when the process has been completed.

More recently, in her introduction to the Penguin edition of *Silas Marner* (Harmondsworth, 1967), Q. D. Leavis quoted the brief and tantalising comments made by Henry James, and then those comments against George Eliot's own account of the origin of the novel:

In his reminiscences *The Middle Years*, written in his old age, Henry James, when starting his memories of George Eliot, refers to her as 'the author of *Silas Marner* and *Middlemarch*', a selection of her novels intended either to represent her at her best or as covering two distinct kinds of her creative art, or both. He goes on to describe her work in general as a 'great treasure of beauty and humanity of applied and achieved art, a testimony, historic, as well as aesthetic, to the deeper interest of the intricate English aspects'. Of none of her novels is this more true than of *Silas Marner*; one could only have wished that he had been specific. What deeper interest of the aspects of England, what aesthetic and historic testimony, does *Marner* represent? That it is not to be dismissed as the mere moral 'faery-tale' or 'divertissement' of many critics, we might have guessed from the quite exceptional nature of its origin, of which we luckily have an account. Our first knowledge of this book is a note in George Eliot's Journal (28 November 1860): 'I am now engaged in writing a story – the idea of which came to me after our arrival in this house [a depressing furnished London house] and which has thrust itself between me and the other book [*Romola*] I was meditating. It is *Silas Marner, the Weaver of Raveloe*.' Thus at the outset Silas is identified by his trade. And we note also that this same day's entry in her Journal opens: 'Since I last wrote in this Journal, I have suffered much from physical weakness, accompanied with mental depression. The loss of the country seemed very bitter to me, and my want of health and strength has prevented me from working much – still worse, has made me despair of ever working well again.' Six weeks later, in writing to tell her publisher of her new book she again stresses the involuntary nature of this new undertaking: 'a story which came *across* my other plans by a sudden inspiration'. She adds: 'It is a story of old-fashioned village life, which has unfolded itself from the merest millet-seed of thought.'

(pp. 11–12)

John Holloway in his introduction to the Everyman edition of 1977 drew attention to the Calvinist doctrine in *Silas Marner*:

There is also a particular reason why a Congregationalist Silas would have been driven to say 'there is no just God that governs the earth righteously, but a God of lies'. We read in R. W. Dale (*A History of English Congregationalism* 1907) that when a member was excluded by a vote of the whole congregation for misconduct, 'the old forms were observed with great solemnity'. There was a particular reason for this. For the traditional Congregationalist, the doctrine that Christ and his Church were one held good, as a direct and literal truth, of every individual congregation. Silas had learnt, as part of his Calvinism, that the decision of the congregation was the voice of Christ. There was no mediate point at which error could enter. When the lots proclaim his guilt, there is nothing for him to believe but that Christ himself has lied. Thus his outburst is wholly convincing testimony to the simplistic integrity of his faith at the very moment of its disintegration and ruin. It has a terrible psychological truth and rightness.

Critics in the recent past have focused upon themes of contemporary relevance in *Silas Marner*: for example, Alan Bellringer in his book *George Eliot* (London, 1993) identifies the complexity of George Eliot's depiction of parenthood and the single parent family in which the step-father plays the female role. In her book of the same title, *George Eliot* (London, 1987), Jenny Uglow highlights George Eliot's concern with social bonds:

> Her fierce class loyalty supports the view implicit in the whole book that organic social bonds are more likely to develop among the rural working population than among their 'betters' who cling to an individualistic ethic of 'rights' which is open to self-interested interpretation. As we find it explored in this novel, the concept of rights loses out as an ethical notion by contrast with the concept of 'nature'. Arguments based on rights (unless refreshed by the appeal to a deeper standard of what is 'right') come to seem like a deep and horrible travesty of morality. The systems of rights are so formal, whether upheld by law or by constitutions, that it is as if they did not exist before they were 'granted' or 'enacted'; rights cannot be foundational in the way that those complex unstated obligations are which grow from shared experience.

(p.157)

Beryl Gray in her 'Afterword' to *The Lifted Veil* (London, 1985) raises the question of the relationship between the motto which prefaces the narrative and the narrative itself:

> The problem with the story seems to be less its literary quality (Henry James, at least, was able to see that it was 'a fine piece of writing', and John Blackwood always conceded that it was powerful) than the apparent subject matter; for in *The Lifted Veil* George Eliot

has accompanied her clairvoyant, first person narrator, Latimer, into a realm where her admirers do not expect, or wish, to find her. Even her biographer, Gordon Haight, sympathises with her publisher's difficulty in having to write to her about it. But *The Lifted Veil* is more than just an exercise in Victorian sensationalism, in spite of its use of the conventions that are readily associated with Edgar Allan Poe or Wilkie Collins or even (it has been suggested) with Mary E. Braddon. It is true that George Eliot's *treatment* of her idea is a departure for her, and therefore requires a corresponding adjustment on the part of the reader. Nevertheless, it is the idea itself which is important to her; and what her letter to Blackwood emphasises is that she wishes to justify the story's painfulness, not its unorthodoxy. The unbiased question that presents itself then is: does *The Lifted Veil* fulfil the idea that the solemn motto expresses? If we look behind Latimer's visionary excursion to the forsaken and the unknown, and behind his unenviable ability to peer into other people's petty selfish minds, I think the answer is that it does; for his story, like that of all George Eliot's protagonists, is essentially a moral journey. Preternatural though his gifts are, his spiritual predicament is created through his misinterpretation or misapplication of what is revealed to him; his curse is not, as he thinks, his clairvoyance, but his inability to reconcile its discoveries with his immediate desire for what does not properly belong to him.

(pp.72–3)

In his discussion of George Eliot's early novels, U. C. Knoepfl-macher highlights what is also distinctive about *Brother Jacob*:

David Faux is perhaps the most unpleasant character in George Eliot's fiction. Swollen with an 'impatient sense that he ought to become something very remarkable', this young man is dissatisfied with his station in life: 'he scorned the idea that he could accept an average' (Chapter 1). But his discontent is unwarranted. Unlike the Tulliver children who were likewise forced to 'put up with a narrowed lot', he is hopelessly mediocre. Tom and Maggie had, after all, evolved above the mental level of a 'superior' miller. This grumbling farmer's son is inferior to all the members of his family, even the half-wit who will come to haunt him. The extraordinary Maggie submits to her fate and returns to St Ogg's. The less-than-remarkable David, whose imagination, like hers, 'circles round and round the utmost limits of geographical knowledge' (Chapter 1) tries to break away from his parents and brothers . . . When he fails to make his fortune, he returns to England under an assumed name and with a face yellowed by malaria.

(*George Eliot's Early Novels*, pp.224–5)

George Eliot's reputation has been under attack from the Left and from structuralist critics in recent years, but this has not unsettled her position as one of the very greatest novelists of the nineteenth century. In his book *George Eliot* (London, 1993), Alan Bellringer usefully summarises some recent views like this:

George Eliot's suspicion of full-scale social theory as too abstract and reductive to provide a guide for action inevitably was deplored by Marxists. At first, they tended merely to disagree with her on the level of political debate. For instance, in 1951 Arnold Kettle supposed that the 'total impact' of *Middlemarch* was weakened by George Eliot's 'undialectical philosophy'; he expressed some impatience that since her view of society was static and her outlook 'mechanistic and not revolutionary', no one in the novel 'can fight Middlemarch or change it'. In fact her outlook was noncommital, not mechanisitic, and she considered revolutionary fighting inadvisable and counter-productive. Raymond Williams modifies the tone, but his political opposition is also very marked. Considering *Felix Holt* in 1958 as an 'industrial novel', Williams criticises the author for patience and caution which are very easily converted into acquiescing in a vicious society; it is obvious to him that George Eliot could not believe that 'the common people were something other than a mob and had instincts and habits something above drunkeness, gullibility and ignorance'; hence her basic pattern was to dramatise 'the fear of being involved in violence'. Mob violence persists, however, as a minority problem, and George Eliot's fear is defensible. In the later *Country and City* (1973) Williams is less interested in George Eliot's putative class bias than in the form and tone of her novels, which are said to reproduce in their disunity the flawed social structures and disturbances of feeling in her subject matter. For example, he finds a conflict between George Eliot's placing value in the past 'as a general retrospective condition' and placing value in the present only as 'the individual moral action'. All that is left is 'a set of personal relationships' in a history that has 'for all valuing purposes' ended. ... The search for contradiction is, however, developed and modified in Terry Eagleton's *Criticism and Ideology* (1976) where George Eliot's forms are held to repress and defuse the 'potentially tragic collision' between corporate and individualistic ideologies, between regard for immutable social laws and regard for romantic individuals' desire for self-fulfilment. Eagleton's argument that George Eliot's 'naturalising, moralising and mystifying devices' are her way out of her failure to reconcile irreconcilable historical conflicts is based on the assumption that social formations are determined by the class war; 'turbulent issues are marginalised'. However varied in subtlety they may be, recent Marxist and Marxist-influenced New Historicist critiques forward a language of metaphoric bellicosity, coded as militancy, action, disturbance, struggle, collision, incompatibility, division, deformation, problem and so on, which deliberately excludes ironic notions like compromise, reconciliation and fairness, and achieves little or no purchase on George Eliot's dense texts with their amused concern for existing and developing social forms. George Eliot presents the reader with characters living in what are immediate social structures, in what Burke calls the subdivision 'or little platoon we belong to in society, the parish, the estate, the profession, the municipality, the market', and she respects the net of free choice, agreement seeking and mutual adjustments on which they rely in spite of the pressures which the individual experiences from prejudice, poverty, debt, vice and crime; she prefers these social forms to deceptive abstractions like collective correctness, political justice, and socialist equality, let alone proletarian victory. Politically, George Eliot is no statist; she anticipates post-socialist ideas of a spontaneous order of tolerant conventions, a community formed by free association where people are entitled to their property and taxes are limited, ideas which Marxist critics showed few or no signs of grasping.

Recent structuralist criticism has also engaged with George Eliot, partly because of her own curiosity as to the instability of meanings, signs and metaphors, but also because of her high reputation for psychological and sociological realism, a concept which has come under adverse, though also rather insecure, scrutiny. Structuralist belief in language as a self-enclosed system which does not transparently grant access to an external 'reality' so that languages and the various discourses which compose them may rather be said to speak us than we them, is highly controversial, but might be thought to have some affinity with the determinist ideas which interested George Eliot in her own time. The anti-scientific element in structuralism is alien to George Eliot, however; she accepted that language shifted with science, not that science shifted with language.

For some structuralist critics George Eliot has therefore been a large target.

(pp.132–3)

Bellringer cogently concludes that George Eliot has not yet 'met her match in the critical world'.

SUGGESTIONS FOR FURTHER READING

The range of George Eliot criticism and scholarship is now extensive and formidable. Readers will need to decide their priorities in terms of perspective and approach. As a contemporary portrait, *George Eliot's Life as Related in Her Letters and Journals* (3 vols., Edinburgh and London, 1885), arranged and edited by her husband J. W. Cross, then revised in 1887, still has the merits of being a first-hand account. A reading of this is complemented and extended by *The Letters of George Eliot*, meticulously edited by Gordon Haight in nine volumes (New Haven, 1958–78). Haight's own account of Eliot's life, *George Eliot, A Biography* (Oxford, 1968), utilises his deep scholarship to modify much in the Cross biography, and has the advantage of historical objectivity.

K. McSweeney's *George Eliot (Marian Evans): A Literary Life* (London, 1991) places George Eliot vividly in the context of her times and in particular her literary ambience. W. E. Houghton's *The Victorian Frame of Mind* (New Haven and London, 1957) is also still useful for locating George Eliot's ideas and attitudes in their social and intellectual milieu, as is Gertrude Himmelfarb's *Victorian Minds* (London, 1968).

Criticism of George Eliot's novels has been influenced more recently by interest in her as a woman writer, and her relation to women's writing generally. But much that was written somewhat earlier about George Eliot from a less gender-specific point of view is still indispensable as a means to understanding her achievement as an artist and her craftsmanship as a writer. Among these works Joan Bennett's *George Eliot: Her Mind and Art* (Cambridge, 1948) is still an acute and challenging introduction, as is F. R. Leavis's appreciation of Eliot in *The Great Tradition* (London, 1948). Knoepflmacher's study *George Eliot's Early Novels* (California, 1968) focuses usefully on her maturing craftsmanship at the start of her career.

Among the critics whose analytical sensitivity to George Eliot's language and style remains outstanding is that of Barbara Hardy in a number of volumes, including *The Novels of George Eliot* (London,

1959), *The Appropriate Form* (London, 1964) and *Particularities; Readings in George Eliot* (London, 1982). In *Critical Essays on George Eliot* (London, 1970), Professor Hardy brings together a number of important essays from different perspectives: those by Lilian Haddakin, Isobel Armstrong and Arnold Kettle are especially valuable.

The best introduction to George Eliot as a woman writer is that given by Gilliam Beer in the Harvester 'Key Women Writers' series (*George Eliot* (Hemel Hempstead, 1986)), which begins with an account of 'The Woman's Question'. Her bibliography draws attention to the range of critical writing on George Eliot from feminist perspectives, as well as more general considerations of women's writing in the nineteenth and twentieth centuries. Elaine Showalter's *A Literature of Their Own; British Women Novelists from Brontë to Lessing* (Princeton, 1977) is particularly notable. Jennifer Uglow's study *George Eliot* (London, 1987) in the Virago Pioneers series is also well written and reflects on many aspects of George Eliot's work, including the feminist perspective.

Alan Bellringer's recent volume, *George Eliot* (London, 1993) for the Macmillan Modern Novelists series is a wide-ranging account which concludes with a useful summary of George Eliot criticism to the present time.

Ashton, Rosemary (ed.): *George Eliot: Selected Critical Writings* (World Classics, Oxford, 1992).

Beer, Gillian: *George Eliot* (Hemel Hempstead, 1986).

Bellringer, Alan W.: *George Eliot* (Macmillan Modern Novelists, London, 1993).

Bennett, Joan: *George Eliot, Her Mind and Art* (Cambridge, 1948).

Brady, Kristin: *George Eliot* (Macmillan Women Writers, London 1992).

Byatt, A. S. and Warren, N. (eds.): *George Eliot: Selected Essays, Poems and Other Writings* (Harmondsworth, 1990).

Gray, Beryl: 'Afterword' to *The Lifted Veil* (London, 1985).

Gray, Beryl: 'Afterword' in *Brother Jacob* (London, 1989).

Gray, Beryl: *George Eliot and Music* (London, 1989).

Haddakin, Lilian: 'Silas Marner' in *Critical Essays on George Eliot*, ed. Barbara Hardy (London, 1970).

Haight, Gordon S. (ed.): *The Letters of George Eliot* (9 vols, New Haven, 1954–78).

Haight, Gordon S.: *George Eliot, A Biography* (Oxford, 1968).

Hardy, Barbara: *Critical Essays on George Eliot* (London, 1970).

Hardy, Barbara: *Particularities, Readings in George Eliot* (London, 1982).

Heilman, R. B.: 'Return to Raveloe', *English Journal* (1957), 46.

Holloway, John: 'Introduction' in *Silas Marner* (London, 1986).

Houghton, W. E.: *The Victorian Frame of Mind* (New Haven and London, 1957).

Knoepflmacher, U. C.: *George Eliot's Early Novels* (California, 1968).

Leavis, Q. D.: 'Introduction' in *Silas Marner* (Harmondsworth, 1967).

Pinion, F. B. (ed.): *A George Eliot Miscellany* (London, 1982).

Uglow, Jenny: *George Eliot* (Virago Pioneers, London, 1987).

Silas Marner

Chapter 1

The weaver's life is placed in its social and historical context. Silas Marner has already been in Raveloe for fifteen years, after coming there in the late 1780s. Before that he had lived as a member of a Dissenting Community in a town in the North. There he had been betrayed by his closest friend, left the town, and started a new life as an independent weaver in Raveloe.

Chapter 2

Silas's present life of solitude at Raveloe; and his pleasure in the gold which he earns from his weaving. His refusal to use his inherited knowledge of herbal medicine (more than once) to diminish his isolation from the community. His reputation for miserliness.

Chapter 3

Squire Cass and his family: Dunstan's attempt to blackmail his brother, Godfrey, over his marriage to Molly, by whom Godfrey has had a child, unknown to Squire Cass, their father. Godfrey agrees to let Dunstan sell his horse, Wildfire.

Chapter 4

Dunstan sells the horse, but before handing him over rides him to his death; goes to Silas Marner's cottage and robs Silas of his gold in his temporary absence.

Chapter 5

Silas Marner discovers to his horror the loss of his gold.

Chapter 6

The narrative moves to the Rainbow Tavern, where the men of Raveloe are discussing local life over their pints of ale.

Chapter 7
Silas appears at the Rainbow, demanding help in finding the thief. (In his anguish he mistakenly accuses Jem.) The villagers agree to help him.

Chapter 8
A tinder-box is found hear the Stone-pits, and speculation intensifies as to whether the pedlar who owned it was also the thief.

Chapter 9
Godfrey tells his father that he cannot repay the money he owes him, and about Dunstan's disappearance. Squire Cass, who still does not know about Godfrey's marriage, urges him to marry Nancy Lammeter.

Chapter 10
The villagers have no success in finding the thief of Silas Marner's gold. Dolly Winthrop goes to comfort Silas, and urges him to participate more in the life of Raveloe, especially at Christmas time. At Squire Cass's home, preparations are continuing for a dance on New Year's Eve.

Chapter 11
Priscilla and Nancy Lammeter prepare for the dance. (Priscilla Lammeter is one of George Eliot's memorable comic creations.) Nancy herself has reservations about being married to Godfrey.

Chapter 12
Godfrey's wife tries to come and see him, bringing her child with her in the cold. She dies in the snow outside Silas Marner's cottage. The child, attracted by the warmth and light, goes inside while Silas is in a cataleptic trance.

Chapter 13
During the dance at Squire Cass's house, Silas arrives with the baby, in search of a doctor. Godfrey and Dr Kimble go to tend its mother at Silas's cottage. Godfrey recognises his wife. Silas determines to keep the baby.

Chapter 14
Dolly Winthrop helps Silas nurture the child. In bringing her up he starts to be reunited with the community; and the love which had been destroyed in him revives.

Chapter 15
Godfrey Cass, knowing that Eppie is his child, continues to act as Silas Marner's benefactor.

Part Two; Chapter 16
Sixteen years later, Godfrey and Nancy, now married, are still childless. Eppie, now eighteen, is loved by Aaron Winthrop. She and Silas begin to think of her marriage.

Chapter 17
Nancy has brought about many changes at the Red House. Priscilla tries to help her cope with her concern about childlessness. Godfrey is deeply affected by this state of affairs.

Chapter 18
The stone-pit is drained, revealing Duncan Cass's body and Silas Marner's gold. Godfrey confesses to Nancy about his earlier marriage, and that Eppie is his child. Godfrey decides to own Eppie publicly, and adopt her as his own.

Chapter 19
Godfrey and Nancy visit Silas to tell him of their proposal. Silas Marner grows angry at Godfrey's concealment and his desire to take Eppie away from him now. Eppie settles the matter by refusing to leave Silas.

Chapter 20
Godfrey and Nancy are compelled to accept the reality of the situation.

Chapter 21
Silas and Eppie visit Lantern Yard where the Chapel from which he was expelled held its meetings. It has been rebuilt and become a factory.

Conclusion
Eppie and Aaron get married. They will both live with Silas and continue to cultivate his garden. Godfrey Cass continues to show his generosity to them all, albeit from a distance.

The Lifted Veil

Chapter 1
The first person narrator tells of his approaching death, which he has foreseen through his faculty of prevision. This last testament is intended

to arouse the sympathy for him which he has never received during his life. His father, a wealthy banker, has always felt him to be a weakling, ill-equipped for the practical necessities of life. While finishing his education in Geneva he falls ill, and his father promises a recuperative tour of Europe.

The mention of Prague triggers an intense prevision of what the city is like; and this is followed by another vision anticipating what is about to happen. His brother, Alfred, is engaged to be married to Bertha. The narrator foresees that she will become his wife; and that their relationship will be poisoned. But the more he falls under her influence, the less he is able to act upon what his other consciousness has told him. On arriving in Prague, he finds every detail of his vision confirmed.

Chapter 2

Shortly before his marriage to Bertha, Alfred is killed in a riding accident; and – as foreseen – Latimer becomes her husband. After the first passion wears off, he begins to see into Bertha's soul, and realises the true nature of the woman he has married. Her contempt for him increases as she realises his ineffectuality. The estrangement between them increases.

Bertha takes on a new maid, Mrs Archer, with whom she forms an intense and possessive relationship. Mrs Archer becomes fatally ill with peritonitis; and Charles Meunier, Latimer's doctor friend, suggests an experiment by which he will try to revive her after death with a transfusion of blood from his own arteries. In her momentary resurrection Mrs Archer reveals Bertha's hatred of her husband and her plan to murder him. They separate, and in the brief life remaining to him, Latimer becomes a wanderer, doomed to see into the thoughts of other men and women. As foretold at the beginning, the narration comes to an end shortly before the narrator's own death.

Brother Jacob

Chapter 1

The narrator introduces his story of the young man whose first ambition is to become a confectioner. Lacking the means for advancement, David Faux decides to steal some of his mother's savings, and set sail for America. His idiot brother, Jacob, discovers David's hiding-place for the guineas, but is persuaded to exchange them for 'lozenges' which he can eat. He does not recognise the significance of what he has seen, and attempts to follow David into exile. David eventually makes his escape.

Chapter 2
David's business in the West Indies has not prospered and he has returned to the market town of Grimworth, where he sets up a new confectioner's business under the name of Edward Freely. The attractiveness of his wares leads the housewives of Grimworth to buy from him what they would previously have baked, and thereby impress their neighbours. Success in business leads Freely to seek the hand in marriage of Penelope Palfrey, the daughter of a wealthy local farmer.

Chapter 3
David Faux responds to an advertisement in which he is named as a potential beneficiary of his father's estate. His elder brother wishes to have no more to do with him; but Brother Jacob, remembering his affection for the brother who had given him 'lozenges', comes to the shop in Grimworth and claims his brother as his own. The unmasking of the true identity of Edward Freely leads to the breaking of his engagement and the rapid decline of his business, forcing him to leave the town. The narrator concludes his tale by claiming it as an example of the way in which Nemesis works.

ACKNOWLEDGEMENTS

The editor and publishers wish to thank the following for permission to use copyright material:

Macmillan Press Ltd. and St Martin's Press, Inc. for material from Alan Bellringer, *George Eliot*, 1993. Copyright © 1993 Alan Bellringer.

Every effort has been made to trace all the copyright holders but if any have been inadvertently overlooked the publishers will be pleased to make the necessary arrangement at the first opportunity.

CLASSIC NOVELS
IN EVERYMAN

A SELECTION

The Way of All Flesh
SAMUEL BUTLER
A savagely funny odyssey from joyless duty to unbridled liberalism **£4.99**

Born in Exile
GEORGE GISSING
A rationalist's progress towards love and compromise in class-ridden Victorian England **£4.99**

David Copperfield
CHARLES DICKENS
One of Dickens's best-loved novels, brimming with humour **£3.99**

The Last Chronicle of Barset
ANTHONY TROLLOPE
Trollope's magnificent conclusion to his Barsetshire novels **£4.99**

He Knew He Was Right
ANTHONY TROLLOPE
Sexual jealousy, money and women's rights within marriage – a novel ahead of its time **£6.99**

Tess of the D'Urbervilles
THOMAS HARDY
The powerful, poetic classic of wronged innocence **£3.99**

Tom Jones
HENRY FIELDING
The wayward adventures of one of literatures most likeable heroes **£5.99**

Wuthering Heights and Poems
EMILY BRONTË
A powerful work of genius – one of the great masterpieces of literature **£3.50**

The Master of Ballantrae and Weir of Hermiston
R. L. STEVENSON
Together in one volume, two great novels of high adventure and family conflict **£4.99**

£5.99

AVAILABILITY
All books are available from your local bookshop or direct from
Littlehampton Book Services Cash Sales, 14 Eldon Way, Lineside Estate, Littlehampton, West Sussex BN17 7HE. PRICES ARE SUBJECT TO CHANGE.

To order any of the books, please enclose a cheque (in £ sterling) made payable to Littlehampton Book Services, or phone your order through with credit card details (Access, Visa or Mastercard) on 0903 721596 (24 hour answering service) stating card number and expiry date. Please add £1.25 for package and postage to the total value of your order.

In the USA, for further information and a complete catalogue call 1-800-526-2778.